THE LORD OF FREEDOM

A COMPLEMENT TO THE BELL TOLLING

The Lord of Freedom

A Complement to The Bell Tolling

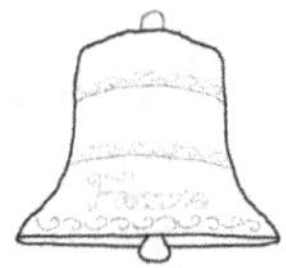 # The Resonant Bell 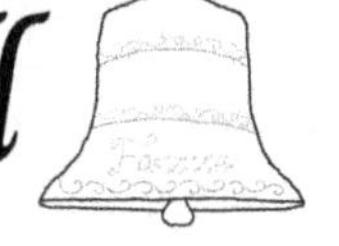

Amena Jamali

The Lord of Freedom

A Complement to The Bell Tolling — The Resonant Bell

Copyright © 2022 by Amena Jamali

Edited by Mary Reid

Cover Art by Lee Contreras

ISBN

979-8-9859244-1-1 *Paperback*

979-8-9859244-0-4 *Kindle Ebook*

PUBLISHED BY AMENA JAMALI

www.amenajamali.com

These stories of how
the Quest of Freedom's Ascension resonated across Icilia
is dedicated with fellowship
to those who recognize in themselves
a need for Divine Blessing.

CONTENTS

AUTHOR'S NOTE AND MAP

Dear Readers:

My thanks for opening this book and perusing its contents. Your consideration means much to me, for the publication of this story is itself an act of gratitude.

When I began to write *The Bell Tolling* in March 2020, I very quickly decided that I wanted to craft a story told from multiple perspectives—both the heroes' points of view and those of characters who are usually considered secondary. Even in the earliest draft, it was apparent to me that a number of these so-called side characters are capable of being the center of their own novels. They are only not the heroes of this series because they live in the time of the divine-blessed Quest of Freedom.

However, as I proceeded further in *The Bell Tolling*'s publication journey, I realized that I could not include most of these secondary perspectives and still compile a cohesive story. With my style of writing, balancing the five primary perspectives of Lucian, Malika, Elian, Arista, and Kyros is enough of a challenge. Balancing fifteen would be appallingly difficult—and yet each of those additional perspectives, as I pleaded with myself, felt so very *necessary*.

Thus was the idea of *The Resonant Bell* born.

The chapters included in this anthology are comprised of eleven perspectives: Darian, Tahira, Eligeo, Ciro, Elacir, Kalyca, Kanzeo, Revera, and Rosalla, as well as one chapter each from Elian and Lucian himself. Their perspectives offer two benefits.

First, they expand the scope of Book One's narration to events occurring outside the Quest's immediate vision, which gives further shape and definition to the political and military reality of Icilia during this timespan. Political maneuvers and military operations do not solely consist of the actions of one or a few, even if they are the leaders, and *The Resonant Bell* chapters portray both the truth of that statement and ensure that the Quest's story shows the agency of other characters as well.

Second, these chapters present alternate perspectives on events that occur in *The Bell Tolling*. Writing and reading them does certainly help fulfill a deep curiosity on what was happening from other characters' views (particularly during the Battle of Ehaya), but the chapters do more than only this: they make the land of Icilia more real, the evils of the enemy more immediate, and the consequences of the Quest's actions more palpable in a heartbreakingly emotional way.

Moreover, united together, the chapters of *The Resonant Bell* depict the true majesty of the Quest. From their own perspectives, sweetened by humility and burdened by their own troubles as they are, it is difficult to perceive why the Quest's names are considered divine, even to each other. But from their vassals' perspectives... the hope that the Quest represents feels all the more real, all the more tangible, because of the broadness of the secondary characters' experiences. We perceive different and glorious aspects of the Quest to which we would otherwise be blind. Through delving deeper into Icilia and these peripheral stories, we are better able to see the forms that light and darkness take and so understand better why exactly the Quest's coming means so much to the people of Icilia. As well as why it means so much to me.

If *The Bell Tolling* is about my faith, my philosophy, and my identity, then *The Resonant Bell* is about my love for the Quest of Freedom. As the ascension of the Quest resonates across Icilia, so, too, does it resonate in my own heart. As I hope it is beginning to do in yours, dear readers.

Because that is for whom this book is intended: not simply the reader of spirituality-perfumed epics and high fantasy, but the reader who knows something of the Quest, or desires to do so, and is noting a stirring of affection within their own heart for these divine-blessed heroes. Such readers will enjoy this book most, and I pray you find the awe and wonder within these pages that I do.

For those reading this book, I offer this advice: *The Resonant Bell* is intended to be read either concurrently with or subsequently to *The Bell Tolling*. Either alongside or afterwards. The inclusion of Segments 1-5 from *The Bell Tolling* is designed to help tie the stories back to the main narrative. Although it is possible to read *The Resonant Bell* first, a number of references, world elements, and plot developments will lack context sufficient to make them clear. Thus, reading *The Bell Tolling* at the same time or first is recommended. I will also post a reading order for the chapters of the two books on my website, in case further guidance is required.

I also offer this warning: because *The Resonant Bell* delves deeper into Icilia and the struggles of her people, many of the chapters contain references to dark topics such as abuse, violence, and depression. More so than *The Bell Tolling*. No explicit language is ever used, but the implications still may be troubling to those sensitive to such triggers. Please care for your heart and your health, dear readers. Choose freely and wisely on your own behalves, and cherish your own dignity.

If you do choose to read this story, remember that, though his world convulses under the pervasive cruelty of the Blood-soaked Sorcerer, Lucian's guidance toward the path of true freedom uplifts souls throughout Icilia. Both those near him and far away rise at the resonance of his name to confront evil and pursue goodness, despite the enormity of the risk to all that they hold most precious. For the blessing promised by his ascension is all the hope they have...

What follows hereafter is translated from *a'Enerérohhe é a'Laètaqqe é a'Raah-é-Fazze*, a complement to the first volume of the annals compiled by the Archivist under the wishes of the Lady of Icilia and the guidance of the Guardian of Names.

With Gratitude,
Amena Jamali
May 2022

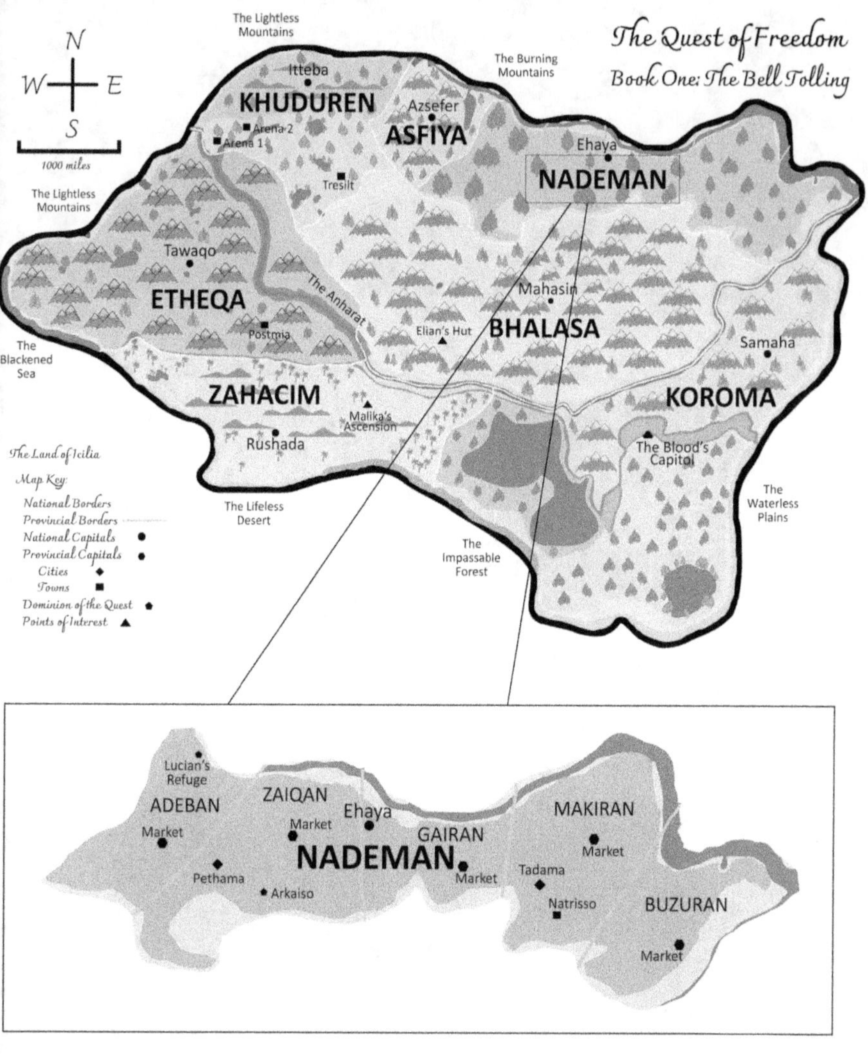

The Quest of Freedom
Book One: The Bell Tolling

N
W E
S

1000 miles

The Lightless
Mountains

The Lightless
Mountains

The Burning
Mountains

Itteba
KHUDUREN
Arena 2
Arena 1
Azsefer
ASFIYA

Ehaya
NADEMAN

Tresilt

Tawaqo

ETHEQA

Mahasin

Postmia

Elian's Hut

BHALASA

Samaha

The
Blackened
Sea

ZAHACIM

Malika's
Ascension

KOROMA

Rushada

The Blood's
Capitol

The Lifeless
Desert

The
Waterless
Plains

The
Impassable
Forest

The Land of Icilia

Map Key:
National Borders
Provincial Borders
National Capitals   ●
Provincial Capitals   •
       Cities   ◆
       Towns   ■
Dominion of the Quest ⬟
Points of Interest   ▲

The Anharat

Lucian's
Refuge

ADEBAN
ZAIQAN
Ehaya

MAKIRAN

Market

Market

NADEMAN
GAIRAN

Market

Pethama

Market

Tadama

Arkaiso
Market

Natrisso

BUZURAN

Market

THE HALLOWED HISTORY

In the beginning, nothing stirred. The divine cleansing of the land had left none who dared to move, for the memory of the purge haunted each breath. But with time, those who survived the purge believed themselves to be spared and then immune to any form of accounting. So, before many years had passed, the land devolved into chaos. Iniquity abounded, and no conscience whispered the truth. There was only darkness.

But then, amid the disorder, came Light. The Light entered the morass in the figure of a man, one who shone. Folding his sleeves up, he gathered a people, a few who were just a little less unruly than their neighbors. He brought them together, he healed them, he nurtured them. Dazzled by his light, they knelt at his feet and pledged to follow him and through him his Master the Almighty always.

The Shining Guide, as they revered him, pleased with this pledge, gave them civilization. He taught them the arts of government and writing, the sciences of farming and metalworking, and the sanctities of family and community. Eagerly they learned, and he smiled and called them Muthaarim, those who shone. He then showed them the treasure that blossomed in their country, the trees which bore athar, the most blessed substance ever known.

He taught them new disciplines, the ways of benefiting from athar and forming their natural magic. Thus, the people flourished.

Yet then came the day on which the Shining Guide bid them farewell. He had completed his task, so his Master called him to another land, and he would answer. The Muthaarim, his heart's children, cried and begged for him to not leave them amid the chaos. The Shining Guide, seeing their misery, smiled and promised them that they would not be abandoned. For one day, the land would unite with them, and, whenever troubles overwhelmed them, saviors would come. And with that assurance, he departed.

Much time passed, and the Mutharrim lost the fervency of their devotion. Thus was the first trouble that broke upon them.

But the Shining Guide's promise was not hollow. Four generations after he had first chosen the Muthaarim to be his people, the Quest of Light arose and fulfilled his promise and prophecy. With the dedication and effort of their lifetimes, three of the Muthaarim, Aalia, Manara, and Naret, spread the blessings of civilization to all the land, which they named Icilia.

So connected, the Mutharrim found companionship with the Areteen, the Ezulal, the Nasimih, and the Sholanar. Seven mighty nations formed, and peace reigned. And the land revered the names of Lady Queen Aalia the Ideal of Light, Graced Queen Manara the Exemplar of Truth, and Honored King Naret the Exemplar of Love only beneath the name of the Shining Guide.

But, as is the way of things, prosperity did not last.

For, only two centuries after the reign of the Quest of Light, the hearts of the people began to turn again from their blessings. Scorning Icilia's laws and traditions, they grumbled at the burdens they perceived themselves to bear of loyalty to their nations, their neighbors, and their land. They coveted what was not theirs, presumed their own pride above that of virtue, and abandoned the protection of the innocent and the weak. And in straying so far from the Quests' hallowed path, they listened when the seductive voice of the Blood-soaked Sorcerer reached their ears. His promise of license, of freedom from duty and responsibility and restriction, of the choice to live exactly as they pleased, seemed like enlightenment.

He was soaked in blood only because he had the power to bring his promise to fruition, they thought.

Lured by the potential for greater riches and glory, Zahacim was the first to join her strength to his. Khuduren negotiated for a share of his gains. Bhalasa let his soldiers into her mountains. Etheqa raised only a feeble defense against his invasion. Nademan lent the benefits of her industry and trade. Asfiya did nothing. Even Koroma, whose rulers had spoken for years against his campaign, did not truly oppose him.

In arrogant blindness, the people of Icilia allowed evil into their hearts and homes.

That evil, absolute, undiluted by the smallest drop of compassion, returned their welcome by destroying their world.

Though the Blood-soaked Sorcerer had restrained his rage and lust while he sought the support of the seven nations, in the fall of Koroma, fifteen years after the start of his campaign, he revealed his true nature. Without the slightest hint of remorse, he brutally tortured and massacred the royal family and the citizens of the capital. The Heir to Koroma, Crown Princess Malika tej-Shehenkorom, a child of only six years, disappeared into his clutches.

The rulers of Asfiya, terrified for the child of sunlight, violet, and silver born amongst them, the future Quest Leader, Lord Lucian aj-Shehathar, sent him into exile amid the giant trees of Nademan and scrambled to rally their citizens. But, though the rulers had awakened to the true threat posed by the southern rebel at the birth of that child, their people had not. Without their support, the only recourse remaining to the rulers was to safe-guard Asfiya's sacred duty, the athar orchards, with their own lives while praying Lord Lucian aj-Shehather would survive the horrors that were to come. With them died the last proof that the Quest Leader yet lived.

Now the conqueror of Icilia's most powerful nations, the Blood-soaked Sorcerer no longer hid his true nature, nor stifled his true desires. Upon his return from Asfiya's capture, he enslaved his first and greatest allies, the warrior princesses of Zahacim, and reduced them to objects of entertainment and pleasure, crushing them so thoroughly that they began to relish their torment. Their people, long since swindled into willing loyalty to their oppressor, spoke not one word in their defense. Only the parents of Princess Arista sej-Shehenzahak dared to retain their love of Icilia by protecting their daughter from his lascivious attentions.

Hearing rumors of these atrocities, the people of Nademan begged their king to defend them, to do something to at least slow the Blood's advance. But their pleas were in vain, for their king had long since abandoned any love for his duty. He did nothing, even unto his own death. And his people, their faith in their rulers shaken, did nothing but cower under the enemy's tyranny.

All but one nation fallen, the Blood turned his attention to Khuduren. His troops, both the willing and those manipulated by magic, were eager to take her as well. For a year, he taunted her, giving respite and punishment in turns, playing with her last loyal forces as though they were but puppets flailing about for his amusement. It was amid this final conquest that the Blood finally found his brother and his brother's family. His brother, long ago turned from the Blood's path to one of piety and compassion, desperately attempted to protect his wife and his young son, but the Blood's wrath could not be overcome, and the battle ended with Elian ben-Janen Izzetís lying broken amid pools of his parents' blood.

As the year 486, C.Q., drew to a close, all of the Blood's enemies lay vanquished, dead or corrupted, while the Blood himself was the undisputed master of Icilia. Exultant in his victory, he laughed and unleashed upon Icilia all manner of suffering and sorrow, crushing the last flowers of hope with torment and agony, turning a land of blessing into one of waking nightmares, smothered by smog. With his deputies extending his will across the seven nations, he raped, stole, and slaughtered, unbound by any law or scruple, fulfilling the freedom he had promised. His violence was meted out with neither cause nor reason, and one such taste left Kyros Dinasiett bereft of both family and dignity as he struggled to raise his infant sister amid a people crushed by fear.

So Icilia suffered.

Until the Quest Leader ascended.

In 499, C.Q., nearly five hundred years after the Shining Guide's first coming, absolute good came forth in form of the second Quest Leader to bestow upon the people the freedom that they had finally begun to realize they truly, desperately needed. With gratitude and patience, Lord Lucian the Ideal of Freedom first gathered together his companions, Graced Malika the Exemplar of Wisdom, Honored Elian the Exemplar of Esteem, Honored Arista the Exemplar of Bravery, and Honored Kyros the Exemplar of Strength, and empowered them such that they strove to overcome their own torments and rise to their places at his side.

With their support, Lord Lucian began his reconquest with the nation of Nademan, building upon the seven years of clandestine aid he, his father, his brother, and his guardians had offered to that land. Though many months passed before the people dared to believe in his promise, Lord Lucian at last succeeded in preparing them for war and, helped greatly by Inase Tahira Enarias, in retaking, province by province and town by town, the whole of Nademan the land of elegance. By Lord Lucian's hand was the Gouge, deputy of the Blood, felled, at great cost, and by Honored Elian's hand the crown prince of the old royal house saved. Beholding the true devotion blossoming in Crown Prince Eligeo tej-Shehennadem's heart, Lord Lucian promised him the Throne of Conscience.

The sun once again shone upon Nademan.

Amid this first part of his journey, knowing well the value of loyalty, Lord Lucian widened his inner circle beyond his companions, his blood, and his guardians to include Tahira Enarias, her brother Kanzeo, Crown Prince Eligeo-nadem, Count Ciro Tolmarie, and his wife, as well as Kalyca Dinasietta, Honored Kyros' sister, and Inase Elacir bi-Dekecer, the first of his vassals.

Thus victorious and wreathed in love, the Quest of Freedom devoted their efforts to reviving the first nation to join their service even as their thoughts turned westward...

Their victory was little more than an inconvenience to the Blood-soaked Sorcerer's campaign for empire without end.

THE PROMISE

From the writings of Lady Queen Aalia the Ideal of Light, supreme ruler and Mother of Icilia:

> Deliverance shall come when the skies grow dark
> The Almighty does not abandon any to slavery
> The contrast between the faithful and the faithless is stark
> Only amid sorrow shall the people of Icilia learn the
> meaning of liberty

> *(Prophesied on Eyyélab, the twentieth day of the tenth moon,*
> *Thekharre, of the year 219 amid the Civilization of the Quests,*
> *C.Q.)*

Though my Lady Queen Aalia the Ideal of Light sent these words to every household, none understood them until the massacres of the Blood-soaked Sorcerer drowned every house in sorrow. Then, the people of Icilia, both in hiding and in captivity, prayed desperately that the prophecy of legend given by the Shining Guide would not go unfulfilled.

The enclosed is a complement to the first volume of seven which present the story of the Quest of Freedom, as drawn from the personal journals and memoranda of their most cherished vassals.

So writes the Archivist.

CHAPTER 1
PROVING HOLINESS

Perspective: Prince Darian sej-Shehasfiyi, brother of the Quest Leader and auxiliary heir to the throne of Asfiya
Date: Eyyésal, the tenth day of the fifth moon, Marberre, of the year 499, C.Q.
Placement: partially concurrent with Chapter 13 of <u>The Bell Tolling</u>

I covered my mouth with a hand and yawned into my palm. Then, lowering my arm with markedly more elegance than with which I had raised it, I buckled my scabbard onto my belt and tilted it so that drawing my sword in a duel would be as easy as possible. Closing my eyes, I leaned back against the tree.

With a diameter of over one hundred-and-seventy feet at its base and a height of over two thousand six hundred feet, the giant probably deserved the name of sentient mountain rather than tree, for its existence stretched the limits of one's imagination regarding what trees could be. But, after spending all of my life, save the early days of my childhood and a few travels, amid the tallest trees in Icilia, even the impossibility of the tallest one did not provoke much curiosity. Particularly not today.

My mind was consumed with worry for my brother.

He had cried last night. All night long. From almost the moment he fell asleep after sunset to just before sunrise.

My younger brother, the savior of Icilia, the future Quest Leader, Lord Lucian aj-Shehathar, had *cried*. Tears had spilled from his beautiful eyes and soaked his pillow, and the sound of sobs in his musical voice had filled our cabin.

Even three endless years of listening to his sobs and screams had not inured me to the horror of his pain. His happiness and his victory were my dearest wishes—I would have preferred to lose my own vision and hearing than for him to suffer as he did.

Yet even that sacrifice would do nothing, for my brother refused to explain the source of the terrors that haunted his nights and days, much less imbibe any draughts that might help him sleep or focus. He seemed to believe that he *needed* to witness whatever he saw in his dreams, and, considering that he had already come partly into his office with his attainment of magical maturity, neither his family nor his guardians dared to question him.

Not because he would be upset—Lucian had the most even temper imaginable—but because his majesty was such that it grew with each passing month and demanded deference even when he did not ask for it.

It was why, though I dearly wished for my brother to simply confide in me, all I could do was try to earn his smiles.

Such an inadequate response.

How I hated that I could not shield him when, for once, it was him who needed such protection and not I.

As yet another mark of his grandeur, Lucian had been prepared for magical maturity by his nineteenth birthday—most royal heirs, including myself, were only ready with great difficulty at twenty, while he seemed to reach the necessary standard, already set impossibly higher because of his office, a year early at his leisure—so our ceremonies were only a month apart. But, while the ceremony had strengthened me, heightening my connection to Icilia along with every aspect of my identity, it weakened him.

I had never thought of my strong warrior brother as *fragile* until he collapsed that day, mere moments after receiving the first measure of his power.

Indeed, he received power yet became frail and feeble—his nightmares and the suffering that appeared to stalk him in the daytime drained his strength, leaving him only a dissatisfied shell of himself. He had not been able to continue his clandestine campaigns to aid the people of Nademan and sow the seeds of his future reconquest, or even continue his studies. Which seemed to compound his frustration.

How I hated to see him suffer.

How I wished that it were possible for him to fulfill his promise without ever tasting the smallest drop of pain.

Resting my head against the tree, I ignored the itchy feeling of weathered bark rubbing against my cap and prayed, *Oh Almighty, Source of Peace, I beg of You the blessing of health and contentment for my brother, the savior who is dedicated to Your name. I beg of You the favor of his ascension, so that he might finally begin his task...* I swallowed, mouth painfully dry. *No matter what that means for our bond.*

It was a terrible prayer. From my rank as heir to my position as Lucian's aide, it was a requirement upon me to be entirely selfless, to be willing to sacrifice even what was most precious to me for the sake of my duty—a distinction of character I dearly wanted for myself. And, indeed, I would sacrifice anything for Lucian.

Yet, though I was willing to give it, how was I supposed to actually *survive* a sacrifice of my bond to him? From an early age, I had given the whole of my self to him, well aware that no one cared for me as much as my divine-blessed brother and that no one ever would. Mother, father, brother, sister, teacher, ruler—he was all of those things to me. And his utter purity meant that he was worthy of such devotion, devotion that otherwise should never have been offered to a mortal child of Icilia.

Lucian was no flawed, mortal incé, and well I knew it. Or at least as much as anyone could understand the Divine.

I blew out a breath and recited my prayer again, desperately hoping that the Almighty would deign to ignore the taint of the one praying in favor of the plea itself.

Lucian's ascension would bring happiness to him and salvation to Icilia, and that was all that mattered.

I was immersed in those prayers when the world changed.

Light spread in smooth waves from the crown of the tree, trickling down the bark in a manner both restrained and magnificent, a declaration of power that did not require ostentation in order to be glorious...

Melodies filled my ears, the sounds of voices raised in hymns —sopranos, baritones, altos, tenors, basses, and contraltos all forming a harmony that was the true complement of the rivers and the winds and the rustling grasses, the very song of life...

Perfumes reached my nose, the deep scents of incense and musk combined with the sharp, sweet fragrances of roses, basil, and all manner of flowers and herbs, everything intended to provide benefit and wholesome joy to the children of Icilia...

Sensation covered my body in bursts of coolness and warmth, pleasant, soothing, the gentle strokes of loving hands that sought to relieve agony and endow relief, the meaning of the strongest magic and the purpose of the highest learning...

As that light, bringing with it such wonders, reached my center, so, too, did a taste spread across my tongue. Pure like freshest water, sweet like athar tears, rich like the purest honey found in the boughs of the tallest of Icilia's trees—it was the flavor of blessed acceptance.

For, as I strained to see the source of these marvels, acceptance was what emanated from my heart.

This blessing was my brother's glory, and I welcomed the proclamation of his holy office with every part of my heart and soul and every piece of my mind and body. I was his to command.

It was why I had perceived so much.

Straightening my spine, I stepped away from the tree and strode to a spot several paces distant. There, amid the incredible silence that succeeded the miracle, I folded my hands over my waist and stood, prepared to wait as long as required for a glimpse of my brother.

As the minutes passed, footsteps crunched the fallen twigs that spattered the forest floor. Then, from amid the few shrubs that survived at the base of the giant trees, emerged my father and all twelve of the guardians. Even the elders Ezam and Almana were present. How blessed we were that all of those traveling for their tasks had returned in these last weeks and that none had yet thought to leave.

We exchanged reverences, I to my father and the guardians to me, and they assembled in a single row, forming part of a circle around the tree, with my father and me on the rightmost end.

All of us were as silent as the forest, hardly daring to breathe out of sheer wonder, as though the slightest puff of air might shatter this fulfillment of our hope.

Then...

With the gentle ease of the sun's rays from long ago...

Then...

He came.

The figure of a man robed and crowned in glowing white descended the tallest tree as though its thick boughs were but the steps of a staircase. Winds whispered around him, green leaves and white flowers sprouted at the touch of his hands, water trickled from his feet, and the entire forest brightened in his presence.

He radiated light like the sun.

Indeed, for the grief-stricken people of Icilia, he *was* the sun.

The white-gold curls of his hair and his beard shone like rays of sunlight descending through the clouds, and his gold-flecked violet eyes were radiant stars, as vast as the night sky and far more compassionate. Holiness and divine favor limned every curve and line of his sacred features, from the gentle arch of his brows to the unwavering firmness of his nose to the soft slant of his smiling lips. His cream skin glowed with the silver candescence of the moon herself. There was no sign of his former weakness, for his form was power incarnate.

He had been beautiful before, but now there were no words on incé tongues for the sublimity of his beauty. One glimpse of him seemed sufficient to inspire faith and hope in the barren soil, to evoke the longing for redemption in those lost to it.

For his glory was such that it was as though our Lady Queen Aalia the Ideal of Light had been reborn. From his hands would come our salvation.

As his name revealed, he was the Almighty's beneficence.

Overcome with gratitude, we—who had long dared to call ourselves his family—fell to our knees, servants at our Lord's coming.

At the motion, his gaze came to rest upon us. And the sweet curve of his pale lips bloomed into a full smile, revealing the edge of his white teeth as he exhaled a chuckle.

Our Lord descended the final steps so that his feet came to rest on the forest floor, a few paces from the giant tree's glossy trunk.

We waited, breaths held in awe, his every movement magnetic.

Then he spoke in a voice resonant with the music of the stars themselves: "May the Almighty bless you."

The prayer was the one he most often intoned, so very familiar, yet now the words carried an odd echo, as though repeated by other beings we could not perceive.

"A'Qahre rad beleqas Isilia on he eyeh," that harmonious voice stated "ru a'laètaqqe é a'Raèdalaan thaner. Onó zaler rasehem a'Qahre rad adiniqas a'ajeh é a'Dalaane-é-Fazze, a'Ewaràwalaane ó a'dinile é a'Zahràdalle ai a'Arafàwalaane é Isilia, a'Kairie é kairiese ai a'Sheheh é Shehile. Elàkan la raëh fazer an a'lalaëh eïla a'Raah-é-Fazze."

The words were a precise repetition, save for the names given to him, of what his ancestor the first Quest Leader had proclaimed after her own ascension.

I could hardly believe this moment had finally come as I answered along with my father and the guardians, "Aalimas a'Qahre! Aalimas a'Raah-é-Alaah! Aalimas Dalaan Lusian ma-Fazélaah!"

How sweet his new name, Lord Lucian the Ideal of Freedom in common Siléalaah, tasted on my tongue.

My Lord beamed, seeming pleased, and the wondrous luminescence of his person dimmed to a soft shine like that of woven athar, revealing the midnight blue robes and cap beneath.

The clothes were the ones he had specifically commissioned for the start of his journey. The first of a matched set of five.

I could not help but laugh. Even amid his distress this morning, he had somehow worn the perfect clothes for the day.

Because he was leaving.

My mirth vanished.

He was leaving.

He was *leaving*.

He was *leaving*!

"My Lord," our father had begun to say, "how may your loyal servants serve you?"

My Lord exhaled another chuckle. "Father," he said, sounding amused, "I require neither reverence nor deference from you. Nor from you, Brother—"

I gasped, overcome that he had remembered me!

"—nor you, my guardians. We are family; your receipt of my name was established long ago."

Though everyone's faces silvered, I knew that our father and the guardians would never be so familiar. Our father had regularly used our Lord's reverential address since his maturity, and the guardians had done so even longer, since his sixteenth year.

Only I had truly needed to change my habit... and he was letting me keep it.

"Lucian," I sighed, savoring the holy name.

My brother flicked a glance and a smile in my direction, before returning his attention to our father. "If you would deign to fulfill this wish, Father, I would ask that you aid me in preparation for my travels. I do not wish to delay in the finding of my companions."

I swallowed, again overcome by the thought that he was *leaving*. The world outside our refuge was so dangerous! And he was going alone!

My father bowed his head. "As you wish, my Lord," he gave the sacred response, then leapt to his feet and ran toward the tree in the branches of which our cabins were perched.

Two of the guardians, Hasima and Fozala, followed.

Lucian turned to the remainder. "I have requests I wish to make of each of you," he said, using the word 'wish' exactly as it was his exclusive right to use. "These are my orders: Da'ana, Eloman, I wish for you to expand our aid operations to Nademani Buzuran and Makiran and begin spreading the rumors of my name. Brother, Taza, Ilqan, expand the same to Nademani Zaiqan and prepare Arkaiso for war. Father and Hasima will continue in Nademani Adeban. Mutal, begin spreading the rumors of my name in Asfiya—I must ask that you travel alone, as you usually prefer. Amalna, Fozala, the same in Khuduren, but only after my companions and I have passed through that nation. Carry a copy of the sacred texts with you. Qaren, you will do the same in northern Bhalasa along with Faqehen. Ezam, Almana, you will remain behind and focus all of your efforts into the research of spells cast through conjury.

"In addition to these orders, I ask that you prepare lessons for my companions. Three of their number have not yet attained magical maturity and will require a condensed version of all that you have taught me. I expect material for their training, complete with references, lectures, and exercises, to be readied by the time the Quest reaches Arkaiso. Brother, Taza, Ilqan, you must be ready to prepare them in every area I have not covered by that time.

"Thus are my commands. Relay them to those not present among you, my father, Hasima, and Fozala, and see them through with all the diligence you will vow in your future pledges."

The guardians and I murmured obedience, none of us surprised, for these commands were the result of years of Lucian's deliberations.

And yet, as Ezam scrambled to record everything Lucian had said, I marveled at the orders: though Lucian had led military campaigns for four years prior to his maturity, those operations possessed only fragments of the scale of a full reconquest—a campaign the likes of which had never happened before and so for which there was no true preparation.

Somehow, moments after his ascension, Lucian was issuing commands for the beginning of the reconquest with such decisiveness that he seemed to have held his office for many years rather than mere minutes. No practice could account for that.

My miraculous brother, I thought, smiling again, despite the fear I felt for his safety and the pain of our imminent parting. Indeed, it was difficult to not smile, for Lucian had remembered me in his orders...

The furious thumps of footsteps echoed through the undergrowth.

Then Father, Hasima, and Fozala burst from the shrubbery and skidded into kneeling positions in front of Lucian's feet, holding aloft several bundles and a large pack.

I hurried to stand and open the first bundle in Father's arms.

Lucian smiled and thanked us in his musical voice before reaching into the folds of cloth.

All of us again hardly dared to breathe.

Happiness shone on Lucian's sacred features as he removed a sheathed sword and drew the blade.

Radiant and magnificent, the silver steel twinkled in the sunlight, as though delighted to finally be cradled in its rightful master's hands.

Lucian quickly unbuckled the sword he had used since his fifteenth year, the sword of the Asfiyan king known as the Prince of Virtue, and handed it to me. He held up the new sword and examined its gleaming length, a single elegant finger stroking the flat of the blade from hilt to tip.

Infused with athar and forged in accordance with the specifications of the first Quest, the sword was one of his symbols of office and a gift for the day of his ascension.

"Praised be the Almighty," Lucian whispered. He touched the emerald inlaid in the pommel. "Receive your duty and your name, Fazálli," he intoned on a quiet breath. "May the Almighty imbue justice into this metal and render it as its name declares, the freedom that is born of goodness." Then, his lips spreading into a rare grin, he tied onto his belt the new sword, his own, the sign of Icilia's protection from the evil that had long plagued her.

Cherishing the moment, I unwrapped the next two packages.

Lucian intoned another prayer, praising the Almighty and offering gratitude, and donned the second and third symbols of his office, the holy ruby ring of the first Quest Leader and the emerald pendant that he himself would make hallowed.

Thus arrayed, his glory shone all the brighter...

"Father," Lucian then instructed, "if you would deign to accept these wishes, would you gather all of the traveling robes, the swords, the rings, the pendants, and my crown into my pack? The rest should be sent with Darian to Arkaiso. Hasima, would you help with the provisions?"

Father and the guardian immediately obeyed, scrambling to fill his pack.

Lucian paused slightly and glanced at the sky.

"Brother," I dared to ask, aware that his brisk, purposeful movements were an indication of his haste, "have you yet broken your fast? If you have not... I prepared some sandwiches for you this morning." I touched the leather pouch that hung from my belt.

He glanced back at me and bestowed a smile. "My gratitude, Brother. Would you offer them to Hasima? I will break my fast as I journey."

I dipped my head and did as he asked.

Lucian stepped forward then and, embracing each member of his circle, bid them a fond farewell. Then, when Father and Hasima finished, he shouldered his pack and embraced both of them as well.

Until only I was left.

I shivered, knowing that all too soon I would be bereft of the only person who cared for me.

His sharp eyes caught that shudder as he turned to me. His smile gentled, and, touching my elbows as though I were now the fragile one, he drew me into his strong arms.

"Brother," he said, "we will be reunited within the year."

"Brother…" I whispered, closing my eyes, "please do not forget me."

There was a smile in his voice as he answered, "That will never come to pass." He pressed a brotherly kiss to my cheek and then stepped back.

Lucian cast all of us a final glance. "My gratitude for your support in my endeavor. May the Almighty bless you and protect you from all harm as you act in the Quest's name."

Father, the guardians, and I proffered bows and hurried to respond with our own well wishes.

"May the Almighty safeguard you in every step, Dalaanem," I murmured.

Lucian gave us a last smile and then, pivoting on his heel, walked away, his luminescent midnight form disappearing amid the giant trees.

I exhaled a shuddering breath before turning to begin his service.

CHAPTER 2
VOWING ACTION

Perspective: Etheqora Revera bia-Tovacera, citizen of Etheqa
Date: Eyyédal, the twentieth day of the eleventh moon, Mirkharre,
of the year 499, C.Q.
Placement: between Chapter 20 and Chapter 21 of <u>*The Bell Tolling*</u>

Gripping the ropes, my wing-mates and I lowered the last wall into place, and the villagers hovering and standing around the house erupted into cheers.

As I wiped the sweat from my face, a smile slid across my lips at the sounds of joy. These cheers at the conclusion of the rebuilding effort were among the only such sounds I had heard from my nest-mates since that day in the summer.

That day.

Even the barest flicker of thought triggered the nausea—and the memories.

I resisted them, desperately clinging to the task of removing the rope from its fastenings on the wall's upper edge.

But no one in Potsmia could ignore the flashbacks.

The rope, untied, fell loosely from my numb fingers as the scenes of fire and pain filled my vision.

On one of the hotter days of the last summer, the governor's colonels had randomly chosen my aerie. Though we had paid every coin of their outrageous and ever-increasing taxes, though we had never raised our voices or our wings in rebellion, they came. Without mercy or any sense of decency.

With their subordinates, spelled once-fellow citizens, standing guard, the colonels had burnt our homes and storehouses of carefully gathered supplies and driven us, sobbing and wailing, into the harsh wilderness around our mountainous home.

Then they had hunted us. For sport. With their soldiers ensuring that none of us ever truly had a chance of escape.

Some of the men and boys who they caught were killed outright. Like my father. But most of them and all of the women and girls were subjected to whatever tortures the colonels devised. They committed unspeakable violence against their captives.

My betrothed, my sister, my friends, and I had prayed for the relief of death. For surely death held the promise of the Almighty's mercy, while survival seemed too painful to contemplate.

Then, fifteen days after that day, on the sixth day of the eighth moon of Belsaffe, came a light, faint, pale, so subtle that it arrived unnoticed.

Yet that light was the first herald of the dawn. Salvation from the Almighty in incé form.

Within the span of three days, that cloaked figure humiliated the colonels in battle such that they and their soldiers fled with nary a threat of return. After driving them away, he freed us from the prisons made from the remains of our own homes. He found us clothing and guarded us as we washed. He fed us, many with his own hands. And with unheard-of magic, he healed many of our wounds.

With his smile and only a few words, the shining man gave us a measure of peace, a peace which our sufferings should have proved impossible to obtain.

And with his strength the surviving villagers mustered the fortitude to bury their dead and begin the arduous task of rebuilding their houses and their hearts.

So many of us, man, woman, and child, had cried on the day of his farewell. My mother begged him to take provisions, but he kindly refused a portion of what he himself had hunted. He embraced each of us. And then he had departed.

The six days this man spent among us had restored both our faith and our hope.

I would never forget him, he of the shining white-gold hair, noble silver-cream face, and calm violet eyes. Though I did not know his name, his beautiful face was the one that brought peace amid my nightmares.

And for that face, I was forming my resolve to act.

The shining man had rescued Potsmia when no one else could or would have, with nary a request for gratitude. For his actions I owed him my allegiance, the allegiance I had only realized later that I should have given. I could not find him, and I was unlikely to meet him again, but at the least I owed him the duty of following his example.

For what the colonels had done should never have happened. It was not something to be accepted or withstood; it was something to be challenged and eradicated from the face of Icilia. No woman, no man, should suffer what my village, my peers, my family, my betrothed, and I had.

So, now that the reconstruction was finished, I intended to prepare and try to gather a team of my peers, my betrothed among them. Then, once the first thaw passed, I would take my own step.

Flapping my auburn-scaled wings, I nodded to those who had stopped to inquire after me. Then I rose on the air currents towards the defensive wall we had been building at the shining man's suggestion. I retrieved a chisel and pot of mortar and melted the snow off the designated portion of the wall with a burst of fire from my throat.

As I scraped the first scoop of mortar between the stacked stones that formed the northern perimeter, I allowed glimpses of that face beneath a dark blue hood to fill my mind.

For him, I vowed, I would take these daunting steps outside my village, even if I faltered in escaping the prisons of my mind.

CHAPTER 3
PERCEIVING DEVOTION

Perspective: Khuduya Kalyca Dinasietta, sister of the Exemplar of Strength
Date: Eyyéfaz, the twentieth day of the twelfth moon, Alshatte, of the year 499, C.Q.
Placement: between Chapter 23 and Chapter 24 of The Bell Tolling

I straightened my back even as I hugged the tiny jar of honey to my chest. Biting my lower lip, I tried to keep my face expressionless, like Kyros often did. But tears still spilled down my cheeks.

The girls laughed, and one of them jeered, "A whiner on top of a burden! That is why no one wants to marry him!"

I shuddered but maintained an even pace. The girls, my age-mates, were mean, but their older siblings were worse. If I ran, they would chase me, and their fists hurt almost as badly as their parents' slaps.

I did not want Kyros to be hurt again while he tried to protect me. Or Lucian to be hurt instead of him.

"Your brother is a liar, Kalyca!" another girl called out. "The Almighty would *never* choose him!"

"And do you know *why*?" another sneered. "It is because a

man so dedicated to a girl like you *must* have something wrong with him!"

"You ruin his life, little cow!"

The taunts felt worse than kicks to my belly, worse than the bone-shattering cold, but I walked unhurriedly to my cottage door. Easing off my snow-streaked boots, I did not react—except for those stupid tears on my stupid face—as I shut the door. Then turned and slumped against the hard wood.

"Kalyca!" Arista's voice.

I clapped a hand to my mouth, stifling a sob.

"Kalyca!" she said again, and a hand squeezed my shoulder, then gently tugged me into an embrace.

Cocooned in the warmth of her strong arms, as loving as Kyros' though shorter, I could no longer hold back my tears. Melting into her, I cried like the whining child I was—and expected her to treat me like it.

But, unlike all the women I had known before, she returned the hug, drawing me closer and pressing kisses to my head. "Darling sister," she cooed, "everything will turn out well. The Almighty answers our prayers."

The words were nothing like what Aunt Cyanna used to comfort her children. But they were so reminiscent of Kyros that I only cried harder.

What am I going to do when he leaves again?

The last seven months without him had been a waking nightmare. Though the villagers were appeased by the currency Kyros had given them from our reserve, enough to ignore me most of the time, their children still yelled taunts outside my window and threw pebbles at my back whenever I went to help in the fields, fetch water, or use the outhouse. My younger cousins played all sorts of cruel tricks, from shredding my clothes to cutting my hair to burning food and blaming it upon me. My eldest cousin even hit me several times. And all anyone did, all Aunt Cyanna and Uncle Leos did, was mildly rebuke them.

I exhaled a shuddering sigh and tucked my face into Arista's neck.

That was not entirely fair—Auntie and Uncle provided for me, protected me from the soldiers, and kept to Kyros' schedule of lessons, sometimes even being kind enough to play with me, and Auntie Aniela and her daughter Enthella shared their biscuits whenever they had a bit of extra flour. I was safe and often even cheerful (though happiness was impossible without Kyros).

I still wanted to run away.

But I knew why Kyros had never left until his visions.

Just as I knew why he would not take me with him.

How I wanted to go with him...

"Kalyca!" called a horrified voice—his voice.

Cringing, I refused to look up from Arista's shoulder (she was only four inches taller, so I *could* hug her this way).

"Kallie..." Kyros sighed, new robes rustling, and said, "Arista, she is not hurt, is she?"

Though I did not want to tell him, I adored that he now had someone to ask, someone who cared about both of us.

"No, Hally," Arista answered, tightening her firm grip, as though she was prepared to protect me from everything. "The villagers had not yet progressed beyond taunts and insults, as you saw."

I loved the endearment, the Zahacit word for 'Brother,' almost more than her embrace.

"Gratitude to the Almighty for that!" Kyros exclaimed. Then he sighed again and muttered, "Will they never cease ruining what peace we gain?" He sounded heartsick.

His pain hurt me more than anything else. Tearing away from Arista's arms, I flung myself into his.

Kyros caught me and lifted me off my feet, holding me to his heart as he had done for as long as I could remember. That place, my face smushed into his chest, my head beneath his chin, and my legs dangling to his knees, was where I belonged, treasured by the brother who was all the family I had ever had, ever needed, ever wanted.

My best friend, my hero, my Kyie.

Wrapping my arms around his neck, breathing in the rich musk of his scent, I snuggled into him, wishing that we would never be separated, that I could simply become part of him.

He kissed my head and then asked, "What is that in your hand, Kallie darling?"

I squeezed my face, which was glossing with embarrassment beneath the filth coating it, against his collar. "A pot of honey, which I bought from the shops."

A shocked inhale stirred the hair leaking from my cap before he exclaimed, "Kallie! You know you are not supposed to leave the house alone!"

"I know," I whispered, "but I wanted to help you prepare. Lucian said he wished for honey, and Aunt Cyanna did not bring any..."

He groaned quietly. "Kallie darling..."

"I am sorry," I squeaked, heart cracking. Even when I tried to be helpful, I was a burden. Always a burden.

He sighed a third time. "There is no need to apologize, my darling." Shifting his arms, he settled me on his hip like a small child.

For once I did not make him put me down. I was *not* a baby, but... if he wanted to hold me like one... I would let him, just for today. Maybe it would make me less of a burden to him.

"Kyros!" Elian cried. "What happened?"

Kyros clutched me more tightly, smearing dirt and soot from my rough, ragged clothes onto his smooth, soft ones, as Lucian and Elian descended the stairs.

His green eyes wide with alarm, Elian rushed to Kyros and me. "What happened?" he asked again as he withdrew the large square of worn cotton that served as his handkerchief from a pocket.

Knowing he had been alone for more years than I had lived—

my brother's new friends had told me their stories after supper yesterday—I expected him to offer the cloth to Kyros.

Instead, lifting a chocolate hand dotted with those beautiful golden scales, Elian began to wipe the remaining wetness from my coarse cheeks. He actually *touched* me, though he often concealed winces when any but Lucian touched him...

I could only stare at him as he dried my tears and then leaned close to me and actually pressed a kiss to my cheek.

No one beside Kyros had *ever* done that—not since I was too little to remember it.

Despite the anguish in his eyes, Kyros' lips curved upwards.

And I stared at that, too. Because, except for the ones he gave for my sake, Kyros *never* smiled and actually meant it. *Never.* It was why I had to do so many silly things, so that he did not fall ill from never laughing.

How the Almighty loved Kyros to give us so much...

"Are you better, my Sister?" Elian asked gently, placing one of his huge hands upon my back.

I nodded silently.

"Gratitude to the Almighty," Elian whispered and gave my cheek another kiss, before stepping back.

"Gratitude, indeed," Lucian said, drawing my attention.

The sweet, sympathetic, *understanding* smile on his shining face made more tears well in my eyes.

No one beside Kyros had ever cared to understand me. And now, no one less than the Quest Leader himself—the hero of every story Kyros whispered to dispel my nightmares and soothe me to sleep—now, the Quest Leader *himself* cared to consider what I thought and how I felt.

How the Almighty loved Kyros to give us so much...

Lucian exhaled a chuckle as he held my gaze, his smile sweetening further.

Of course he knew my thoughts. I was happy to share them with him.

Keeping one arm wrapped around Kyros' neck, I held my

other hand out to him. "I bought the honey," I said. Then realized I could not possibly be doing this the right way, because rulers did not just *take* things—

Before I could pull back my hand, Lucian accepted the tiny pot, encasing it in his long, beautifully elegant fingers. "My gratitude, my darling Sister," he replied, "though I would ask that you seek your brother's permission first. He worries much for you. You did not tell us that you had left, and our use of magic to find you could not assuage his fears, for we could not come to your aid without attracting the attention of the soldiers."

Oddly, like the look he had given me after I had disturbed Kyros amid our lessons earlier, the words were scolding in a way that did not make me feel small—so much loving understanding filled his every expression that I knew all he wished was for me to be safe and well and blessed. His scolding did not break my confidence but instead built it stronger.

Like Kyros'.

So it was easy to say that I would do better and truly mean the words.

Kyros, Lucian, Elian, and Arista all favored my response with more smiles and more kisses—fulfilling every daydream I had ever had about what my parents and other siblings must have been like.

How the Almighty loved Kyros to give us so much...

Then Elian carefully took me from Kyros (again shocking me), his strong arms carrying me as effortlessly as my brother's did, and together we followed Lucian to where he and Elian had been sorting through the things the Quest would carry with them on their journey.

Settling gracefully on the edge of my parents' old bed, Lucian explained what they were doing and asked if I had any thoughts about what they should do next. Then both Lucian and Elian listened when I suggested fixing the old, broken flasks from Kyros' childhood.

If not for the shock of Aunt Aniela's request before luncheon,

I would not have believed anything that was happening. No one beside Kyros had *ever* thought that I was more than a pest underfoot, another irritating rat that stole food the village could not spare, much less valued my presence and listened to my ideas.

But Lucian and Elian actually, openly, let me help. Even after I accidentally spilled a flask full of water all over the pouches in Lucian's pack and dented one of Elian's pots. Not only did they not hit me, they did not even become angry. Their smiles never faltered even as they cleaned my messes.

It was too much to believe that anyone could ever think well of me beside Kyros. It was too much to believe that I could be safe with anyone beside him.

How the Almighty loved Kyros to give us so much...

When Lucian and Elian were satisfied with their packing, we went downstairs to where Kyros, Malika, Arista, and Elacir were repairing weapons, fletching arrows, and washing clothes.

At Lucian's entrance, the four of them leapt to their feet. Then, shocking me again, Malika and Elacir ran to *me*, and Malika scooped me into her arms.

Arista told us what happened when we returned from the stream, Malika said hurriedly in Lucian's link. *Are you all right, my darling?*

My throat closed at the depth of affection in her words—the words of a woman who had suffered more than I could ever understand, more than anyone ever could, without anyone ever asking her that question. Her concern for me when her skin was gray with illness and her voice stolen... I could not believe it. And my amazement was all the greater because she glowed: despite her ill health, she wore a radiance bright enough to rival Lucian's own... and yet she deigned to ask after me.

How the Almighty loved Kyros to give us so much...

At my continued silence, instead of pressuring me to answer, Malika squeezed me more tightly, before kissing my forehead, setting me on my feet, and giving Kyros a look of worry.

My brother pressed his lips together as his beautiful gray eyes met Malika's equally beautiful blue ones. Though neither of them spoke—there was not a single twinkle of magic about them—they seemed to understand each other perfectly.

I adored how he now had someone to understand him so well. Though I did everything I could, I had always known that my brother was too far beyond me for me to ever really grasp him. It was how he had been able to raise me, though he had been only a child himself.

Kyros dipped his head in response to something in Malika's expression. Then he turned toward me, his lips curving into the narrow but intensely loving smile that, matched by the creases that spread from the corners of his gray eyes and the serene sparkle within them, was my most favorite thing in the entire world. When he wore that fatherly smile... it was like all the evil things in the world lost all their power to hurt me.

How I would miss it when he left again!

"Come, Kallie," Kyros said, using the nickname that was just ours, "let me show you how to sharpen this sword." Bending, he folded his long legs and sat on the floor in front of a cloth on which he had placed several smooth stones and a pair of swords. He patted the ground by a sword, and I scampered to his side. "Now, Kallie," he began, gesturing at the sword closer to me, "this is our mother's sword, and I intend to leave it and our father's with you. You must take care of it because it is made of iron. First, this is how we must sharpen the edge..."

I relaxed as I listened to the smooth melody of his rumbling voice. He had taught me so many things in that low musical voice, from properly shucking corn to skinning rabbits to baking bread to reading and writing, and I could not imagine any more days passing without hearing it...

Around us, Malika, Arista, and Elacir returned to their work, and Lucian and Elian joined them, murmuring in quiet voices, as though they did not want to disturb Kyros and me... as though they respected our bond as no one else ever had.

Having heard ever since I could remember that our bond was

somehow impure and tainted, that we did things with each other that siblings should not do... with such horrible things echoing in my ears, Lucian's, Malika's, Elian's, Arista's, and Elacir's respect was too a precious a jewel to believe I could ever have.

How the Almighty loved Kyros to give us so much...

When Kyros had taught me everything he knew, Lucian and Arista beckoned me to their sides and showed me more ways to care for weapons. Next, Arista helped me sharpen small stones for the points of my first arrows and tie silky feathers to the thin sticks of their shafts. Then Elian took me upstairs again to teach me the purpose of the various herbs he carried, as well as what was safe to eat on plains and in forests.

By the time Kyros called us for supper, my mind was full and my heart warm from everything I had been blessed enough to learn. As Lucian recited the prayer and Kyros placed a bowl of steamed vegetables in front of me, I was certain that *everyone* around the table loved me.

Kyros was really right to say that we had a new family. It was no longer just the two of us, alone, against all the terrible evils that filled the world—there was no thanks great enough that I could give for that.

But what I can *do is make sure my brother is not keeping secrets as he usually does.* Though Kyros told me everything—*everything,* from how bitterly he grieved our parents and our siblings to how badly the villagers abused him—he confided in no one else. Aunt Cyanna and Aunt Aniela only knew half of his reasons for demanding the assurances he had for my safety.

But that should not be how he treats our new family...

Deciding on how I wanted to begin, I opened my mouth and said, "Lucian, Malika, Elian, Arista? Elacir?"

Their quiet conversations stopped as they all turned toward me. My brother gave me a curious look.

Savoring their attention, I could not help a big grin. The words "I love you!" spilled from my mouth.

All five of them smiled, seeming actually delighted, and

returned the words. Kyros bestowed upon me another lovely fatherly smile.

Bolstered by the affection, I took a deep breath and asked, "Did Kyros tell you what the villagers are like?"

Everyone except Lucian startled.

Then Kyros sighed and rubbed his forehead. "I do not want to tell them, Kallie."

"You should, though, Kyie," I said, meeting his gray eyes with my own. "We are a family, and we love each other, and we trust each other to protect us."

Kyros closed his eyes and blew out a breath.

Around the table, our new family curiously watched us both.

"It is only fair," I pushed, sure from his expression that he saw my point. "You cannot let them face the villagers tomorrow without telling them."

Kyros rubbed his forehead again, then sighed and flashed me a rueful smile. "As always, wiser than I am." Then he glanced at his new friends, a deep entreaty in his gaze. "I did not want to burden you with more pain than you already bear."

Malika smiled softly and, lowering her spoon, touched his hand. *I would much prefer to share that pain than leave you alone in its grasp.*

Elian and Arista murmured similar things, and Elacir returned Kyros' look of entreaty with his own. Lucian, however, met my gaze and smiled in approval.

I beamed in answer.

Though that smile quickly vanished when Kyros lowered his head and began to speak.

It was one thing to have lived through our suffering; it was quite another to hear what it was like for him. His pain hurt worse than anything else, and he hurt so much *more* than I did...

With his memories in the air, I could only wonder at how terrible the choices before him were: he could not possibly take me on what was sure to be a dangerous journey, even one with the most powerful warriors imaginable, but he also could not leave me in Tresilt because even Aunt Cyanna did not truly respect—

The sight of her pledging to Lucian flashed before my eyes.

This is why, I realized suddenly as Kyros described the sorts of evil threats the villagers had made against me, *this is why Lucian took Aunt Cyanna's pledge, though he does not like her, and also why Lucian agreed to Aunt Aniela's plea. If they are loyal to him, they would care for me and protect me from the soldiers. Or at least this was one of his reasons why.* Curious, I looked up from my bowl to Lucian's shining face.

Despite the pain dimming those glowing features, a small smile curved Lucian's pale lips as his gaze met mine. *Do you truly think I would choose your brother and then abandon you without protection?* he asked in the link only he and I shared.

I pressed a grin into the sweet-tasting magic. *No, Lucian! That is why you are our sun.*

In response he impressed the most wonderful thing into the link: the sight of his beautiful smile widening and spreading, showing a hint of his white teeth, as the gold flecks in his violet eyes sparkled.

Even as my brother spoke of the horrors of our history, that one image blew away all of my unhappiness, like bad smells scattered by the wind's perfume.

As I saw that sacred smile, my foresight sparked. Invoked by the inspiration of his gaze, energy flared and mixed with magic, sighing softly, like the breaths passing through my nose while I fell asleep, yet with all the force of the rising gales born whenever my brother ran across the plains.

My vision flashed white.

Then...

Kyros' smile faltering as he whispered, "I am sorry for leaving again, Kallie, with even less notice than the first time," his face mere inches from my own...

Kyros' wondering grin as light burst from his person, shining like the sun, blazing around him as though he were a star himself, dazzling, searing, flaming, as he became what he was meant to be...

Kyros' laughter as he marveled at the boughs of a tree that looked like it was made of glass...

Kyros' fatherly smile, dazzlingly happy despite the new lines around his eyes and nose, crowned by a white helm and circlet adorned with vibrant jewels, coming closer as he leaned down toward me...

Kyros' affectionate glances toward a woman whose cold blue eyes seemed to thaw as she walked at his side...

Wings of purple scales curving around me, not coming close enough to touch yet almost cradling in their nearness...

The Quest enthroned, each of their faces bright with joy, the hallowed chairs beneath them wide and strangely made without part of their armrests and sides...

The golden sun rising over fields of yellow corn, every wisp of smog absent like in one of Kyros' legends, as warm, familiar fingers gripped both of my hands...

My vision flashed white again.

Then the magic faded, dissolving upon Lucian's pleased expression.

Those were certainties, were they not? I asked, recalling the solid quality of all that I had seen. *If Kyros goes with you?* I bit my lower lip. *And—I could not tell when most of them will happen—I do not know enough magic for that—but the first will be soon, will it not?*

Lucian impressed a nod into the link.

I stared into his divine-blessed eyes. *I want that future,* I whispered with all the longing in my heart, the bright happiness flavoring all but the first vision still present on my tongue. *Will the Almighty give it to me?*

Kindness shone in those violet stars. *Yes, if you do not waver in your faith.*

What he asked was something more than what I could give: Kyros had been my only family for as long as I could remember, and being without him for even a few months was a nightmare without waking. Being without him for more months, even years... while fearing that he was in dangerous places doing dangerous things... how could I possibly survive it?

Yet how could I beg him to stay?

His sacrifice of going and mine of staying would bring back the sun. And it was what the Almighty wanted and Lucian needed... just as it was what *Kyros* needed...

How the Almighty loves Kyros to give us so much...

As those wondrous words flashed through my mind, I knew what choice I would make.

The Almighty loved Kyros, so I would believe the Almighty would make Kyros happy by reuniting us someday.

In response to that thought, Lucian beamed just like the legendary sun. Sharing in his joy, despite their confusion, so did the rest of my new family. Including my Kyie.

CHAPTER 4
PROFFERING DEDICATION

Perspective: Inase Elacir bi-Dekecer, confidant of the Quest
Date: Eyyéfaz, the twenty-seventh day of the twelfth moon, Alshatte,
of the year 499, C.Q.
Placement: between Chapter 26 and Chapter 27 of The Bell Tolling

Though I was *right* in front of Elian, he did not meet my gaze. Forehead wrinkled, scales a dull ochre, he looked only at his bowl—the bowl he had taken from *my* hands—as he ate. There was none of the charming, if awkward, chatter that he had shared with me only weeks prior.

I suppressed a whimper. It was too much like my cousin—that was how his betrayal had started, with a refusal to look at me, as though the very sight of my face was abhorrent to him... Yes, pain rather than the cold, hard glint of jealousy filled Elian's eyes, but it could so easily change—

Moving my hand from the ladle, I pinched the skin of my arm hard, brutally crumpling a scale. *It is blasphemy to think such things about the Potentates!*

But the recrimination did not kill the thought...

Holding in a sigh, I gripped the ladle again and poured the final bowl of stew before proffering it to Kyros.

Though pain glittered in his eyes as well, he looked at me and gave me something of a smile as he accepted the bowl. He dearly missed his sister, the parting raw once more, and those accursed villagers' words were salt on the wound, but his kindness to me had not faltered.

Like Malika, Arista, and Lucian himself.

Only Elian had changed.

I prepared the final bowl, scraping the bottom of the pot, and lifted the wooden spoon to my own lips.

The stew was excellent, one of Elian's best, as delicious as my own mother's cooking, but it felt like dry wood as it slid down my throat. A texture I remembered all too well from last winter, when bark had been all there was left to eat.

Amid the silence that stifled all but Lucian's and Arista's discussion, it was too easy to lose myself in memories of those dark days... and of the darker ones that came after...

Around me, the Potentates quietly finished their meals, attended to the day's last chores, wrapped themselves in their blankets, and fell asleep. They exchanged kind glances and words, with each other and with me (except Elian), but little conversation stirred, those accursed villagers' insults lingering like a dark storm cloud around us as they had since Tresilt.

How I hated those people for hurting my saviors. Each of the Potentates was sacred, our sun and moon and stars amid the darkness, our path free of the enemy's brutal reign, and their sister carried a greater gift of that goodness than any of us ever could, and the villagers had had the gall to *insult* them. Not just refuse to proffer the allegiance and service for which they were born—no, indeed, they had to *insult* our Rulers and their sister.

How I hated them.

But it was Lucian's mercy to let them live. And, indebted to that same mercy, I had no choice but to quash the urge to exact vengeance. Even as Elian's pain and distance shredded what was left of my heart.

I scrubbed the last dish clean with a handful of snow, dried it, and tucked it in Elian's pack. My last assigned task completed, I sat back and glanced around.

Having finished their chores faster than I had, Malika, Elian, Arista, and Kyros lay in repose next to the horses, which were tucked beneath blankets for the night, and the whole world was quiet.

Quiet like the tomb.

I could not sleep. The memories were too fresh on this night.

It was *the* night, after all.

Turning to Kyros' pack, pressing my wings more tightly around my sides for warmth, I removed a jar of salt, which we had replenished from a salt deposit only yesterday, and retrieved the slabs of meat drying on a stone by the low-burning fire. With brisk motions, I began to cure the meat, preserving the leftovers from the morning's hunt so we could travel faster for the next few days.

Because of our hasty departure from Tresilt, the chore was now given to whoever was assigned the first watch. Lucian had chosen to take it tonight, but he had stepped away a few minutes earlier, and it seemed shameful to remain awake and not take care of the task for him.

The repetitive movements soon proved to be inadequate distraction.

The black memories crept closer.

My mother's scream as she thrashed amid the throes of blinding hunger, the fetid stench of death reeking from my father's body, the darkness in my uncle's eyes...

My cousin's leer as he watched me cry on my betrothed's shoulder... the disdain on her face as he mocked me before the aerie...

The drum of the soldiers' wings... the bruise of their fists, and how all of my neighbors had closed their ears to my pleas for help... the places the soldiers had touched me and the burn of the blood as it leaked from my wings... the choking terror of those days in which I had believed everything, from my home to my sanity, to be lost... how close I had been to giving up.

Elian's face, crown-patterned gold scales bright despite the freezing rain, had been what saved me. What returned me from the brink enough to beg for salvation at Lucian's hands, what brought me this second chance at life—both in how Lucian had roused me from the stupor of the dying and in how he had somehow deigned to bestow upon me the blessing of calling the Potentates themselves my family. He involved me in every aspect of their lives, from embraces to lessons, and he himself tutored me in the use of my stunted magic. Such unimaginable blessing.

Elian was the one who had given all of this to me. Through his gentle gaze the Almighty had restored to me more than what I had lost. He was everything to me.

And now he would not even look at me.

I could not lose him. But I did not know how to hold onto him—I had not even been able to ward off betrayal from the girl I loved or the cousin I treated as my own brother. How could I presume to matter at all to Elian when my own beloved and blood thought me worthless? How could I dare to call myself his brother?

All I could do was make myself so invaluable that convenience maintained my place at his side.

Hence the chores.

Ignoring the throb of my fingers and the sting of my bleary eyes, I packed more salt into the sides of the steak, precisely as I had seen Elian do. Once the piece was done, I reached for another.

A soothing hand touched my shoulder.

Startling at the sudden rush of comfort, I jerked my head up.

Lucian smiled warmly as he sat beside me, gracefully folding his legs as though the hard dirt was in actuality a throne worthy of his use.

"Little Brother," he said, beginning with the endearment I so loved, "I did not accept your pledge so that you would labor without sleep in this manner."

I shrunk from that affectionate gaze. "Sorry," I muttered, loathing myself for troubling him.

"No, Little Brother," he said, the rich sound of his chuckle easing the weight of my sorrows, "I do not ask for your shame. Instead, may I join you?"

I stared at him. It was *his* meat.

Laughing again, Lucian gently pried the salt from my frozen digits. Dipping an elegant finger into the jar, he collected half the remaining slabs and started the process of preserving them. With more skill than even the hunters of my former aerie.

"Elacir," he said as he worked, "would it please you to hear a story?"

I nodded dumbly.

A smile spread his lips. "In my childhood, one of my cousins, a prince three years my elder, was enthralled by crowns. He did not quite understand what they meant, but he did know that our parents, the parents of my cousins, and our grandfather treasured them and that the few officials allowed to know of me respected them. That was apparent to him even in his seventh year. His enthrallment—he thought they were beautiful, shining, sparkling, filled with athar magic. He also knew that I was meant to wear a crown as well. But, not knowing where the first Quest's jewels were kept, he resolved to create replacements. Rallying his sister, our cousins, and my brother, he led them in making dozens of wreaths of every flower imaginable..."

Lucian proceeded to describe how the young heirs had ambushed him in the middle of a lesson, whisked him to a secret court session, and then tried to coronate him with the flower wreaths. The result had been the future Quest Leader, barely three feet tall in his fourth year, staring bemused at his grandfather from within a pile of flowers higher than his head. Though Lucian himself had begun to giggle, despite his sneezes, their parents and their grandfather had sternly reprimanded the heirs as they rushed to dig him out. The royal cousins had apologized but eventually tried to repeat the same ceremony.

Though I had never seen anyplace so beautiful as Asfiya's capitol nor experienced such peace, I was captivated by the sound of his voice and the vivid images it invoked. For uncounted minutes, I lived and breathed as Lucian had, lost in his memories instead of my own. Or, rather, found there by him.

Completing that story, Lucian shifted to another, again from before Asfiya's capture and again of his brother and his cousins.

It was so easy to forget my woes and sorrows in his presence.

Smiling and laughing, Lucian finished a final tale as we stowed away the last of the meat, salted and wrapped in thick athar cloth. Then he clasped my shoulder and said, sorrow coloring his voice, "May the Almighty bless your parents."

Of course he knows. "My gratitude, my Lord," I answered, shuffling closer to his touch. Beneath its influence, the cruelty of their deaths did not seem to haunt me as much...

"They prayed for your life, Elacir," Lucian said, the gold flecks in his violet eyes glowing.

I dropped my gaze, too guilty to behold his divine face. "I ate the last bit of bread, my Lord. I should have ignored her begging, left it for my mother at least when my father's health failed."

"Would you truly have denied her last wish?" he asked. "The end of her time in this life had come; the Almighty called her, and none can refuse the Almighty's call. Her last moments were filled with the satisfaction that she had cared for you as best she could. Your father felt the same. Would you deny them that pleasure?"

"No..." I swallowed, then fell into his embrace. Though I usually showed nothing but lighthearted cheer, or grave attention where appropriate, every tumultuous feeling well hidden, I could not help but seek his comfort. My resolution to look only at the uplifting in my life, made when I had pledged to him, was crumbling under the weight of my memories, and he was my only support.

He did not refuse me, tugging me close to his chest and stroking the scaled ridge of my wings. Though I was too unworthy to look upon him, he let me cry into his robes, rocking me back and forth exactly as my mother once had.

When the tears stemmed, he tipped my head up and said, violet eyes bright, "Do not fear, darling Brother. He will never turn his back upon you."

"But I have what he most wants," I whispered, all my desperation welling in my heart. "I can fly, and he cannot. How can he not be jealous?"

Lucian shook his head. "Elian does not possess the capacity for jealousy, and least of all in this."

"How can that be!" I cried. "What is a Sholanar without wings..." My chest shuddered under the weight of my sobs. "I would give him my wings, my Lord! If only I could cut them from my back and attach them to his! But I cannot! If only he would not turn away from me for what I cannot do..."

A deep sympathy on his shining face, Lucian drew me yet closer and kissed my forehead, as though I really were his sibling, like the ones of which he had told me stories.

Soothed by his compassion and by the blessing of his arms, I almost had the strength to believe his words.

Almost.

It was too good to be true.

Before the scar of my parents' deaths had healed, my family betrayed me. The experience had forever marked me—I always lost everyone I loved. Either I betrayed them, or they betrayed me...

Elian was too precious for me to survive a betrayal. He was my world... but my world tended to reject me.

Though it was blasphemy of the highest order to not believe Lucian.

CHAPTER 5
CONTRIVING SHIELDING

Perspective: Nadeya Tahira Enarias, citizen of Nademan
Date: Eyyéala, the seventeenth day of the first moon, Lushatte, of the year 500, C.Q.
Placement: between Chapter 32 and Segment 1 of <u>The Bell Tolling</u>

I tipped the chalice toward me, surreptitiously examining the metal and the color of the water within.

A thin film of white powder coated the base of the vessel.

Poison to kill me, corrupt my judgment, or sedate me and leave me vulnerable to rape? I thought wryly. *Which this time?* I casually switched the glass for another and repressed a disgusted frown at the foul odor rising from it. *Yet another poison, only more obvious.* I surveyed the portion of table closest to me. *Well, that is the last chalice available. No water tonight, it seems. At least I managed to get an untampered plate. Or,* I laughed bitterly within my own mind, *perhaps that is only what I think. Their poisons are expanding far faster than I can catalog—*

A shrill scream cut through my thoughts. Pained, desperate, pleading for help.

I did not look up, though the indifference scathed my soul. I was the Gouge's strategist, the chief architect of his armies, the commander of his commanders, the pillar that reinforced his throne, and I was utterly powerless.

My production of unideal strategies was useless in halting the massacres, my attempts at manipulating the staff into aiding his captives were increasingly unsuccessful, and I had no way of knowing whether the only person for whom I truly cared at all still lived. My life's purpose was evaporating much like the water of the rivers. There was little point to continuing to protect myself, save my unwillingness to allow the Gouge to choose my end.

I do not know how to continue, oh Almighty. I suppressed a wince as the woman screamed again. *I beg of You a chance to serve Your name. I have tried to do so in protecting my brother and in lessening the cruelty of the monster's plans, but it is work without hope. Please, oh Almighty, I beg of You hope.*

Though I prayed, I doubted the prayers of such a stained soul as mine could ever be heard.

Another scream, this one too familiar, shook the long dining hall.

I held back a sigh. *It seems there is yet another frustrating attempt at convincing the staff's healer to attend to his wounds in my future.* I despised the crown prince, the son of the man whose negligence was the direct cause of Nademan's woes, but I could not leave him completely without support.

Just as I could not entirely abandon either the people of Nademan or the Gouge's other captives. Though I loathed them in my darker moments, for all of them were almost as complicit in the enemy's evil as the traitor king, declining to resist the monster out of a selfish, mistaken desire to preserve their own safety, I could not wholly refuse to do anything for them. Yes, I kept my interference on their behalf as minimal as possible, for my greatest responsibility was to my brother, but still I acted. Perhaps it was solely out of a lingering sense of duty to the Almighty, often without even a drop of compassion, but I did act.

Despite the cruelty surrounding me in the Gouge's court, I had not forgotten my family.

In a pious attempt to protect their town and their nation, my parents and my sister had rejected the thought of simply acquiescing to tyranny and had sparked a rebellion in the year following the Blood's conquest. They and their supporters had been truly loyal to Icilia, resiliently fighting a hopeless battle for ten years against forces too powerful to confront, striving to free those who too quickly betrayed them to the enemy... until, finally, one single act of misplaced trust had led to discovery by the Gouge.

In accordance with the habit that had earned him his appellation, he gouged out all of their eyes. Then slaughtered them and hanged their bodies from the walls of the old Nademani castle-tree. Then he threw their eyes at the rebels' surviving families, who were herded together like animals and forced to watch every moment of his brutality.

His crimes did not end there: immediately upon the heels of the execution, he and his colonels had committed violence against the youth and children in front of their relations, calling one family after another from the overcrowded cells.

Knowing that Kanzeo and I were next, and at nine and nineteen the preferred targets, I had devised a method of escape.

Frantically memorizing every movement of the guards that I could, I discerned the moments in which they were most careless: when removing the corpses of those who had perished from their wounds in the cells. Thinking the task onerous, they never checked whether the bodies were truly dead.

So, as the guards strolled through the cells, I scooped up blood, both fresh and congealed, from the puddles left behind by the other occupants and streaked it on Kanzeo's and my clothes, imitating the splatter of the most grievous injuries. Then I pinched a specific nerve in my brother's neck, rendering him unconscious, and pretended to have died.

Some minutes later, the soldiers arrived at our cell, unlocked the door, and exclaimed in dismay at our bodies. But, without questioning how those who had not yet been summoned by their master could be so injured, they threw us into a cart full of corpses. Then piled more corpses atop us.

I was glad Kanzeo was unaware, for I was clinging to what discipline I had at that time to not cry out at the stench and the feel of cold, clammy flesh and seeping blood.

The guards brought the corpses to a storage chamber a floor below the prison tower.

Twenty-nine stories remained between us and the ground. That little bit was all I knew of the castle's arrangement.

The moment the soldiers' footsteps faded, I roused Kanzeo. Then, mustering every drop of my powerful Nasimih kind magic, I attuned myself to the whispers of the living tree and listened. Gathering all the sounds I heard, footsteps and voices and the clinks of objects, I plotted a mental map of the area around me and the soldiers' and the staff's movements within it. I predicted where they would go and when based on what I was hearing, previous observations that I had made, and my general knowledge of how people behaved. Hours passed.

At the right moment, when a lull emerged, I took Kanzeo to the next floor below.

Then repeated the process. Again. And again. And again. Pausing only when the need for sustenance required that I locate the nearest pantries, trash storage chambers, or the soldiers' dining rooms just before they were cleaned. Water we drank from faucets in the castle-tree's advanced bathrooms.

Slowly, with great patience and focus, I snuck Kanzeo and myself down through the floors. Days passed, and the soldiers returned to a more normal pattern of activity as the last of the prisoners were murdered. Even then, I did not dare to reveal myself by attacking anyone, trusting rather in my mind than in my physical strength, worn away by days of imprisonment.

Finally we reached the last floor.

There I spent hours watching the grass move outside and the guards change positions, until I had discerned another weakness:

at mealtimes, the guards ate at their posts. They did not expect any attack, so they did not have any alert rotations watching outwards. And they did not trim the grass of the glade outside the castle in any direction but that of the main city. It was tall enough in many places to hide an adult woman.

Tracking a particular guard's schedule of relieving himself, I slipped my brother and myself out a side-door moments after the soldier stepped away for his needs.

Then, pushing my brother to his knees and urging him to follow, I crawled through the grass, carefully avoiding any visible ripples.

We reached a lesser gate and waited again.

When a cart of corpses passed, I climbed onto it and pulled my brother up after me. Moments after it reached the pyres on the edge of the glade, I rolled both of us off and led us again through the grass to the tree line.

Listening again, I crept through the trees toward the boundary, avoiding patrols and folk alike, not trusting anyone to offer us sanctuary.

But, by this time, after so many days of fear, hunger, pain, and filth, Kanzeo was exhausted. He was so small and so terrified, and I had been so harsh with him in my attempt to save us. He was stumbling as I dragged him forward, delaying during the precious seconds when the soldiers were out of hearing range.

Moments after we crossed the boundary, Kanzeo tripped on a thick branch and collapsed.

That, along with his stumbles, lost us too much time.

I was pulling him to his feet when, exactly as my calculations predicted, a soldier passed that section.

We were caught immediately and taken to the Gouge.

When we were dragged before him, he almost killed us on the spot. Then his anger cooled, and he leveled at me a look of vicious consideration.

"That was quite a strategy, for a woman," he said. "It's been two weeks, and no one realized you were missing."

Then he had, all of a sudden, declared me to be his official military strategist, burdened with the task of managing the positions of all of his forces. To ensure my stellar performance, he held my brother hostage. Should I fail, my brother would receive the personal, torturous, rapacious attention of the Gouge. And, obviously, so would I.

Our lives had been waking nightmares ever since.

Kanzeo was all alone, living in a tiny hut amid the open forest under the malicious eyes of squads of soldiers, and forced to provide everything for himself, from food to clothes to medicine to money. Though I was allowed to see him every few months, I was a slave without wages. Besides a few smuggled pieces of meat or some fronds of medicinal herbs, I had nothing to give him. Not even, as the years passed, open affection.

But at least he still lived. Beaten to the point of blood and bruises every other month, but still alive and sane and not raped.

How cruel is this age that such is actually a desired state, I thought grimly as I daintily swallowed the last bites of the grilled chicken I had been allowed today. Then, unfocusing my vision so that all I could perceive was a hazy blur, I glanced up and swept my gaze over the chamber.

"Enjoying the entertainment?" a dark voice sneered from across the table.

For the love of Icilia, no. I refrained from rolling my eyes. *That is merely a ploy to fool you into thinking I am watching.* But as much as I wanted to speak aloud that retort, my only answer was, in an entirely emotionless tone, "Entertainment, is it, General Perveries?"

He chuckled cruelly. "It seems you are as cold as your reputation, General Enarias."

I did not react, calmly finishing my supposed inspection of the room before returning my gaze to my plate.

"Tell me," the recently appointed western regional commander began, chair legs scraping the floor as he took a seat, apparently sated after partaking of his share of the malice, "as we have rarely had a chance to speak before, how *did* you find your-self in his Depravedness' service? How did a young woman like yourself become respected and feared across the whole of this territory?"

Such a poor attempt to learn my secrets. Yet, to protect Kanzeo... "His Depravedness offered me a chance to use my skills to their maximum," I replied, sounding disinterested. "That is my preferred source of pleasure, General Perveries."

The commander curled a lip at his name—not many months after his appointment, he had given himself the epithet of the Smasher in the western provinces—but he could not object to its lack of use at the Gouge's own table. Yet, still, he was angry.

I hid a smirk as I waited for him to recover. If he really wanted to unseat the Gouge, he needed more discipline. For all his lasciv-ious pleasures and debauchery, the Gouge possessed a degree of cunning and control over himself only exceeded by his rival gover-nors'. And by mine.

The western regional commander seethed for a moment, before visibly composing himself and saying, "And why did you think his Depravedness could best offer you that pleasure?" His tone became sultry as he leaned closer. "Is there no one else who could offer you more, General Enarias?"

I raised my gaze and examined him dispassionately. I hated the Gouge and held no loyalty to him, but it would be foolish to defect to General Perveries. For one, he was nearly as cruel, the primary source of the increase in massacres over the last year and a brutal suppressor of any mention of defiance (it was why the Gouge had originally appointed him two years ago). For another, he had the reputation of actually *reading* documents, which meant I would not be able to slip as much past him, and he had been disobeying my orders for too long to believe he would not betray me even if I made his rule possible. For a third... he would not succeed. The Gouge enjoyed letting rebellions, both by his soldiers and by the citizens, proceed for a time before killing everyone involved (as he had with my family). And, regardless,

Perveries lacked any magic whatsoever, much less conjury, so he had no chance at all of controlling the army or of entering the Blood's inner circle even should he succeed.

Under my impassive perusal, the general started to bristle once more. "Well?" he snarled.

"His Depravedness has granted me what I want," I said, as nonchalantly as though this was a question regarding furnishings and not treason. "It would be difficult to find a better agreement."

A brutal rage filled his eyes—he had believed that, as a woman, regardless of my intelligence, I would be easily bullied—and he opened his mouth to speak.

Noticing a shadow in the corner of my vision, I began to stand.

"Ahh, Perveries!" a voice that was blacker than night called. "Are you the one who has managed to *tempt* Enarias into joining us?"

Caught unaware, Perveries leapt to his feet, quickly wiping the anger from his face and replacing it with an insincere eagerness. "I'm certainly trying, your Depravedness!" he chirped.

I hid another smirk. *What a fool. How does he not realize that, with that comment, the Gouge is saying that he heard Perveries' treasonous words? And...* I blinked as the Gouge cast me a look that would have been called *affectionate* on any face but his cruel one. *... he apparently heard my seemingly loyal response as well and was pleased by it. Though* I *would be the fool to think that means any mercy—*

"So, Enarias," the Gouge said, reclining in his throne and thumping his booted feet on the royal table, "have you visited your brother lately?" A sneer accented the words.

Having heard this threatening question too many times to count, I felt not the slightest swell of panic as I answered neutrally, "I have not seen him recently, your Depravedness." I knew better than to say that he had not allowed it in over three months, or to actually request a visit of him.

In the last four years and seven months, I had perfected a

balance of casting my brother as both unimportant and indisposable. That balance was the reason the Gouge kept thinking him a valuable hostage without questioning the depth of my loyalty. If he believed my brother was important, he would break his vow and torture him simply to hurt me and enjoy my pain. Showing too much love for my brother would eventually cause him to suspect my deceit, as even he knew coercion did not buy allegiance. Yet on the other side, if he believed my brother was disposable, he would break his vow because he no longer needed to refrain from the cruelty he so desired to inflict in order to keep my obedience. Showing too much apathy toward my brother, such as refusing a visit, would lead him to believe he had succeeded, through repeated exposure to horrors such as this supper, in corrupting my soul and breaking my adherence to virtue. A balance as sheer as the edge of a blade.

Proving that I had accurately misled him, the Gouge shrugged in response. "Visit him tonight then." From his careless tone, he had lost interest—really lost interest, not attempting to deceive me into thinking so—in what he was saying.

While my heart lit with joy. "If it pleases your Depravedness," I said, rising, "I will leave quickly so that I return in time for the delivery of messages scheduled for tonight."

The tyrant waved a long-clawed hand. "Yeah, yeah, Enarias," he said, drawling the 'yes' not out of casualness, as most would, but to show how little he respected the very language he spoke. "Don't disturb me about reports tonight."

I curtsied and, though I longed to fly toward my brother, I forced myself to walk at my usual measured pace in the direction of the exit.

"Your Depravedness, may I escort General Enarias?"

I almost froze at the question but managed to calmly turn and face the table. Though my heart screamed against the thought of Perveries coming anywhere near my brother, I knew the Gouge would not refuse. It would be yet another way to remind me of my place beneath his boots.

Exactly as I had predicted, the monster tossed a smirk at me and answered, "Yeah, go with her. Take a squad."

That is permission for him to take a squad of his own loyalists. I curtsied in acceptance. *How far do I need to go to deceive him...? For he absolutely cannot end this night thinking that Kanzeo is important—as his attentions tonight prove, he is finally trying his hand at stealing my allegiance. What is my best course...?*

The western regional commander bowed and, grinning cruelly, stood next to me. "Lead the way, General," he drawled.

I nodded to him and walked onward, rapidly calculating the best plan, not allowing my composure to falter even as he fell in step half a pace behind me, close enough to breathe on my exposed hair, and summoned ten soldiers with a few barked orders at the guards stationed outside the dining hall. With that squad forming around their commander and me, ostensibly for my protection, the enemy soldiers and I exited the castle and proceeded toward my brother's shack.

Perveries did not even pretend to be ignorant of where it was.

Experience has proven, I concluded, *that the tactic that would most effectively ensure the least notice is the most painful. He has made me his target, so I must ensure that he does not believe he can force me to his side by abducting and torturing my brother. He* must *believe that Kanzeo is not my vulnerability.*

The group drew closer to the grove of sickly cedars that grew around the old hunter's outpost.

It is only for tonight, I thought, trying to brace myself. *Perveries is the only one who still has any interest, and he will be leaving tomorrow to address the new rebellion fomenting in Adeban. He will probably not return. The Gouge will likely soon murder him.* How strange and wrong that, for once, the thought was a comforting one.

The hut appeared through the trees, and Perveries raised a fist.

The soldiers halted.

"Go on, General," the commander sneered.

I lightly bit the inside of my cheek, a reminder to show no

emotion, and summoned my composure. Keeping my face entirely emotionless, I stepped forward and twisted the rusted iron handle.

The door swung open.

Kanzeo was standing but a foot past the entrance. Every patch of skin visible through his ragged clothes was blue and purple with recent bruises, cuts glistened red with barely clotted blood on his forehead and cheeks, and his frame was so painfully thin that he resembled the bare branches of the winter forest.

But he lived.

Gratitude to the Almighty for that...

I knew the moment his gaze came upon me.

A desperate adoration lit his dear eyes, turning them the soft cerulean color of the long ago morning sky, and a loving smile curled his sweet lips, bringing such dazzling joy to his expression that his injuries seemed barely noticeable amid the happy glow.

He loved me still. Despite my failure in protecting him from this evil, despite all the years alone, Kanzeo still loved me.

For the briefest moment, I savored my brother's presence.

Almighty, Shining Guide, I whispered within my mind, *Aalia, Manara, Naret, please, for him.*

His lips parted, forming the shape of my name.

If he spoke, it would break my will to do what I must.

Before the beloved sound of his voice reached my ears, I pivoted on my heel.

Then left.

Left.

Simply left.

Not bothering to close the door behind me.

A whisper of a strangled shriek cut through the gloom of the night.

I did not stop. I did not look back.

My expression remained frozen in its emotionless cast.

I reached the soldiers and uttered a single word: "Well?"

A scowl burned on the western regional commander's face as

he stared at me, furrowing his brow as he scrutinized my countenance.

I held steady.

Disappointment soured his visage, and a foul word fell from his tongue.

Then he turned and issued more orders, fury twisting each word, and the soldiers herded me back to the castle-tree.

I complied, limbs moving without conscious direction, eyes observant yet blind, as the bleak taste of ash and soot filled my mouth.

How many more times will I have to break his heart to save him, oh Almighty?

Though I could not cry, a howl of utter misery and anguish rose from the depths of my soul.

What have I done, oh Almighty! What have I done! What have I done to he whom I love most...

My heart was shattering in my chest, my bones crumbling, my lungs suffocating under the deluge of guilt, my eyes beholding only the devastation in Kanzeo's gaze as I callously abandoned him yet again...

How I pray he will abandon me and escape! The plea tore from my soul. *How I wish he would just forget me and leave! He is worth so much more than this charade of a life...*

In the atrium, Perveries stormed away, seeming ready to rage over the failure of his ploys tonight, and his soldiers dispersed, eager to return to their dissipated pleasures, leaving me alone.

Though the castle echoed with the sounds of raucous laughter and tormented screams, I was, for once, alone.

My impassive composure did not so much as flicker.

The only outward sign of the turmoil brewing within was the way my hand brushed a small, round bulge over my middle, the only indication of the presence of my pendant beneath my dress.

Navigating the dense corridors, I avoided both soldiers and staff members alike as I continued to my study, a tiny office on the twenty-fifth floor that was not large enough to store all the documents I was required to keep.

Only once the door closed behind me did I let a single tear fall.

But only one.

The next moment, I wiped my face, poured a glass of clean water from a hidden jug, and sat to review the sealed packet waiting upon my desk.

The packet was only visible because of its red seal amid the papers scattered across the wooden top—papers that I had neatened into tidy stacks prior to leaving for the so-called banquet.

It was the Gouge's way of telling me that he was watching, that I had no privacy even in this minuscule space allocated out of spite in my first year of slavery.

Too used to such methods of intimidation, I sipped from my glass as I broke open the seal, slid out the first sheet, and, stroking my pendant, began to read.

This is quite *odd*, I thought as the words of the reports poured through my mind. *Since the past moon of Etshatte, the Gouge has begun to receive more and more of these* communications, *these messages from the other governors' highest commanders, even the governors themselves... and he has returned every single one of them. When before, only five months prior to the first packet, he refused to inform the Clawed, the Manic, and the Slicer about the grain blights that started in Nademan and were predicted to, and certainly did, destroy their harvests. He was willing to let even his master's own soldiers starve out of his hatred for his rivals. For many years, the* only *exchange of information occurred through soldiers gossiping on the borders. Yet now... the governors are talking. Actually talking. And there are more communications I have seen him receive and send than the ones tossed to me to read and answer. It is surely a sign of greater evil to come...*

As I pored through the briefs from Khuduren on rebel activity, I began to construct a strategy for the steps that the Gouge could take if the unrest spread to Nademan. It would not be particularly creative or efficient, but I had realized in the first months that the Gouge needed a strategist because he was not truly intelligent himself. He would never know the difference. He would never realize that my supposed loyalty masked absolute and unmitigated hatred stronger than anything his subordinates felt. I would not truly serve him.

It was a fine line to walk, with my brother's life and mind at stake, but walk it I would. There was no evidence whatsoever that I was far more brilliant than I appeared to be.

The forbidden books of Icilia's old history with which I had honed my affinity for strategy as an adolescent had instilled in me a devotion to the Shining Guide and to the Quest as well. I was in an untenable position, but I would not entirely abandon my duty. Kanzeo, from what I remembered of him, would approve of that.

The outlines of the strategy were ready in my mind as I reached the end of the reports.

I began to put the papers aside.

Then my eyes touched the final line, scrawled by a general of the Slicer as an addendum to a report written in the middle of the last moon: "As a final note, the rumors behind this little rebellion, your Depravedness, are interesting, though highly unbelievable and ridiculous. There is actually a claim in the air that the Quest Leader is alive! I have sent soldiers to find the villagers who let such nonsense slip and, as I have assured your peer my liege, will soon have the matter controlled."

The papers slipped from my fingers.

I stared unseeingly at the wall as my unemotional mask broke.

The Quest Leader is alive?

Can it be true?

After the capture of Asfiya and the massacre of her royal family, my parents and all of Nademan had presumed that, if a Quest Leader had been born, she or he was certainly dead. Or worse. It had been the most terrible sort of horror to think that such tragedy might have befallen our savior...

But there was a rumor that she or he was alive? A rumor that had never been circulated before... a rumor that rang of truth in the deepest parts of my heart...

If it was true... it was such an answer to my prayers that I could hardly dare to believe it.

But if it was true... I could not empower the Gouge's troops even as much as I did, not without risking my soul and my one chance at freedom.

I started to modify the strategy. But then stopped.

Was I willing to now risk my brother to such an extent? Was I willing to do *more* than conceal this news from the enemy for as long as I could, however long that might be?

I swallowed, tightly clutching my pendant as I remembered all that had happened tonight.

Oh Almighty...

Then I expanded the modifications, producing vulnerabilities that the enemy himself would never notice but would be glaringly apparent to a true warrior.

Though my heart was still raw with pain, my course was settled: in the service of the Quest Leader, I would risk even Kanzeo. I would take the greatest risks for the chance to throw myself at the Quest Leader's feet and beg for mercy for the both of us.

As I sat to draft the proposed plan, I prayed to the Almighty that the rumor would prove true.

Only the Quest Leader's coming could free my brother and me from this waking nightmare.

CHAPTER 6
PROVING COMPETENCE

*Perspective: Prince Darian sej-Shehasfiyi, brother of the Quest
Leader and auxiliary heir to the throne of Asfiya*
*Date: Eyyésal, the twenty-second day of the first moon, Lushatte, of
the year 500, C.Q.*
Placement: same as Segment 1 of The Bell Tolling

The sword clunked as it landed on the ground.

"You have not improved, your Highness."

Despite all the confidence I so dearly wanted to portray, my shoulders hunched at those words, fisting my trembling hands, newly bruised from the spar.

"How do you expect to serve our Lord if you cannot equal your mother's skill?" Low, quiet, even, disappointed words.

I did not drop her gaze only because I had been taught that a prince never should.

"When he returns, your Highness," Taza said, "do not be surprised to find yourself without a place at his side." That brutal warning delivered, she walked away, leaving me alone, coated in mud, on the sparring field.

Suppressing my emotions, I waited until the base commander's ring told me she had left the inner circle of the fortress' trees.

Then, swiping my sword, I ran for the tallest, the only one with branches sturdy enough to sit upon at its crown that were not visible from the ground.

It had been one of Lucian's and my favorite spots whenever we had visited this base.

And it was the place I now went to remind myself of him.

He never let Taza, or any of his other guardians, treat me so poorly. But, in his absence, there was no one to remember me. No one to see my value. No one to care for me.

I could not remember anything different. From my earliest memories, Lucian had been the center of my family's world. Parents, grandfather, aunts, uncles, cousins, courtiers—those trusted enough to know of him lived and breathed for his sake, devoting every possible moment to his education, training, and comfort. Though he was the youngest of our family, he was our ruler, our hero, our salvation, Asfiya's hope and Icilia's soul. And, in his shadow, amid such enamor for his light, I was forgotten.

Save by him.

Though Lucian was the future supreme ruler of Icilia from the day he was born and I a lackluster spare prince, he had cared for me. He had always included me, always wanted my presence, always comforted me amid my fears and doubts. Even as he prepared for his destiny, he had never treated me with even an iota less than the respect an elder brother should have.

Even after his maturity, when he was endlessly plagued by nightmares so terrible that he roused himself with his own screams, he soothed away my terrors and ensured I received the training I desired.

Even after his ascension, when he became the Quest Leader entire, he remembered to speak to me and fondly bid me farewell.

He had adored me far more than I merited.

Small wonder then that I had never been jealous, in even the slightest degree, of the younger brother who was in every way more than I could ever dream of becoming. Indeed I wholly embraced the role for which I had been raised, his aide, shield, and the herald of his court.

Thus, for Taza, the woman who had come closest to becoming a second mother, to say I had no place at his side... was there nothing I could do that would ever be enough? Even the most rancorous of the guardians, the elderly scholar Ezam Talaméze, called me Icilia's next master of magical scholarship, of such magnitude was my skill in designing and deciphering the inner workings of spells, second only to Lucian's own. Even Taza herself acknowledged my prowess in military planning and strategic command of Lucian's fortresses. Yes, to my frustration as well as theirs, I could not seem to achieve true proficiency in battle —as though there was some unknown *thing* I awaited—but surely what I did excel in was enough? Surely *I* was enough?

The tears welling in my eyes spilled onto my cheeks.

As desperately as I wished to be reunited with Lucian, I feared that, when the moment came, I would find that I truly was *not* enough. For how could an incompetent spare prince retain any worth before the Potentates of the Quest? How could a sibling bond forged by blood compare with those sprung from divine blessing?

I was as Ezam once raged—a burden, valueless save for my blood, and my life would have better served Lucian if I had given it in Asfiya's capture as the other heirs did. Not even my own father saw me as anything more than an unnecessary respon-sibility.

"Lucian..." I breathed. "Lucian..."

Only his name ignited enough strength in my heart to begin the preparations I had so long delayed: composing the lessons his companions would need.

My lips curved down in a bitter scowl. I did not lust after the Potentates' offices—I would never so disrespect the divine blessing bestowed upon them—but I wanted as little to do with them as possible. Yet, before his departure, Lucian asked his family to help him provide education and training to his companions. And, probably knowing my distaste for the task, the guardians decided to leave the burden of preparation and most of the teaching on my shoulders.

I would fulfill the duty regardless—it was what an aide did. As long as my brother had use for me, I would serve him.

Closing my eyes, I finished a mental list of the materials and topics requisite for history, entrusted the notes to the perfection of my memory, and then turned to literature and the sciences. I would need to confer with Lucian about the topics on which he had already lectured...

As I switched to the subject of magic, the base commander's ring, which linked me with every inch of athar-infused tree and soil that comprised the fortress, heated on my hand.

Ilqan must have returned from his patrol.

Twisting my long slim fingers, I tapped the top of the emerald adorning the simple silver band.

The living base responded, eagerly warming to my attention like the beloved pony of my childhood, recognizing my royal blood, powerful athar magic, and sincere interest in her welfare.

Unable to help a slight smile, I asked for the veins of wood, water, and athar to relay the sounds of Ilqan's conversation with Taza.

Such intrusion, particularly upon spouses, was certainly not a holy act on my part. But they refused every question I asked about the status of the guardians' task, spreading rumors and clandestine aid to Nademan's towns on Lucian's behalf since his ascension. Far beyond simply not involving me, though rumors and aid did not require a level of weapons skill beyond my reach, they seemed determined to keep me ignorant.

The trees shook in disapproval but obeyed, knowing my reasons with the form of sentience they possessed, and brought to me the guardians' voices:

"... yet more evidence," Ilqan was saying, "of the troops' withdrawal to the garrisons at Pethama and the Zaiqani market. The forest is nearly empty of soldiers."

"You also stated the forest is no less safer," Taza said, voice firm and impassive as it was when she spoke in her capacity as general rather than wife or doting guardian.

"It is not," Ilqan said, sighing. "The new commander of the forces west of Ehaya has given direct orders for troops to harass and torment as many townsfolk as possible. Some of the soldiers I attacked were carrying these letters."

A shuffle of paper.

"Is he countermanding direct orders from the Gouge's strategist?" Taza asked, incredulity breaking through her stern focus.

"Quietly, yes, and complicating any sort of aid we might give," Ilqan said. Then he sighed again. "This development atop signs of the soldiers communicating across borders and our attempts to discover more about their plans failing... What are we going to do, Taza? How will Lucian pass safely through these lands?" It was a testament to his fear and concern that he spoke Lucian's name instead of his reverential address.

Though I disliked Ilqan (as much as anyone could detest the man who had held one's hand on countless trips to the outhouse), my heart softened, for I shared the same worry.

"That is something, Ilqan," Taza gently replied, "in which we must trust the Almighty to ensure the safety of the Almighty's own chosen."

"That is true," I whispered, leaning my head against the trunk.

Sensing the intensity of my emotions, the tree swayed gently, trying to soothe me with the rocking motion of a mother's arms.

I could not help a chuckle. "It is not the sort of worry to be rocked away, Arkaiso."

Wind whistled through the trees, blowing my beard and the stray locks of hair leaking from my cap in more attempts at comfort.

My smile widened. Amid all my doubt and anguish, how blessed I was to receive this profound response. Such depth of connection, as Lucian explained, was uniquely mine, unrivaled even among other heirs.

"I know, Taza," Ilqan said, "but it is not easy—"

I noted the shift in his tone, anxious to affectionate, and ended the relay.

Moments later, the emerald pendant pressing over my heart vibrated.

My breath caught. *That is Lucian's pattern! All my gratitude, oh Almighty!*

Fumbling with the silver chain and its amethyst and athar beads, I grasped ahold of the emerald and tapped it.

"Blessings, Brother."

The rich harmony of that voice relaxed all the tension riddling my body, bestowing a peace I had not felt since the moon of Thekharre, when he had informed us of the Quest's union.

"Blessings, Brother," I whispered into the jewel, "and especially so for your birthday." Unable to suppress the words, I then exclaimed, "I thought you would have arrived by then!" I had never been apart from him before on that sacred day, and the guardians and I, unwilling to risk his safety by initiating contact, had had a miserable celebration.

Lucian exhaled a laugh, the most beautiful sound. "My apologies, Brother. I will arrive in time for yours."

Contented, I beamed as I had not in months, despite the spell's drain on my energy. "So I will see you soon?"

"Yes, Brother," he answered. "I estimate two weeks until our arrival."

I nodded. "What do you wish?"

A smile sweetened his beloved voice. "Prepare the rooms alongside your own in the commander's quarters for six. Elacir— the boy of the Sholanar I mentioned in my communication to Father in the moon of Mirkharre—will share a room with Elian. Also prepare the study with all necessary books and the chamber adjacent with the larger maps. As for the kitchens... Darian, I also ask that you welcome my guests."

"How many?" I asked, a bit crestfallen at the thought of more demands on his attention.

"Thirteen," he answered. "Eleven women and two men, whom the Quest saved from the ruins of an Adebani town, Filisso. You might recall the skirmish we fought near her boundary in your eighteenth year."

I gasped. "Filisso is destroyed?" The news was not uncommon, but... though six years had passed, I remembered the town so clearly—I had never forgotten the face of the woman I had helped save, and it was one of the only twelve missions on which I had been allowed to come.

"Yes," he said, voice grim, "and we could save only a few."

Calculations whirred in my mind, and bile crept up my throat. "Was that day... was it perhaps *after* your birthday?"

Lucian sighed. "We arrived in Filisso on the sixteenth of the moon of Lushatte."

My pulse roared in my ears. "Lucian! Your birthday is meant to be celebrated! The day salvation came! Not lamented upon! Did at least your companions congratulate you?"

"They did," he replied, a smile evident once more in his words. "I am blessed, Darian."

My worry for his sake immediately turned to fear for my own, and I hated myself for it.

"Darian—" Lucian began. Paused. A moment passed. Then he said, sounding distracted, "Brother, I must ask for your pardon. Kyros' farsight is about to fail, and the rebounding magic will have the force to crush bone. I must address this."

"As you wish, Lucian," I forced through numb lips. "Arkaiso will be readied in accordance with your wishes, both for your stay and for war."

"My gratitude, Darian," he said, still preoccupied. "May the Almighty be pleased with you, Brother."

Barely had I returned the greeting before he ended the contact.

I thumped my head back against the trunk, even the trees' soothing whispers bringing no smiles.

I will watch him forget me. And indeed what love would he deign to keep aside for me now that he has his beloved Malika, Elian, Arista, and Kyros? The siblings for whom he spent three years in prayer? I am but a placeholder.

And yet I would obey even when he no longer cared for me.

Lucian was Icilia's savior, but he was my savior first.

CHAPTER 7
INTENDING DUTIFULNESS

*Perspective: Crown Prince Eligeo tej-Shehennadem, Heir-apparent
to Nademan*
*Date: Eyyédal, the twenty-third day of the first moon, Lushatte, of
the year 500, C.Q.*
Placement: between Segment 1 and Chapter 33 of The Bell Tolling

The sharp pain of a brutal kick erupted in my lower back. I stumbled forward and collapsed onto my knees, scraping them against the uneven wooden floorboards. Before I could process the pain, a hand grasped my hair, yanked my head backwards, and plunged it into the cleaning bucket.

Overcome by the shock of the sudden attack, I inhaled a breath full of filthy water and tried to move my head. The hand was unyielding, and I began to struggle, desperate for a free breath. My limbs thrashed on the ground, but even in my instinct-driven state I remembered to not reach up and try to remove that hand.

In my air-deprived mind, I wondered if today would be the day he would kill me.

The hand's pressure disappeared, and I thrust my head out of the water. I coughed, thumped my chest to eject the water from my lungs, and coughed again. With the discernment that comes with repeated practice, I judged precisely when my lungs were clear and ignored the taste of dirt that coated my mouth and throat.

Recovering, I cautiously looked around, my gaze sticking to the floor.

Two feet to my right was a pair of gilded boots.

I froze as soon as I noticed them.

Despite my near drowning, I held my breath. *Anything* could trigger worse abuse, and my body was still healing from his last bout of violence.

"Pathetic *boy* who is supposed to be a crown prince," the blacker than night voice jeered. Every syllable dripped with the promise of excruciating pain, every intonation shivered in pleasure at the thought of causing that pain.

I suppressed a series of shudders. I feared that voice more than any other sound in the world, but I could not let the unadulterated terror overcome me. Fleeing might save me from a painful evening, or it might only prompt *more* torture.

How pathetic was my lot that I had been the victim of conjury so many times that the mere thought of him provoked nearly uncontrollable panic.

"Stupid crown prince," the dark voice laughed.

Then those boots moved closer again.

Before I could react—not that there was a reaction to be had—one gilded boot kicked my chest.

The savage blow threw me onto my back, sending me skidding for several feet before my head collided with the stone wall.

I gasped for breath as my vision flickered rapidly between senseless images and darkness. Agony pulsed from my chest and streaked down my spine from both the first kick and the scrape of the rough boards.

I could not breathe. My throat was too dry. My lungs were empty of air.

Panic clawed at my throat, and I convulsed on the ground, unable to breathe.

My vision blackened, and I lost consciousness.

When I roused, I was soaking wet—the dirty bucket had probably been upended over my prone form—but at least air filled my lungs. Though my body still throbbed with pain.

I cautiously sat up and glanced around.

The boots were gone.

Gratitude to the Almighty.

I relaxed marginally and leaned forward. Placed my hands on the stone floor and slowly folded my legs beneath me. Then lifted myself onto my hands and knees.

He might have emptied the bucket, but I still had to clean the floor of the throne room, and all I had been allowed was just this one bucket. I could not retrieve more water, by *his* order.

What heartbreaking irony. I was the crown prince, yet I scrubbed the floor of my own throne room.

But then, that image contained the story of my life.

I had been eleven years old when Nademan had fallen to the Blood—or, more accurately, crumbled to pieces before him. I remembered all too clearly the day of the conquest. Just as I remembered why it had happened: Nademan had fallen because my father had done nothing to stop the enemy.

Oh, yes, after the fall of Koroma his advisers had finally persuaded him to field an army. But he had made every excuse to not fully fund it, train it, or deploy it. He was too confident that the Blood could never cross the thorns that protected the Dasenákder, and he was too sure that the monster was not that great of a threat, whatever the monarchs of Asfiya and Koroma said.

His arrogance had cost us everything.

His life, certainly, for the Gouge brutally clawed out his eyes and removed his head after the Blood had sacked the capital and summoned the royal family for a reckoning.

His nation, certainly, for the Blood's soldiers overran it, raping, torturing, murdering, and burning everywhere they went.

His family, certainly, for the Blood had tortured and massacred my grandparents, my aunts and uncles, and even my cousins who were but infants at the time.

His wife, even, for my mother fled the capital just before it was sacked and had never returned.

But also me. He had never considered what would happen to me and to my siblings.

The four of us had been claimed by the Gouge as his pets. His objects of pleasure and torture. His slaves.

And so, since the fall of Nademan, nightmares had become our lives.

None of us ever knew whether we would live to see the next day. We never knew when the next meal would come. We never knew a relief from pain.

The castle that had once been the background of our idyllic childhood was now our prison.

We had no one—not even each other, really, for the stress of survival shredded the bonds of family and friendship we had before so treasured. And the staff, forced to remain in the castle, certainly blamed us for the loss of our country.

In the Gouge's court, there was no loyalty and no love.

I rubbed the cleaning rag against a slight stain in the wood until the mark disappeared, then pressed the cleaning rag against the tatters I wore as clothes (the rag was in better shape) to soak up water and moved to the next board.

Scrub, soak, scoot.

At least the repetition distracted me from the pain.

I dearly hoped that I had not broken a bone. Those took forever to heal, particularly since my bones were brittle. Indeed, I was but a bundle of bones, more a skeleton than a man of twenty-five years—my frame of five feet and eight inches, short for one of the Nasimih, carried very little flesh.

Scrub, soak, scoot.

I brushed back my unevenly-cut, greasy golden-blond hair from my eyes, which still burned from exposure to the unclean water. The skin of my cheeks abraded against my fingers when I smoothed the sparse hair of my beard so that it would not catch in the rag when I raised it for another soak.

Scrub, soak, scoot.

I was almost to the wall when the black voice spoke, bored, "Report, Lieutenant."

I almost jumped—I had not known that he was still in the room!

I tried to control my breathing. Fainting in front of him was dangerous, for I had no idea what he might do to me while I was unconscious.

I was fortunate that he had only soaked me in the dirty water earlier. He could have done unspeakable things to me—he had before, both while I was conscious and while I was not.

I did not know which state was preferable. Someday I could wake from a beating only to find myself facing the Almighty's judgment for a poor, useless life.

Trying not to draw attention, I continued my scrubbing. The Gouge was not speaking, so I could focus intently on my motions.

Soon I would be done, and then I would drag myself to my broom closet of a room to recover. If he allowed me to escape.

Scrub, soak, scoot.

I was trying to pry off a piece of mud when the Gouge began to guffaw with an unholy glee. "That is ridiculous," he snickered. "No matter what folk spread rumors, the Quest Leader is dead!"

I froze at the name that the Gouge had so casually tossed out.

The Quest Leader. The hero of Icilia, the Shining Guide's promised one.

That name was never mentioned.

Not by the people of Icilia. Not by the Blood's soldiers.

To the people of Icilia, that name was both hope and despair, for the Quest Leader was supposed to be our savior, yet no one knew if she or he had even been born, much less survived the

Blood's conquest of Asfiya. And even if she or he had survived, why would the Quest Leader care to save such a broken, disloyal people as we?

The Blood's soldiers, in diametric contrast, hated that name. If the Quest Leader had indeed been born, had survived, and had chosen to have mercy on the people of Icilia, her or his coming meant the end of the Blood's age of unrestrained pleasure. So, the Blood's soldiers feared what that name could mean.

Thus, the Gouge's sudden mention of this taboo name sparked my curiosity, though I usually cared about so little.

I buffed out the piece of filth and moved to the next board while straining my ears to hear more of what was happening.

The Gouge was still snickering. "What rebel has grown so bold? Tell me, what name are these stupid Nademani folk actually crowding around now?"

The lieutenant hesitated oddly. Then he took an audibly deep breath and said, "Your Depravedness, may your days of mauling never end..." He had to pause for the Gouge to stop cackling over the address, ordered for his amusement. "The rebels spread a... strange name, one that is not of Nademan." He dropped to one knee and, bowing his head, held up a piece of paper to the Gouge.

The Gouge took it with a scowl.

I hurriedly turned back to the floor. The monster knew how to read, but he hated it and often took out his frustrations over the necessary task upon me.

Then, unable to resist, I peeked back at him as he opened the paper and read the contents.

The Gouge's brow furrowed. The soot-gray splotches that dotted his blacker-than-night skin simmered like the scorching ash clouds from the Burning Mountains beyond the northern border of Icilia. A sure sign of anger and pain to come.

Then he snarled, "Never speak of this name again! This 'Lord Lucian the Ideal of Freedom' is a myth! A lie! Anyone caught speaking of it or writing it is sentenced to immediate death!" He leapt to his feet and growled, the sound long, drawn-out, and animalistic.

Though a cruel and terrifying brute of a man himself, the lieutenant shook in his boots and muttered his obedience.

I froze in place, too scared to breathe. Even as something sparked in my heart.

The Gouge snarled.

Then, instead of turning to me, he stalked out of the room.

The lieutenant quickly followed, trying hard to not look afraid.

I glanced up and noted both that the hall was empty and that eight boards were left.

I scrubbed them quickly.

Then fled, the bucket and the rag clutched in my hands.

Through the wide wooden halls, still scratched and cracked from the conquest over fourteen years prior, I ran, avoiding the routes of the patrols and dodging the few staff members I saw.

My circuitous route required a few minutes more, but I was soon back in the closet that I had been allowed to use as a room this year, without anyone having seen me.

I dropped the bucket and the rag by the pile of rags and dried leaves that I called a bed, then sank down upon it and covered my face with unclean hands.

Even the pain that assaulted my body and the torment lurking at the corners of my mind faded away as I considered what I had heard. And my reaction to it.

The Gouge himself had spoken that name, but... it was *beautiful*. The sounds that formed it made up hundreds of other names and words, yet they were special when they comprised this name. Something about it seemed... divine. As though the sounds, when strung together for this name, were imbued with holiness and power. As though it bore the Almighty's favor.

Indeed, the name was a spell, though the magic of it was one far beyond my understanding.

The very sound of it sparked hope. A taste I had long ago forgotten.

I took a deep breath.

Then, daring this risk, I whispered, "Lord Lucian the Ideal of Freedom."

Even speaking it was easy, like the smooth flow of milk, on my injured mouth and bruised throat.

That spark of hope flowered in my shriveled soul. The welling of love that accompanied that hope brought the first hint of a thaw to my frozen, broken heart.

I cared for no one, not even myself, my faith in the Almighty only just smoldering. But I could not help but care for the bearer of this name.

The change alone justified my belief in him.

I took another deep breath past the internal bruising.

Then I slipped off the bed and rummaged beneath the lowermost rags for the knife I had once smuggled for myself, when I had still been young and foolish enough to think that the Gouge could be easily overthrown. I had hidden it again only minutes before the Gouge had thrown me into this room four months prior.

I found it and pulled it out to inspect it. It was not very sharp, and rust coated the poor metal blade. But it would do for a start.

I raised the knife in the starting position for a defensive maneuver. I swung it once and then winced as my hand seized and dropped the wooden hilt.

I quickly snatched it before the blade could clang against the floor. Then restarted the maneuver.

When the knife fell again, I tried again. Then again. And again.

My plan was simple: I was weak. I needed to become strong enough to fight, and that required relearning the weapons I had studied before the conquest, attempting to catalyze once more, and smuggling more food than I had previously dared to take. Alongside that, since I was the Gouge's pleasure toy and preferred slave, I would use my access to his chambers and meetings to collect information.

Because I intended to serve the Quest Leader.

I doubted that I could escape the castle to find him, for I was too closely watched a prisoner to leave unnoticed. But I did not doubt that he would someday come to Ehaya, for Nademan's capital was strategically located and was where the bulk of the Blood's garrison was stationed. For the day on which he came, I wanted to be prepared—with both information and strength. Such would give credence to my plea.

I intended to serve him, if he was merciful enough to accept me. Not as a crown prince—my father had effectively destroyed any credibility I could have had as a ruler—but as an infantryman or a stable boy or a cleaner. Indeed, I would be a coat-stand for his army if that were all he was willing to allow me to be.

He was my only chance at freedom, my only chance at fulfilling the duty that was the long-choked core of my soul.

He *had* to be real.

The Quest Leader *had* to come.

I begged the Almighty for the boon of his acceptance.

CHAPTER 8
PROVING PRINCELINESS

Perspective: Prince Darian sej-Shehasfiyi, brother of the Quest Leader and auxiliary heir to the throne of Asfiya
Date: Eyyédal, the seventh day of the second moon, Etshatte, of the year 500, C.Q.
Placement: partially concurrent with Chapter 34 of <u>The Bell Tolling</u>

Slipping in first one arm and then the other, I shrugged on the robe overcoat and smoothed the folds over my chest. The athar robes were a plain chocolate, embroidered with only a single line of flowers at the collar and hems, but they would suit this most important occasion, as my brother would be wearing travel robes and so would his companions.

They would match. Five sides of the same whole.

I would stand out like a leafless tree amid the verdant glory of the summer forest. Out of place at the side of the only person who had ever given me a place.

If only I could continue to belong with him...

I exhaled a sigh. *Remember, Darian,* I spoke to my heart, *whatever he decides, you must accept. You may not have pledged yet, but it is your duty to think and feel and act as if you have. His smallest wish is your highest command.*

Clinging to those words, I mustered the strength to stand and complete my remaining tasks before their arrival. Lucian had sent a message after dawn that he would arrive today, and everything had to be perfect before he came.

A quick inspection showed that the bedchamber I had prepared for Lucian, the one we had usually shared in prior stays, appeared empty of my possessions, which were all well hidden within the sheets of wood that paneled the walls. Every surface was clean, without a single trace of dust or dirt, and arranged exactly as Lucian preferred.

Stepping outside, I checked the other commanders' suites. The rooms beside Lucian's and mine, chosen for the Quest Second and the Exemplar of Bravery, required some rearrangement of the bedclothes, but the clothes, weapons, and herbs Taza had set out were perfectly situated. The chambers for the Exemplar of Esteem and Inase bi-Dekecer needed nothing, nor did the ones for the Exemplar of Strength.

On the floor below, Lucian's books were ready in the study, and, on the one below that, the kitchens were well stocked with supplies and provisions. The pots of vegetable soup and trays of pies and wrapped potatoes simmered on the cooking hearths (Arkaiso managed to ignite fire without actually burning anything, and the resulting flame was somehow perfect for any sort of slow cooking). There was enough for Lucian's guests as well as he himself, his companions, the guardians, and me.

Several trees away, I confirmed that the laundry tubs (each formed of living wood and connected to the system of natural streams that fed water to every part of the base) were filled and prepared with soap. Then I surveyed the stables and ensured that the three stalls for Lucian's horses had adequate grain and water. Finally, I swept through the rooms set aside for Lucian's guests, arranging the last linens and the pitchers of water.

That is everything, I thought to myself as I consulted my list. *The military defenses have been ready since the moon of Alshatte...*

Arkaiso's trees rustled, asking an eager question in the soft whispers of sound.

I glanced up at the snow-laden branches and allowed a faint smile to curl my lips. "Yes, darling, I think you will meet Lucian's standard."

The trees rustled harder, as excited as I was.

My smile widened.

"Your Highness!" Taza called.

That smile slipped. Taking a steadying breath, I turned to face her. "Yes, Taza?" I replied with a calm I did not feel.

The former general wore a terrifying scowl as she strode toward me. "Your Highness," she said, "with respect, the base is not ready."

"With respect, Taza," I answered, trying not to quake as she halted in front of me, "Arkaiso *is* ready. The rooms for my Rulers are clean and furnished with the guardians' gifts, and the rooms for their guests are as—"

"Your *Highness*," Taza bit out my reverential address, "with respect, the base is *not* ready." She jabbed a finger at the trees. "Over sixty percent of the trees are filled with dust and cobwebs and are absolutely filthy. You have not dedicated the effort that you were expected to give."

Her words were a dagger in my ribs, and I desperately tried not to recoil. "Taza, cleaning and preparing even these many trees all by myself is—"

"A prince does not offer excuses, your Highness," she seethed. "How do you expect to keep your brother's favor if you cannot meet his standards?"

My knees gave way, and I fell to the ground, unable to stand at the sound of the words that proved my deepest and most painful insecurities to be true. "Taza, please..." I gasped. "Please..."

"Do better, your Highness," she spat. With those cutting

words, slicing into me when I was so very vulnerable, she pivoted on her heel and left me, walking toward the commander's tree.

I stared after her. Not a single drop of the affection that she had once bestowed upon me had sparkled in her eyes... She had been gone for weeks, spreading rumors with Ilqan for Lucian's sake, and she had not at all missed me as I had her...

I swallowed, my lips twisting into a grimace of pain, as bile roiled up my throat. I gagged, the caustic liquid pouring into my mouth, and retched onto the white snow.

Lucian... Dalaanem, please...

Twigs brushed together overhead, murmuring concern, and a slight breeze tugged back the soft curls of my beard.

I retched again, expelling the last of my morning meal. I cleaned my mouth with several mouthfuls of untouched snow. Then I leapt to my feet and ran.

The trees whispered a frantic question, asking where I was going.

I stumbled through the trees, only keeping any sort of balance because little bursts of wind pushed me upright every time I fell, and reached the bottom of Arkaiso's tallest tree. Without pausing, I scrambled upward, fingernails scrabbling at the bark.

Groaning slightly, branches bent unnaturally to push me upwards.

I arrived at the highest bough and flung myself onto it. I pressed my back against the trunk and desperately tried to steady myself.

Every gasp of air I inhaled did not seem to do anything to fill my lungs.

I could not breathe...

I could not breathe...

I could not breathe...

Lucian! Lucian, Dalaanem, Brother, please! *You said you would not leave me...*

But how could he not?

I had spent six months at Arkaiso, but I had not even

managed to clean his base. All the endless days of magic and sweat I had given to the task had not been enough.

Just as *I* was not enough...

The trees trembled around me, streaming comfort into the connection between us, and the tallest began to sway back and forth, attempting to soothe me with the rocking motion.

"He will not accept me, Arkaiso," I whispered, closing my eyes. "How could I ever have believed I could mean anything to him?"

Arkaiso shook furiously, vehemently denying my words and expressing her belief in me through the means available to her.

But I could not comprehend it. The woman who was like my mother did not believe in me...

Tears spilled down my cold cheeks and soaked my beard and collar as I curled in on myself and cried.

I did not dare to invoke Lucian's name again.

All I could do was cry... rocked by the fortress who loved me yet alone and lost...

All alone...

I surfaced from my misery only when Arkaiso mentioned, quietly and carefully, the entrance of a figure formed of light.

My breathing hitched in something that was, for the first time in hours, that was not a sob. "Is it him?" I asked.

Arkaiso rustled slightly before impressing an image into our connection: a man who shone like a star, emanating the same holiness and succor as Lucian's, yet decidedly not him. His eyes were a calm gray, with a silvery gleam, and his hair and beard were metallic ash-blond. His presence was both gusting winds and the solidity and steadfastness of roots deeply anchored in the soil, a pillar of resolve who did not shake even under the greatest of calamities, reminiscent of the constancy found in a father's embrace, accented with the soft clarity of a thoughtful gaze...

"The Exemplar of Strength," I breathed.

And on the heels of that realization came the thought that I did not want to meet him. A being so pure as he would see my faults with even greater poignance than Taza had, and surely he would tell Lucian of my unworthiness, ending any vestige of chance I still had of retaining my brother's affection.

It was cowardly.

I would have to meet my Honor regardless, once Lucian reached Arkaiso, and I would be his teacher for the next many months.

But I could not seem to muster the strength to leave what refuge I had.

Cowardly and unbecoming of a prince. All the more reason for Lucian to cast me aside.

I still could not move.

Despite the misery she shared with me, the base shuddered in delight as my Honor walked past her boundary and entered the ring of poisonous trees. Relishing how he reminded her of Lucian, she deflected every drop of poison from him and his guests.

Her joy grew ever more effervescent the closer he came. When he reached the edge of the inner circle, she actually glowed with happiness (even though he could not see it). And, when his expression brimmed with awe, she vibrated with so much elation that her trees seemed almost ready to move.

Despite my pain, I smiled.

His eyes on the vast inner trees, my Honor sent forth a ripple of wish magic, which tasted of the muted, gentle sweetness of farsight.

"He is our Lord's companion, Arkaiso," I said through the hoarseness in my throat. "Let nothing impede his path."

The fortress, who had been of the same opinion, gladly obeyed.

The faint hint of obstacle to his magic faded, and my Honor proceeded to examine the whole of Arkaiso.

The trees chattered in our connection, excitedly asking if I thought he liked them.

Watching the subtle shifts of expression on that holy face, I answered, "I would think so, darling."

The trees' bliss only increased.

Then Taza and Ilqan approached my Honor.

"I cannot watch," I whispered, my eyes burning with more tears. "Forgive me, my darling. I do not want to ruin your joy."

The trees murmured their understanding, and I slipped the commander's ring from my finger, temporarily dulling our connection.

I could not discover the energy to move any more than that. Or to wonder why my Honor had arrived without his Leader.

Climbing down now or asking questions would have meant facing Taza as she and Ilqan had to present a dirty base to my Honor, and I did not have the strength for it. I could not bear to see her disapproval again. Not so soon.

So I waited, as still as a carving, until I was estimated that my Honor would have reached his quarters. Then I descended the tree.

Ilqan was waiting at the bottom.

I froze on the last bough.

A brow arched. "Your Highness, it was your duty to greet our Honor and show him to his chambers."

My mouth fell open. *I forgot about that! I have never done that before...*

"You have never forgotten a duty before," he echoed my thoughts. "Performed inadequately, yes, but never abandoned. See that it does not happen again, your Highness."

Then he, too, pivoted and walked away.

Leaving me stuck on the branch.

For what seemed like an age, I could not move. I could not think. I could not breathe.

Because Taza's words were already becoming true.

As soon as Lucian heard of this, he would be angry enough to discard me. My Honor was his sacred companion, and I was no one.

No one...

What use could a lesser prince ever believe he had?

Nothing...

Arkaiso jabbed a twig into my back and flung me off the tree —then caught me with a thick bed of moss. Before dumping a branch full of snow on my head.

I sighed and wore my ring. "Sorry, darling."

She emptied another branch. Then promptly used several breezes to dry the outer layer of my robes.

A smile twitched at my lips. At least I had her, my precious Arkaiso.

The trees rustled, mollified by the burst of affection. Paused. Then rustled harder.

My eyes widened. "He is almost here?"

She answered with a harder shaking, informing me that the forest around her, though less sentient, was clearly perceiving the light of Lucian's passage.

I jumped to my feet and bolted for the commander's tree.

How much did I complete of the final inspection? Before Taza arrived, I was checking the last portion... yes, I really did finish. But what about supper? Did it burn? There is no time to cook another!

Entering the tree and tossing off my boots, I threw myself up the stairs and tripped into the kitchen.

Everything was as it was four hours prior. Arkaiso had infused a large part of her reserve of catalyzed energy into the food, thereby preventing any mishap in my absence.

I beamed, overcome by her kindness, and replenished her stores. Then I set about adding the final ingredients to the soup and removing the pies and the potatoes so that they would cool.

Arkaiso trilled, a sound more magical than physical, when Lucian and his companions arrived at the edge of the inner cluster.

I scrubbed my hands clean, pulled off my apron, and darted down the stairs. Skidding to a halt on the final one, I smoothed my clothes and settled into a proper princely posture, hands folded over my waist, back straight yet head tilted forward, gaze slightly lowered. But I could not muster the required smile.

I really should have been at the boundary to greet him... If only I had not wasted so many minutes mourning my own uselessness...

Two sets of matched footsteps on the stairs beside me jolted me from my melancholy thoughts.

Recognizing the tread, I tried harder to compose my expression.

Taza and Ilqan marched past me and out the door with no more acknowledgment than a pair of cold bows and a terse "your Highness."

I sighed. *I do not know why I repeatedly expect anything different...* But I did know why: with my father's aloof disinterest in his own sons, and the lack of society I had faced since early childhood, the guardians were my sole chance for affection of any kind from anyone other than Lucian and his sentient fortresses.

It was to my shame that I could not content myself with what I had.

That covetousness would only become even more detrimental when Lucian turned away from me.

I closed my eyes and tried to soothe myself with a hymn.

More footsteps resounded in the stairwell, these so light as to be mere taps on the wood.

A feeling of deep serenity swept through the innermost depths of my soul.

Those footsteps screeched to a halt on the step above mine, and a rumbling voice uttered, "My apologies."

I turned to behold the glowing figure of the Exemplar of Strength with my own eyes.

He was even more beautiful than Arkaiso's magical impressions had conveyed. His skin was a soft beige, which had gained a faint glass-like polish as he met my gaze, and his ash-blond brows formed broad arches over the smooth silvery gray of his eyes. Gleaming blond hair, lashes, and beard complemented the gentle curves of his features, and slight crinkles around his eyes and lips indicated the depth of his care for those whom he loved. Though his form was intimidatingly tall and muscular (particularly for one of the Nasimih), that face gleamed with a fatherliness that rivaled Lucian's own.

He resembled Lucian more than I ever could.

Just as he would be a better brother than I ever could.

Though my heart was welling with love for this wondrous man, I could not help but dislike him. His presence was a reminder that I no longer had any use in Lucian's court. I wanted as little to do with him as possible.

I dipped a stiff, formal bow and stepped aside.

In response, he blessed me with a warm, deeply affectionate smile, the sort of gift reserved for a treasured sibling.

Dazzled, I was slow to turn as several pairs of footsteps entered the tree.

Then my world changed.

My Honor the Exemplar of Strength was folding his arms around a woman who was Lucian in female form.

With eyes as blue as the undimmed sky of long ago, only a few degrees of color from Lucian's violet, and curls of fiery gold that were the sunrise to Lucian's daylight, she was his fulfillment. His heart. His soul. His Second. His beloved Malika. The holiness and divine favor in his face were matched by those in hers. From the curve of her brows, the angle of her cheeks, and the firmness of her nose and chin, to the power and authority of her presence, my Grace resembled our Lord as completely as though she *was* him.

That was not something that had ever been said about our Graced Queen Manara the Exemplar of Truth.

And the gray pallor of her face, the dullness of her hair, the thinness of her figure, and the bleak void in her magical signature did absolutely nothing to blemish her majesty.

I reeled, stumbling backward.

Only to be further shocked by the next person to embrace the two Potentates.

She was the image of the warrior royalty of old, a glimpse of

Icilia untainted by darkness, pure and unfettered bravery. The very sight of her heartened the most beaten heart, defeating the crushing fear that threatened to break an enfeebled spine. From the amber of her eyes to the olive-bronze of her skin to the mahogany of her hair, she was the Divine's challenge to the evils of conjury and rapaciousness, the valiance of Lucian's heart formed into flesh, radiant like a star. My Honor the Exemplar of Bravery.

Even as I struggled to understand what I had seen so far, there came the last of the five.

The last yet the first, a man like the moon and like the starry blackness of the night sky, the holy shadow cast by Divine Light. The golden crowns of his scales were the lanterns that brought illumination to the cruelty of the abyss, the chocolate of his skin was the shade in which the hopeless found rest and redemption such that they could witness the glory of Lucian's sun, and his green eyes were life itself. His every movement emanated such compassion, such uncorrupted kindness, that I almost collapsed to my knees, weeping for his favor.

The bind on my Honor's discolored wings and the fearful exhaustion of his magical signature did absolutely nothing to dim his magnificence.

Indeed, despite the anguish and weakness that clung to the four's physical forms, all I could behold was the perfection of the Quest. The redemption of Icilia, the bestowal of the Shining Guide, the freedom of the Almighty. They were the Divine's promise fulfilled.

As Lucian folded his arms around his four companions and a younger man with the bearing of a prince, love for the Potentates filled every particle of my heart.

And then came a sense of inadequacy that devastated every shred of my soul.

For how could a lackluster spare prince ever presume to stand in their presence? How could a bond born of blood retain meaning before bonds forged by divine favor? How could a child cast aside by the father of the Quest Leader and by the greatest scholars and warriors of Asfiya ever aspire to be of worth to the Rulers of Icilia?

Taza was right. I was nothing.

It would have been better for me to die in Lucian's place when Asfiya was captured than to live as a waste of his time during his reconquest.

I only did not turn and flee because of my training as a prince.

Lucian embraced Ilqan and then strode in my direction.

I did not have the daring to go greet him as I should have.

The four Potentates and their confidant disentangled themselves and turned to watch him.

I could not bear for them to witness the moment Lucian cast me aside.

Because, as he walked toward me, the gold flecks in his violet eyes glowing bright and the pale curve of his full lips slanted into a soft smile, that was the only possible outcome.

Even so, I could not help but fret for his sake in my connection with Arkaiso. When he had ascended, he had blazed with such strength as to exceed the very foundations of Icilia. Yet now... deep creases lined his cheeks, connecting the sides of his nose to the corners of his lips, and there was a tinge of immense weariness to his presence...

Shamefully, as he halted before me, my mind snapped back to my imminent heartbreak.

My lips shook with the effort to repress my sobs as I tilted forward in a bow. *I will serve you regardless, Dalaanem...*

"Blessings, Brother," Lucian said, rich voice sweet with a musical chuckle. "Since when have I asked my elder brother to bow to me?" His blessed hands grasped my elbows in their firm, soothing grip, and he tugged me forward into his chest and wrapped me in his warm embrace.

He was hugging me.

Hugging me.

Hugging me as though he loved me still.

As though I had not lost my place at his side.

It was all I wanted.

Closing my eyes, I melted into his hold, my posture and composure falling to pieces in his strong arms. "Blessings, Lucian," I dared to answer.

Gentle fingers stroked circles into my back as he reignited the links between us. *I have missed you so, Brother*, he murmured.

I swallowed, unable to express what those words meant to me. *I-I have missed you, too.* Childishly, I could not help but add, my heart pouring out its troubles to him as it always did, *It was so lonely without you.*

They mistreated you, did they not? he replied, sounding even wearier than his face showed.

I did not want to answer. Lucian loved his guardians, and rightfully so, for they had dedicated their lives to his education and his service, and to him they were the most wonderful parents imaginable.

Their only flaw was that, no matter what he pled for my sake, with every passing year they grew harsher and harsher toward me. And he could not truly correct them, for to do so would break their hearts while he still so dearly needed their service and would for many years to come. For that reason, knowing that they were the first army of his Quest, I had begged him in our adolescence to not interfere on my behalf.

It was an old issue, and I did not want to revisit it.

He sighed softly and pressed his lips to my forehead, before drawing back. *If it would please you, would you give my greetings to Arkaiso?*

The fortress quivered with delight, a child overcome with the wonder of an affectionate caress.

Exactly like such a child, I could hardly speak to offer the proper, formal words of welcome from a military commander to his liege.

But, though I was showing myself as a fool, as evidenced by

the disapproval in Taza's and Ilqan's expressions, there was only joy on Lucian's sacred face.

He really was happy to see me. At least for now.

It gave me hope that he would have use for me for a while longer.

CHAPTER 9
CHASING REDEMPTION

Perspective: Khuduya Rosalla Eminietta, citizen of Khuduren
Date: Eyyélab, the eleventh day of the second moon, Etshatte, of the year 499, C.Q.
Placement: between Chapter 34 and Chapter 35 of The Bell Tolling

I blocked a blow with my first sword and swung the second sword towards my opponent's head.

With a sickening squelch, his life ended, his blood on my hands.

Panting, I lowered both blades and stared at his corpse.

The crowd of off-shift soldiers cheered.

But I did not move to acknowledge them until I heard the telltale slow, rhythmic applause of the governor—a sound I had trained myself to distinguish.

I immediately pivoted and knelt to him. *Do not stand, do not stand, do* not *stand—*

The Slicer stood. His boots thudded against the ground, each step an ordainment of doom, as he descended the steps of the dais and walked onto the arena floor. There was no barricade to cross: none but the most foolish gladiators tried to attack him directly amid their matches.

He stopped in front of me and purred, sick pleasure in his oily voice, "Well done. Attend me after the feast."

I held my breath until he walked away.

Then I scrambled out of the arena through the tiny hole meant for the gladiators.

The jailer motioned to the table in front of him with the flick of a lazy finger.

Without the thought of protest, I surrendered my blades. Then I held out a wrist instead of fleeing to my cell.

A smirk contorted the jailer's cruel face. Lumbering to his feet, he buckled a manacle with a leash on my wrist.

Then he dragged me upstairs, instead of downstairs, to the gladiators' baths.

Though it was the only area in the entire complex that was actually clean, with a proper pool of water and a supply of soap, my stomach roiled, for only those given the decided lack of honor to *attend* the governor were taken to the baths.

Yet, despite the dread choking my throat, I bore the stumbling pace with the weary endurance of one who has been so dragged hundreds of times. Which was no exaggeration for a gladiator approaching her sixth year in a prison where we were dragged everywhere from the arena to the outhouse.

The jailer buckled the end of the chain to an iron loop by the side of the pool. "Wash well, or I'll do it for you," he menaced.

I repressed a shudder as I saluted.

The jailer left with a sadistic chortle.

Releasing a deep sigh, I leaned against the wall. I closed my eyes and allowed a single tear.

I cannot continue.

My hands were soaked in blood—I had killed so many of my own country-people in my desperate struggle to survive the gladiator pits. I could no longer count how many I had killed. Though bloodlust stole my inhibitions in battle, enough that I could kill even those who had once been my treasured friends, afterwards I could not help but be haunted by what I had done.

As did the horror and agony of frequently being chosen as the governor's nightly object of pleasure. I had endured it to survive, yes. But I could not stand the sight of my own reflection. How I wished to scrape away my own skin.

I cannot continue.

Guilt and shame tightened a noose around my neck as surely as the executioner.

I would rather die than live another day in this life.

Tears streaming down my grimy face, I prayed for relief, for freedom, even as I doubted that the Almighty would deign to hear the prayers of one so stained as I.

Death would be a sure escape...

But, however tantalizing the waters of the pool looked, however seductive the thought of letting them fill my lungs, the residual meaning of my mother's teachings on the laws of the Almighty echoed in my mind.

My only recourse was to pray. But I was not sure I deserved freedom, however much I wanted it.

Wetness dripped down my torso, and I shuddered at the innocent blood that coated my leather armor.

At the very least, I needed to wash it off.

I took a step towards the pool. Then froze as the manacle fell off my wrist.

My eyes wide, I stared at the shackle... which the jailer had not properly closed.

He had made a mistake. Though he *never* made mistakes.

A grin, the first true joy to curve my lips in five years, stretched my mouth as I muttered a prayer in gratitude.

Then I strode from the room, eager to take advantage of my opportunity: I was expected to be at the baths, and the gladiators' movements were so controlled by unbreakable chains and personal escorts that no one patrolled the complex.

I quickened my pace, even as I stepped more lightly to muffle my footsteps, and entered the cell blocks.

Though I did not know anyone else's name, I would free as many of the others as I could.

Then I would find a way to rally them and enact justice upon those who had destroyed us. I would chase redemption even if I never found it.

Even though I did not dare to dream that there was truth amid the governor's recent spouts of vitriol—that the Almighty had possibly deigned to favor Icilia with the Quest.

CHAPTER 10
FINDING PROTECTION

Perspective: Count Ciro Tolmarie, mayor of Jurisso and noble of Nademan
Date: Eyyéthar, the eighth day of the third moon, Zalberre, of the year 500, C.Q.
Placement: between Chapter 37 and Chapter 38 of The Bell Tolling

I murmured the prayer that I had often heard my grandfather recite at the bedsides of the sick. Or, after the Blood's conquest, the tormented.

Reaching the end, I blew gently on the young woman's sleeping face and smiled sadly. As much as I had disapproved of Penna's marriage to my dearest friend, she did not deserve this.

No woman did.

I rose to my feet and dipped my head at her parents' murmurs of gratitude. I clapped her father's shoulder in passing and walked into their small living room, where Penna's husband, Bron, waited for me.

He folded his arms when he saw me. His expression forbidding, he demanded, "Count Tolmarie, you are not going to ignore what we saw last night, are you?"

I allowed a brief grin to split my lips. "You know better,

Nadeyi Zitarie." Though we were as close as brothers, his question was one that merited a more proper address.

He nodded, satisfied, and let me pass outside.

I walked out onto the platform and, with the light feet that only the Nasimih had, easily swung my body over the steep ladders and swinging wooden walkways that made up my beloved town in the treetops. Though I moved with abandon, hardly regarding the need for keeping at least one of my limbs grounded, my mind remained a whirl of anxiety. Counting and counting again, I marked the face of each person I saw, frantic to ascertain that no one else had disappeared, even as I habitually acknowledged their respectful nods.

Too much tragedy had befallen our town for me to feel sure in my people's security. The world in which we lived resembled nothing of the quiet peace of my childhood. Oh, yes, that peace had been only a relative one—the pervasive rumors of the enemy had brought greater terror with every passing year—but still it would have been preferable to this fear-choked existence...

Just as I reached the last walkway before my family's hut on the highest platform of the centermost tree, a young girl flung herself up a nearby ladder and threw her arms around my knees.

"Count Tolmarie!" the girl, my adopted five-year-old daughter, Fionna, wailed, gripping me so tightly that pricks of pain tapped up and down my limbs. "There are strange noises in the forest!"

I forced a calm smile, my heart pounding wildly, and gently tugged at her wrists. "I will check, my dear. Would you go to—"

"Take me with you!" she begged.

I hesitated—her plea struck my heart—but shook my head. "Please return to Auntie Belona, my dear." Then, carefully removing her hands, I turned and sprinted toward the town's boundary.

If something really was there, the boundary was where she would be least safe.

Though I understood why she wanted to come with me.

If something really was there, no place at all would be safe.

And she knew it well. Not seven months past, she had witnessed the murders of both of her parents before suffering unspeakable horrors herself, and even the folk of my somewhat more virtuous town shunned her, fearing that her misfortunes might become their own. My wife and I were the only ones who cared for her, and she believed I could protect her.

I could not protect anyone.

As I ran across the walkways and down the ladders, in my wake the able of the town gathered. Several of them urged the children into the most secure huts we had, built amid a thicket of tree limbs in the center of the tree cluster, while the rest hurried behind me.

If something really was there, we would be a useless defense, untrained and unarmed as we were, save for a few sharpened sticks, but at least our families would have a chance to escape the enemy for a while longer. Though not really much of a chance at all.

I scrambled down the last ladder and darted across the wide ring of cultivated field that surrounded our tree cluster, over the dying remnants of the old boundary hedge, to the fringe of the forest.

"Ciro!" Bron called out, panting. "Wait!"

Ignoring him, I skidded to a halt just within the tree line and peered into the gloom of the woods.

Nothing.

I closed my eyes and inhaled deeply, easing into the series of breaths that would help me expand my Nasimih senses, as my grandfather had taught me.

Nothing.

Branches creaked in the distance, a few prey animals scrabbled beneath shrubs, some birds pecked at tree bark, a bear took lumbering footsteps over the forest floor—normal sounds.

I exhaled a relieved sigh. "I do not hear anything strange."

"Neither do I," Leana Erevias said from behind my shoulder.

"Nor do I," Chana Thrasaria added.

"Nor I," Bron commented.

The rest of the men and women exhaled sighs of relief as well.

"I am sorry," a small voice whispered from behind me.

I turned and realized Fionna had followed us, even to the edge of the town's glade.

Though she had disobeyed my orders, I only sighed, opened my arms for her, and, when she ran into them, lifted her into my embrace. More than the other orphans, she was delicate, so very sensitive, and scolding her so soon, even in a gentle and caring tone, would shatter her little heart. I would discuss the seriousness of her behavior with her, but several hours later, when the terror had faded some.

Fionna hid her face in my beard, clutching my collar, and whispered again, "Sorry, Count Tolmarie."

"Do not be sorry, my dear," I responded, rocking her slightly as I would my baby. "We might be mistaken this time, but your next warning might save all of us."

None of the adults around us protested—the last time we had ignored a warning, not a week prior, Penna had been stolen.

If we startled at shadows and jumped at strange noises, it was because they truly were to be feared. We were not safe in our own beds, and we would do well to remember it.

Slowly, lingering a little, casting wary looks at the forest, my town's defenders dispersed, beginning the walk back to their huts for luncheon.

I stayed only a moment more before doing the same.

No sentries remained behind—with the famine of the last two winters having claimed a fifth of our more able citizens, every hand was needed in the fields, the coops, and the forest (though this last was so perilous that hunting teams were rarely sent). The moment I finished my meal, I would myself return to my own share of the plowing and sowing, and my wife would join me with our nursing child and the six orphans we personally raised. None but children younger than five years could be spared from working, so desperate was our state and so difficult it was to grow even the most resilient crops—and so grim were our lives that even the children too old for carrying baskets and too young for work were subdued as they clung as closely as they could to their laboring parents, the joy of infanthood choked by fear and sorrow not long after their first words were spoken.

Fionna was quiet as I completed the trek back, still grasping my collar as though fearing she might be torn from me. Only when I paused to remove our shoes and coats at the threshold of my family's hut did she whisper, "Thank you, Count Tolmarie, for listening to me."

In answer, I merely kissed her forehead, before gently placing her on the floor and nudging her toward where the other children had gathered around a bowl of steamed vegetables in the corner of the tiny living chamber.

She squeezed my neck one more time and then hesitantly approached the others, who shifted among themselves so that she had space to sit.

All six girls were so quiet that the sounds of chewing were the only noises they made.

I sighed, praying that they could have had a childhood of laughter and play like my own. Then I turned to face the opposite corner, where my wife knelt on one of the many cushions that covered our floor as she changed the cloth diaper of our baby, Dorona, who waved both arms and legs as she lay atop our one low table.

Sensing my gaze, Belona quirked an eyebrow but did not look up from removing the soiled diaper. She had probably heard the alarm, but, instead of panicking, she had likely followed our safety procedures with diligence—trusting me to find Fionna—and, as soon as the alarm was proven false, she had immediately returned to her tasks, efficiently caring for our family and our town.

I smiled, comforted by the sight of my capable wife and our youngest daughter, and knelt by her side. Lowering my head, I brushed my lips over our baby's forehead and lightly poked her belly. "Blessings, my soul!" I greeted.

Dorona giggled—the sound pure bliss to my ears—and raised her tiny fists toward my face.

She had not yet forgotten how to laugh, the natural happiness of babies still within her, and how I wished I had the power to protect that innocence.

I unwound the curly strands of my long beard, which fell halfway down my chest, and then leaned in closer and let her grasp the trailing strands. Then, while Dorona yanked at the hair, I murmured, "Penna is recovering. Still sleeping poorly but recovering. The fit of torment she experienced after her return seems to have receded some."

"Did she confirm the story?" Belona asked quietly as she slid a fresh cloth diaper beneath Dorona.

I hummed a yes. "She told Bron that the Mutharrim men, the Areteen woman, and the Sholanar man treated her with utter kindness. Her recovery is proceeding much more quickly than expected because they healed her wounds and offered her food and affection as they escorted her home. She reported that the men addressed her as 'sister' and that the touch of the one who carried her was like sunlight. Just as his appearance was. She felt no fear in his presence, nor did she feel any of the aversion that many women now experience at the proximity of men who are neither spouse nor family. The story is very similar to what we heard from your cousin in Ruyisso just before Penna's return."

"Do you think that it is true, then?" Belona asked, her eyes on Dorona's matching ones.

Dorona yanked at my beard particularly hard, and I winced but still laughed to amuse her. Belona quickly finished clipping the cloth diaper in place, redressed Dorona's tiny form, placed a linen cap on her head, and swaddled her in a blanket. Then she handed our child to me.

Cradling her, supporting her head with one elbow, I gazed

down at her happy face and gurgling smile as she buried her tiny fingers in my beard and sputtered.

Transfixed, my heart welling with gratitude for the Almighty, I answered, "I think we need to seize the hope that it is true."

Belona touched my cheek, drawing my attention, and smiled wryly. The expression pulled slightly at the scar that slashed through her right cheek, a remnant of the blows that the soldiers had dealt her four years ago, just before we married.

I still remembered the horror of those days... I had rushed excitedly home from a trading journey only to learn that my betrothed, the woman I had loved since we were children together, had been stolen by the soldiers. Wild with fear, I abandoned all the town's earnings and scoured the forest for her, against the advice of many, and found her curled beneath a thorny thicket after three endless days of search. Her clothes were torn, her body injured too badly to witness with a sane mind, so deprived of food and water that she did not stir even as I lifted her into my arms. She had nearly perished, and recovery for both mind and body had seemed impossible.

Many tongues, even her parents', had wagged that the son of the mayor should choose another bride. She herself had seemed to expect such betrayal, though she had known me for all of our twenty years.

I refused to hear such talk and insisted on marrying her, declaring my intentions in front of the entire town.

It was then that I realized that my parents had *allowed* the soldiers to take her.

So deeply had they fallen into the trap of acquiescence to the wretched Gouge that they were willing to sacrifice a child whom they loved for the lie of peace. And neither was Belona the only such woman, nor were my parents the only such nobles.

Though I had controlled my tongue then, I immediately began planning a revolt. Gathering my friends, both from my own town and from towns across the province of Zaiqan, I led a quiet effort to depose the ruling generation of nobles, speaking both against their growing abuses and of the old virtues of our nation. Since the soldiers in Nademan preferred to patrol rather than preside over each town, my message spread quickly, igniting passions long smothered and beliefs long buried.

Such was our stealth and our success that, gratitude to the Almighty, within sixteen months, under the enemy's nose, eighteen of Zaiqan's twenty-six surviving towns had followed Jurisso's direction, and the remaining eight declined to contest the change.

It was not peace—better than all the prior years since the tyrant's conquest, but not peace.

The old generation had not retired quietly, many, including my own parents, inciting discontent and committing such crimes as to require exile and even execution. Moreover, in retaliation for our defiance, in the year following the revolt, the wretched Gouge personally slaughtered four more towns and instructed the commander of his western forces to further concentrate their malice upon our women and our children. When that commander did not prove himself cruel enough, the wretched Gouge replaced him with one far more ambitious, General Perveries, who actively pursued every whisper of rebellion.

So much tragedy had befallen us in that year that funerals had become more common than births. There had been no tears left to shed.

Yet, somehow, despite all this evil, the people of Zaiqan had become increasingly more united. For we knew that, while we died in great numbers, acquiescence would grant only slower deaths.

Our patience had garnered some reward: in the last year, the province's circumstance had improved some, the western regional commander's attention and that of his master diverted elsewhere by more incendiary rumors, and many of the young couples among my friends had finally had their first children.

Including Belona and I.

More than a year after I married her in defiance of my parents' dictates, she had finally given birth to our first child—Dorona, her salvation and my heir and soul.

For, like the province's own state, our marriage had been full of pain.

Though Belona had accepted my hand, returning my loyalty with devotion, she had struggled to find peace with me even as she helped me with our revolt. Nightmares and flashes besieged her, and she fell deeper and deeper into torment as she mourned the child that she had lost shortly after our wedding, both loving and loathing the first baby she had ever carried.

I had stayed by her side, praying day and night and lamenting that I had neither protected her nor could bring her peace.

Dorona's birth had finally brought her that.

And now we feared again.

For it was a terrible age to have a daughter. To have any child at all, as much as we considered them blessings, but particularly a daughter.

Not that the Blood's soldiers were kind to sons—oh, indeed, they tortured men and boys as well. But daughters, particularly the prettiest, were more vulnerable, more susceptible, to being stolen or demanded as tribute or tormented in front of their families and killed. The orphans Belona and I raised were only the ones who had survived.

Far be it to wish for them to be happy when their survival itself was questioned.

Everything I had done for my province had done nothing to shape a safer future for my daughter, little Dorona. Particularly because I feared that she would be uncommonly beautiful. She possessed her mother's sky blue eyes, honey tan skin, and fine features and my rich brown locks—even at the age of six months, she was charming and adorable to behold. She would likely grow lovelier with each year, and no amount of soot would be enough to hide it.

My wife had not escaped notice. I doubted that my baby

would either. As my other daughters and my branch-sisters had not.

I had to do something so that my daughters, so that no woman, would ever suffer such violence again. All of the girls and all of the women of my town depended on me, their count and father, to find a way.

Oh Almighty, may it be Your will that I have finally found the way...

A gentle tap of my cheek brought my attention back to Belona's lovely blue eyes.

She was smiling sadly, her expression replete with the pain that was more familiar than her joy.

I shifted so that I could hold Dorona with my right arm and wrapped the other around her too-thin waist.

She scooted closer to me and tilted her head back, closing her eyes and inviting a kiss.

I lightly pressed my lips to hers and savored her closeness, how wonderful it felt to be with her—

Dorona grumbled and yanked again on my beard.

I chuckled quietly, savoring the strength of her personality while it remained undulled, and turned my face toward her, as she seemed to want. "She has quite the grip, Belona."

My wife rested her scarred cheek against mine. "She does, indeed, Ciro," she whispered, gazing at our baby with an enthrallment greater than even my own. A sigh left her lips. "That name is our only hope, my love. Those rumors, which we regarded warily before and which we have now seen proven before our own eyes, are the only way we have found."

"So we must take it," I said quietly.

"You know it as well as I," she answered.

"I do, but..." I paused, the words thick in my throat as I watched Dorona, again merry, offer us a precious toothless grin. "If we commit to it, we must be prepared for war. There will be no freedom without war."

"Then let us commit," Belona replied. "We must have that freedom. At any cost."

I swallowed. "At any cost, my love? Would it not be better if I left Jurisso behind, abdicating my title to you, and joined with only my own name and the friends who chose to come with me? I fear to bring any more retaliation upon our neighbors."

Belona cupped my bearded chin with her strong fingers and angled my head so that my gaze met hers, without disturbing Dorona's grip. "In any age but this," she spoke, "that would be wise counsel, Ciro. But in this age, we cannot do less than devote everything we have to his cause. We cannot act with half a heart."

"Even if the war takes us from Dorona?" I asked, deeply troubled, even our baby's playful tugs on my beard failing to evoke a smile.

She smiled mirthlessly. "Rather the war for freedom takes us from her than the soldiers take her from us."

I flinched, the truth of those words a dagger to my heart.

Her expression softened. "Ciro, my hope is to secure such favor that he agrees to shelter our entire town. While we remain here, regardless of what we do, we will always be a target for the soldiers. But we cannot beg for his protection if we are not willing to offer the whole of our loyalty. He will surely care for his vassals; every one of us must become among their number to earn that care for our children. And, alongside that, Ciro, the pledge of a whole town would be eminently valuable to a military campaign, both by swelling the ranks of his army and by inspiring the rest of the province. We must do everything we can for his victory. We cannot act with half a heart."

I pursed my lips, my mind awhirl with her arguments... my heart swayed all the more by her words because, despite all my efforts, she was slowly growing thinner and thinner as she poured the health of her body into our child...

"I know that you desire to shield me, Ciro," Belona murmured, her enchanting blue eyes warm with affection, "but my place is at your side, and our daughters and our town are more important than our safety. More important for you, and more important for me."

My thoughts and my heart settled as she had prescribed, and, unable to contest her reason, I sighed and smiled wanly. "As always, you are wiser and more intelligent than I. I would be lost without you, my love."

At the resumption of Dorona's grumbles, I adjusted her so that she laid against my shoulder and began to bounce her. The irritated sounds subsided, and she cooed as she gripped my beard and my clothes in her tiny fists.

Belona's cheeks glossed, but her gaze remained steady upon mine as she lifted both brows. "So?"

"So we are committed." I brought to the forefront of my mind the sacred sight with which we had been blessed the night prior, the shining face of the man who had returned Jurisso's daughter with nary a demand for reward. And I affixed in my ears the name which I desperately hoped that man bore.

Then together Belona and I kissed our baby's head and whispered the words that would seal our fate, whatever the Almighty had ordained it to be: "Wherever you are, our Lord the Quest Leader, Lord Lucian the Ideal of Freedom, savior of Icilia, we beg that you might deign to accept our allegiance in the Almighty's name."

I hoped, as she did, that we would find him soon. That he would care to protect us. That he would accept us among the ranks of his soldiers. And that he truly was the promise of the Shining Guide fulfilled.

For our daughters and for all the daughters of Nademan.

CHAPTER 11
PROVING WORTH

*Perspective: Prince Darian sej-Shehasfiyi, brother of the Quest
Leader and auxiliary heir to the throne of Asfiya
Date: Eyyélab, the ninth day of the third moon, Zalberre, of the
year 500, C.Q.
Placement: same as Segment 2 of The Bell Tolling*

"My Lord," Taza said as soon as Lucian turned away from greeting his companions, "I beg your pardon. The guardians outside Nademan beseech you to grant them an audience—Amalna and Fozala have news of a rebellion fomenting in Khuduren and only an hour in which to present it. They fear that any longer will expose them to the enemy's patrols sweeping their surrounds."

Lucian pressed his lips together, an odd light shining on his beloved face, which still retained a shadow of gray. "Such news certainly requires immediate discussion." He started to swing his heavy saddlebags onto his shoulder.

It was an opportunity. So, before anyone else could offer, I blurted, "I can carry your packs to your quarters!" We actually shared a chamber, as I had arranged and Lucian had allowed, but I was careful to avoid any such mention—after learning of Lucian's imminent arrival, Taza and Ilqan instructed me to give up my room in the commander's quarters entirely.

They had not even asked where I had slept in the month since.

Pushing aside that hurt, I let my eyes drink in the sight of his smile as he allowed me to take his bags.

For one moment, the world held only us, brothers forever.

Then Lucian gave me a single nod and, beckoning Arista and his guardians, walked briskly in the direction of the training arena. "Khuduren is not the only nation with a possible opposition. Etheqa, too, seems..."

I was left staring after him.

Why did you not ask me to come with you?

"Prince Darian," Kyros said, using the little formality a Potentate was required to use for an auxiliary heir, "would it please you to join Malika, Elian, Elacir, and me for supper?"

'No, it certainly would not!' was what I desired to say every time one of them asked. But that was disrespectful, and Lucian would hear of it. So, instead I dipped a reverence, murmured a polite refusal, fisted a hand in Farib's reins, and strode as fast as I could toward the stables.

The horse dragged me to a halt and, flicking his tail in my face, trotted back to whicker at Malika, his mistress, leaving me scrambling to remove my saddlebags.

Neither the Potentates nor Elacir nor the staff said anything, but, from their sympathetic glances, they clearly noticed my humiliation.

Such an embarrassed chill spread over my face and neck that it almost burned my skin.

Once I managed to retrieve my possessions, I clutched all four bags and, leaving aside the horse, trudged toward the commander's tree.

How pathetic you are, Darian. A caricature of Lucian's virtue and dignity like your appearance suggests.

Hunching my shoulders, I stared at the ground, the sight of Lucian walking away flashing repeatedly before my eyes.

It was just as Taza had predicted: I was losing my place at his side. Oh yes, he had thought to include me when he issued his commands for excellence, and he did ask about how his companions' lessons progressed—but those were the demands of office. He had only a few minutes for me otherwise. Nothing like the long hours we had once spent together on this very base, laughing as we studied, practiced, and prepared...

Even to the fulfillment of my role he gave little relevance: as the herald of his court, *I* should have presented the townsfolk's proffering of service. But I had not had the chance to even open my mouth before he spoke. As his aide, I should have been in attendance at every meeting. But he had not called me even once.

He was losing interest in me.

Small wonder then that I could hardly bear the sight of the Potentates. Outside of lessons and training, I wanted as little to do with them as possible. I avoided even Elacir for his presence usually meant Elian or Kyros were but a step behind.

Amid such aversion, the last two weeks—spent watching Lucian lavish all his time on Elian while being expected to somehow survive as Arista eked more skill out of me—stretched my nerves almost beyond what I could withstand. And, now that I had returned, I would be required to continue Malika's lessons in strategy and fortress command.

Yet another sign of how Lucian was replacing me.

As she excelled in the few areas which I had mastered, he would have less and less need of me. Soon enough, with the rapid pace of her learning, Lucian would order me to surrender the commander's rings and keys in my custody, leaving me almost entirely without use.

I had only one way left to prove my worth—the fulfillment of the vow I had made regarding Malika's curse.

Though in truth my motivations were many: my own place, certainly, and the admiration for the Potentates that had rendered their suffering, particularly Malika's, heartbreaking to witness. But most of all was my fear for Lucian's health.

The plan we had begun nearly a decade ago for Nademan's reconquest was no small endeavor, requiring massive effort from both he himself and all of his vassals in every area from military action to magical preparation—but what Lucian was doing now was several steps beyond. The demands he heaped upon himself, as he had done since the retaliation from Malika's curse, were so great as to be unhealthful. That was apparent even without giving credence to my suspicion that he was concealing something from none less than the Potentates themselves.

My place at his side was too uncertain, however, for an objection. The best I could do was relieve a fraction of his burden, and the most effective manner in which to do so was the application of all my skill in magical scholarship to the breaking of Malika's curses.

Connected deeply enough to my will to sense the sway of my thoughts, the trees of Arkaiso whispered in appreciation of my intentions.

My embarrassment fading, I could not help a soft smile. From the way they had overwhelmed me upon my return with even the smallest sensations, the movements of butterflies and bees, the trees of Arkaiso had truly missed me. They were becoming as attached to me as the histories said they had been to their first commander, the legendary Prince of Virtue, the Asfiyan king who was Lucian's and my ancestor.

Reaching the commander's tree, I climbed the stairs, two at a time despite the heavy packs, to my shared bedchamber. Once there, I quickly refreshed myself and arranged Lucian's possessions, separating out the weapons and clothes that needed cleaning. Gathering the bundle in my arms, I left to bring them straight to the laundry and the armory. Though Halona Tikariat, the woman whom I had appointed as chief of Arkaiso's staff, would collect such loads tonight, Lucian's belongings had first priority.

Caring for such minute matters was what an aide did.

Upon my return to the commander's tree, as I crossed the common area among the suites, footsteps on the stairs caught my attention.

The athar in the wood thrummed in delight, shining white in my magical vision.

"Arkaiso, *every* time one of the Potentates walks anywhere?" I asked, quietly chuckling as I retrieved my research journal, my preferred quill, and a half-empty inkwell. "Particularly her?"

The fortress drenched me with a sort of smug satisfaction, before posing a question.

"No, they cannot see your greetings yet, darling," I answered, "but may the Almighty soon bestow those gifts upon them."

The trees creaked a little and then settled, praying in their own way.

Prince Darian, were you speaking to Arkaiso? Malika asked in our private link as she stepped into the common area. Her eyes were bright with curiosity, as eagerly attentive as during any lesson. Gratitude to the Almighty, she did not find my most cherished subjects boring.

"Yes, my Grace." I bowed and then elaborated, unable to resist that enthusiasm for knowledge, "Living fortresses always respond more faithfully to those commanders who treat them as incé."

The tree groaned softly, an agreement.

I impressed a smile into the connection as though it were a mind-link. "The original design of these Nademani clusters was that living trees, able to recognize friend and foe, would serve a chosen commander's will. But, because they are indeed living, the trees soon began to exert their own judgment. Thus, although usually merely possessing the commander's ring allows access to the base's defenses, the trees may choose to entirely revoke such access. Or, conversely, with pleasure and trust they may grant near total impunity. Much as incé themselves do."

And you are one of the commanders obeyed with impunity, she said, gazing at me with a sort of... that could not be admiration, could it?

Cupping a hand over my heart, I bowed slightly and replied, "Yes, my Grace... my Grace, might I implore you for a few minutes of audience?" I could not hide the hint of fluster in my tone.

Malika nodded and led the way to the chairs Kyros had arranged for us by the tall, narrow window that gave a view of Arkaiso almost as spectacular as the one from my most favored tree.

Dipping another bow, I sat across from her, opened my journal on my lap, and began, "My Grace, I beg your indulgence in answering a few sensitive questions."

Please ask, Prince Darian, Malika encouraged, smiling kindly, hands clasped over her lap. Though I only ever spoke with her out of duty, she always radiated such comfort and peace...

I swallowed hard at the similarity to Lucian. "If you would deign to tell me, my Grace, I would like to ask about the curse on your voice."

Malika froze, and that easy smile fell from her lips. Shuddering, she wrapped her arms around herself, then sighed and nodded. *Of course, Prince Darian... I confess that I am not all too sure when he placed it. I only know that, sometime after I found I could not speak, he told me that I would never become a magician. Much... many of the memories are too dark to understand. Without light as well as without... compassion.*

Flipping to a fresh page, I recorded her answer. "That itself is most illuminating, my Grace..." I paused and cracked a wry smile in an attempt to soothe her nerves in return. "That choice of word was not intentional."

She chuckled, her shoulders relaxing, and asked curiously, *Why do you inquire about this curse though? Is not the one on my magic of higher priority?*

"I have decided to try something different, my Grace," I answered. "I theorize that, of the three curses between you and our Honor the Exemplar of Esteem, this one may be the simplest. Diseases that affect the vocal cords do exist, while nothing natural impedes the flight of properly formed wings and the use of one's magic. Thus, I hope to gain a proper taste of his magic from this curse."

Malika nodded. *Hmmm, that is quite reasonable...*

I tried not to silver at the praise like the neglected little boy I was.

Any other questions, Prince Darian? she asked.

"Yes," I said. "If you would indulge me, my Grace, I would like to observe you attempt speaking. By sight as well as by feeling your throat as you attempt the sounds. Please do not think the request to be one made with improper intentions."

She nodded, a bit hesitantly, but with enough decisiveness to convince me of her consent.

I moved my chair a bit closer and placed a cool hand on her throat, slipping my fingers beneath her high collar. "If it is in accordance with your will, would you try to speak the alphabet?"

Malika grunted and then opened her mouth in pronouncing the first rune.

Vibrations met my fingers, rippling through the delicate tissue. *She laughs and screams and sighs, so indeed the cords do work, and well. I have noted in the past that her muteness concerns words. Speech. A reasonable conclusion because the Blood hates language... of course he would attempt to ruin her dignity as an incé by taking away something as fundamental as speech.*

"Please continue," I encouraged, masking my rising ire.

She formed the next runes, and more vibrations met my hand as they should have. Yet...

There is something... odd about the movements of her mouth. I know what she is saying—I know the history behind every one of these runes—but if I did not, would I be able to tell...

At that precise moment, Elian, Kyros, and Elacir emerged from their rooms.

"What are you doing, Malika, Prince Darian?" Elian asked.

Only curiosity filled his tone, not the suspicion and anger I expected, but I could not help the defensive response: "I am only attempting to learn more about my Grace's curse."

"Ohhh..." the three brothers breathed and gathered around us, sweet smiles curving their lips.

Even as those smiles warmed my heart, I opened my mouth to shoo them away (though it would be disrespectful). Then paused. *What if I...* "My Honors, Inase, can you guess what our Grace attempts to say?"

They intently examined her face, then shook their heads.

"Sorry, Malika," Elian muttered.

My eyebrows drew together. "Hmmm... my Grace, would you switch to the names of the Quest? But not in order?"

Malika did as I asked.

"I cannot tell," Kyros said, cheeks coarsening.

"Nor can I, your Highness," Elacir said, scales dimming.

"Sorry, Malika," Elian repeated.

No need to apologize... Prince Darian, Malika asked, *what did you conclude?*

Withdrawing my hand, I pursed my lips. "Nothing definite yet... but..." *She can utter the words, but those words do not make sense on her lips... what if...*

My gaze shifted to Elian, and I remembered Lucian's description of the magnitude of his healing. Then scrambled for my quill, ink, and journal. As I scribbled my thoughts with perfected elegance, I wondered, *If what I am starting to hypothesize is correct... could we actually break this curse?*

Nothing would please and aid my savior more. And nothing would do more to secure his regard for me.

CHAPTER 12
VOWING ADHERENCE

Perspective: Etheqora Revera qia-Tovacera, citizen of Etheqa
Date: Eyyéqan, the fifteenth day of the fourth moon, Likberre, of the year 500, C.Q.
Placement: between Chapter 41 and Chapter 42 of The Bell Tolling

"Oh Revera," my mother whispered, clutching my hands, "oh Revera, what will I do without the both of you?" She gave a sob and, dropping my fingers for my lower back, pulled me into her embrace.

With her cherry-red wings wrapping tightly around me, the feathers that marked her Mutharrim descent sliding softly against my scales, I could almost pretend that I was still a child, unknowing and uncaring of any danger from which she could not protect me. I could almost imagine that all was right with the world. That I could stay without consequence.

One of the worst tragedies of the last year was that her embrace no longer brought me peace.

I slipped my hands beneath her wings and squeezed her tightly. "Mama, you must keep faith that we will be reunited once more."

My mother wailed and held me tighter, a reaction that cut at my already-bruised heart. She had once been one of the most assured and confident people I had ever known—so strong and brilliant in matters of both trade and politics, even with the enemy's tyranny crushing our spirits, that the mayor had considered stepping aside for her. But my father's brutal death, which she witnessed, had broken her in ways I could not fathom, despite my flourishing bond with my own husband.

I exhaled a sigh, lightly stroking her wings at the ridges where they connected with her back. But, as impatient as I was to leave after the lengthy and difficult winter, I did not say anything and let her cry endless tears onto my newly-made leather armor.

Finally, many minutes later, Mama seemed to remember where we were and why we were there. Drawing back, she tipped my chin down and kissed my forehead. "May the Almighty safeguard you and, through your hands, safeguard uncounted others," she whispered. Then, letting go of me, she embraced my younger sister and her baby.

I sighed again and turned to my mother-by-marriage.

Instead of greeting me with an embrace, Mother coolly surveyed me, expression and posture as rigid as the bladed staff she had once wielded in the nation's army.

I straightened under her regard and met her gaze with the fire rekindling in my heart.

After a moment of keen examination, her face softened as satisfaction lit her hazel eyes. "You have prepared well, Revera, my daughter. If anyone can accomplish this mission, it is you."

I smiled softly and dipped my head. Then, moving hesitantly, I slid my arms around her slim waist, bent down, and rested my scaled cheek against her translucent one.

Mother exhaled heavily and returned the hug. She offered me a cursory squeeze before going to her son and giving him an equally brief embrace. Then she stood back. "May the Almighty protect you, my darlings."

That simple pronouncement was a signal to the rest of our aerie. Exclaiming tearfully, they touched their cheeks to mine, clasped my hands, or dipped their heads, bidding farewell first to me and then to each of my six comrades.

The mayor of Potsmia, Count Benor bi-Kolacer, a young boy who had been forced by our tragedy to take his father's mantle at fifteen, approached me last. Exhaling quietly, he bowed his head. "I do not know what I will do without you, Big Sister." His fiery orange scales dulled to the color of rust against his gaunt, taupe-brown cheeks.

I forced a smile, memories of him scampering after my friends and me, eager to be included in our play, flashing across my vision through the haze of sorrow. "Our village is loyal to you as they were not to your father, Benor—our pain has made us aware of the enemy's influence as nothing else could. They will support you, and I will return when I can."

Benor took a deep breath and nodded, not commenting on what we both knew: there was no guarantee of my survival, just as there was no guarantee that the soldiers would not finally remember Potsmia's escape from their noose and return to subjugate her.

I drank in his beloved face one last time, as he did mine. Then I bowed formally, whispered, "May the Almighty bless you, Count Kolacer," and waited for his reply and dismissing nod before turning to my wing-mates.

Though all of the other villagers, Sholanar and other kinds alike, had already stepped back, knowing what little daylight there was would soon wane, Mama was still tightly clutching my scowling sister to her chest. Netara's baby, a little boy I had named Ator, was in my husband's arms.

Noticing my attention, Afra, a young woman of the Nasimih and the last person I had expected to want to come with me, leaned toward me and muttered, "We are ready to leave as soon as she lets go."

I suppressed a burst of irritation—Afra had lost both parents because of the tragedy, one to murder and the other to her own hand—and replied, "Check for soldiers with your farsight, please."

Afra nodded curtly and strode to the side of her Sholanar half-brother, Cethor, who began to wind a rope around their waists in preparation for flight. To their right, Glora and Dalor, another newlywed couple like Astor and me, both Sholanar, shouldered their packs and even slightly spread their wings.

As much as I did not like to admit it, Afra had a point. I was the one who had loudly declared that even cherishing what days we had left with our families could not come above service to our nation in this desperate age—would it not be the height of hypocrisy if I let my own mother delay our departure more than she already had?

Bracing myself for more of her tears, I parted my lips to speak.

Just as that moment, my husband, Astor, stepped toward Mama and rose onto his toes to whisper in her ear.

My mother sobbed and sniffled but finally nodded at whatever he was telling her and then relinquished her grip on Netara.

My sister, even more impatient than she had been before the tragedy, let loose a loud, insensitive sigh. Then her gaze caught on her son.

Mama, Astor, my friends, the village—everyone, even me, held our breaths.

Netara stared at the sleeping child for a long moment, revulsion and affection battling in her red-amber eyes. Until, as usual, the revulsion triumphed. She sneered, only seeing the reminder of the worst moments of her life, and turned away without even a murmur of farewell.

Not a murmur of protest arose, not even from my mother and my husband, who adored the baby. We had been forced to watch as she was raped; how could any of us do anything less than empathize? As the shining man had so gently said, to inflict blame and censure upon a sufferer of violence was the very opposite of piety. They did not deserve the dishonor, he had said, that so many chose to heap upon them.

Her beautiful face twisted with anger, Netara strode in my direction. But before she reached me, she spread her burgundy wings and jumped into the sky. From the sharp fire of her expression, I had only a few moments before she left without me.

Oh, Netara... I wanted to groan. I understood my sister's pain, truly I did—the visible difference between our torments was that she had conceived and I had not—but our mission was too important and too dangerous to allow pain to sway our judgments. How I hoped she would not so quickly forget her promise to me.

Exhaling another sigh, I beckoned to Astor.

As aware of my needs as always, my husband quickly but carefully placed our nephew in Mama's hands and walked to my side.

Not wasting a moment, I folded my arms around his torso and lifted his much shorter body so that his head, protected by a supple leather helmet, was pressed to my collarbone. With practiced movements, I looped a rope around his waist and my middle, tying us together for greater security in flight. Then, murmuring a final farewell, I opened my auburn wings and pushed off against the ground.

Cethor, Glora, and Dalor did the same.

Flapping hard, pushing against the still air, we rose higher and higher, until Potsmia and the solemn figures of our family and neighbors were the size of tiny insects, a full two thousand feet below.

Five thousand feet was the absolute highest we dared to fly. Though Sholanar wings and bodies were made to soar many thousands of feet above the ground, the clouds of the enemies' smog hovered at only eight thousand feet, shrouding the peaks of all the taller mountains from view and often drifting downward in coiling, snake-like tendrils of smoke, rendering only the air closest to the ground safe for flight.

So long ago had the sky been clear that I did not even remember what it was like to live without the oppressive weight of the smog.

"Finally," Netara grumbled as we reached her. "Finally, we can get away from here."

I stifled the urge to correct her, and, from the pinched looks on their faces, Afra and Dalor were squashing the same impulse.

Astor, however, dared to say, "Tara, Sister, if you would allow, a moment of planning would be invaluable." His soft bass voice did what none of us could: soothe the eagle after her wrath had been aroused.

I smiled slightly, proud of how he could calm the hottest hearts (in actuality sometimes, for some of the Sholanar in our village spat sparks when angry), and glanced at Afra.

Her expression sourer than usual, Afra pointed to the north-west with a thumb. "Some Areteen soldiers are attacking the town there. The one that is properly uniform, with only Nasimih." What she left unsaid, but what we all knew, was that uniformity in an Etheqore village meant anyone of every other kind had been either killed or stolen.

I took a deep breath. "We should stop them." I nodded a few times to myself. "Confronting them is our purpose for leaving like this." It was one thing to plan but quite another to do...

My friends nodded, not raising an objection, though they looked as nervous as I felt, and maneuvered themselves so that they were arranged behind me in an arrow-shaped formation, two on each side. The arrangement would allow them to glide on the air currents spilling off my wings and to better follow my direc-tion in flight and battle—an honor usually accorded only to great rulers.

I was not one of those great rulers. The last time I had tried to lead anyone, the soldiers had caught every single one of us. Every single one...

"You can do this, Rev," Astor whispered, just loud enough that his voice reached my ears. He molded his legs tightly against mine (not an intimate gesture—simply the best way to reduce drag in flight, like the way I had wound my short kinky hair in a tight, flat bun under my leather cap).

I clutched him more tightly, drawing comfort from his solid presence, as I had since I was a child, and tilted the base of my wings so that I turned toward the northwest. In the next flap, I drew my wings together so that they were perpendicular to my back. Then slammed them inward, shoving myself forward in my chosen direction. The momentum caused me to lay flat on the wind current, my body parallel to the ground.

Behind me, the others sped forward in the same manner. But while I kept flapping, gaining speed through more hard flaps, the rest glided, enjoying a respite from pushing against the still air.

It was only fair—ultimately, they were leaving Potsmia in this manner for my sake. Netara, Dalor, and Afra felt a burning need to leave, yes, and Glora and Cethor were coming because of them, but none of them would have left in this way and for this reason if not for me. And as for Astor...

Despite the discomfort produced by the strain on my wings, a small smile curved my lips. "Have I thanked you yet for promising to come with me, Asty?" I spoke lowly in his ear.

He chuckled softly. "Only a thousand times, Rev. Though I do not know why you think my refusal to allow you to leave without marrying me first counts as something to be grateful for." A note of embarrassment tinted his voice.

I laughed, remembering how he had, with uncharacteristic fire, actually demanded a wedding in response to my declaration of leaving for this mission. That moment, and the wedding itself, had been nothing like romantic daydreams we had both once wanted, but it suited who we had become since the tragedy— distilled pieces of who we were at our cores, cut sharp like broken glass.

"Well, at least it earns your laughter," Astor said, muttering, but in a pleased tone.

I briefly pressed my chin down over his head. "Of course it does, Asty. It does not matter how you renewed your proposal—I am forever grateful that you still wanted to marry me. Even though..." my voice faltered.

"The men in those other villages were fools," Astor said quietly, "to lose their beloveds over thefts of innocence. How could I do anything but be at your side? The shame you feel is something I share for the violence I, too, suffered, but it is something neither of us deserve. What we deserve is healing, to overcome this degradation, as difficult as attaining it currently seems."

I could not answer for the tears choking my throat at the affirmation he so loyally gave of my worth. How was I so blessed to have him? He had lost his father, his uncle, and all of his brothers and cousins, leaving him and his mother the last of their family and the last of the Areteen in our village, and yet his first thought was of me.

Me, troublesome, rebellious little Revera, always a bad influence and embarrassment to her family. Netara was impatient and prone to anger, yes, but, even before the tragedy, I was the one who attracted the soldiers' fury with my unruly tongue. The one who protested injustice when injustice was the only way we lived.

I had never understood why Astor had defended me the first time, when my complaining about the way my fellow young Nasimih were smacked when they dropped their weapons nearly resulted in my baby sister's death. I was already eight years old and should have known better, the elders said, and I had been about to receive the most severe of punishments—the binding of my wings—until Astor began to cry on my behalf. His quiet disposition, despite his age of seven, had lent his tears extra weight, and so he had saved me.

Both then and countless times after.

He did not even notice that, because my height was greater than this, he had to look up to meet my gaze, the objection many other men were beginning to have. He had even taken my surname as his own, though many other men were now refusing to follow this marriage custom. He thought the world of me, and the way we had begun to help each other heal since the tragedy had only increased that. Even when I forgot to do so, he always believed in me.

I truly was so very blessed...

"Rev," Astor breathed, his awed voice breaking through my thoughts, "is it not beautiful?"

I glanced down to see what had caught his attention and realized he meant the land itself.

The curves of the gently rising mountains, the sharp edges of cliffs, the smooth slopes of the hills, the thick forests, the gleams of lakes and rivers—it was all dimmed by the smog, its beauty and variety as shadowed by the enemy as the hearts of the people themselves were. And yet Astor found it beautiful. As the shining man had.

I smiled and parted my lips to respond.

"The town is just beyond this next ridge!" Afra called out.

Both Astor and I tensed—reminded that, though we had let ourselves ignore the sharpness of our purpose for a while, this was no romantic couples' flight. War was what lay ahead.

Without a word, Astor tangled his legs with mine (again, not an intimate gesture—unless his legs were secured, no matter how he excelled at keeping them in place during the flight itself, they would fly painfully forward if I needed to pull up from a dive).

Appreciating once again how well he knew me, I peered at the forest as we crossed over the ridge.

The moment I saw a break in the trees, the incongruous circle of a Nasimih town boundary, I dove forward.

My friends followed—griping at each other over bumps and jostles, yes, but still smoothly enough that the dive did not break the coordination of our flight. A better performance than our practices.

As we dipped into the trees, the destruction below came into view.

A squad of Areteen soldiers were tormenting a large group of terrified Nasimih. Chasing and herding and corralling them like animals. Swords ready to inflict pain upon those who fell as they ran.

Even sheep were treated more kindly.

A strange heat began in my head and scorched down my body, burning my skin and scales, at the sight. No matter their sins, no one deserved to be treated this way.

That heat cleared my mind of fear and hesitation, even about their greater numbers, and I ordered in a calm, clipped tone, "Drop Astor and Afra. They fight below, and the rest fight from above."

In response, Netara, Glora, and Dalor broke our formation, screamed a war cry, drew their swords and axes, and swooped down upon the soldiers. Cethor and I first undid the security ropes and dropped my husband and his sister and then immediately joined the attack. Seconds later, Astor and Afra, who had rolled to break their fall before jumping to their feet, did the same.

The Areteen soldiers whirled around at our charge.

Shock and disbelief contorted their faces.

Then mockery.

My friends and I slammed into them. Ducking, parrying, using height and flight to weave around blows, we swung around the enemy as we had each other on the training field.

But our skill did not match theirs. A few months of training, even with my ability to breathe fire, was not equal to their years of experience. We could hold our own, but not well enough to win based on skill alone, particularly with their greater numbers.

The only reason we won at all was because we were a squadron of three kinds, while they were of only one. While they fought only from the ground, both the ground and the sky were ours.

Even so, by the time the enemy lay dead, my friends and I dripped blood from a number of injuries—several dangerous enough that Cethor immediately gathered us together away from the battlefield and began to slather us with poultices.

I opened my mouth to speak but stopped, staring with horror at a long cut on Astor's arm. My right wing had been pierced with a throwing knife, a far more grievous wound if it did not heal well, but his blood was so much more disturbing...

"Orders, Revera?" Afra demanded, breaking my stupor.

Shaking my head, I scrambled to organize my thoughts, shoving aside the pain of a familiar wound until my turn for treatment came (my wings had been pierced many times in this way last summer before the shining man came). "Afra, speak to the townsfolk—if I recall correctly, this town has been uniform for a long time. I do not recognize any of them, and they seem frightened by the rest of us." I gestured toward the Nasimih, who were huddled against their trees, staring at us with such abject terror that they had not even fled.

A terrible sight, but not an unusual one. The governor's edict that all Nasimih train as warriors broke them by either shattering their courage and will to defend themselves or by hardening them past the reach of any incé compassion. The second was what had happened to Afra—she was only even distantly interested in my mission because the shining man's kindness had managed to melt her heart.

She still rolled her eyes at the order before stomping toward the terrified townsfolk.

I turned to Glora—only to see her launch herself at her husband, wrap her arms around his neck, and kiss him deeply. Dalor responded just as eagerly and folded his wings around them both.

Cethor ignored them as he bandaged Netara's thigh, while Netara herself gagged, looking disgusted. Then she narrowed her eyes at me. "Are you not going to do the same, Vera?"

Astor and I exchanged an uneasy glance. We had kissed once before, the night after our wedding... and regretted it. For all that we had longed for marriage and its delights, for all that we thought each other beautiful and found comfort in each other's embrace, we just... could not be intimate. The tragedy had broken this for us. At least until we found greater healing.

But that was hardly something I wanted my bitter younger sister to know.

So instead I said, suppressing both my discomfort and the

blinding ache building in my wing, "We need to discuss the battle."

At the words, Glora and Dalor ended their kiss and turned back to the rest of us. "It went poorly," Dalor stated simply, tightening the wing pressed around his wife's back.

"We won, didn't we?" Afra replied sharply, speeding back across the field. Behind her, the Nasimih were climbing back into their town, at least unfrozen by whatever terse words she had given them.

"It was a narrow victory," Netara shot back. "Too many injuries, and we don't have a healer. Just you and your farsight."

Incensed, Afra seemed ready to yell—before Astor murmured a few soothing words.

Dalor glanced at them, then said to me, "We need better attack plans."

"The shining man did much more than simply attack," Glora added. "You are asking us to fight greater numbers; we need to learn more from his example."

"What does that mean?" Astor asked quietly as he held his arm out so that Cethor could bandage it. "Should we train more and return?"

The question stunned everyone.

But, though my eyes lingered on his wound, as his did on mine, I knew the answer. Shaking my head, I said, "If we do, we will never get started."

If we did not adhere to our purpose, we would waste all of the effort the shining man had given to saving us.

CHAPTER 13
CONTRIVING STRATEGY

Perspective: Nadeya Tahira Enarias, citizen of Nademan
Date: Eyyéfaz, the tenth day of the fifth moon, Marberre, of the year 500, C.Q.
Placement: same as Segment 3 of The Bell Tolling

Though my heart burned at the act, my face was blank as I curtsied to the Gouge. "Your Depravedness," I said, my voice perfectly emotionless, "I have prepared a suggestion for the next set of orders."

His head leaning on one fist, he waved at me and yawned. "Hurry *up*, Enarias," he drawled.

I knelt before his throne and offered up the stack of documents.

He seized them, scowled at me, and flipped through the pages. "Withdrawing to the provincial fortresses?" he muttered and cast me a sharp glance. "Why?"

I held steady—such was his usual manner. He hated reading, so he only skimmed my proposal, picked out a few key words, and then demanded an explanation. Since he never actually read the documents, there was much I could slip past him.

"Several of the lieutenants' reports show that the rebels are attacking our supplies." This was true. "By gathering together, the squads will pose a more tempting target and so will be better able to lay ambushes." Such attacks would have been effective... but not with the methods I had outlined in the orders.

"Will they get rid of the nuisances faster?" he asked lazily—a ploy for luring his less competent soldiers into self-incrimination.

Well accustomed to his games, I answered, "The rebels will pursue larger caches of supplies, in a continuance of the pattern that they have shown in pursuing the smaller. Your soldiers will draw them in like flies to honey and so conquer them." The fortresses contained far more than supplies, so I had no doubt that the silent heroes would attack, rescuing the captives within while also decimating the Gouge's forces.

The Gouge's soldiers were no match for these heroes: since the first moon, quite a few of the patrols had gone missing across Nademan. Only a few ever escaped, the few whose records were marked in the barracks for special food and drink—the magically manipulated. Their testimony indicated that their attackers rarely numbered more than three. Indicating the heroes were exceptionally powerful warriors.

As should be expected of the Quest Leader and his servants.

But the Gouge and his commanders were too stupid to draw such educated estimations, and I would not help them. If they did not read their own military's reports and analyze the whispers catalogued within, then I would not do it for them.

For indeed, as much as I could, I was sabotaging the Gouge. I had never been loyal to him: I served him only because he held my little brother Kanzeo hostage, threatening to wreak the worst sorts of violence against his life and sanity in order to ensure my obedience. But even in that service, I had always walked a fine line—I constructed his strategies and managed his troops but with only slightly more creativity and efficiency than what he and his colonels could manage. And because they underestimated my brilliance, and that of women in general, they had never guessed that I produced plans beneath my own standard.

Yet now I did more. Halfway through the first moon, I had heard confirmation of the Quest Leader's coming in the form of his name, a name too resonant in holiness to be fabricated. So I had not hesitated.

My Lord Lucian the Ideal of Freedom was the one who possessed my loyalty. Though, should I have the blessing of entering his presence, he would certainly regard me with suspicion and censure.

Indeed, my Lord likely already did—according to what Kanzeo had once heard and told me with a sob during one of the few meetings we were allowed, I was infamous among many of the towns.

But still I did not hesitate.

As long as I continued to leave no evidence and provided partially viable strategies, I could balance long enough on the edge for the Quest Leader's reconquest to reach Ehaya.

It was a risk, but a calculated one—not taking such action would slow down my Lord's reconquest, each passing day another that left my brother and me exposed to the Gouge's whims. Moreover, inactivity would leave us without a defense in my Lord's court. Not to mention how each further month of the Gouge's rule cost the blood of innocents.

I was all too aware of that. Though the military was nominally in my hands and though I controlled their postings, I did not control their movements. I had not been able to stop their pillaging before, and, now that I was shuffling forces to create vulnerability for the Quest Leader, I could not stop the amassed forces from... *enjoying* their pleasures. Like the destruction of the town of Filisso—which I suspected my Lord had seen, from the reports of residue there. Yet another accusation against me, yet more blood unnecessarily spilled.

Bile rose in my throat, but my expression remained even as the Gouge perused the documents again.

"Enarias," he drawled, "what about the border? You want to withdraw forces?" The edge of danger to his tone threatened a display of conjury, the soot-like blemishes on his void-black skin shimmering like mirages of water.

In the corner of the throne room, a man, little more than skin stretched over bones, jumped. He glanced frantically around himself and then scrubbed the floor with renewed fervor.

Crown Prince Eligeo tej-Shehennadem—the son of the man responsible for our troubles, abused and tortured and *hated* so much that it was impossible to believe that he had once been called the hope of Nademan.

The man from whose situation I would do anything to protect my own brother. Including both serving the Gouge and walking the line of betrayal to him in order to usher in the rule of the Quest Leader.

If my life was forfeit, so be it.

With that strength starching my spine, I responded, "Your Depravedness, the forces were withdrawn because your spies in Bhalasa assure you that your inferior rival the Clawed is feuding with your inferior rival the Slicer over failed intelligence. Your inferior rival the Clawed has transferred his own forces from his border with you to his border with your inferior rival the Slicer. Thus, it is proffered to focus on the threat of these rebels, to crush them and show what they blindly ignore, your awesome might."

The anger cooled on the Gouge's face. "Hmmm. Fine, Enarias." He tossed the papers at me and leaned forward as I caught them, the cracked edges of his lipless mouth spread in a leer. Then he said something that scalded my ears, despite the five years I had spent in such close quarters to his court.

I did not flinch, unlike the broken figure of the crown prince. "Your Depravedness," I calmly replied, though what I wanted to do was scream that I would *never* willingly accept such a lecherous invitation, "I must beg your forgiveness. There is much still to do to bring about this strategy such that it does credit to your glory, and a single moment of distraction might threaten all of your stunning achievements. And I would certainly be... *distracted*."

The flattery worked as it always did, and he leaned back,

appeased. "Off with your boring self then, Enarias," he snickered. "Make my glory obvious in front of my rivals. And give your brother my greetings." He repeated his usual threat, though it was becoming more absent-minded as the years of my seemingly flawless service passed.

I curtsied from my kneeling position, picked up the papers, and stood. I backed away from him, never turning away and never straightening as I moved toward the double doors of the throne room.

The Gouge smirked after me, then cast the broken crown prince an amused look. He rose from the throne and kicked the poor man in the ribs, drawing a shriek. Laughing, he leaned down, hooked his fingers into the piteous prince's collar, and dragged him along the floor toward the small room behind the throne's dais. The door clicked shut on both the governor's massive figure and his pathetic captive.

I suppressed a wince. For all that Crown Prince Eligeo tej-Shehennadem was hated, for all *I* hated him, I pitied him also. I was under no illusions about what the Gouge did to him. The crown prince was the living remnant of the civilization that the Blood and his governors so despised—the Gouge took out all his hatred on him. And that hatred, that utter disdain and contempt, was like the unfathomable pools of molten rock beyond Icilia's borders: unextinguishable and unbearable.

The prince deserved pity. All his siblings, but him especially.

Perhaps my Lord would deign to free him as well.

Because, I thought dryly as I finally left the throne room, ignored the guards' sneers, and walked to the commanders' war chamber, *no one else will lift a hand to protect him. Not his siblings, not his former staff, not I.* It was despicable, but in the Gouge's court the freedom that nurtured love and compassion did not exist.

The only person I cared to save was Kanzeo, and that motivation still smoldered because the Gouge had not yet beaten it out of me.

I sighed and checked my papers one last time outside the chamber, ignoring more sneers from both these guards and passing soldiers. Frustrated at my lack of a reaction, several of them tried to tug loose the tight blonde braids of my bun, unprotected by cap, bonnet, or handkerchief as my hair was. I ignored them as well.

My Lord's location, I had deduced, was in southern Zaiqan, and he was amid a transition in operations from clearing a swathe of area around his base to reconquering provinces. He possessed the beginnings of a military force, but it seemed reliant upon his and his servants' skill. He certainly did have a secure fortress.

If the Almighty blessed us so, his progress would soon accelerate with my planned vulnerabilities. Surely the townsfolk of the various provinces would not be so foolish as to avoid pledging much longer.

And soon, if the Almighty blessed us, my Lord would be on the way to Ehaya.

Then freedom would be within my grasp.

Neatening the stack of papers, I entered the round chamber. The men inside grudgingly quit their crass exchanges and turned to me with snorts, sneers, or leers. Not one of them rose from their seats around the rectangular table. Indeed, per his habit, one of them kicked my assigned chair as I moved to sit on the right-hand side of the head.

My expression did not change as I smoothly steadied the seat and handed the papers to the top general, who took them with a roll of his eyes.

"His Depravedness approves?" he grumbled.

I dipped my head. "Yes, Sir General."

He grunted and began to distribute orders according to my proposal, with many a sideways baleful look directed at me.

Indeed, I thought with an inward grim smile, *though the townsfolk hate me for this, like they do the crown prince, my place is timely for the Quest Leader's service.* I laughed within the privacy of my thoughts. *How ironic. The commanders hate me for my posi-*

tion, and the townsfolk do the same, but I am the one with the power to remove obstacles from my Lord's path. Such power that I may do so with near impunity.

The commanders grumbled and growled but could not find fault with the orders. But many still cast me lascivious glances or glares of murderous wrath.

I suppressed a sigh. For all of my bluster, how I hated my place. Other than those brief moments with Kanzeo, years had passed since anyone had treated me with kindness and respect. Well, also since I had deserved such treatment.

But still how I longed for esteem.

As I always did when such yearning came upon me, I subtly moved my hand to the stomach of my simple gray gown, where a tiny emerald hung from a long cord looped around my neck. Trembling slightly, my fingers stroked that emerald, caressing the perfect half-sphere.

The round shape reminded me of laughing violet eyes lit with brotherly affection and set in a shining silver-cream face adorned by sunlight hair and the thin wisps of an adolescent beard. Instant comfort from the memory of the only person whose kindness remained untainted in my mind.

Warmed by solace, I dreamed of the coming of the Quest Leader.

CHAPTER 14
IMPLORING MERCY

Perspective: Nadeyi Kanzeo Enaries, citizen of Nademan
*Date: Eyyéthar, the eighteenth day of the fifth moon, Marberre, of
the year 500, C.Q.*
Placement: between Segment 3 and Chapter 43 of The Bell Tolling

The heavy blow landed on my face and sent me flying into the wall.

Finally.

I had waited for this moment since the moon of Zalberre, secreting supplies and medicines so that I would be ready to leave as soon as they were done with me.

Another punch hit my cheek, throwing my head to the side as blood filled my mouth. Hands gripped my throat, deepening the bruises the city-folk had left.

I whimpered piteously, giving them the reaction they desired, but I hardly felt the pain. I had suffered such beatings since my tenth year—by now, the blows felt familiar. More familiar than my beloved sister's touch.

As my eyes squeezed shut to avoid the next blow's damage, her face glowed in the forefront of my mind.

Tahira.

My sister, my hero, my protector. There was no limit to the love and devotion I held for her.

From my earliest memories, she had been everything to me. While our parents and our elder sister pursued their righteous attempt to resist the Gouge, Tahira had acted as my sole caretaker, bathing me, dressing me, feeding me, and lavishing upon me all the affection a child could want, even when I distracted her from her studies. With a kind hand on my back, she had instead helped me read my first words and shared her books with me, teaching me everything a noble of Nademan was supposed to know. And, though I found myself a slower learner than all, the letters twisting and scrambling beneath my gaze, she had never once become impatient or spoken a cruel word.

Never once until the day we watched our family die.

On that day, even as I reeled from the horror of what I had been forced to see, she had acted to save me, tricking the prison guards and sneaking me through the vast hallways of the castle-tree, scolding me sharply whenever my nine-year-old body stumbled or slowed, desperate to take me to a safer place. Though exhausted, weakened, and sorrowed, she poured such determination and discipline into our escape, spending days upon days and taking no risks, all because she wanted to be certain we would not be found.

She had been captured only because she had wanted to take me with her.

Yet still, when the Gouge had recaptured us, she sacrificed the purity of her soul for my sake. She vowed to empower his tyranny just so I would remain alive and unviolated. She had given her conscience for me.

For me, a little boy worth nothing in any eyes beside hers.

I simply had to protect her in return. It was my only purpose, the sole reason I continued to endure all the lonely, endless days without her.

And finally, after nearly five years, my chance had come...

The soldier, his breath rancid with some sort of toxic herb, shook my limp form and then abruptly slammed it against the floor. Hard enough to splinter bones.

Agony shot through my spine, eliciting a less contrived shriek, but the padding beneath my clothes, carefully hidden stitched animal hide cases full of wads of abandoned feathers, shielded my bones and organs from the worst of the damage.

The second soldier leered down at me, lifted his booted foot, and brutally kicked my ribs. Once, twice, thrice... then a fourth kick aimed at the sensitive section at the top of my legs.

My scream was wholly genuine this time. That one always hurt, no matter how much padding I tucked around that area and no matter how accustomed I was to it.

The first soldier sniggered, obviously enjoying the sound of my pain, and reeled back his fist. Then let it swing into my middle.

His partner jeered and joined him, and the two of them pummeled my face, chest, and middle with fists that were closer to blocks of stone than incé hands.

Though I gave the appropriate reactions, mentally I relaxed. When this pair of soldiers arrived at this part, they were nearly done and were only taking out their frustration that they were prohibited from wreaking the deeper violence of rape upon me. Punches and blows above my waist were easier to handle, and a bloody mouth only had to be washed, so I preferred them.

In the meanwhile, as I waited for them to finish, I lost myself in old memories of my sister...

A dozen punches later, the soldiers slammed my supine body against the floor twice more and then left, banging the hut door behind them.

I closed my eyes and simply breathed.

In... out... in... out... in... out... in... out... in... out...

Remember, Kanzeo, I said to myself, *remember that this is your chance.*

A successful beating, one that I did not avoid, usually meant that the capital commander would not bother to send any more patrols in my direction for the next four months—the abuse seemed, in his mind, sufficient to prevent me from escaping and crush my spirit enough that I remained a useful, pliant hostage. Which meant that I would be able to escape without the soldiers learning of it.

And, just as important to my mind, the beating provided some small chance that a report of my continued survival would reach my sister's ears. I had, of course, little way to know for sure whether it did—even when she was brought to visit me, Tahira was under such scrutiny that she could hardly speak anything at all—but how I hoped. That would make the pain worthwhile...

A few more moments passed.

Then, inhaling deeply, I pushed myself upright and, pressing a hand to the wall, managed to stand.

There, that is the first step. Now for medicine.

I limped across the tiny hut to where I had concealed my medicines—balls of ointment wrapped in waxy leaves and prepared as Tahira had done in my childhood and as I had once secretly watched the city-folk do.

Removing the floorboard that protected them from the soldiers' inspections, I sank to the ground with a sigh and found the ones for bruises. I untied the little bits of string that sealed the leaves shut and dipped a finger into the pungent greenish paste. Scooping slightly, I took a sticky blob and rubbed it on the bruises ringing my throat.

The sharp scents of lavender, yarrow, comfrey, and plantain, though sloppily crushed and mixed, soothed me enough that I could dare to attempt the next step of shrugging off my clothes and padding.

My breath caught as the rough cloth and the coarse hair on the pelts scraped the fresh wounds. But I did not cry out. It did not hurt *that* much.

I scooped more ointment into my palms and spread it over my chest, my sides, my legs, the sensitive part...

It is a bit worse than I hoped. But no bones are broken, the skin is not cut anywhere, and... I rubbed a hand over my calves. *I should be able to walk. Gratitude to the Almighty.*

With a nod to myself, I used the last of this stash of bruise medicine and cleaned my mouth of blood with water from a flask. I dressed in my rags and my thin cases of padding, the best clothes and armor I possessed, and wiped my hands of paste on the last bruise on my cheek.

Then I removed another board. From the hole beneath I took out a large, shapeless sack, and in that I dropped the remaining tinctures, letting them fall atop bundles of more poultices, dried herbs, provisions, my one spare set of clothes, and some rabbit pelts for trade. Reaching again into the hole, I lifted my one weapon, a sturdy wooden branch that could knock even a wolf unconscious. Finally, once I had replaced the boards, I rose to my feet, swung the sack over my shoulder, gripped the stick in my hand, and walked toward the door.

I could not help a glance back.

The dingy wooden hut, perhaps some royal hunter's temporary quarters from the age before, stank of blood, pain, and the soldiers' toxic herbs. It was the only place I was allowed to be, the residence granted by the Gouge out of a mockery of mercy, but I was never here unless I needed to be found by the soldiers. I slept on a thick branch high in the treetops, and I stored my pelts, my food, and my medicines in a hollow carved within the trunk there (I had hidden my travel supplies and medicines within the hut only once I decided I would take this beating).

Neither place was home.

Home was in Tahira's embrace.

Not that she had given me one of those in nearly five years.

I swallowed, stuck out my tongue at the hut, and left, letting the door bang shut behind me.

The display of temper was perhaps childish, but it was the only way I had to express my dislike. And no one had ever taught me how to be an adult.

Not that I wanted to be one. My heart longed for those far away days of being a baby wrapped in Tahira's arms... How little I had appreciated her then.

"This is your chance, Kanzeo," I whispered to myself. "Your chance to change everything, to go back, to return her love."

With a prayer that she would never receive a report that I was missing, I walked deeper into the forest, away from the capital.

Unlike the sunny, life-filled wood in what Tahira had described of her own childhood, a deep gloom shrouded the forest floor despite the midday hour. The few birds that dared to trill a song very nearly whispered their melodies, and the wilting shrubs concealed even fewer animals, most of which looked like they had hardly eaten since winter. Though the summer months were almost upon us, the forest was more yellow than green, and the leaf litter was mixed with splinters from the cracked wood of the painfully thirsty trees. And, in places, blood.

Even in the forest, it was impossible to escape the signs of the monster's tyranny.

I shuddered at the sight of a bear lying dead in a pool of its own blood, flies feasting on its rotting carcass, and hurried onwards.

The prey animals were at least not left to decay, despite how cruel the soldiers often were in killing them, but the predators were just... abandoned. Turned into sport, hunted mercilessly, and then just abandoned.

More than only the people needed saving.

More than only Tahira.

But it was only for her that I went.

The Quest would have mercy on the people, the animals, and the trees, simply because that was who they were, but no one would have mercy on my sister.

I knew what they called her in the city. 'Traitor' was the kindest insult I had heard.

When all she did, all she has been doing, is protect me. The agony of that thought inflamed a wound that was deeper than any bruise or cut could ever be...

I reached the line of withered shrubs that marked the edge of the capital territory, the furthest I had been in nearly five years, and looked out into the open expanse of the Dasenákder.

And I could not move forward.

Though there were no soldiers within sight (too lazy in these last couple of years to properly patrol), I could not cross.

I could not move my feet.

It was as though roots bound them to the ground, preventing me from taking a single step.

No, no, no! I-I-I must leave! I must! I must! I simply must leave! Come, Kanzeo, a single step! A... single... step...

But I could not.

Because the last time I took that step, I had ruined my sister's escape and so deprived her of her chance at freedom. Crossing the boundary felt wrong, malicious, as though I was shoving her behind and stealing her chance.

And because once I took that step, I would be beyond everything I knew. Everything I knew how to survive. Everything I *could* survive.

Beatings, insults, isolation, illness, hunger—these things I knew. Since the Gouge had turned me into a hostage, I had survived things that I had never imagined a person could. With what fraction of Tahira's strategic mind I possessed, I had managed to make routines and patterns that helped me withstand all the torment the enemy heaped in my direction. My body was slowly growing stronger despite the wounds and hunger, and the loneliness hurt just a little less with every passing year. I was even coming to welcome the pain. I *was* surviving.

But, once I took that step, even if I did not bring the soldiers down on both Tahira's and my heads, I would be at the mercy of horrors of which I knew nothing.

And how would I? I was only fourteen years old, and no one had ever taught me how to properly hunt or make weapons or fight or even how to cook. I did not know where I was going, all of my guesses about the Quest's movements based on brief snatches of rumor, and I had no plan for what I would do if I could not hear any more in the closest towns. Indeed, I hardly knew the difference between north and south amid the daytime darkness beneath the forest canopy.

If something wanted to hurt me once I took that step—and something certainly would, for the world was full of danger—there was nothing I would be able to do to stop it. No stick could compensate for a weak body that seemed incapable of ever gaining an adult's strength.

I was defenseless.

A tear splattered on my collar, and I inhaled a sniffle as I realized that I was crying.

I had not even left Ehaya, and I was already a failure. Just like I had been during the escape.

There was nothing I could do to save my sister.

Presuming that she even wanted saving.

Presuming that she still cared for me.

She has not said she loves me in so long...

I covered my mouth with both hands, stick dropping with a quiet thud, as my breath came in gasping heaves.

... perhaps because she no longer does.

The last time I had seen Tahira, sixteen days after the Day of Light, her face had been entirely expressionless even when she looked at me. There was no tenderness, no affection, no *love* at all in her blue eyes, and her lips had not curved in the slightest. She had only opened the door, glanced at me, and left.

The sister who had adored me so as a child had acted like I was *nothing* to her.

Nothing.

Did it even matter that reports of my continued survival reached her? Perhaps she actually relished the news of my beatings. Such things did happen in the Gouge's court—the horrors people saw there tended to harden their hearts. And she, unlike the family members who all of those city-folk speaking in anguished murmurs had lost, had a solid reason to hate me. If not for me, she would have never been trapped here. She would have succeeded in her escape, and no one would have ever found her again.

Her suffering was all my fault.

How could I be upset if she blamed me?

My legs wobbled, unable to bear my weight any longer, and I sank to the ground and curled up, holding my knees to my chest, as if that would keep my heart from shattering.

It did not.

Leaving behind a hurt that would not dull and become almost pleasant like all the other wounds.

I wailed softly and buried my head in my knees.

If she forgets about me, there is no one else...

Tears soaked the thin rags and stung painfully as they disturbed the ointment covering my bruises. But I made no attempt to stop them, the pain welcome, almost a balm in its familiarity...

If she forgets about me, there is no one else...

I wondered if it was finally time to abandon my struggle for survival. No one beside Tahira had cared whether I lived or died— if she no longer loved me, my efforts were as worthless as I was...

If she forgets about me, there is no one else...

A great, heaving sob tore from my lips, and I welcomed the thought that a soldier might hear it, like last time, and finish what the blows of their comrades had started. It hurt too much, and I could not continue...

Trembling from the force of my sobs, I braced myself for the last blow I would ever have to endure.

But...

No blow came.

Instead...

Like the toll of a bell echoing from a far away place, the quiet voice of my mother reached my ears from a long ago time:

"The Almighty is the One Who is still present when no one else is."

"The Almighty is the One Who is still present when no one else is," I whispered, my lips almost too numb to move yet tingling with those words.

As they had tingled with the Quest Leader's name: Lord Lucian the Ideal of Freedom.

It was not the sort of name that could be false.

And it was the greatest proof of my mother's words.

For the Quest Leader was coming, and his coming was the sign that the Almighty had not abandoned Icilia.

The Almighty had not abandoned Icilia despite the reality that many, like the duke and the city-folk, had walked the way of the Gouge with their lack of compassion and esteem for anything sacred. They did not deserve salvation and redemption, because they were the true traitors. Indeed, everyone beside my parents and my sisters had crumbled before the enemy. Yet the Almighty still bestowed a savior.

If the Almighty had not abandoned them, then surely the Almighty had not abandoned my sister—no matter what the city-folk said about her or what she felt about me, she would never truly serve the Gouge. Tahira was the one who had fervently relayed to me our parents' teachings on loyalty to Icilia. However cold her heart became, this part of her would not change. So, despite her terrible circumstances, she was undoubtedly ruining the Gouge's plans beneath his very nose, and her efforts had surely only increased once news of the Quest reached her. Though I had no way of proving these things, in my heart I knew for certain they were true. There was no question that she deserved an appeal made to the Quest on her behalf.

I was the only person who could do that for her.

I choked in the middle of a sob and coughed to clear my aching throat, then lifted my head to stare across the boundary.

I am the only person who can appeal to the Quest on her behalf.

I stared at the wood dust swirling in the dim light that permeated the gloom, overcome by the thought though it was one I had had before.

I am the only person who can appeal to the Quest on her behalf.

I drew in a shaky breath.

There was no guarantee of the Quest listening to me, and there was also the hastily suppressed fear that she could be punished for my absence, as well as the agonizing possibility that she did not care for my help, but...

Though all of the affection that once brightened her gaze had long ago evaporated, she was the only meaning my life possessed. I had survived so long for her; surely I could survive a little longer outside my familiar circumstances for her sake? Surely I could dare to cross the line that held so much torment for me in her name?

The risks were necessary. The Quest was coming, but it was unclear whether they would prioritize the reconquest of Ehaya herself—so many soldiers would have to be prepared, and there was always the threat of conjury. Without a reason, they would come, but not soon.

While the possibility of the Gouge discovering her true allegiance only increased for Tahira. Though even without the possible horrors of such discovery, she did not deserve to remain any longer in the Gouge's ash-laden shadow.

No one beside the Quest could or might even be willing to save her.

And only I could make the appeal.

Though my heart palpitated, my pulse fluttering erratically in my throat and pounding in my ears, and I could not seem to breathe, I clambered to my feet, grasped my stick, and, whispering the Quest Leader's name for courage, took the first step over the shrubs and across the border.

Gratitude to the Almighty. I sighed, shoulders slumping with relief. *At least I did not die or alert the soldiers the moment I crossed. As I did last time.*

Then, straightening my back, not daring a glance behind, I walked onward.

Tahira might have forgotten about me, but I had not forgotten about her.

She might no longer love me, but I loved her as I always had.

For her, in the Almighty's name, I would do anything.

CHAPTER 15
FINDING JUSTICE

Perspective: Count Ciro Tolmarie, mayor of Jurisso and noble of Nademan
Date: Eyyéfaz, the twenty-second day of the sixth moon, Kadsaffe, of the year 500, C.Q.
Placement: between Chapter 45 and Chapter 46 of The Bell Tolling

I fidgeted anxiously with my silver mayor's ring, unable to stand completely still despite both my noble and military training. *Please, oh Almighty, please,* please *protect him...* I doubted that he needed my prayers, but I prayed all the same, the love I held for him rendering me desperate to protect him...

Arrayed in neat, orderly ranks behind me, the soldiers of his army seemed just as immersed in prayer. Very few appeared to even notice the jeers and insults slung by the enemy squads gathered on the opposite side of the improvised arena, closer to the castle and the city.

The contrast between our behavior and theirs was stark, as was everything else about the Quest's army and the Quest themselves. Where the enemy was cold, cruel, and vicious, the Quest was kind, gentle, and virtuous, promising compassion even to those who disrespected them and deserved their presence the least.

And this impression grew all the stronger with each week I spent at my Lord's side.

How blessed Belona and I had so quickly become. When we had set out to pledge to the Quest, leaving our children with Belona's great-aunts, we had feared we would never return. Yet, not three days after our departure, we found them—really, *they* were the ones to find *us*—and the Quest accepted us without question, welcoming us into their confidence as though they had always known us. Without hesitation, they fulfilled our most ardent prayers and offered their protection to all those for whom we had sought it. They truly were the Shining Guide's promise fulfilled.

It had been the greatest honor to proclaim my allegiance in front of the market of Zaiqan and use my influence among the nobles and citizens of my province for their name.

And, in return, the Quest Leader had kept me at his side amid his campaign.

After his companions left for their own shares of his reconquest, my Lord had traveled to each of the towns of northern Zaiqan and gathered a division of troops, new forces beyond those who had already joined his companions. Young men and women, all between the ages of seventeen and twenty (as well as some of the more enthusiastic girls and boys of fifteen and sixteen), many of whom had been the juniors among my revolutionary peers, flocked to his banner, enthralled by the possibilities of education and empowerment that flowed in his wake.

My Lord did not disappoint in his response. With a gentle smile on his lips, he welcomed these youths with all kindness, soothing away lifetimes of neglect and pain, and trained us in a way that was actually enjoyable and exciting. Through games and tournaments he refined our skill such that, within a few weeks of beginning, we were prepared to confront our oppressors. Though at first my Lord had borne the brunt of every skirmish, soon his soldiers fought reliably by his side and pushed forward his reconquest, capturing armories and winning outposts, freeing captives and towns at every step.

Then we reached the city of Pethama.

There the western regional commander, second only to the wretched Gouge in his cruelty, awaited us.

Instead of the quick surprise attacks that before fueled our progress, we had but one option: a siege. Something that scared my fellow soldiers and me more than even the sight of blood, the scents and sounds of battle, and the feel of flesh giving way before steel.

My Lord, however, had known exactly what to do.

Within minutes of our arrival, he gave instructions to begin building a thick wooden wall around the city and to ready ten squads as infiltrators. Amid the showers of arrows, he explained that the wall would serve to protect our camp and to distract our enemy so that the infiltrators could make their way into the city. There, they would divide into two groups: one to encourage revolt against the enemy in the Quest's name, without weapons, and another to strategically attack the enemy's soldiers while wearing the simple uniforms our Lord had designed. This dual prong of infiltration was his real plan.

How well it worked.

Despite the enemy's seemingly endless number of arrows—they had control over the production of Pethama's smithies, the only places where metal was forged in all of northern Icilia—within ten days, the city fell into chaos and the enemy forces were brought to their knees.

That was when my Lord issued a challenge to General Perveries: let the heads of the two forces meet in single combat, and the winner would be master of the city without further bloodshed.

The commander, cornered yet arrogant and full of confidence in his weapons skill, had not hesitated to accept.

Thus, now, a day of message exchanges later, half of each force were gathered outside the siege wall around a field cleared of stones and shrubs for the duel, the enemy taunting and the Quest's soldiers praying as each awaited their commanders...

A roar of rage sounded from the direction of the castle.

The enemy troops leered at us in eerie unison before splitting and pivoting, forming an aisle down which walked the western regional commander.

Six inches over six feet, hulking, dressed from head to toe in black steel armor, monstrous sword more than twice the size of any of ours, expression twisted with a haughty cruelty too reminiscent of the Gouge... General Perveries was a walking nightmare. The reason we had been so late to dare to behold our Lord's favor.

I cupped my hands together over my heart and desperately prayed, *Please, oh Almighty, bless Your own savior with victory. Please, oh Almighty, bless Your own...*

The soldiers behind me snapped to attention, split to form an aisle, and pivoted to face the man who passed between them.

But, instead of the wary cheers the enemy had given their commander, the Quest's soldiers saluted and cried, "Praised be the Almighty! Blessed be the Quest Leader!" Tears filled their eyes as they looked upon him, drinking in every movement of his person and every hint of his smile.

Fear struck my wildly beating heart at his arrival.

General Perveries' armor was the best I had ever seen, while my Lord wore only his usual robes.

Yes, I knew that the athar of my Lord's clothes was more resilient than any metal could ever be.

But... it was nearly impossible to remember that with Perveries looming like black smoke on the edge of my vision.

My Lord reached where I stood in front of the companies and offered me a smile. "Blessings, Count Tolmarie," he greeted. "Is everything prepared?" He seemed not the slightest bit disturbed by the malice in Perveries' glare, as serene as always.

My Lord's peace gave me strength. Enough that my pulse

calmed and my mind settled, resuming focus upon what he had ordered me to do.

Bowing, I answered, "It is as you wish, my Lord."

"Excellent, Count Tolmarie," my Lord said, seeming pleased. He rested a hand on my shoulder, squeezed slightly, and then strode calmly into the arena.

My breath wheezed in my chest, and I almost wished that Belona were with me and my daughters in my arms, my peace amid these dark moments. After what he had done to us in these last two years, I was terrified of the western regional commander, like all of my peers the Quest's soldiers, and to watch my Lord walk to face him...

Perveries barked an order to his troops and stalked toward my Lord, insults and crass words spilling from his mouth.

My Lord halted twelve feet from the monster and drew his sword. Letting it hang loosely at his side, he met the enemy's glower with a calm smile. "By the Almighty's name, shall we begin?"

Perveries sneered. "What we *shall* do is choke you on your stupid promise before the day is done, pretty boy." Then he attacked.

The ground seemed to shake, to my horrified eyes, with the force of his footsteps as he charged at my Lord, huge sword raised for a vicious slice.

My Lord, still smiling, merely raised an eyebrow.

"Taste your death!" Perveries swung his sword downwards in a brutal arc, a move intended to lacerate his opponent from shoulder to hip, and—

Quick as a flash of light, my Lord leapt back and away, neatly dodging the blow.

Perveries stumbled, sword bereft of a target, then chased him those few steps and snarled, "Fight me, coward!" He lifted his sword overhead.

In the dim illumination provided by the smog-filled sky, the cruel blade gleamed sinisterly, like the sheen of poison on a snake's fangs.

I caught my breath. *That does not merely* look *like poison—it is poison!*

Before I could scream a warning, Perveries crashed his sword down toward my Lord's head.

My Lord stepped sideways again, another dodge. Then, in a silver-smooth movement, he swept his sword upright, raised it overhead, and swung it down at his enemy, wind whistling off the edge.

Eyes widening, Perveries scrambled to straighten himself and managed to block the strike in a harsh clang of steel on steel only a hand's breadth above his nose. Despite his greater height, his arms visibly trembled with the weight of the powerful blow, more powerful than any of his.

My Lord pressed downwards, smile replaced by a stern expression, then disengaged with a high-pitched scrape of his sword and struck toward his knee.

Perveries' visage contorted with pain as he blocked that slice, movements slower than before.

My Lord swung upward and again down at his enemy.

Before Perveries could react, the sacred blade cleaved him in two.

Both halves of his body thudded to the ground in an explosion of blood and bile.

Somehow none of it touched my Lord.

Both armies stared, mouths open, jaws slack, eyes huge.

His sword had riven even steel armor! It had cut through bone and sinew as though they were but soft bread!

All of the general's reputed weapons skill had been no match for my Lord's prowess.

My Lord gazed at the bleeding corpse for a moment, his lips moving slightly with what was likely a prayer, and then glanced at the enemy soldiers. "Do you surrender to me, troops of the Gouge?" he asked calmly.

The enemy soldiers startled at the address, attention snapping to my Lord's shining face, a fear sparking in their faces—the faces that were a source of terror to countless people—a fear that savored to my peers and me of justice.

On the opposite side, my Lord's voice jolted the Quest's soldiers from their shocked stupor. Placing our hands on the hilts of our swords, we braced ourselves.

That fear, the soldiers' fear, the fear of justice, smoldered into anger.

"Never," called one of the enemy. Then another. And another. Until the whole force was screaming, banging swords against swords, stamping their feet, all three hundred and fifty soldiers roaring their defiance.

"Is that your answer, troops of the Gouge?" my Lord inquired.

"Death to the Quest!" cried a voice from the front of the force —the highest-ranking captain, from his placement, standing at the head of his soldiers as I did before my Lord's.

My Lord nodded. "If that is your answer, then our agreement is no longer binding." He cast a glance and a warm smile over his shoulder. "Ready, my sisters and my brothers?"

Those sweet words, which he bestowed before every battle, bolstered our courage—arrayed behind him, all two hundred soldiers straightened and unsheathed their swords, no longer fearful, suddenly prepared to face the worst of our tormentors in a way we had not since the start of the siege.

My Lord's smile widened. Then he looked at the enemy and, without any response of anger to the crude insults they had begun to throw in his direction, raised his blood-dyed sword. In his resonant voice he proclaimed, "For the Light!"

The cry reverberated over the battlefield, echoing as though the trees repeated it and shocking the enemy back into silence.

My Lord charged into battle.

And his soldiers followed.

The half-company stationed in the treetops released a flurry of arrows, felling many of the enemy before they could even react to the attack (the advantage of height was ours for the first time since the beginning of this siege).

The soldiers posted on the ground shifted into a run, blurring with our kind magic, timing our movements exactly as my Lord had instructed, so that those immediately behind him were on his heels and those to the sides were a few paces behind, constituting a triangular formation with the force of an arrow. And I was the blade at its tip, following in the footsteps of my Lord.

Together we pierced through the enemy ranks, tearing their rows to pieces just as they raised their swords to fight, slaying soldier after soldier in sprays of crimson blood, cutting through their counterattack like a thrown dagger slicing through flesh.

Within moments, the enemy force was in an uproar, pinned against the siege wall, none of their captains able to rally their troops well enough to muster a counter. Their usual method of using either height or numbers to overwhelm us was failing, no challenge for my Lord's grasp of battle tactics, and not many minutes passed before we reached the wall.

Gripping notches in the wood, my Lord led the way over the barrier and dropped onto the other side. Most of the two companies followed, the rest remaining behind to dispatch the enemy soldiers who had survived our initial assaults.

Beyond the palisade was tumult and bloodshed.

As my Lord had predicted, Perveries had been so confident in his victory that he had stationed his troops all along the other side of the wall, ready to swarm over it and massacre our forces at the first news of his victory—he had had no intention of keeping the agreement.

Anticipating this betrayal (the pact had been but a means to lure the enemy into a battle on his terms), my Lord had commanded the ten squads of the infiltrators to prepare themselves for outright battle.

And so they now fought, valiantly against a force that outnumbered them four persons to one. Even with my Lord's childhood guardian, Safira Hasima Sareneze, fighting alongside them, they were unable to hold their ground.

Without hesitating a single moment, we ran to help.

Though nearly two hundred soldiers crossed the wall, it was my Lord's coming that reversed the flow of the battle.

For, unlike his soldiers, who dueled earnestly for every little victory and every foot of progress, my Lord stalked across the battlefield with the ferocity of one of the lions of legend, his every blow the death of at least one of his enemies. None could stand before him, as none could stand before the Almighty's justice.

Inspired by the sight, many of the city-folk joined us, attacking their persecutors with branches, iron pots, and whatever other implements they could find.

It was wondrous to behold: the people of Nademan finally gaining courage because of our sun...

Once the battlefield was almost clear, Safira Sareneze and I gathered six squads, and we took initiative in scouring the castle-tree, clearing every room on each one of the twenty-five floors, both main trunk and tower. None of those we encountered surrendered, but, at my Lord's direction, we spared and imprisoned a few soldiers who he deemed to be tainted and not among those acting of their own will.

Within a matter of hours, the city was won, and my Lord's name was ringing throughout all of Pethama.

It did not seem real, but it was.

Though the blood soaking the ground brought the choke of nausea to my throat, and though tears burned my eyes at the grief of those of my peers who had lost their friends or relations, I was almost happy as I made the long trek from the castle to where my Lord's tent was situated in the center of his army's camp, a full mile from the city's boundary.

The next task will probably be scouring the castle for papers and moving into its barracks, but... I sighed to myself. *I do hope we are not here for more than a few days. There are a few more towns to liberate further south and some more outposts to defeat, and the faster we address them, the faster we might...* I squeezed my eyes shut for a brief moment. *How I miss them...*

Now that the battle was over, it was impossible to not sink into my endless longing for my family... Belona, Dorona, Fionna, Sonora, Donna, Risona, Rona, Kalenna—each of their precious faces flashed ever before my eyes, my strength and my anchor, the marker of my home.

And whatever moment they did not rule my thoughts was consumed by the names of Jurisso, each child and woman and man for whom I was father and protector, whom I loved second only to my family and my Lord and my Honor Arista, and for whose presences I longed, regardless of whether I liked them individually or no. They were my purpose, and I was bereft of them, for my branch-mates were either at my Lord's fortress of Arkaiso or with his companions on their various campaigns. Not a single one was with my Lord's division, so I had not seen any of them in more than two months.

How I missed them.

But my yearning was the least of the prices I was paying to fight for them, so I bore it without complaint.

I am finally acting to protect them. My actions might even bring back their laughter. For that, my gratitude should contain no impurity. And I am doubly blessed that, in this battle at least, none who were dear to me have fallen.

Suppressing more sighs, I walked onwards, returning salutes, murmuring words of condolence, and offering suggestions wherever I saw my young peers confused about an action they needed to take. As my Lord had taught, they were beginning burials for both our own dead and our enemies', but such matters of morality always felt more complex outside of his benevolent gaze. Everything was clearer in his presence.

Truly everything, I thought as I approached his quarters. *Even my love for my family and my town has gained clarity it did not possess before I was blessed by his presence...* Smiling at the reflection, I knocked lightly on the wooden pole that held up the thick fabric. "My Lord, may I be given leave to enter?" I asked.

His rich, musical voice answered, "Enter, Count Tolmarie!"

Raising an edge of the flap, I ducked inside, removed my boots before stepping onto the rug spread over the ground, and dipped a bow. Then immediately startled and protested, "My Lord, let me do that!"

My Lord chuckled as he submerged his sword in a basin of water placed on the small wooden stand that served as his writing table. "It is every warrior's own task to care for her blade." Lifting a small piece of rag, he began to gently rub the metal, removing spots of congealed blood in long scarlet streamers (though blood was usually so difficult to clean, beneath his fingers it seemed almost eager to be washed away).

As often as I saw him do this, after every battle, I still stared. He had merely to glance, and he would find a hundred people ready to serve him in even the smallest of ways!

A kind smile on his lips, my Lord tilted his head toward a second basin next to the first. "The archers were eager to help, so I asked them to bring one more. I thought you might join me."

That would be an honor! But I could not seem to muster enough sense to speak those words as I dumbly crossed the tent to stand beside him. Clumsily I drew my sword and began to clean it as he had instructed me.

My Lord's smile widened, a spark of what could only be called affection in his jewel-bright eyes, as he switched to scrubbing his cross-guard.

Overwhelmed by the attention, I quite uncouthly blurted, "I did not think you would be here more than a few minutes!" My cheeks glossed as soon as I realized how I had spoken, and I stammered an apology.

Instead of offense, only amusement lit his shining face. "The soldiers were quite adamant this time that I should come only for the funerals. I knew you would come in this direction for your report, so, once I had spoken to as many of the grieving as were present, I decided to await you here."

I almost cut my thumb on the sharp blade. He was waiting for *me*?

My Lord chuckled softly and raised his sword, gleaming silver and green without a hint of red, from the murky vermilion water. He set it on his cot, lowered the used basin to the floor, and replaced it with a fresh one. With a murmured word, he removed his robe overcoat and began to wash it of blood and dirt as well (though it was nearly pristine, filth rarely daring to approach his person).

It was an astonishing sight, to see the Lord of Icilia so casually dressed and engaged in such ordinary chores, and even more astonishing to think that *I* was the one allowed to see him so.

My Lord bestowed another affectionate glance upon me and then seemed to focus upon his chore.

Between the sounds of rubbed fabric and scraped steel, a silence spread between him and me that felt... if I dared to say it... like the camaraderie of friends. Though of similar age, he and I were of vastly different ranks, he my liege and I his vassal, and our experiences of this world did not parallel... but relaxing with him like this was easier than I could have ever imagined... It left no doubt that he knew me, not merely as one of a number of soldiers, but on an individual level, for who I myself was.

In his presence, with my love for him and my Honor Arista blazing alongside my devotion to my family and my town, I knew hope as I never had before. For, as his defeat of the commander showed and his decision to care for each of his vassals revealed, with his coming there would finally be justice in my nation.

CHAPTER 16
FINDING PEACE

Perspective: Count Ciro Tolmarie, mayor of Jurisso and noble of Nademan
Date: Eyyésal, the twenty-sixth day of the sixth moon, Kadsaffe, of the year 500, C.Q.
Placement: concurrent with Chapter 46 of The Bell Tolling

I scowled at the numbers (even as I thanked the Almighty that I still remembered how to read them so well). "This is not as many sets of armor as we had planned, my Lord."

My Lord pressed his lips together as he flipped through the main report. "The smiths claim that they do not have enough ore, is that not so?"

"Yes, my Lord." I tapped my forehead in an effort to relieve my headache. "From everything the captains and I have gathered, the smiths have faced perpetual shortages of ore since the Blood's conquest, with the governor of Bhalasa only sending more at his own whim. Consequently, the smiths use either their reserves or old pieces of weaponry to fulfill the enemy's demands, and the last set of those demands exhausted almost everything they had. They are willing to take all the armaments we have gathered over our campaign and reforge them for us, but they have little capacity for new work." Those armaments did require reforging because they were remnants from the enemy's armories—my Lord refused to allow the collection of weapons and armor from the enemy's corpses, and most of his soldiers were almost as repulsed as he was by the thought—but the effort the smiths promised would not produce as much as we had hoped.

Certainly sensing some of my thoughts, my Lord glanced at me from where he was seated on his cot. "You seem rather more discontented than even these numbers warrant, Count Tolmarie. Tell me."

In response, soothed by the encouragement, I blurted out my suspicion: "I think the smiths have more ore than they say!" At the questioning raise of an eyebrow, I added, "Experience has taught them to be cautious with their reserves. They do not know what the future holds, so they are unwilling to commit fully to your victory."

He nodded thoughtfully. "I can speak further with them, if you believe it to be useful."

"Please," I breathed, unable to help the adoration I knew was filling my expression. His very touch could transform dust into gold.

My Lord smiled and dipped his head. "Of course, Count Tolmarie. If the Almighty wills it, we will be prepared with this armor when her Grace declares the Quest's armies ready for our reconquest of Ehaya."

"If the Almighty wills it," I echoed and shyly returned his smile. Even after so many weeks in his presence, how over-whelmed I still was at his attention...

A knock came upon the tent pole, and a muffled voice asked for leave.

Startled by the unanticipated noise, I leapt to my feet and nearly dropped my papers into the half-full pitcher of water placed atop the desk (a reprehensible mistake, as paper was scarce).

My Lord leaned slightly in my direction and took the papers. His violet eyes twinkled as he replied, "Let her enter!"

Curious about the wording, just as the flap was raised, I turned.

And saw Belona enter.

I froze, unsure whether I had strayed from the waking world into a dream, one of the bittersweet visions that often captured me amid the night...

Her lovely lips curved in a hesitant smile and uttered in a quiet voice, "Blessings, Ciro, my love."

I remained frozen.

A tiny, dimpled arm rose behind her shoulder and waved a fist, and a little voice grumbled a familiar loud complaint.

Dorona.

I lurched into motion, stumbled across the tent, and threw my arms around both of them, squeezing them against my chest, clutching them as though a little pressure would allow me to become one with them, never to be parted—

Although my wife hugged me just as tightly, her no-longer-thin form melting into mine, the baby carried in the basket slung across her back wailed crossly, sounding vastly displeased.

Laughing with a breathless relief, Belona and I drew back from each other, and she carefully lifted the infant over her shoulder into her arms. Then, with a shy smile, offered our child to me.

As embarrassing as it was, I froze again.

Three months had passed since I had seen either of them.

Not long after Belona and I had met my Lord in the middle of the moon of Zalberre, the Quest had decided to leave for the spring market of Zaiqan. Though every couple in my town had already made arrangements with their relations for the care of their children, my Lord encouraged my wife, other women with infants and toddlers, and the young adolescents to remain behind at his fortress with the elderly, while the rest of us traveled at his side. Then, instead of all returning, the able of my town had divided among the contingents formed to support each of our Lord's companions, and I myself had followed our Lord.

So I had not seen Belona and Dorona in three months.

My baby had grown so much in my absence—no longer needing swaddling and perhaps not even suckling, if Belona had succeeded with her plan for an early weaning, which was possible as she seemed much healthier than when we had parted, as though she were no longer sacrificing her life for our child—and I feared she would not recognize me.

Three months was a long time in the life of an infant.

Dorona fussed a little, rubbed her eyes with her adorable fists, and looked up at me.

Those blue eyes that mirrored her mother's blinked.

Then she held out her arms to me in an unspoken demand.

Exhaling a soft cry, I swept her into my embrace and held her to my heart. "Blessings, my soul!" I exclaimed.

My baby grumbled again in response and then began to coo, one little hand sinking into the strands of brown beard rolled neatly beneath my chin and the other gripping at the leather pad covering my shoulder.

Tears spilled down my cheeks as, with her warm weight in my arms, I felt at peace for the first time in months.

They are actually here...

Wait.

Why are they here?

Remembering what had taken place on a field but a mile distant and not a week prior, I opened my eyes and frowned. "What are you doing here, Belona?"

Her blue eyes sparked with irritation, perhaps at my stern tone, but her answer was calm: "Three weeks past, his Highness Prince Darian sej-Shehasfiyi called me to our Grace's study and informed me that our Lord summoned me to Pethama. Our Lord wished for my presence and stated that my place is now at your side. That is why I am here."

I blinked, shocked. My Lord had not mentioned anything like that to me, and I could not see why he thought Belona's presence was necessary—except for my own sake, and that was hardly important—but then my Lord did not always explain his decisions. As was his right. And, regardless, I was certainly grateful that he had summoned her and was delighted to see her.

But still...

"Why did you bring Dorona with you, Belona?" I asked. "Apologies for my tone and the questions, my love, but... you know better than I how unsafe all of this is!"

A tension left Belona's posture, and she seemed to relax as a wry smile quirked her lips. "Our baby, Ciro, is quite as stubborn as you are. She would not let me leave! Though she stayed quietly with my aunts when we searched for our Lord, this time she refused to remain behind. If I dared to be absent for more than a few minutes, she ceased to eat, drink, or sleep and threw endless tantrums. My aunts could not keep her. So, after much difficulty, I asked our Grace and his Highness, who advised me to take her with me. A squad of soldiers escorted me, and the woods were cleared, so," she shrugged, "we have been quite safe."

I sighed, seeing her point, and smiled ruefully down at Dorona's brown head. "As demanding as the grouchiest of counts and not yet a year old." Praying in gratitude for how she had kept her personality, I bounced her, to her delighted squeals, and then asked, again frowning, "What of our other daughters?"

Belona reached up to straighten the leather cap on my head that was the best our army had done so far for a helmet. "They seem comfortable now at Arkaiso, and willing to stay with my aunts, so I decided not to disrupt their lives any further. Ciro," she met my gaze, "they are happy, my love. They even laugh now, almost as happily as Dorona. You do not need to worry."

Her words indeed dispelled the last of my anxiety. All I needed was the safety of my family, and all I wanted was their happiness...

Belona looked past my shoulder and dipped a curtsy. "May the Almighty bless you, my Lord."

I startled and turned, my cheeks glossing at the disrespect we had given by ignoring him... only to freeze once more.

For his eyes were full of pain.

He inclined his head. "The Almighty's blessings upon you, Countess Tolmariat." A sorrow accented his melodious voice as he spoke her name.

My brow furrowed. *That pain seems familiar somehow...*

My Lord glanced down at Dorona's small form, smiled warmly, and extended his arms. "If you would allow?"

I stared at him. Did he really mean...?

Belona jabbed her elbow into my side. "Ciro," she hissed, "this is a wonderful opportunity! Do not waste it!"

I jolted at the prompt and carefully placed our baby in his hands.

Without the slightest bit of uncertainty, my Lord lifted the child to his shoulder and bounced her, drawing sweet giggles, as expertly as though he played with infants every day. Astounding, not least because he was neither a father himself nor surrounded by children. It was another divine quality of his.

Indeed, the whole scene seemed divine-blessed. For the Quest Leader himself was holding my daughter, a girl born in an age of pain and blood, and they were both laughing, his white-gold beard falling lightly over her lustrous brown hair, her face pressed into his neck as his hand rested on her back, her coos answered by his whispers of "my little sister." What protection I had needed, what peace I had been seeking—it was that sight, the Lord of Icilia treasuring my child like his own, and, having seen it, I could have perished with a smile on my lips.

My Lord kissed Dorona's head, over her little cap, and then glanced up.

And again pain dimmed his blessed eyes.

"My Lord..." Belona spoke from beside me. "Why do you look at me with such pain?"

I startled at the question, shocked yet again. But proud of my wife's daring as well. I myself could not have fathomed asking.

My Lord pressed his lips together and exhaled a quiet sigh. Then he gestured with his bearded chin toward the pair of chairs placed across from his cot (usually used by his commanders and me). "If it would please you to sit, I will explain."

Belona and I did as he ordered, and he himself took a seat on his bed, our baby still cradled in his arms.

Somehow, despite the informality of the setting, he presided over the tent as though it were a throne room.

My Lord pressed another kiss to my daughter's head. Then, meeting Belona's gaze, he spoke, "I was with you on that night."

I inhaled a shocked breath, while Belona's cheeks coarsened, all gloss disappearing. The memories were too near for us to not understand what he meant.

The silvery glow of my Lord's beige skin faded, like sunlight interrupted by a black cloud. "One of the blessings bestowed upon the Quest Leader is her dreams. Dreams that allow her to experience something of the lives of her people, to know their passions and their fears, their joys and their sorrows. It is meant to be encompass all strong emotion... But, in this age, my dreams have always been of the worst horrors my people suffer."

"And one of those dreams was of me," Belona breathed, her voice hardly more than a whisper.

"Yes, Countess." My Lord wore a smile full of agony. "Not many nights after my nineteenth birthday and my ceremony of magical maturity, I dreamt of your sufferings as you suffered them. It was my first such dream, and my sixth at all fueled by this aspect of my magic."

Belona's eyes widened, her mouth falling open. Shocked. Speechless. Horrified. Heartbroken. Stricken with a torment that had never truly faded.

As I was.

My Lord combed his fingers through the tiny curls that were starting to peek out from beneath Dorona's cap. His eyes were distant, his gaze almost glassy, as he spoke, "Before that night, I had known that such nightmares existed—I had fought from the shadows against our enemy for four years already, so I was not naïve. But I had not seen the reality... a dream only four nights prior had begun to teach me what such violence meant." Tears, each a source of soul-burning agony, spilled down his cheeks.

As tears spilled down our own cheeks. But we did not speak, both knowing instinctively what the other needed—the same need, to know what he had perceived and what he had felt.

Perhaps sensing that need, he continued, "When I first opened my eyes in this dream, I was entirely disoriented. It was dark, the patch of forest was one I had not seen before, and there was so much noise... Flashes of flame strobed across my vision, leaving me nauseous, and I still understood little of what was happening to me.

"Then I saw you. Skin coarse, eyes bloodshot, too terrified to scream... and entirely without clothing. Shadows loomed above you and approached your form with malicious jeers... For a moment, I was too horrified to react. I was already partly the Quest Leader in actuality, so to see such a thing... it tore my heart into little pieces that have still not healed.

"I tried to come to your defense. Throwing myself between you and them, I yelled a war cry and drew my sword... only to realize, in a moment of bone-deep horror, that it was but a dream. Though all I was seeing was truly happening, at the very moment I was seeing it, I had no physical presence. I could do nothing.

"So I sat beside your head and cried. I whispered comfort that you could not hear and sang the most calming hymns I knew. I tried to remain with you, thinking that I at least should bear witness if no one came, but I could only maintain my dreaming state until dawn. The next night, I attempted to return to your side, for I had noted your auric signature, but no dreams at all came. The night following, I dreamt of another."

An agonized gratitude filled his expression. "I thought you had perished that night, and I mourned your death. I did not know your name to find you, as the ability to know names came later... I only learned that you still lived in the days after my ascension, when I searched all of Icilia with my magic to learn what had become of those of whom I had dreamed. It has been a great blessing unto me to not only have learned of your life but also to have seen you well and received your pledge."

In the wake of his words, there was silence.

Silence as I tried to comprehend what he had told us and as Belona simply stared into the distance.

Silence.

Then Belona uttered a choked sob.

Falling from the chair onto the ground, she shuffled toward him and pressed her face into his knees. Shuddering, she began to cry.

Unable to bear her tears, I rose, knelt beside her, and wrapped her shaking frame in my embrace. But I had no peace to give.

It was too much.

Her torment and the thought of my daughters suffering the same... some of whom already had, and some of whom still might... the knowledge that so many women already had... it was too much.

It was too much.

Who could survive this pain?

My Lord balanced Dorona with one hand and caressed our faces with the other. "That night, my sister," he said quietly, "is the first night that I specifically vowed to purify Icilia so that no one would suffer in such ways ever again."

Belona sobbed harder, shaking in my arms and against his knees. "Why does such evil exist, my Lord!" she wailed. "Why did I suffer it! Why must I fear that my daughters, too, will never be free of it!"

I gazed miserably up at him, unable to answer, unable to escape those same cruel questions. Neither a platitude nor the reality of what had happened could fulfill her plea, and I had nothing else to give her.

An answering sorrow shone on my Lord's face. "Suffering, my sister, is both the cause and the consequence of sin. Each of us, through the actions we take that are less than pure, generates this harmful energy, and it accumulates, in a person and in a lineage, until a free choice causes it to manifest in evil. Evil that is glad to wreak destruction and spread pain and fear to all it touches. And, in its wake, we suffer, sometimes as a recompense for harm we have done and sometimes through no fault of our own. In both, my sister, is the Almighty's justice.

"Though the Almighty is the author of goodness, not at all the author of evil, evil and suffering, too, fall under the divine command. However, though it is within the Almighty's power to eliminate such pain, doing so would imperil justice, as punishment often must take the form of suffering, giving restitution to sin and learning from our mistakes. Thus, instead, the Almighty strives to balance evil and suffering with light and justice, letting suffering lighten the weight of sin and enacting justice upon those who torment the innocent. It is a delicate harmony to maintain, for, with but the slightest error, our free choice would be stolen in the name of peace."

I shook my head. "I would prefer peace to free choice." His words soothed much of the desperation in my heart, and they appeared to smooth the pain from Belona's expression, but this point of discontent still burned within my chest.

"A world of peace, free of sin and evil, indeed seems appealing, does it not?" he replied. "But be wary, my brother, and do not discount the blessing of free choice too quickly. For, without free choice, the beauties of love, virtue, and devotion would also not exist. Without choice, the gravity, the willingness to sacrifice, the disciplined and intentional adherence to a path that renders these qualities so sweet would be bereft of meaning.

"You know well what I mean—you yourselves have embarked on such paths. But in this world of peace those paths would be lost, for what illuminates those roads and sustains our feet along them is our identities. And without choice, the preferences, sentiments, and beliefs that form each of our identities would be arbitrary, some given to virtue and others to vice, and thus the joy of a life well lived would be extinguished as though it never was.

"In the grand balance of the cosmos, there would be no salvation. No way for our souls to earn a share of the hereafter. No way to become more than we are, that eliminated alongside any method by which to become less. It would not be peace, my friends, but slavery of another form."

"But where can peace exist at all amid such evil?" Belona whispered.

My Lord smiled. "In the love between friends, between spouses, between parents and children, between lieges and vassals, and between the faithful and the Almighty. That love, when true, ignites the fervor for virtue, and that in turn shines the light necessary to counter evil wherever it may be found. When you search for peace, my friends, seek it between you and me."

Those words pierced through to my heart.

He will be our peace.

He will not abandon us to our doom as our last king did.

He will always be with us.

It was the assurance I had needed, the assurance that my people had needed.

I had known it before, yes, but to know it so intimately in relation to my greatest fear and my worst memory... That was a boon for which no words of gratitude could ever fully suffice.

A wail tearing from my throat, I pressed my face into the side of his knee, besides Belona's, and cried, weeping away the last of the misery that had plagued me since the day I found my betrothed gone and myself awoken to the harsh reality of my world.

"My Lord," Belona whispered amid my sobs, "thank you. For being with me when I had no one else, and for not being ashamed of me. I-I cannot tell you what- what it means—" Her voice broke, and a moment passed before she continued, "what it means to know that you cared, that you, the Lord of Icilia, cared. Thank you for caring, for not avoiding the burden of my suffering."

I said nothing, for it was her moment. I had lamented her pain, but she had suffered it... With the voice of my heart, I whispered my gratitude for how his words had remedied what I never could, the sharing of her suffering by being there with her and experiencing those evils at her side. All that I could express was unequal to the task, but still I tried, knowing with greater certainty than ever that my Lord Lucian the Ideal of Freedom knew the prayers trapped within our hearts.

My Lord chuckled softly. "My sister, my brother, this is nothing for which to thank me. With whom will I be if not with you?"

I lifted my head to stare at him in wonder yet again.

Besides me, Belona caught her breath, just as astonished.

My Lord smiled and stroked our cheeks, first hers and then mine, in a motherly gesture that felt more wonderful coming from him, even with the youth of his face, than it would have from our own mothers. Then, with a flick of his gaze, he directed our attention toward our baby.

Our Dorona who was sleeping soundly in his arms, little face tucked against his neck, who had not stirred even once despite our tears and cries.

"Ohhh," Belona breathed, eyes wide. "She actually slept!"

My Lord exhaled a laugh. "Not quite the grouchiest of counts, is she, Count Tolmarie?" His eyes sparkled as he repeated my words.

I laughed myself, though quietly in order not to disturb her. "Perhaps not... but even the grouchiest count would be willing to rest peacefully in your shadow. Indeed, if I may say, it is almost symbolic for how all of Nademan is finally able to be at peace now that you have come."

His cheeks actually tinted silver at the praise! And he cupped his hand over his heart!

I smiled, savoring my savior's every joyous expression...

Then Belona asked, frowning, "My Lord... if I may?" He nodded, so she continued, "There is a question I have about what you said about your dreams. What happened to me... How- how often does it- does it happen?" She swallowed, still pained, but such courage now blazed in her eyes that I did not suggest that we avoid discussing the matter further.

My Lord sighed, his smile once again leaving, as he pressed his other hand to Dorona's back, as though to shield her. "It happens far more often than you have estimated. And particularly," his brows drew together, "to women who are nobles or will marry nobles."

I caught my breath. "Like Belona?"

"Yes." The ever-present peace on my Lord's shining face transformed into a terrifying, restrained fury. "Like so many others, you were targeted. The Gouge suspected that there was a chance you had magic."

"But neither Dorona nor I do!" Belona exclaimed.

"Is this why my parents allowed them to take her?" I asked, the creeping horror of that realization returning stronger than before...

My Lord smiled grimly. "Yes. The Gouge thought, as those who have no conception of love do, that magic would be the only reason a noble would marry a woman without some sort of visible political connection. I ask your pardon for this comment, Countess Tolmariat."

Belona shook her head. "There is nothing my Liege cannot say... My Lord, why would he do this?"

A deeper anger lit his features. "The violence has become, over the last decade, no longer random. The Blood is pursuing all women with the possibility of magic for a far eviler purpose: he wants them to have children. Children who he wrongly believes, in his disdain for free choice, will serve him because of the violence of their conception."

Belona and I stared up at him, stunned by such depth of cruelty... such deprivation of what was sacred to women and children...

"How can there be peace amid such evil?" I whispered with numb lips, desperately repeating Belona's question.

"In the Quest's shadow," my Lord answered. "For freedom

from such destruction of the dignity and esteem of incé and of free choice, for these mothers, these children, and their families, is given unto our hands by the Almighty. It is our purpose to balance this injustice."

As they had given healing to Belona's and my pain, so, too, did his words promise to bring light amid a darkness that seemed without end.

CHAPTER 17
CHASING PURPOSE

Perspective: Khuduya Rosalla Eminietta, citizen of Khuduren
Date: Eyyéfaz, the sixth day of the seventh moon, Narsaffe, of the year 500, C.Q.
Placement: between Chapter 46 and Chapter 47 of The Bell Tolling

The rising voices of my comrades grated against my ears like the whistling sound of a hundred bloodthirsty arrows.

Not the most accurate comparison, but it was the first sound that my mind remembered. A particularly brutal torture.

Indeed, I remembered it so well that the whistling was replacing their voices in my mind as they grew ever louder in their quarrel—

"Silence!" I roared.

The sounds of my comrades' voices ceased. And that unbearable whistling ended as well.

Glancing around at them, I scowled and folded my arms across my chest. "This cannot continue."

The eighteen members of my band either scoffed or looked away. But none dared to raise their voice as they had only a few moments ago.

I continued, "We have narrowly avoided most of our pursuers and managed to defeat those we cannot avoid over the last five months. We have survived. But only barely. Can any of you count how many times we have nearly starved since our escape because we do not know how to hunt? Or how many times we were nearly caught in the rain or snow because we cannot remember this terrain? We wander in circles. And with each week we descend deeper into madness. Our lot has not much improved from the cells."

The claim was bold, but none of my comrades objected. Most of them could not meet my gaze.

I tapped the hilt of my stolen sword as I looked around the circle, letting the hardness of my hazel eyes reinforce my message. Then said, "We need a purpose."

At that, they stirred. Half of them scoffed, and several others rolled their eyes. Jonrel Kretiett muttered, "What purpose?"

I did not let their expected skepticism dissuade me. "You know what I think: our escape was a miracle, a blessing from the Almighty. We need to use that miracle, to do something with it that is more than killing a few soldiers. We did not win our freedom to squander it. You heard the rumors in the arena just as I did. There is enough discord in the soldiers' movements that we no longer doubt them."

My comrades were silent in a rare moment of contemplation.

I waited with what meager patience I had—I knew that they would see my way in the matter.

My release from the manacles five months ago had indeed been miraculous. But what had been more so was that I had avoided recapture. And beyond even that was how I had freed all of the other forty-two gladiators in the arena before the alarm had sounded. With so many unchained, we had managed to liberate the rest, evade the guards, and steal a few weapons. Some perished on the way out, but the rest of us made good our escape before the Slicer or any conjurors arrived.

Our fortune in escaping was proof that miracles were real, that the Almighty still heard some of our prayers.

We had mourned those who died, and a few of us, including me, prayed for them, but mostly we rejoiced.

Then fifteen of our number, all newer gladiators, had started a quarrel. They declared they would return to their homes, where they would still be welcomed. They urged the rest to do the same... in quite brutal terms.

The other nineteen, including me, had rejected the notion. Whether we admitted it or not, we had spilled too much innocent blood to ever feel welcome at our homes. Some did not have homes any longer, for they had been taken from destroyed villages, and others, like me, could no longer remember where home was. Some simply knew that they could not meet the gazes of their families again.

The debate had raged for days, with many nearly coming to blows. Until, feeling responsible, I had taken charge and declared that everyone would choose for themselves. Those who believed they could go back would leave with our weapons, and the rest would follow me.

We had agreed and split. I immediately then led my new band to attack a few patrols and steal their weapons so we would not be defenseless.

But not defenseless was *all* that we were. In the months since our escape, we had come close to starvation many times, for few of us actually knew how to hunt, even in spring and summer. Only the weakened kind magic of the Ezulal amongst us, including me, kept us from dying of dehydration. We had almost died of exposure to the elements many times. We were disorganized, prone to arguments, melancholic, reckless, and more than a bit wild. I was their leader, since I helped them escape and they felt they owed me, but only a few regularly obeyed orders. Causing yet more arguments.

Maintaining a calm head, especially when that head often reeled from memories of brutal torture and crushing melancholy, was nearly impossible. Still, though, knowing we were all alone together, I tried. These eighteen youths were my only hope for a family and my only chance at gaining a purpose.

I just needed them to commit.

So, after several minutes of tense silence, I spoke again, "I have a target."

My comrades' gazes sharpened as they looked at me.

A smile that was more a feral baring of my teeth than anything else spread my lips. "Let us bring the fight to our enemies, that monster's soldiers. Let us break open another arena and free more gladiators."

My comrades' gazes gleamed with interest, and many of them began to smile in the same feral way as me.

We did, after all, lust for blood. The soldiers' blood.

So perhaps my motives for attacking the arena were more revenge than justice or the righteous desire to free others.

But I could purify my motives as I went. What was most important was to start something worthwhile before we squandered the remains of our lives in pointless little clashes. Or worse, turned to pillaging our own people.

Such an attack on an arena would be folly.

Two others and I had magic, but it was long suppressed. We were good fighters, but our movements were often sloppy and learnt through desperation and so could not be called actual skill. We were physically weak and thin and not especially coherent. But we were also too brash and desperate to choose some less risky path. We had little enough reason to be cautious—that was indeed why we had stayed together.

Once everyone was wearing that same gruesome smile, my comrades began to make noises of agreement.

My feral grin widened. "Outstanding. Then let us avoid the latest group of soldiers and be on our way."

Mikkel Sigien, my self-appointed lieutenant, rubbed his hands and cackled. "Let us start planning." His grin matched mine in the anticipation of violence.

My comrades whooped. Then picked up what few possessions we had gathered over the months.

Soon enough we were on our way, away from the fertile but desolate shores of the Anharat, near where it entered Icilia in the shadow of the Lightless Mountains, toward the second largest of the eight gladiatorial arenas, each a proper fortress.

A foolish mission. No one had ever tried such an absurd thing. No one ever tried to *enter* a gladiatorial arena, only leave.

But we were going to do it regardless.

We had to act.

How else were we supposed to gain a name worth anything in front of the Quest Leader?

Without a name worth something, why would he deign to save us?

CHAPTER 18
PROVING SELFLESSNESS

*Perspective: Prince Darian sej-Shehasfiyi, brother of the Quest
Leader and auxiliary heir to the throne of Asfiya
Date: Eyyésal, the tenth day of the seventh moon, Narsaffe, of the
year 500, C.Q.
Placement: between Chapter 46 and Chapter 47 of* The Bell Tolling

Murmuring words of thanks to the cook, I shifted my grip on the tray of porridge bowls until I was sure my hold was secure. Then, with a nod in response to her curtsy, I set off in the direction of the commanders' tents.

The camp around me, scattered among the bases of the large trees, was still waking, as the sun had not yet fully risen, but it bustled with energy. The few soldiers who had been to the kitchen tents before me were leisurely enjoying their breakfast with their families, their children taking advantage of the day-long pause in our march to run, shrieking, through the tents. At the same time, the soldiers on guard rotation at the camp boundaries or the central quarters were exchanging with their replacements, while the smiths were already hard at work, beating metal at their transportable anvils on the opposite side of the camp from the stables, coops, and kitchens.

Neat, efficient, yet pleasant and welcoming—the entire scene so well suited my brother and his companions that I almost laughed. I had read a hundred accounts of military campaigns, from those launched for important issues to those begun out of petty insult, and all of them had fallen far short of the discipline, organization, and initiative I saw before me. Though originally the Quest, the guardians, and I had spent hours on instruction regarding the duties required for such a large camp, only ten days into the journey the army now functioned without the need for much supervision or direction. It was why my brother could begin to dedicate his time while riding to advanced lessons for his companions and Elacir, and it was why the guardians and I could begin to spend ours training new magicians and tutoring younger soldiers in the basic studies of our civilization.

They are already showing themselves to be very devoted students, I thought, unable to help a small, fond smile as I passed several campfires surrounded by the youths I had started to teach. *They are slow in learning how to read and write, but their enthusiasm for the laws and the economic structure of Nademan is much greater than I expected. Some of them may even have the zeal required to begin restoring some of the lost arts and sciences...*

One of the young women glanced up from where she was giggling into her friend's ear. She startled at the sight of me and jolted to her feet. "Your Highness!" she gasped, bending in a bow.

As though her reverence was a ripple in a pond, the women and the men around the fires scrambled to stand and bow, only narrowly avoiding spilling their bowls on the ground.

I could not help a sudden surge of shyness. I was accustomed to bows and curtsies—the guardians had prepared me well, and these same youths offered them every time they came for a lesson —but there was something about the informality of the meeting that felt unusual, a quality more intimate than the reverences I usually received. There was a sort of admiration in their eyes that I had never seen before...

That is not true, I realized as I followed Lucian's example and smiled warmly. *My Grace and my Honors look at me in this manner as well. I have simply not wanted to acknowledge it for all these months...*

The young soldiers beamed and bowed again, excited by the acknowledgment, as I walked onwards.

I had proceeded only a few paces when a pair of children, sister and brother, ran up to me.

"May we carry your tray for your Highness?" the little girl asked, cupping her hands together in the traditional gesture of pleading.

Her brother merely gave me a beseeching look, blue eyes huge in appeal, as he sucked his thumb.

I smiled down at them. "Not today, Nademile. Our Honors would like some privacy this morning." I would usually let children help me carry the Potentates' trays, for it was an excellent chance to acquaint them with their Rulers, but from the look in my Honor Kyros' eyes as I had left, he did not need onlookers to his anxiety.

"Ohhh," the girl breathed, eyes wide, and nodded seriously. "Blessings, your Highness!" She grabbed her little brother's wrist and pulled him into a bow alongside her, before scampering away.

With a smile after them, I continued forward, easily balancing the laden wooden tray, until I reached the flap of my Honors' tent.

Before I could attempt a knock, the cloth sprung up, and Elacir gestured me inside. "Your Highness!" he exclaimed, seeming relieved. "You can help us!"

I raised an eyebrow as I placed the tray in his outstretched arms. "With what do you require help, Elacir?"

"Kyros!" Elacir hissed. "He is panicking!"

I lifted both brows, removed my boots, and slipped past him into the tent. Then blinked and tried to comprehend what I was seeing.

My Honor Kyros, the ever serene and composed Exemplar of Strength, was pulling at his hair and pacing back and forth at the far edge of the tent. A groove almost deep enough to collect rainwater had been worn into the earth beneath his feet, evidenced by the way the thin carpet was folding inwards as he tread upon it.

My Honor Elian seemed at a loss for what to do as he stood a few feet away, his hands filled with our Honor Kyros' formal robes, sword, and crown.

"Panicking indeed," I muttered, surprised.

At the sound, both Potentates turned toward me. Both of their sacred faces flashed with relief. And my Honor Kyros actually flung himself in my direction.

"Prince Darian!" he cried, his arms wrapping tightly around my body. "Prince Darian, what should I do? I am not ready!"

I blinked, now actually alarmed. "My Honor, why do you think you are not ready?" I asked, trying not to squirm in the unexpected but oddly welcome embrace. It was strange to be hugged so by a man as fatherly as he. "You have met every known standard for magical maturity that is prescribed for crown heirs, and our Lord believes you are ready. What more assurance could you have?"

My Honor Kyros sighed and leaned further into me, relaxing, the tension in his body seeming to drain away. "Those words are exactly what I required."

"Sorry, Kyros," my Honor Elian said, shame gleaming in his vivid eyes. "Sorry that I could not reassure you so well."

"No, Elian," my Honor Kyros sighed, "I could not expect reassurance from you for something neither of us have experienced. That only Arista or Prince Darian could do."

My mouth almost dropped open in shock.

"That is true," my Honor Elian replied, giving me an adoring glance—further deepening my shock.

"And, well," my Honor Kyros' lips curled in a small smile as he continued, "at least now I will be of use to you when it is your turn."

"From your blessed lips to the Almighty's divine mercy," my Honor Elian whispered, sounding wistful.

"May the Almighty grant so," Elacir added from behind me.

Although none of them seemed to require me to speak, as the guardians would have, I repeated the prayer. As difficult as it was to be around the Potentates, I was well aware that I did love them. Unworthily, yes, but still deeply. The months of their absence had taught me so all too well. It was why I brought meals for my Honors, helped Elacir set up their tent and bedding each evening and clean their weapons and clothes, and coordinated similar service with Countess Tolmariat for my Grace. Or, at least, whenever they did not finish such chores before I could address them.

My Honors favored me with affectionate smiles—further cementing that devotion with every drop of kindness.

Then my Honor Kyros gave me a final squeeze (a rather odd experience, as I was both leaner and slightly shorter than him), before releasing me and reaching for his clothes.

I promptly pivoted on my heel, giving him the privacy he would want, and began to set out the porridge bowls in the center of a circle of cushions, arranged by the back of the tent, that we used as a dining area.

A few moments later, my Honor Kyros joined me, and we started the meal, both of us carefully avoiding looking behind us even when our Honor Elian yelped.

My Honor Elian only grudgingly allowed Elacir to help him dress and to care for his wings; he would not welcome the presence of anyone else, save Lucian himself. The one time I had attempted to help had prompted such shame and revulsion to crumple his features that I did not dare to ask again.

So, though my Honor Kyros and I both repeatedly winced, our fingers tightening on our spoons, at the faint sounds of his gasps and whimpers, we continued to eat.

As soon as I discover the key to our Grace's curse, I will *address yours, my Honor,* I vowed. *I do not understand why such gentle touches on the numb flesh of your wings hurt you so, but I will do whatever I can to serve you.* The words would have embarrassed him if I had spoken them aloud, but my silence did not reduce their fervor.

Even so, my heart burned that I could not act. My Honor Elian was the first star of the Almighty's freedom. He deserved not a drop of the suffering that he was so cruelly forced to drink...

Only when he slumped onto a cushion in our circle did the strained silver of my tensed knuckles fade.

My Honor Kyros glanced concernedly at his brother but said nothing. Elacir wore the same expression as he proffered a bowl to our Honor Elian and then retrieved his own share. My Honor Elian himself fidgeted uneasily on his cushion, his scales a dull ochre.

I pressed my lips together and sighed, letting the sound break a too-familiar tension. "Are there any more preparations remaining?" I asked.

My Honor Kyros set aside his spoon and bowl as a quiet anxiety returned to his features. "I underwent the ritualistic cleansing last night, after you slept—Lucian himself went with me to the river—and I have the prayer memorized... umm..." He bit his lower lip, distractedly resettling his crown on his head. "Is there something I am forgetting, Elian?"

My Honor Elian smiled fondly. "Have you asked Prince Darian, my Brother?"

I raised an eyebrow. "You have already asked me."

My Honor Kyros murmured a word of thanks to his fellow Potentate, then turned and offered me a nervous smile. "Would you accompany me as my teacher?"

My mouth almost fell open.

The tradition was that royal heirs chose the teachers they most valued to escort them to the ceremony of magical maturity. It was every court scholar and warrior's dream, a grand honor, the pinnacle of a teacher's life and the highest possible recognition of excellence in one's chosen disciplines. But to be so chosen by one of the divine-blessed Potentates? That was an honor too great to comprehend. And so soon after my own maturity? That could not be believed.

I blinked, certain that I had misheard him. "Is not Taza walking with you as your teacher?"

"She is," my Honor replied with an almost painfully eager hope in his voice, "but I would be blessed if you would as well, Prince Darian. She instructed me in my magic, yes, but you taught all of us how to rule."

I shook my head, unable to believe what he was saying. "Surely Ilqan would be a better—"

"No, Prince Darian," my Honor cut across my speech (the first time I had heard him interrupt anyone at all in all of these months). "You are my choice." A bashful smile tilted his lips. "I cannot do this without you."

I swallowed, so overcome by the wonder of those words that I could hardly nod. No one beside Lucian had ever chosen me for my own merit. No one, not even my father. So my Honor Kyros' doing so... there were not enough words in all of the twenty years of my education to express sufficient gratitude.

My Honor Kyros' smile brightened, a lovely sympathy rendering his eyes as soft as a mother's hug and as unmistakably full of affection.

It was enough to bestow a sense of invincibility upon a neglected child.

I straightened, stacked our empty dishes, and ushered the Potentates and Elacir to their feet. "Our Lord and our Grace must have prepared the site by now. If it would be in accordance with your orders, would you lead us?"

The three men listened with, strangely enough, delight, not merely mere good humor, and turned to check each other's robes for wrinkles and splatters of food. My Honor Elian wore his crown and buckled on his sword, while Elacir neatened our bedrolls. With brisk movements, I switched to a more ornate set of robes, which featured silver curls of embroidery on the collar, sleeves, and cuffs.

As I placed the matching cap on my head, I turned and found my Honor Kyros holding up an athar cloth pouch.

"I know that you usually dislike it," he shyly requested, "but would you wear it today?"

I numbly reached forward and accepted the pouch. *How can they still startle me with their sweetness after so many months...* Pulling open the velvety strings, I drew forth my heir's circlet—a thin band of silver adorned with a single central setting of luminous athar—and wore it for the first time since my own maturity ceremony.

Then, with a deep breath, I extended my arm to my Honor Kyros.

He immediately wrapped his right hand around my wrist and leaned into me, letting me bear some of his weight, a symbolic demonstration of how my teaching supported his throne.

Elacir opened the flaps, and the four of us wore our boots and stepped outside.

To the cheers of the soldiers who had gathered around our tent.

My Honor Kyros froze, an absolutely endearing expression of embarrassed pleasure creasing his features.

I could not help but grin. My own maturity ceremony had been a somber affair, dimmed by the weakness on Lucian's face after his own, so I was doubly glad that my Honor Kyros' would be well celebrated. He had labored so much for it.

The same joy was reflected on Taza's face as she stepped to my Honor's side and offered her arm to him.

Though he properly gripped her forearm, he seemed too star-tled to remember the next action.

"Walk, Brother," Elian prompted in a whisper.

My Honor Kyros jolted forward, and the soldiers instantly arranged themselves so that a path formed in the direction of the camp's center, where our Grace had ordered a ring of one-foot-tall stones to be placed last night, about five minutes' walk from the commanders' tents. The area was surrounded by logs for the commanders' seating and, beyond that, by a cleared space where the soldiers could gather to observe the ceremony.

On that path we walked amid cries of "Bless the Exemplar of Strength!" and "Hail the prince of Asfiya!" and "Salute the general!"

Cool silver spread over my face, so overwhelming was the sound of my title being included in those tributes.

But quickly my attention focused upon my Honor, whose cheeks grew coarser and coarser as we approached our destination. All of his earlier composure slipped away, leaving him again almost shaking with fright.

Until we arrived at the circle of stones and Lucian met his gaze.

From that one look, my Honor seemed to gain enough confidence to stand straight, skin glossed and eyes determined.

I had felt the same way during my ceremony.

Lucian smiled gently and flicked his gaze around the circle, directing us to look.

As tradition required, my Honor Kyros' lieges, our Lord and our Grace, had decorated the ring with little circlets and bouquets of fragrant flowers and verdant leaves, arranging them over the stones and strewing them over the cleared earthen floor like ribbons of luscious color. Roses, marigolds, tulips, daisies, lavender, violets, sunflowers, peonies, lilies—more than I could name and in more colors than I could grasp. A thick pad of blooms marked where my Honor would kneel in the center of the circle in front of his lieges.

Inhaling the sharp, beautiful scent, I wondered how many of those flowers had blossomed specifically for this occasion— though my ceremony had occurred at the end of winter, and all of the blooms my father had saved for me from Lucian's had wilted, Lucian had still somehow managed to adorn my circle with a meadow's worth.

There were even more for my Honor's.

Tears gleamed in my Honor's eyes, and he swallowed, throat bobbing, as he whispered, "Thank you."

My Grace, who stood with her arm entwined through our Lord's, beamed at him and pressed an elegant finger to the emerald pendant gleaming over her collar.

A voice spilled from it, sweet, bright, effervescent, and bouncing with excitement. The voice of Kalyca, Kyros' adorable little sister.

"Blessings, Big Brother!" she called out.

Those tears spilled over the rim of his eyes and down his cheeks. "Blessings, Kalyca darling!" he answered through a strangled sob.

"Blessings for your ceremony!" she replied. "I am proud of you!"

He seemed overcome—though she said those same words every time he contacted her.

Smiling slightly, I used a handkerchief to dry his cheeks. "See, my Honor, it will be perfect," I reassured.

As my Honor pressed his lips together in an effort to compose himself, Lucian's gaze slid to me.

And, like my Honor, I was overcome. There was an unmistakable gleam of pride in those violet eyes...

It was all I wanted, my heart's prayer over these many months as I strove to prepare his companions despite my own shameful fears and jealousy...

If my Honor's affection rendered me invincible, then Lucian's bestowed holiness itself.

It was all I wanted.

And yet, as I looked into those sacred eyes, I could not help but wonder... why had he not accepted my pledge? He had presided over my maturity ceremony in the role of my liege, and there had always been an expectation between us that he would one day hold my entire allegiance, but he still had not taken my pledge. He had accepted our father's, Taza's, Ilqan's, and Hasima's when they had each reunited with him, as I had learned a week prior, but he had not even mentioned mine.

That was not the whole of it: he and I had always, *always*, shared tents and performed chores together while traveling. Yet... once my Grace and I had joined him, my Honor Elian, and Elacir on the march to Ehaya, he had asked me to choose my own tent and to not worry about caring for his needs. I understood not wanting to share sleeping quarters—though she had her own tent, my Grace often slept on a second cot in his because of her unbearable nightmares—but to not let me even perform my duties as his aide? To give those tasks to his soldiers instead? Particularly as illness clung so visibly to him? Was I truly worth so little? So easily cast aside as Taza always said?

Who would want me if the Lord of Icilia did not? Who would care for me if not him?

My Honor Kyros' anxious squeezes of my wrist brought my attention back to him. Certainly, at least for this moment, *he* needed me. That was more important.

Dropping my eyes from Lucian's, I leaned back slightly and looked toward Taza.

The guardian offered me a rare, wondrous smile—which warmed the depths of my heart—in agreement.

Then, together, we helped our Honor Kyros remove his boots and urged him forward over the stones into the hallowed circle. Though the approach seemed to daunt him, he followed our direction, drawing upon our arms for support as he had our teaching.

The moment his foot touched the first flower, the soldiers gathered around us cried, "Praised be the Almighty! Beloved is the Shining Guide! Glorious is the Quest of Freedom!"

My Honor Kyros' face glossed. And then reached the smoothness of glass as Kalyca repeated the words.

My Lord and my Grace, beautiful faces shining with joy, beckoned him forward over the flowers, and Taza and I lowered him into a kneeling position on the soft blossoms at their feet.

Waves of sweet floral perfume rose up in thick clouds around us with each movement.

"A'Qahre ediniqasimas u'haseh onó am, Ajaanem," Taza and I intoned the ceremonial words in sacred Alimàzahre.

Then we stepped back and returned over the stones to where the rest of Lucian's commanders waited to take their seats on the logs. At a nod from our Lord, we bowed and sat alongside our Honor Elian, my father, Ilqan, Hasima, Elacir, Kanzeo, and Count Ciro Tolmarie and his family. A number of the Quest's captains and the head of the smiths stood directly behind us. Behind the captains were all of the Quest's soldiers and their families, save for the sentries, arranged in even ranks rippling outward in concentric circles.

Once we were all in position, Lucian glanced down at his companion. A sweet smile, joyous and loving, which he only ever gave those four who complemented his soul, curved his lips, and he spoke, "A'Qahre beleqasemas Ajaanam Kairos a-Majéalaah e a'archel purer é enalheham. A'naaleh é a'Qahre ai a'husneh é a'Zahràdalle ai a'loreh é a'Raahile enpureqasemas u'am zilu am banàkanerad onel am aneqasu kanne. A'Qahre ideqasemas am u'beleh onó a'Silàretet é Isilia," here, he smiled and added beyond the ritual, "be am kaneqas ó Dalaanam ai Fidaanam ai ó Raaham."

A shy smile bloomed upon my Honor Kyros' handsome face as he gazed up at his Leader.

A moment of intense affection, too intimate to behold yet too dazzling to look away, passed between them.

Then, through the link he had specially crafted to connect the entire army for this occasion, his Second issued the ceremonial order, *"Ne a'onàmirile é a'Qahre, a'Zahràdalle, ai a'Dalaana-é-Isilia, efikrerim likelam ai qabeham! Melchelam kaneqasemas é alheh ó a'Qahre."*

Though my Grace herself was not magically mature, only participating in this rite at Lucian's insistence, her voice rang clear and bright in the link, with the same echo that underlay Lucian's voice when he prayed.

She does not speak, I realized, *like someone not whole. Her speech in sacred Alimàzahre is perfect, with the melody of magic. That should not be possible for one whose magic and voice have been stolen...*

A shift in my Honor Kyros' kneeling figure as he raised his head snapped my attention back to him.

I clenched my hands together, suddenly anxious myself. *This simply has to work. My Honor's maturity would provide untold benefit in the coming battle, and I know Lucian has so wished for it, even though nine months of training is hard-pressed to compensate for twenty years and—* I jumped slightly as warm fingers suddenly rested atop mine. Noticing the chocolate and gold, I gave a questioning look to my Honor Elian.

He offered an embarrassed smile. "Sorry," he muttered and began to retreat.

My heart welled with a compassion it had gained from him. In the absence of our Honor Arista, who he dearly missed, and with the rest of his new family part of the ceremony, I was his only chance at an elder sibling's comfort. So, placing aside my own reluctance, I grasped his hand and lightly stroked the soft scales.

He beamed and scooted closer to me, and Elacir on his other side moved with him. Together, both of their broad frames loomed over my slender one.

Letting myself revel in how utterly soothing their presences were, I returned my attention to the ritual.

My Honor Kyros rested both of his hands, palms facing upwards, on his thighs. Then, his chest rising with a deep breath, he recited, "En manarrel ó a'Qahre, em azeqas a'taëh é albelem ai rohehem ai a'jameh é nohehem ai zatelem an a'labiëh é Isilia. Em rad wuldemiz é he husner retet, em rad eleqas a'raëh é a'Raahile, ai em efikreqas a'beleh é a'Zahràdalle. Tharel kuseqas hayànohilëm, qanel aleqas qalàzazatelem, ai fazel kureqas neràrohilëm zilu em banàkanemas ke a'Qahre aneqas. Saleh unpureqasemas puràtaëh idel em kaneqas."

Breathing heavily, my Honor Kyros bowed his head.

And waited.

And waited.

And waited.

And waited...

A pleased smile twitched Lucian's lips.

Then light burst from my Honor, blazing through the gathering like the fiery sparks of a flare of sunlight, dazzling, searing, flaming—

The world turned entirely white.

In that whiteness was a melody sung in a clear, ethereal voice, intoning words too, too, too *bright* to understand, and a peace so fragrant of honey and incense that—

And suddenly I returned to my own circumstance, feeling my lean frame and athar clothes.

But the world was different.

Because the man who knelt amid the flowers was no longer incé.

Light glimmered off of every curve and line of his form, as though little particles of sun whirled around him on shifts of unseen wind. His face, though unchanged in physicality, appeared somehow clearer, a veil pulled back from his beauty so that it shone with full brightness. And his presence... oh, his presence. Such resolute strength emanated from him that it seemed as though he alone could be the foundations of the mountains, the anchor of the adrift and the home of the lost. Unconquerable, indomitable, invincible—the pillar of Icilia in this age where everything seemed but dust blown by tendrils of foul smoke. The Almighty's constancy given physical shape...

It was like Lucian's ascension and maturity had occurred together.

I startled with a shock as I realized that that was *exactly* what had happened. This, this, this *miracle*, was a fulfillment of Lucian's blessing, as *each* of his companions' would be. They were *all* divine-blessed! The woman who stood with Lucian and the man who held my hand would someday become as exalted as their brother had just become, as their Leader and their other sister already were.

Though I had known this before, my mouth still hung open as a powerful contralto voice reached my ears.

Through the medium of Lucian's pendant, in common Siléalaah sang my Honor Arista, "Oh Almighty, blesséd be those who rule by Your name."

Though we still blinked rapidly in shock, the gathering responded as we had practiced, "Rule in Your name."

"Rule for duty and love," she continued, "rule for virtue and the world above."

We answered, my own trembling lips chanting the same words, "Rule in Your name."

"Rule for Icilia, rule for the Quests and the world above."

"Rule in Your name."

"Rule for the people, for the land and trees and beasts, oh Almighty."

"Oh Almighty."

As the most sacred name echoed amid the trees, my eyes somehow again met Lucian's.

He smiled and tilted his head slightly, gesturing with his bearded chin toward the hallowed man who he was helping to stand.

A memory flashed, a vision of when that hymn had been sung for me.

And I wondered, those sweet words still ringing in my mind, why he had sought me with his gaze when his beloved companions were all around him.

CHAPTER 19
INTENDING SERVICE

*Perspective: Crown Prince Eligeo tej-Shehennadem, Heir-apparent
to Nademan*
*Date: Eyyéfaz, the twenty-seventh day of the seventh moon,
Narsaffe, of the year 500, C.Q.*
Placement: same as Segment 3 of The Bell Tolling

For countless minutes I was in too much pain to think. Agony ripped through my limbs and coiled through my torso... at once too much to bear yet all too familiar.

But, though the Gouge's cruelty had not abated one degree, this time was different. For I had something to which I could cling: the Quest Leader's name.

As I returned to a state of coherence, my lips fluttered with that name, like a prayer.

I opened my eyes and cautiously tested each limb, before inhaling deeply.

The expansion of my torso sent pain shooting through my chest.

I winced. Those were definitely broken ribs. The Gouge's kicks had fractured the healing breaks from his last blows, and my ribs were dreadfully fragile. But, from the dull familiarity of the pain, the injury was not more serious—no bones piercing my lungs, for one. Whenever that happened, I had to grovel for healing from the one elderly staff member who had the magic. She was always disinclined to help me, and only taking on chores that I could hardly afford to shoulder ever persuaded her...

I tested more of my body, twitching my hands to pat my sides and my skull. There were bruises and bumps, but no cuts or burns. Which meant that he had not gone beyond conjury and his usual tortures.

Blessed.

I moved to push myself up.

"I do so think your little checks are hilarious," said *that* voice, menace given the form of sound.

I froze. Whatever calm I had evaporated. *He has not left yet!*

That voice, so full of desire that it was cold, continued, lifting into a mocking croon, "Pathetic little prince, poor baby without protection, heir to nothing."

His taunts turned so crass that I wanted to burn the ears that had heard such things. Then he stepped forward... and his boot, the sole lined with metal nails, hovered over my exposed left hand. Taunting with the cruel prospect of escape.

There was no escape to be had.

His boot stomped down over my bloodstained fingers.

Audible snaps mingled with my scream.

The Gouge laughed and walked away.

My chest heaved as I tried to come to terms with the pain, but each breath only increased the agony.

Lord Lucian! my mouth uttered in a silent screech. *Oh Almighty! Please do not abandon me!*

Again and again I repeated the words... until the pain did ease, enough that I could regain control of my breathing.

Whimpering, I cradled the broken hand to my chest.

Then, bracing the one working hand against the hard wood, I pushed myself into a sitting position.

Oh, gratitude to the Almighty, he is gone, I thought, sighing—and winced again, regretting that sigh.

My head swam with pain, but I forced myself to stand. He had not dragged or summoned me to his personal chambers in several weeks, so I needed to take this opportunity. These rooms were the best place to search for information. The Gouge despised written messages, but he did keep them. The most important of those papers were likely to be here—he did not trust his soldiers, he did not use a study, and the rest of the papers were anyway handled by Tahira Enarias.

Tahira Enarias—the Gouge's brilliant chief strategist, who was trapped here just as much as I was.

Though my siblings, the staff, the soldiers, even the Gouge himself, thought she delighted too much in the challenge of her position to care about the implications of her actions, I knew her true motivation: her brother's life and sanity. For I had been present, scrubbing the floor in a corner, on that day five years ago when the Gouge ordered her and her brother to be dragged in front of him. I had seen the expression on her face when she accepted his offer of a position. And I heard enough from the Gouge and the soldiers to know that she still visited her brother, as often as she was allowed.

She was better than I: she was not so ruined by the Gouge's cruelty that she had forgotten her sibling, whereas I... sometimes I had to rack my memory for the names and faces that had once been so precious to me. But moreover, she used her position in the Gouge's court to protect the people of Nademan—my mind was not so far gone as to not realize that the strategies she presented the Gouge were only just more efficient than what he himself knew how to design.

She was only a commoner, her noble title and duty destroyed with her village, while I was the crown prince. Yet she acted for the whole of Nademan while I had done nothing for my people.

If anyone at all in the capitol deserved salvation, Tahira Enarias did—even more so now as she attempted to render the

Gouge vulnerable to the Quest Leader's conquest. She was risking both her brother and herself, but that did not cow her into abandoning the Quest Leader's service.

I admired her, though I had never spoken to her—the Gouge scrutinized every person to whom I spoke for any stirring of sympathy toward me. She had too much at stake to risk such examination.

Though, perhaps, if I found any useful information, I would consider hoping that she might take that risk. The Quest Leader's reconquest was of paramount importance.

Clinging to my conviction, despite the pain, I shuffled to the nightstand, the desk, and the dresser. With my one working hand I pulled out each drawer and scanned the jumbled contents.

As I did so, a memory bubbled up in my mind: as a child, long ago, I had poked through these same drawers, in search of clues and trinkets at my father's behest. On one rest day he organized a treasure hunt for the children of the castle, and we giggled as we scampered through the castle. Indeed, the halls rang with joy—my parents, aunts, uncles, staff, and the visiting nobles laughing uproariously at our antics. The day had been so much fun...

Where had that father and king who had cared for his family and his people gone? To where had that man who desired to bring joy to his loved ones disappeared?

He had vanished long before his murder. All his murder had done was end his body; the man himself had already died. His name was unsalvageable—there was no question in anyone's mind that he started us down this path. This was not a story of eventual discovery of his blamelessness: his guilt was clear. Even I, once his most devoted son, hated him for what he had done.

He had stood by and let Nademan be destroyed. He was just as much a traitor as the royal families of Zahacim and Bhalasa. And with his treason came my own damnation. His actions had cursed all of his blood.

No matter what I did, how could I expect the Quest Leader to ever accept me? I did not deserve forgiveness; I was not like the long-lost Heir to Koroma or the massacred heirs of Asfiya—my parentage was not of heroes but of traitors.

I had not even tried to compensate for that. Instead, I had allowed sin to consume me.

I was too unworthy to look upon the shoes of the Quest Leader, much less his face. He was mustering an army, but I had no place in its ranks.

A pain even greater than my broken bones skewered my heart.

Curling my fingers around the knob of the last drawer, I opened it and spied the edge of a stack of paper, just as a few muttered words reached my ears.

I froze. I knew the Gouge's voice better than my own—undoubtedly, he was the one speaking.

I should have scurried away by now! Regardless of what he did to me, he always expected me to be gone within minutes of his departure!

Closing the drawer and lifting my other hand to my mouth, I frantically looked around the room. I needed to hide; I could not even imagine what would happen if he caught me snooping...

There was no space behind the furniture, and he could come and sit on the chairs in the corner—

My eyes lit upon the athar cloth bed-skirt. Moving as fast as I could, I limped over to the bed, lay down on my back, and scooted underneath, letting the drape fall to cover my body.

My heart thundered in my ears as, but moments later, the door slammed open.

Heavy footsteps thumped across the wooden floor and made a shrill screech.

Then a hand, blacker than night, appeared beneath the cloth.

I bit my lower lip, the faint taste of blood filling my mouth.

The hand groped about under the bed and latched onto something near my head and pulled it out. Stones collided against wood.

Remembering my conviction, I raised the drape by a fraction of an inch, just enough that I could peek out from beneath it.

The Gouge was taking a blue stone from a wooden chest—presumably what he had removed from below the bed—and lifting it to an eye. He examined it, then grunted in satisfaction. Replacing the stone, a sapphire, he pocketed the chest. With a growl he spun on his heel and left the room.

Outside the door spoke another voice—certainly the voice of one of his conjurors, though I could not tell which.

The Gouge responded in his bone-crushing timbre, "Of course not; we have her brother. And anyway that—" he used a foul word that demeaned women— "enjoys what she does. She gets pleasure, somehow her—" foul words regarding intimacy and what ought to be private about a woman's body— "so I will let the generals use her plans. But I will not stay for this battle, as much as I want to confront that upstart. His Viciousness requires this to be delivered."

The other voice mumbled a few words.

The Gouge snarled, "I am the master of this territory; I control it, and I will not lose it to some—" again, a foul term, this one demeaning men.

Then several sets of boots thundered away.

Silence.

I dared to shuffle out from beneath the bed.

A bellow pierced the walls of the castle: "For the Lord of Freedom!"

A smile, the first in a decade, spread across my lips. *He is here.*

I scrambled to my feet. Limping over to the dresser, I pulled open the last drawer—in answer to my prayers, it contained sheafs of documents.

They were not important enough for him to take, but perhaps they might still be of benefit?

Making a quick decision, I stuffed the papers down the collar of my tunic and more in the waistband of my trousers. A few remained, so I shoved them into the sleeve of my useless arm, which I pressed against my heaving chest. Glimpsing the knife lying carelessly atop the nightstand, I clutched it in my working hand, though I could not repress a shudder of horror—the blade was stained with my blood.

No! Keep your focus, pathetic little prince, I chanted to myself.

Then I shuffled out the door as the walls began to glow.

I did not know what would become of me by the end of this day, but these papers would reach the Quest Leader's soldiers.

And, if she allowed, I would help Tahira Enarias do the same.

CHAPTER 20
CONTRIVING CONCORDANCE

Perspective: Nadeya Tahira Enarias, citizen of Nademan
Date: Eyyéfaz, the twenty-seventh day of the seventh moon,
Narsaffe, of the year 500, C.Q.
Placement: concurrent with Chapter 49 of The Bell Tolling

"For the Lord of Freedom!"

Though my face was as expressionless as ever, a drop of joy warmed the achingly cold void of my heart at the reverberating cry.

This is the last day, I told myself. *The last day. Either the Gouge will punish me for my defiance or the Quest will censure me for my treason. My suffering is finally at an end.* The bitter taste of failure still filled my mouth, as it had since the Gouge had told me that Kanzeo was missing, but at least I would have one final opportunity to do what little I could in service to the Quest.

Perhaps if I died, as seemed all too likely, the Almighty would grant me one last glimpse of my brother's face. Even if I were not blessed to be reunited with him in the hereafter.

Such a glimpse might be my only chance to see him again. For although I was praying that Kanzeo had merely decided to abandon me and escape, there was too great a chance that the

Gouge had finally murdered him and was waiting to tell me when it would most suit his cruelty. His harsh questions about my involvement might have been only a deception. It was all too possible. The Gouge did indeed enjoy playing with his prey.

It was why he had not acted more strongly against my Lord, why even now he was absent at his generals' emergency war council, even as his enemy charged toward the castle's walls.

That fact was not lost on the generals gathered around the council room's table.

"Has he really abandoned his own capitol?" one of the lesser ones muttered. Then promptly clamped his mouth shut, fear flashing in his eyes, as though the Gouge might hear him from afar.

That is a caution Perveries should have practiced, I thought dispassionately. *He was blessed that the Quest Leader slew him, not the Gouge. And that in turn is a lesson these... people... would have done well to learn.*

The head general seemed too frantic to give attention to his subordinates' grumblings. "Are you certain?" he demanded of a messenger. "Absolutely certain?"

"Yes, General," the soldier whispered, eyes huge with fear.

The head general emitted a noise closer to a wolf's growl than any incé sound and slammed his gauntleted fist against the table-top. "How dare the elite squad disappear at the start of battle!" he roared.

I almost jolted. *The* elite *squad is missing? The elite squad of* conjurors? *As well as the Gouge? That is a very poor sign! What sort of evil has he now planned...? Surely he has not left the castle as the elite squad has! Even for him, abandoning his throne like this does not quite make sense...*

Attempting to decipher his motivations as I was, I listened to the generals' heated argument on which battle-plan to use with only half of my attention. They underestimated me: they might have reluctantly accepted the strategies I wrote beforehand, but they would never ask for my opinion during an actual battle.

Thus, my presence here offered an ideal opportunity to gain intelligence without having to aid in the counterattack.

The situation painted by the messengers reporting to the council was quite interesting: foregoing previously existing methods, the Quest seemed to have decided to use a four-pronged strategy for their assault. Nearly a legion's worth of soldiers were attacking the lower part of the castle-tree, another half-legion descended from the towers, a final company penetrated the city—and they were all preceded by a small squadron who had reached the castle walls first. A squadron that, from the way the castle walls were shining, surely included the Quest Leader himself.

Unlike any previous battle in Nademan's history, the castle-tree was siding with the attacker. For, after a decade and a half of inertness, out of a hibernation entered only out of a desperate need to protect herself, Tejénadda was waking up. Her true master had come, and she was ready to serve him.

I needed to do the same.

The moment the generals decided on where to send the remaining conjurors—the most important aspect of their entire defense—I slipped from the room. My movements were so soundless, so unassuming, that they did not see me leave.

Once I had exited into the corridor and walked far enough away from the guards, I ducked into an unused room. There, I quickly re-tied my hair into a knot (the generals had picked at the bun before their quarrels on tactics had absorbed them), covered my head with a ragged kerchief, and retrieved a dull knife and a sack from where I had hidden them the previous night behind a dusty, empty bookcase. The kerchief was the best I could do at ensuring I looked like a follower of the Quest—the Blood forbid the wearing of every form of headdress, save helmets—while the sack contained the most valuable of my papers, the plans detailing the Gouge's troop and supplies movements and the messages from the other governors' commanders. The two items, as well as the information I had just gained about the enemy's plans, comprised my last attempt to serve the Quest. The knife was of little worth, too dull to cut well, but it would likely help me past the obstacles I encountered.

The first such obstacle arrived moments after I re-entered the hallway.

"General Enarias!" a voice called. "General Thunaries demands that you return! You can't just go and *hide* in the middle of battle!"

I turned and directed such a cold glare at the soldier that he froze mid-step. His sneer faded into trembling lips, and he quailed at the complete lack of empathy in my gaze. The fingers that were about to tug on my hair fell limply to his side.

My hand flashed forward with a jolt of Nasimih speed and slammed the wooden hilt of my knife against his temple. His crumpling to the floor elicited no emotion whatsoever from my heart. Even the sound did not startle me.

Calculating that I had little time to waste, I simply turned and walked away. I did not expect to survive the day, and I had nothing to lose now that my brother was gone.

Listening carefully to the sounds echoing through the hall-ways (a tactic I had much refined since my attempt at escape five years prior), I quickly located the chief of the staff in a private staffroom on the twentieth floor. Though she was precisely where she was usually was so early on an Eyyéfaz morning, the gaunt woman was agitatedly pacing back and forth and murmuring to herself. Sixteen of her subordinates anxiously watched her, tense and ready to flee like deer at the approach of wolves.

I did not allow the slightest particle of hesitation to impair the surety of my step as I entered the room. "Nadeya Pitelariat, you must lead your comrades into hiding."

The woman, who had always hated me more than all of the other staff members, whirled around and scoffed. "How dare you come here, General Enarias? How many times must I tell you that we have no room here for your treason?" Her gaze repeatedly darted from my eyes to my kerchief.

I ignored the bolder than usual insults. "Hiding is your best chance at survival, Nadeya. If you join the Gouge's attack, you may not live until nightfall; if you try to flee, the Gouge's soldiers will not let you escape."

Though visibly shocked by my use of the enemy's appellation, rather than his preferred reverence, she sneered. "And why should we believe you, traitor—" The next word she uttered insulted my honor as a woman.

I ignored that as well. "You do not know who is attacking or how the Gouge's soldiers will respond. It would be better for you and your assistants if you hid in the small closets—the ones that are too small to be used for ambushes. But," I bit off the word for a cold sort of emphasis, "it is your head. Do with your last moments as you will."

Those words delivered, I spun on my heel and walked out, not bothering to gauge her reaction or listen to what she thought. I wanted to protect them, but not out of compassion—they had quietly served the Gouge and disregarded so much of the suffering he inflicted. They deserved mercy as little as I did. But if they were out of the way during the battle beginning above and below, it would eliminate one difficulty for the Quest's army.

The apathy regarding their welfare was also, of course, a sign that the Gouge's horrors had begun to corrupt my soul. I had resisted his influence in many ways, but not in this, a matter of compassion toward those I did not respect. Yet another reason the name of 'traitor' applied so well to me.

Behind me, Nadeya Pitelariat loudly uttered several expletives, then barked, "Tell all the staff to hide in these smaller closets..."

Now for my intelligence. I glanced at the ceiling. *The Gouge took the cursed crown prince to his chambers sometime last night, from what the generals were discussing, so I cannot help him... Perhaps there is enough left of his mind to realize that he should hide.* But, regardless, I did not care—I only thought to help him because virtue dictated that I should, not because any vestige of reverence or kindness. His safety was not my priority, nor was what became of him.

The only priority I had left was the Quest.

So, steeling myself, I carefully picked my way through the halls, following at a distance the squads who ran to reinforce the enemy's troops against an attack on the lowest floors. Though I could not afford to be caught by one of the soldiers—I knew how to use a sword and a knife, but years had passed since I had been able to properly practice—their movements were the fastest way to locate one of the Potentates. For, as noted during my studies of their movements, instead of sending servants to do their bidding, the Potentates always fought first, leading their troops from the front ranks. Admirable, and possible because of the scope of their war so far.

Despite my exclusive use of back corridors and staircases, I descended rapidly through the castle and quickly reached the site of the main attack.

Blood stained much of the living wood, and corpses littered the halls.

Most of the bodies wore the vermillion skulls of the Blood's insignia.

This will be a nightmare to clean, I thought unsentimentally as I picked my way through the battlefield. *Perhaps the potent soaps that the Gouge forbid last year might be valuable once the battle is won. But I can only pray that someone finds them, for I doubt I will have so much chance to speak. If I have any chance at all.*

Death was imminent, looming over my head like a branch hanging from its tree by only a strip of bark.

I descended another story to the second floor.

The hallway into which I entered was glowing.

It was merely a faint shine, the dimming remnants of luminescence, but, for one who had been enthralled by the stories of the Quest of Light as a child, it was a clear sign of one of the Potentates' passing (just as the arrival of this sacred day, the anniversary of the first Quest Leader's birth, was a clear indicator of their attack). Even the blood and gore could not obscure that light.

Tracking the sounds of weapons and footsteps, clutching my satchel and my knife, I walked down the corridor toward the atrium.

The light of the walls grew stronger.

And then, by the door to a balcony, I beheld him.

A figure who was more a ray of divine Light than incé, his presence reverberant with the steadiness of the deepest roots, the thickness of the sturdiest tree, the utter surety of the purest love. From the nobility of his handsome features to the calmness of his warm gray eyes, he was part of the path through which salvation came.

The crown that adorned his ash-blond curls exactly matched the description of what our Honored King Naret the Ideal of Love had worn.

And though he stood over six feet tall, taller and more muscular than most Nasimih, there was nothing about his armored form that attempted to frighten me. Even his raised sword appeared soothing.

But my sins were unforgivable.

The sight of him cracked the mass of ice that was my soul and melted the unfeeling stone of my heart, bestowing a joy and contentment the likes of which I had not known since that day I looked into violet eyes. But death was imminent.

At least I had perceived the grandeur of the Quest before my death. Even though both my brother and that violet-eyed boy were lost to me.

It was time to submit myself to his judgment.

Only moments now...

Those clear gray eyes met mine.

And then, and then, instead of anger, instead of disgust or revulsion or hatred—instead of anything I could have expected—he smiled. Actually smiled. And dipped his head in a sign of what was usually respect and lowered his sword. From his blessed lips came the words, "Blessings, Nadeya Tahira Enarias."

My composure slipped as I startled, caught truly by surprise for the first time in half a decade. *He knows my name! A name that, despite my infamy, few know outside the castle. And, despite that cruel reputation, he spoke it with the demonym, another sign of esteem...*

But seconds later, my façade returned, more out of forcefully learned habit than any need for protection, and I managed to sweep a smooth, deep curtsy and utter the proper greeting, "May the Almighty bless you," with the correct reverence of "my Honor," as though my mind was not almost scrambled with long-suppressed emotion.

I had not spoken aloud the Divine's address in so long...

"I am delighted to meet you, Nadeya Enarias," my Honor said in response, exhaling a chuckle, the kind expression on his features as bright as the long-ago stars.

Those words were so unbelievable—*no one* was ever happy to see me, likely not even Kanzeo after my last dismissal—that my mask faltered again, my emotions leaking just a little onto my face as polite disbelief. But my façade returned as quickly as it had left.

Take advantage of the moment, Tahira! I commanded myself. *He seems to be actually listening! This is your chance to serve!* Forcing my mind into a semblance of order, a skill perfected by necessity, I replied, "The distinction is mine, my Honor. And, if it would be in accordance with your pleasure, I ask for a moment of your time."

Again with that incomprehensible kindness he nodded in permission. "Speak."

He is letting me speak, but will he actually trust my intelligence? As he absolutely must? *From his behavior toward me, he does not seem to know who I am—which is not what I was expecting... Oh Almighty, may I not err! He* must *believe me!*

I inhaled deeply, unusually needing the gesture to steady my nerves. Then reported, "My Honor... the Gouge's squadron of conjurors plan to approach your position."

The gentle smile on his blessed face slipped. But, gratitude to the Almighty, instead of anger or fear, it was replaced by a thoughtful expression, a distant one, as though he saw something beyond his immediate surroundings.

A farseer, I noted, remembering how my father had looked while wielding his magic. *Then speaking of the conjurors is sufficient; he must already know the movements of the other troops. So, should I tell him of the Gouge's absence? But that is not something I know... If I said the tyrant was gone and my Rulers actually believed me—which no longer seems quite so impossible—and then he re-appeared, my Rulers would not expect him and so would be impeded in countering with an effective response...*

A slight wrinkle formed between my Honor's arched brows, tightening the creases around his glowing eyes (perhaps the simultaneous use of another type of magic, of foresight? If so, a sign of incredible power). "There are conjurors by the throne room... but my Lord engages with them." His shoulders shook for a second with fright—fright he had not felt for his own sake—before he stilled them.

Terror arose in my own heart at his news, that the precious Quest Leader was fighting the monsters of our world, as great a terror as what I sometimes felt for Kanzeo. But I had more intelligence to deliver: "My Honor, the Gouge has three squads of conjurors under his command. He sent two squads, divided into four squadrons, to find my Rulers, per established plan." I included only the most relevant points. He did not have so much time. "The remaining squad, his elite, is... not in the castle."

"Hmmm... If they are not in the castle," my Honor considered, shockingly not disregarding my words, "the best we can do is inform our Lord. As for the ones coming in my direction..." he exhaled. "I can address their attack."

The thought of him, my Honor, whom I was already coming to revere, fighting them was as terrifying as that of my Lord doing so. But... despite my fear... how magnificent was his courage, to willingly confront these enemies! And, indeed, from the assurance in his gaze, he would certainly win.

So deep was my admiration that, for the first time in five years, a small smile lifted the edges of my mouth as I replied, as the Quest's etiquette guided, "As you say, my Honor."

His gaze grew distant once more—I thought it likely that he was using mindlinks, whether his own or another's, to communicate. This news was the sort to relay to one's commanders, and he had not summoned a messenger.

The abstraction lasted for but a few moments before he refocused upon me. "My gratitude for this warning, Nadeya. It is invaluable."

My face was only a degree or two short of impassive, but my melted heart sobbed with happiness. For he had believed me, and his belief meant that he would be safer. I would at least have accomplished this much before he learned of my true identity and decided to execute me.

Kindness glimmered in his soft eyes as he continued to speak, "Nadeya Enarias, if it would please you, I would ask that you wait here, wherever it is safe."

Shock jolted my heart once more, but I remembered to at least nod.

The second I did, he slipped out onto the balcony.

I stared behind him, overwhelmed by the whole encounter. Not only had he not ordered my death but he had also believed me. *Believed* me. Trusted me. Cared for my safety.

Though this favor was given only because he did not know who I truly was, still how I cherished it...

I closed my eyes. *Finally I have seen the Quest. And what was faith is now joined with fact: the Blood cannot rob Icilia of salvation, for the Quest Leader lives.* I did not dare hope to see my Lord himself, but merely the knowledge of his life and the proof of his companion's glory was more than enough. It was the fulfillment of so many prayers...

The first peal of steel against steel outside the balcony door reminded me where I was.

Ruthlessly quashing my emotions with practiced efficiency, I spun on my heel and walked to the nearest staircase, climbed to the third floor, and found an abandoned office that was precisely in the middle between two balconies. Though dark, dank, and dust-filled, it would provide a good view of the battle.

I chose a spot against the wall by the open hole of a window, the glass long broken, and seated myself so that I could see outside without betraying any movement.

The pale light streaming into the atrium from the smog-covered morning sun illuminated a fascinating engagement: the Gouge's soldiers clearly had the advantage of numbers and height, attacking from the upper balconies with volleys of arrows and, as the battle progressed, by climbing down to the lower levels. But my Honor's troops were, far from being overwhelmed, well able to hold their position and minimize casualties. Through a series of seamless, perhaps even coordinated, strategically well-calculated movements, they returned fire and, when the enemy climbed down, herded their opponents onto the weapons of their comrades. Again and again were these movements repeated. And yet, unlike the Gouge's troops, my Honor's companies did not lose their patience. They did not abandon their orders.

The show of my Honor's skill was captivating, and thinking of how to improve on his tactics was even more so, but it was not enough to distract me from watching for the conjurors' approach.

Where are they... Oh Almighty, may my Honor not be caught unaware by their attack. I beg of You to augment his magic so that he sees them come...

Amid the heat of battle, the Quest's troops abruptly rushed inside the castle in a thunder of footsteps. The moment the last of them left, my Honor climbed down from the second story balcony on which he had fought and ran into the center of the atrium, dodging arrows all the while. His hands were frantically checking his armor, which, I realized, gleamed in a manner unusually luminescent for metal...

A door opened on the far side of the atrium, and four conjurors stepped out.

The enemy soldiers retreated with squeals of fright. Though

both the soldiers and the conjurors fought for the same tyrant, the soldiers were scared almost to death of their superior officers—they well knew that the conjurors did not differentiate between ally and enemy in choosing victims. It was a lesson I, too, had learned.

I clenched my hands around the hilt of my knife as I remembered the taste of conjury. *Please, oh Almighty, I beg You to safeguard your Chosen...* If only I could do something other than watch!

A black cloud billowed up from the conjurors' bodies and swept toward my Honor.

His crown flashed, and a shield of white light coalesced around him just before the smoke struck.

Not a single wisp touched him.

I exhaled a heavy breath in relief. *As he said, he can address their attack. Belief I had, but to see his response is the fact reinforcing my faith.* A flare of white light from his armor cut through another smoky cloud. *Ah, so that was why he was checking his armor... Ah, gratitude to the Almighty, he teleported in time! Two killed, two more left...*

Unable to look away, I watched anxiously as my Honor struggled against the conjurors.

The moment he fell to his knees amid a cloud of black nearly stopped my heart.

But, by the Almighty's blessing, my Honor was victorious.

Smiling a little, I waited until his soldiers were preoccupied with his order of burning the monsters' corpses and then descended to the first floor. Passing through one of the lesser external doors, I stood beneath a balcony, where few would notice me in the shadows. I did not dare hope that my Honor would wish to speak with me again, but he *had* said to wait, and he should not have to look for me...

When smoke, this time purifying, began to rise from the ravenous fires, my Honor turned. And strode in my direction.

My heart melted once more at his approach, enough that a

small smile accompanied my curtsy. "Praised be the Almighty," I whispered as he halted in front of me.

"Indeed, praised be," he replied, bowing his head at the Divine name and smiling.

I braced myself for when that wonderful smile would turn to the coldness of displeasure.

Still smiling, he regarded me for a moment. Then he said, "Nadeya Tahira Enarias, I have met your brother, Nadeyi Kanzeo Enaries."

Kanzeo... My brother's name in that blessed voice shattered my composure. *No one, not even the Gouge, knows my brother's name! So, for my Honor to know... he must have met him. That means he must know what happened to my brother! But, if he has met my brother, then he knows, without question, who I am! For Kanzeo would have told him!* Choking on the fear and relief rising in my throat, I fell to my knees at his feet. *Please, please, oh Almighty, may he have mercy on my brother! Even if he cannot on me.*

Contrary to anything I could have ever expected, my Honor laughed softly and knelt in front of me, bending so that my eyes were at the same level as his. "Please, Nadeya," he said with a sweet respect, "this is not necessary. Nadeyi Enaries explained, and the Quest knows he speaks the truth."

Kanzeo explained... I struggled to comprehend those words as tears welled in my eyes. *Kanzeo explained... whatever he said was believed... and, for me to receive such kindness, whatever he said was in my favor...* That, even more than my Honor's gentleness, was too much to believe.

My Honor continued, gray eyes warming with even more kindness, "For that reason, I offer you my pendant as a sign of safe passage." While I blinked in shock, he slipped it from his neck and clasped it around mine, careful to avoid touching me in any way. "Show this to any who stop you and use it to ask for direction to my Grace. She will protect you."

For the first time in five years, tears spilled down my coarse cheeks as I clutched the emerald of his pendant. Though it was uncouth, I could not help but stare at him.

How many times had I prayed for someone at all to respect me? And now... a Potentate of the Quest, a Ruler of Icilia, was treating me with dignity when I did not deserve any, when my own actions should have forever robbed me of worth in his eyes.

How generous the Almighty was!

I tried to express some portion of my gratitude, but it had been too long since I had last spoken of such uplifting sentiment. All that I could manage to utter were words that sounded too much like a demand: "My brother?"

Unlike the men with which I had dealt these past years, my Honor did not even seem to notice the offense, instead answering, "Safe with my Grace and one of her guards and awaiting you." He beamed, appearing excited for my sake.

I swallowed and nodded, hoping my reaction did not disappoint him—though I was so very relieved to know my little brother was safe, I could not help but question whether he really wanted to see me...

But, then, maybe, perhaps he did. Everything today, save the Quest's attack itself and the enemy's movements, had defied my expectations, from my Honor's news of my brother to his trust in my intelligence about the attack of the half-squad—

Half-squad? But in the battle I saw four... I tilted my head and counted the pyres. "My Honor," I asked slowly, "those are four pyres. Where is the fifth?"

Leaping to his feet, my Honor spun and counted as well. His lips tightened, anxiety filling his eyes. "Seek my Grace, Nadeya," he ordered abruptly, a clear dismissal.

I curtsied again and obeyed. As much as I wanted to help, I would be of no use in a fight against even ordinary soldiers, let alone conjurors, and I did not like the thought of testing his patience.

Remembering the direction of the Quest's charge, I decided to cut across the castle-tree's base by following in reverse the path of my Honor's attack. The hallways grew increasingly bloodier the closer I came to the outer wall, and I was hard-pressed to keep my gown clean, but none appeared to challenge me, scared off by the violence that had already occurred here.

Only ten minutes after leaving my Honor's side, I exited the castle.

And stopped short.

For amid the trees, rising from the far edge of a large glade to the northwest of Ehaya, was the flag of the Quest: the flower-crown embroidered in white on a field of deep green trimmed with gold edges. Beautiful, resplendent, majestic, aglow with showers of sunlight that were piercing through the smog overhead.

A contented smile lit my heart, if not my lips, at this second proof of the Quest Leader's life and coming victory.

CHAPTER 21
CONTRIVING ATTUNEMENT

Perspective: Nadeya Tahira Enarias, citizen of Nademan
Date: Eyyéfaz, the twenty-seventh day of the seventh moon,
Narsaffe, of the year 500, C.Q.
Placement: concurrent with Chapter 50 of The Bell Tolling

Drawn to that flag like a bee to nectar, the sight of it soothing away much of my trauma from previous fraught journeys into the forest, I hurried across the large outer greensward, jumping over the now tiny hedge (of course the Quest Leader had been able to shrink it) as I walked over the imprints of the Quest's army's many boots.

Again, with all the fighting occurring inside the castle and the city, none challenged me.

Until I reached a pair of sturdy, ten-foot-tall wooden gates set discreetly within the tree-line, just before the flag's pole.

"Halt!" cried several soldiers stationed on nearby branches.

I hesitated, unsure whether a name would be expected, then simply raised my Honor's pendant so that it caught the dim light.

The soldiers gaped at it, mouths wide open, for a long moment. From their expressions, they both clearly recognized it and were shocked to see it in the hands of an unknown woman.

One soldier pivoted and called out, "Open the gates!"

A creak sounded along with the groaning of moving wood, before the gates swung open, parting wooden walls that so seamlessly blended in with the forest that I found it difficult to say where one ended and the other began.

I quelled my emotions and strode confidently into the midst of those who would hate me if they knew my identity.

But, though the eyes of the guards followed me warily, I passed unimpeded into the camp.

A number of trees wrapped with platforms and stairs stood deeper into the forest, each constructed with interesting new variations on Nademan's existing architectural styles, but I could only focus on one tree, directly behind the gates, from the direction of which the sounds of many murmured voices were audible.

I quickly located the stairs and climbed.

One story, two stories, three, four, then the fifth and the massive platform onto which the stairs opened.

Opened onto a forest's worth of women and small children, who stood and sat about, quietly chattering and playing with tiny wooden toys.

I blinked. *These are my Grace's guards?*

One of the women caught sight of me and spun to face me, a gleaming sword appearing in her hands.

Ah. I marveled at my Lord's ingenuity. *No one fights harder than mothers with children to protect. And with this method they are close enough to support the main force while remaining safe as well.*

More women drew swords, their faces setting in grim lines as they shoved frightened little children behind the shields of their own bodies.

Ahhh, Enarias, bane of Nademan, I thought, heart burning at their reaction. *But no longer.* I raised the pendant.

The women startled, much like the guards at the gate. Then, exchanging glances, they lowered their swords and parted, leaving me an aisle forward.

I walked it, ignoring their sharp gazes, keeping my own focused on where I was being led, the front of the platform, the part that looked onto the flag and the glade.

Then I saw her.

My Grace.

The blue sky, the seat of the sun, holiness and hope incarnated into one person—the clear resonance of voices heard and treasured, of thoughtful compassion and affectionate prudence—the wisdom brought by divine Light glowing in the blue of her eyes and the red-gold of her hair beneath a crown that matched our Graced Queen Manara the Exemplar of Truth—

My Grace.

Like our Honor, the sight of her melted my heart, dissolving the defenses that caged me more than protected me and replacing them with her own power. She would not abandon me.

I could not explain why I felt so, but the truth was one I could not deny.

She turned, brow furrowed as she glanced at a woman in armor, a silent order in her vivid eyes.

Then those brilliant eyes came upon me.

And she smiled.

Warm, welcoming, generous like the summer sun of a long-ago age.

Smiling.

She was *actually* smiling.

And with that one smile, without the utterance of a single word, I knew that she not only knew of my efforts these past months and years but acknowledged and accepted them. What little I had done the Quest counted as service.

In their eyes I was no traitor but a devoted vassal.

And they were grateful to me.

Only the steel of my composure kept me upright and able to dip into a proper curtsy.

My Grace gave a glance to the armored woman at her side, who cleared her throat and spoke in a stern contralto voice,

"Our Grace Malika the Exemplar of Wisdom, supporting her Honor Kyros the Exemplar of Strength's judgment, in love of him—"

I almost startled, just now realizing that this was the first time I was hearing my Honor's name!

"—welcomes you, Nadeya Tahira Enarias, to the encampment of the Quest of Freedom. With such loyalty as you have already shown us, you may be certain that you will always find shelter and succor in our presence. May the Almighty forever bless you and your brother."

At those final words, my Grace beamed and flicked her gaze to her right.

Inhaling deeply, I slowly turned.

And there, clinging to the side of a woman who wore a baby's carrying basket on her back, was Kanzeo.

He beamed, joy and adoration lighting his dear eyes, bringing a happy glow to his features that accented the subtle filling of his form and rounding of his cheeks, signs of a safety, health, and nourishment of which he had been long deprived.

It was what I most wanted in the world.

There were no words sufficient to express my gratitude to the Almighty and the Quest for this.

Whispering my name in his sweet voice, my little brother left the woman's side and took a step toward me.

Then a dark cloud flashed across his features and stole his joy. Replacing it with wary caution.

His smile faded to a sorrowful grimace.

Halting, Kanzeo stared up at me.

The heartbreak of our last meeting filled his eyes with tears.

That heartbreak would never leave if I did nothing to chase it away.

Our last meeting had convinced the enemy that I no longer loved my brother; was it any surprise that it had convinced my brother as well?

If I did not want the pain in his eyes to linger, I had to act.

So I parted my lips. But the words I wanted to say remained trapped. And my expression was colder than ice.

Frantic, I tried again. And again. And again.

All the while, the anguish on Kanzeo's face grew.

Until he finally turned away, looking to our Grace as tears fell from his eyes.

No, no, no! I exclaimed within my own mind, my heart screaming behind my silent façade. *No, Kanzeo, do not abandon me! I am sorry, so sorry, for treating you this way... The Gouge did much to me, but he could not kill my love for you. Please do not look away... Please... Please, oh Almighty, help me!*

A warm hand touched my elbow, the blessed feel of it so gentle that even I, wary of every sort of physical contact, did not recoil. Instead, soothed, I turned and found myself looking up into the kind blue eyes of my Grace.

Smiling softly, a deep sympathy glimmering in her eyes, she tugged me into a gentle embrace, encircling my soul as well as my body with her blessed touch.

Though she did not speak—I was coming to the horrifying realization that she could not—her message felt clear: I needed to try again, this time with faith that I would succeed.

Squeezing me gently, my Grace hugged me for a moment more, before stepping back.

I took a deep breath and turned back to Kanzeo.

My brother silently watched me, his face wet with tears and his expression brimming with agony.

Oh Almighty, Lord Lucian, Graced Malika, Honored Kyros... Chanting the divine names, I wrenched apart my lips and forced out in a low grumble, "I love you, Kanzeo."

Coarse little sounds, unworthy of him.

But my brother's face lit up, as though his most desperate prayer had been answered, and, laughing joyfully, he sprang forward and threw his arms around my waist. "I love you, Tahira!"

It was all I could do to lift my arms and hold them stiffly against his back.

He no longer seemed to mind, holding me tightly, as though determined to never let go, and pressing kisses to my chin, the highest part of me he could reach. With every breath he murmured, "I love you, Tahira."

Exhaling a quiet sigh, I relaxed in his arms, thawed slightly by his love. *He is so, so good to still love me, to even champion me in front of the Quest... Oh Almighty, I do not deserve a brother like him, but how grateful I am for him...*

Laughing and crying, Kanzeo snuggled against me for several uncomfortable moments more, before finally letting go of my waist. Only to slip his hand into mine and pull me toward our Grace, who had resumed her position by the platform railing.

She glanced back at us over her shoulder and smiled. The armored woman at her side spoke, "Gratitude to the Almighty for your happiness. So says our Grace."

Kanzeo grinned, almost bouncing where he stood. "Thank you, my Grace! And please tell our Honor that, too!"

My Grace nodded, seeming to return his joy. Then she glanced at me and raised an eyebrow. The armored woman said, "Nadeya Enarias, it displeases me to ask this amid your reunion, but, if you would deign to perform yet another service for us, would you aid us in organizing a portion of the Quest's troops? My Lord, my Honor Elian the Exemplar of Esteem, and my Honor Kyros the Exemplar of Strength have just learned that the Gouge has left Ehaya, so all of their troops are now under my personal command. Since many troops yet remain and many supplies must still be found, would you aid me? So says our Grace."

How kind she is to even ask! Curtsying deeply, one hand spreading my skirt while the other remained with Kanzeo, I answered, "As you will, my Grace." *Perhaps I might even have an opportunity to devote attention to why the Gouge actually left... I cannot comprehend why he would, but there may be a gap in my intelligence, and this reason would surely be valuable information for my Rulers...*

"Excellent!" my Grace exclaimed through the armored woman's voice. "If you climb to the platform above this one, you will find paper and ink. My little brother, Inase Elacir bi-Dekecer —" she gestured behind me, and I turned to see a young man of the Sholanar nodding enthusiastically— "will join you to receive your first orders."

I prepared myself to let go of my brother's warm little hand.

"Kanzeo," the armored woman continued, "is connected via mindlinking to Inase bi-Dekecer, so you will be able to communicate with him from afar. So says our Grace."

I blinked, certain I had misheard. "My brother can come with me, my Grace?"

Her smile softened as she nodded.

I stared. *She is not separating us... There are other ways to handle the relay of orders, and she surely knows them, yet she gives my brother a role... She does not think we should be apart in order to push me to perform better. Indeed, she actually* intends *to keep us together!*

It was then that I knew that my prayers had been answered beyond anything I had ever thought to ask: the Quest of Freedom had liberated my brother and me not only from our waking nightmare but from my sins and our heartbreak. And now, heaping mercy upon mercy, in bringing us together, they were giving us an opportunity to seek the Almighty's blessing and a new purpose in their service.

It was then that my heart, cold as it was, became fully the Quest's, my love blossoming beyond an acknowledgment of rule to true, fervent adoration.

The salvation that the Quest of Freedom had given me I would devote to their victory.

CHAPTER 22
INTENDING COHERENCE

Perspective: Crown Prince Eligeo tej-Shehennadem, Heir-apparent to Nademan

Date: Eyyéfaz, the twenty-seventh day of the seventh moon, Narsaffe, of the year 500, C.Q.

Placement: concurrent with Chapter 50 of The Bell Tolling

A spasm of pain tore through my body, lighting every nerve like a white-hot brand. My consciousness receded in a desperate attempt to cope.

When thought returned, the monster's bloodied blade was slipping through my shaking fingers.

Before I could even attempt to catch it, it clattered on the wooden floor.

Footsteps slowed outside the parlor, then approached the door of my hiding place.

I froze, even as pain worsened the tremors racking my limbs.

The door was flung open, and two soldiers entered—wearing uniform soaked in blood and marked with the scarlet skull and putrid yellow thorns of the enemy.

Snatching up the knife, I held it up, my one working hand trembling, at a paltry attempt at defense.

Recognizing me, the soldiers sniggered and stalked toward me, eyes bright beneath their helms with bloodlust.

Bloodlust that was too familiar.

It was the Gouge himself who stalked me. I knew he was not present, but he was what my mind perceived.

Desperate to get away, I stumbled backward and tripped, falling onto my bottom. The wads of paper stuffed into my trousers folded beneath me.

The Gouge's nightmarish form blurred and dissolved into the sight of the soldiers jeering and raising blood-red swords over my head.

My one working hand would not lift to protect my own life—

Red bloomed on their chests.

Gasping, the soldiers fell forward—only to be replaced by two more.

But their armor was different—unadorned save for a small green flower painted over their hearts. A difference mirrored by the odd lack of mockery in their expressions.

A moment passed before I realized that lack was actually concern. Actual concern—concern for me.

I blinked, confused. *How do they not know who I am? The born royals of the Shehennaden house all possess a very distinctive color of gray-green eyes. And the golden-blond of my hair and the honey-brown of my skin so clearly mark me as my father's son. I look too much like him to ever escape his shame.*

Gazes flickering over my form, the soldiers approached me with their arms held out, as though I were a wild animal, injured and prone to snapping. "Nadeyi," one said, "you have no need to fear. You are safe now. The Quest of Freedom establishes their rule over Nademan—in their mercy, all of us are freed."

"The- the Quest?" I squeaked. They- they were the Quest's soldiers?

The other nodded. "Yes, our Rulers. Would you come with us? There is security and freedom to be had in their shadow."

I could not believe I had actually found the Quest's soldiers—

though I had taken the papers, I had truly feared I would perish before finding them, my body left as sport for the enemy.

"Come with us," the soldier repeated.

Though I still awaited their disgust, I nodded and let the knife fall (I did not want to appear malicious when they learned of my identity). If the Almighty allowed, I would finally have my chance at serving the Quest.

The soldiers stepped forward and, with small pulls and pushes, urged me to my feet and out of the room into the corridor.

Their touches, though perhaps intended to be gentle, caused me such discomfort, such pain, but I withstood it, praying desperately that they would take me to their commander.

Beyond the next intersection stood a large group of soldiers, all also in that plain armor adorned only with a flower. Amid them stood two taller men, massive as tree boughs, their skin dark like the stateliest trees and covered in tiny dots of color. From the back of one, the one whose dots were purple, emerged similarly colored large limbs that reminded me of the wings of the birds I had seen as a child. The other man appeared to have those same bird-like limbs, too, but covered by an enormous silky blue cloak. How different they looked from the soldiers and from me...

They are of a different kind, I realized. *Not children of the Nasimih —they are of a kind whose name I cannot remember, and, unless everything has truly changed, not of Nademan either...* I swallowed the bitter taste of impossible hope. *They would not welcome me either.*

The group of soldiers parted for the ones taking me, who brought me to the cloaked man.

Who wore a crown. A helm of a crown. A crown unlike any I had ever seen... Silky smooth material formed its ridges, curls, and base, not metal, and the gems... Oh, the gems! No royal ever wore such bright stones! No royal ever wore rubies, emeralds, or diamonds, for such jewels were reserved for the Quest (a fact at which the Gouge had on occasion sneered). So for this man to wear them...

The man turned.

Oh, his face, his beautiful face... every line and curve of it, from the gold dots arranged in the pattern of crowns that formed elegant clusters across the smooth chocolate planes of his forehead and cheeks, to the tight umber curls of his mustache, beard, and hair, to the round curves of his cheeks, his nose, and his full lips curving in a small, sweet smile—every line and curve of it spoke of kindness, as though it had never known cruelty. It was the face of the divine, crowned by a helm too dazzling for eyes as tainted as mine to perceive without sin.

The face of a Potentate of the Quest.

"A captive," one of the soldiers who had brought me here said, lightly pushing me in the man's direction.

I was already crumpling at his feet, unable to bear his majesty and my sins, unable to not show this reverence. Paper bent and crinkled inside my clothes, but I hardly noticed.

Oh Almighty, how You have blessed me... As much as I wanted to hide from his gaze, my heart brimmed with gratitude for how this much beauty was so briefly gracing my worthless life...

A gentle finger touched my chin amid the ragged, blood-streaked strands of beard and tipped my head up.

Barely had I comprehended the immense comfort of that touch before he spoke in a sweet tenor voice, the wind chiming in the highest treetops, "Blessings, Nadeyi."

My lips trembled as tears spilled down my cheeks. "My-my-" I stuttered, trying to learn his rank from his crown. But I could not even remember the correct addresses for the Quest! Oh, how was I going to—

"My Honor," the man whose wings were uncovered supplied, his tone bright and kind. "You speak to my Honor Elian the Exemplar of Esteem, Potentate of the Quest."

Which meant he truly *was* our Lord's companion. The Divine's inner circle. Sacred.

Too sacred to sully himself with my nearness—

A full smile curved my Honor's lips, his forest green eyes shining like stars.

I shuddered at the weight of his presence and his name. But, in the same breath, hope sparked in my heart, hope that he might accept what little service I could proffer... that, maybe, just maybe, he and our Lord would accept me.

How could I not dream of such lofty things! His gaze was so kind! Just so wonderfully kind...

"What is your name?" my Honor asked in his musical voice.

Enthralled, I opened my mouth to answer.

Clinks of metal and heavy grunts reached my ears. As the Nasimih faces over my Honor's shoulders and cloaked wings filled with anger and distaste. And dozens of hard gazes skewered my short, scrawny form.

All the hope that had so briefly blossomed in my broken heart withered. Cowering, I crossed my arms over my chest and hunched, trying to make myself as small a target as possible to deflect what wrath I could, without shaking away my Honor's blessed touch.

Alarm flashing in his lovely eyes, my Honor looked up at his soldiers. "What disturbs you? What is the reason for such a reaction?"

So my Honor's kindness had not come despite my identity, just in ignorance of it. Already I mourned the loss.

At their commander's questions, the soldiers exchanged glances. Then one said, with audible fury, "My Honor, those eyes are a clear sign! This man is the former crown prince, the firstborn son of the shamed king!"

My Honor frowned. "The shamed king... who is... oh."

The recognition in his divine voice hurt worse than the Gouge's slaps. Flinching, I curled into myself as much as I could without disturbing my Honor's finger, savoring whatever comfort he would deign to still offer before the beating came. *How I hate my eyes—if only the Gouge had taken them as he took my innocence! How I wish he would have gouged them out!*

Still frowning, my Honor seemed about to speak, the anger I feared brewing on his sacred face.

Then a desperate fear exploded in his eyes, shattering the anger.

The winged man recoiled, star-patterned dots turning a flat, lusterless navy, and the soldiers' faces creased with the same fright, their rancor toward me momentarily forgotten.

Despite my own fear, I dared to whisper a prayer that whatever plan of the Gouge that had so terrified them would fail.

Particularly if it in any way sought to harm the Quest.

The terror slowly drained from my Honor's face, replaced by a relief too intimate to witness.

In response, the winged man and the soldiers slumped, almost falling over with an echo of that same relief.

My Honor blinked, black lashes sweeping across his cheeks, and seemed to return to his immediate surroundings.

"What happened, my Honor?" several of his soldiers immediately asked.

He beamed in answer, his brilliant smile a draught of unquenchable hope. "My Honor Kyros of Light defeated the four conjurors who had attacked him."

Oh gratitude to the Almighty. I did not dare to sigh, desperate to avoid drawing their attention back to me, but I could not help the tension leaving my rigid body. The Quest was safe, at least from one plan.

My Honor tilted his head then and seemed to consider something, the gentle kindness that seemed so characteristic of him filling his eyes.

It was a sin to covet what was not mine, but I reveled in the sight...

The winged man tapped my Honor's shoulder and proffered a smile, and my Honor glanced at him, their eyes exchanging a look full of a gentleness again too intimate to witness.

I was too starved to turn away, however. I had been too many years without even a taste of affection. Certainly no one cared for me.

"Nademile," my Honor said then, his gaze on his soldiers, "let us take Nadeyi Eligeo—"

How noble my name sounded on his blessed tongue! The first time in fifteen years it had not been used to mock me...

"—with us, back to the camp."

I froze. *He cannot possibly have said that.*

"My Honor!" several soldiers protested, and one added, "He is unworthy of your presence! Much less your care and attention!"

How right they were. It was presumption to even stand on the same ground as him.

But my Honor Elian spoke something different: "That is for my Lord to decide, not us. And regardless, my Lord would be appalled if we left him in this condition, when he has not raised a weapon or uttered an insult. Until and unless my Lord says otherwise, Nadeyi Eligeo is to be treated as a freed captive, a guest of the Quest's army."

... A guest? Not a captive or a slave or a prisoner? A guest? A guest—someone whose presence was actually welcomed?

Had anyone ever esteemed me so?

A guest of the Quest's army—it was more honor than of what I had dared to dream.

He... he did not cast me aside...

I could not help the tears of gratitude that blurred my vision and spilled down my cheeks. Somehow, despite all my sins and failures, the Almighty had deigned to grant me this blessing.

My Honor smiled and moved his hands to my shoulders. His gloved knuckles faintly, ever so faintly, brushed my broken fingers.

Pain seared my body, emanating in a wave of fire from the twisted bones, so all-consuming that it devoured the comfort of my Honor's touch.

Despite the profound depth of my hope and happiness, I could not suppress a whimper.

The shining smile disappeared from his lips as his gaze swept across my face.

Even as I lamented losing his smile, I startled at the realization that his gaze did not hurt me. There was something so pure, so *wholesome*, about how he looked at me...

My Honor scowled suddenly.

It terrified me.

But, before I could shrink back from that fearsome expression, his dots and fingers began to glow a pale green, much sweeter than the color of my nation in its bold vibrancy.

Is that... magic? I wondered, for once distracted from my pain. *Does the Quest have a different color for their magic than the seven nations do?*

Then my Honor touched my forehead and spoke, "Kazaqer lamile ai akakaser hadile, damile unuzuler ai lananareh ider, paresilerim, pariderim, parobanerim, parejiderim, pareneru be ore anemizu kanne."

On the final word of the spell, his green light pierced through me. But, completely unlike the black of conjury, its touch was pure, untainted, innocent pleasure—soothing, comforting... restoring.

A gasp left my lips, my back arching, as the feeling overwhelmed my senses, consuming every thought so that all I knew was the pleasure...

Then the light faded.

I mourned it.

Until I realized what it had done for me.

For the first time in fifteen years, there was no pain. No groaning bones, no throbbing bruises, no screaming cuts. No agony in my most private areas. No buzz in my ears from blood-loss. No haze at the edge of my vision.

Oh, yes, a faint tenderness, tiny blips of ache, reminders of countless older injuries, remained. But, compared to what I had suffered for so long... I had never been so well.

It was the most amazing thing to have ever happened to me.

And it came from the gentle hands and kind gaze of this shining man.

As I bowed my head and whispered my thanks, I knew that I would always be his devoted servant. He was my salvation, the light of redemption amidst my sin. I loved him as I had loved no one else. He was more than parent or sibling or even my nation to me.

My Honor Elian chuckled softly, the sound as soothing as his magic, and, with his grip on my shoulders, lifted me to my feet.

I scrambled to maintain my hold on the papers, unused to both such gentle nudges and the freedom to move without compensation for pain.

Shuffling papers back into my sleeve, I glanced up just as my Honor's hands fell away and the winged man grasped my arm.

I almost whimpered, startled by the unfamiliar touch.

The winged man drew me to his side, his grip firm but not hurtful, and tugged me forward as my Honor's soldiers resumed their march. But, though he began that march at my Honor's side, the winged man quickly fell back, slowing his steps, until he followed the last rank at a distance great enough for privacy.

I followed his unspoken cues, desperately hoping that he shared our liege's opinion on sanctuary for me. He was so much taller and stronger than my usual tormentors that I would be even less able to protect myself should he decide to hurt me...

The winged man took a deep breath, then turned to me.

I suppressed a flinch. How I wished my Honor had not left me alone with him!

His eyes meeting mine, the winged man smiled with some of our liege's kindness. "My name is Elacir, your Highness."

I did flinch at the bizarre address. Rarely used in fifteen years, even as a taunt.

Elacir grinned playfully and lightly pushed my shoulder with his own. "You *are* a crown prince, your Highness." His hazel eyes twinkled with mischief. "I never thought I would be able to say I knew so many members of Icilia's royalty. There is our Grace, our

Honor Arista the Exemplar of Bravery, our Lord's father, our Lord's brother... and you, your Highness! It is quite the blessing."

I stared at him. *He is certainly* not *a child of Nademan.*

Elacir winked, then said seriously, "Our Honor bid me to accompany your Highness to our Grace's presence. The soldiers know me, so I may serve almost as a seal of protection for you. Please do not part from my side."

I nodded slowly, eyes huge, some of my terror fading at these words. Those who wanted to hurt me usually did not conceal their intentions.

He grinned again and tilted his bearded chin to the papers clutched by my other arm. "Might I help you with those, your Highness?"

My first reaction was to tighten my hold, fearing an attempt to snatch them. Then, exhaling, reminding myself how high he seemed in my Honor's favor, I nodded again. These papers were for the Quest, so he would likely not destroy them.

Still wearing that lighthearted grin, Elacir tugged the papers from the sleeve of my recently broken hand and tucked them into the front of his armor. Then he drew me even closer, as though ready to stand between me and harm.

I wondered dazedly if I had strayed into a dream. His touch was difficult to withstand... but it did not hurt. It did not send prickles of unease or outright terror down my spine. And he himself did not openly loathe me. Indeed, he seemed to... like me.

What generosity he must have had to *like* me!

Lost amid such utter and overwhelming change in my circumstances, I only remembered the most urgent of my news when we approached the threshold between the tower and the main castle.

Mustering all my courage, I cried out, "My Honor, I have to tell you something!"

Evidently hearing my ridiculously squeaky voice, my Honor Elian turned from the front of his force in my direction. His eyes met mine, and, in kindness upon kindness, he seemed prepared to listen.

A black cloud appeared beyond him.

Conjury.

I froze, unable to breathe. The mere sight so frightening that my heart seemed to entirely halt.

A heavy wind flung me at the far wall.

Yet my head did not crack against the wood.

So I was watching as the cloud enveloped my Honor.

I screamed—as did Elacir and the soldiers.

Such potent conjury, so black, so cruel, so hungry—who could survive it?

Please, oh Almighty, please protect him!

A twinkle of silver flashed amid the cloud, and a dagger impacted the conjuror's shoulder.

The cloud faltered.

Footsteps echoed from a nearby stairwell.

Then a shining figure—brighter even than my Honor—streaked into appearance and sliced the conjuror's head from her neck, which dissipated the black cloud.

Without a single moment of pause, he turned and dueled the six conjurors following on his heels.

White lightning flashed around his form, and the blackness could not touch him.

He was at once too beautiful and too terrifying to behold.

And, as he shone and struck and conquered, there was no question of who he was.

The Quest Leader.

I had finally seen him.

All that I had imagined of his glory was ashes compared to the true grandeur of his majesty. If the Divine had ever chosen a vessel and a conduit, it was he, Icilia's only path to the Almighty.

Even as breath filled my lungs, the first free breaths I could ever remember, I did not dare to breathe. His presence was full of freedom, but I did not deserve to be free.

My Lord slew the last conjuror and turned to us. Though perspiration beaded his forehead, his smooth, flower-adorned armor was pristine, unmarked by blood, and not a single curl of white-gold hair or beard had fallen from its place. His crown, white athar lined with gold, was a ring of stars encircling the sun.

So enamored, I could not understand what he commanded in his rich, musical voice.

My Honor and his troops scrambled to obey him.

I moved to do so as well but startled at the sound of crinkling paper.

The papers... the warning.

I closed my eyes and whispered curses at myself for this forgetfulness. Everything was overwhelming and overpowering, but my responsibility to the Quest and to Nademan remained the same. Indeed, considering what wonders my Honor had already given me, my duty to serve him was all the greater. As was my burden of atonement.

But how could one so lowly as *I* approach my Lord?

My Honor and Elacir were preoccupied with my Lord's command, and the soldiers would have neither the motivation to help me nor the daring to speak with him themselves.

I had to try alone.

And it was my place—as I had striven to fully remember since the Quest Leader's name reminded me of my duty, I was Nademan's last crown prince. Though my people hated me, it was my duty to beg for his favor in their name. No matter that he had already given it.

That began with this measly service.

Taking a deep breath, not trusting my legs to carry me, I began to crawl, my head bowed with all repentance, toward where he stood, leaning against a wall, exhaustion apparent on his shining features.

I loathed myself for disturbing him, but I dared to think that he might wish to hear my news.

All too quickly, the harrowing seconds passed, depositing me at his feet.

My Lord tilted his head down and gave me a warm smile.

The world spun as though I fell from the tallest tower—or as though I was thrust into the air, raised by soaring bird-wings abruptly from the ground beyond the forest canopy.

He spoke, "May the Almighty bless you, Crown Prince Eligeo tej-Shehennadem."

Compassion filled that rich voice as he used my *title*—he, the Quest Leader himself, the Heir to what my father had betrayed. My cursed name sounded so sweet on his blessed lips.

The pace of my heart increased until it felt like it would explode from my chest, its roar throbbing in my ears.

Calmly, as though he had not just fought the sort of villain that had sent my entire nation into hiding, my Lord continued, "I wondered when I would meet you. His Honor has certainly performed a thorough healing."

He... he wanted to meet me? Meet me? But- but- is it not his intention to be rid of me? Beneath the purity of his gaze, my entire body burned, so blackened with sin as to be unsalvageable.

How much it hurt. The Quest Leader himself had come, and I had nothing with which to avail myself of his mercy—

Except my warning.

Trying to rally my scrambled thoughts, I opened my mouth to speak. Then closed it, not having the strength to dare. Then opened, reminded of my duty. Then opened, closed, opened—

"Speak," my Lord said kindly.

At the encouragement, I dared to cry, "My Lord, the Gouge is gone!"

My Lord stilled, his gold-flecked violet eyes suddenly distant, as though seeing something beyond the tangible. Then he raised his head and across the hall met my Honor's gaze.

Lips pinched together, my Honor Elian nodded.

My Lord inclined his head. Then, turning to me, he bent and

grasped my chin, then tilted my face up so I could look nowhere but into those violet stars.

Sensation too powerful and complex to comprehend flashed like a lightning bolt through my mind as his gaze seemed to pierce through all my layers of misery and pain into my very soul.

As alarming as the moment was, I welcomed it. His fingers were firm but gentle and soothing beyond all measure, and his gaze was... There were no words to describe how it felt to be *seen* by it.

My Lord nodded to himself, lips pressed into a thin line, and straightened, dropping that sacred hand from my face to his sword. "My gratitude, Prince Eligeo." A stern focus hardened his features. "Your Honor, come. Inase bi-Dekecer, seek her Grace's will. The Almighty's blessings upon all of you."

Then, as quickly as he had appeared, he left, striding toward the stairwell.

I exhaled a shuddering breath. As painful as his leaving was... *The Quest Leader himself believed me!* Finally I had done at least one thing worthy of my besmirched crown for Nademan.

"Crown Prince Eligeo," my Honor Elian said, commanding my attention, suddenly now using my title for a reason I could not understand.

I scrambled to stand as he walked toward me.

Though anxiety glittered in his green eyes, he smiled as he reached forward and helped me to my feet. An exhale left his lips, and then he embraced me.

Green light exploded again within my body, so intense that stars twinkled before my eyes.

My Honor Elian tightened the arms that were the first to hold me in fifteen years, then withdrew.

I blinked my vision clear—to find him gone and every wound, every sore and cut and bruise on my body, healed.

I could not understand what to think about this blessing. He had no reason to waste his energy before such a mighty battle on me...

CHAPTER 23
INTENDING ATTUNEMENT

Perspective: Crown Prince Eligeo tej-Shehennadem, Heir-apparent to Nademan
Date: Eyyéfaz, the twenty-seventh day of the seventh moon, Narsaffe, of the year 500, C.Q.
Placement: between Chapter 50 and Chapter 51 of The Bell Tolling

"Your Highness," Elacir whispered urgently, steadying me as I stumbled, then whisked me behind him and said to the soldiers, "Our Grace wills command of our Honor's forces to my hands. Sergeant Ekesaire, you will lead our charge and scour the last of the castle with our Honor Kyros the Exemplar of Strength's forces. My guidance will come from afar; his Highness the Quest Leader's father will arrive in but a few moments and include you in the commander's link."

One of the soldiers—who had spoken first against me—stepped forward and saluted, before pivoting to face his peers. Not a single hint of doubt spoiled the readiness of their obedience.

Elacir breathed a sigh and turned back to me. "May I carry you, your Highness?" he asked. "Our Grace's will is that I bring you to her side, and this is the quickest way."

Barely able to cope with all of this change, all I could do was nod.

Despite the tension wrinkling his forehead, Elacir forced a smile before sweeping my piteously thin form up into his arms. Holding me like a child to his chest, he spread his plum wings and jumped into the air.

A shriek tore from my mouth—it was too much like falling! And not the falling into my Lord's gaze—it was like when the Gouge had thrown me from the highest balcony and let me scream myself unconscious before catching me—that sort of falling!

My Honor Elian! I screamed within my own mind.

"My apologies, your Highness," Elacir whispered in my ear as he maneuvered through the castle corridors, just below the high ceiling. Many of the halls were marred with fresh puddles of blood and broken weapons, and in places we passed over the heads of battling soldiers. But Elacir's speed was such that, before any could note our presence, we were already gone.

Though his touch was so unfamiliar and the movement so frightening, I realized that I now felt... *safe* with him. Indeed, a long-forgotten instinct in my soul was beginning to stir and whisper that he and I were kindred, that we could understand each other.

Such a foolish thought.

Elacir swooped through the main entrance of the castle and into the atrium. Then, before I could blink, we were outside.

Outside. Where the air did not smell like decaying wood and stinking uncleanliness. Where, though the smog choked most of the sun's light, the world was warmer, where the trees rustled softly under the whispers of breezes, where the perfume of green and growing things filled the air...

It was not as idyllic as my memories—the enemy's tyranny had left its mark on everything, from the leaves to the grass to the sky, but to someone who had only ever been outside in the last fifteen years for some sport of the Gouge... it was miraculous.

Almost as miraculous as my Lord and my Honor Elian.

"Thank you," I whispered, my words lost to the wind.

But Elacir still seemed to have heard, for he tightened his embrace.

Flapping rapidly, he angled around the castle-tree, climbed higher into the sky, and sped northwest in a great arc over the glade surrounding the capital toward where a large, beautiful green flag was aloft in the wind. Before I could discern its details, however, he dove into the sparse canopy. Weaving skillfully through the branches, but moments later he alit atop a tiny platform high up in a tree on the edge of the clearing beside the pole of the great flag.

I craned my neck to see that flag properly.

"Your Highness," Elacir said quietly as he set me on my feet, bringing my gaze to his face, "as much as you can, come before our Grace like the prince you are."

Already wrapping my arms over my chest, cowering as always, I merely blinked, startled by the advice.

He sighed. "May I help, your Highness?"

I nodded, eyes again huge.

With gentle pressure, he straightened my arms and spine. Then, with an encouraging smile, he led me down the ladder to the next platform.

A group of women and small children, all of the Nasimih and most wearing some form of armor, surrounded a figure standing by the far railing.

"Nademile," Elacir said, his smile both warmer and more formal, "would you permit us to pass?"

At his voice, my branch-sisters glanced back, returned his smile, and stepped aside. Though they did not bow or curtsy, murmurs of "Inase" accompanied by the reverence I had once heard attached to the title of "prince" followed us as we walked toward the railing. In Elacir's wake, they barely cast me a single glance, trusting him implicitly.

It was a blessing that they had not yet noticed me. Passing

through their ranks was terrifying because they were all taller and stronger and could so very easily hurt me.

Even as this fear threatened to choke me, I marveled at their respect for one so young—despite the difference in kind, Elacir seemed hardly eighteen, his beard still patches of curls covering the sides of his cheeks and his jaw with even less evenness than my own sparse, dry strands.

As we crossed the platform, two familiar faces near the front drew my attention: Tahira Enarias and her little brother, Kanzeo. Though her arms were wrapped around her brother's torso, her face was cold, emotionless, the icy blue eyes only a little less flat than they had been before. She looked so much like a statue. But, still, something about the way she was leaning slightly into her brother's embrace told me she was not only safe but happy.

And I was happy for her.

Elacir tapped my elbow so we both halted slightly behind the Enarios siblings.

The two of them turned from each other to the tall figure by the railing.

A figure who wore a crown much like my Lord's and my Honor's but with silver accents instead of gold or white.

A figure of breathtaking majesty, shining with a light mirroring my Lord's own.

My Grace.

I did not hear what words were exchanged.

For, as I dared to gaze upon the Second of the Quest, I realized that I knew her. Her jewel-blue eyes, the red of her gold hair, the angular curve of her cheeks, the thinness of her nose... she resembled my Lord, yes, but she also resembled a child I had met long ago, a tiny little girl who had beamed up at me as she hugged me farewell amid an expansive green garden...

Malika tej-Shehenkorom.

I had been only seven years old when I traveled to Nademan for the celebration of her fourth birthday, but I had never forgotten her.

How I had mourned her when Koroma fell... How I had feared for her, lost amid torment surely greater than even my own... I was a prince, and I had suffered so, but she was a princess, and I had not dared to imagine what horrors had befallen her. Surely agonies even greater than my sister's, for Malika was a *crown* princess, scion of the civilization the enemy most hated, and her tormentor was the Blood himself. For so many years, I had prayed that she would perish instead of suffering any further...

And now she was here. As the Second of the Quest.

Once my equal, now my Grace.

My lips curved into a smile for the first time since we had last met.

Elacir glanced back at me and startled. Then he grinned and said, "Your Highness, I hope this means you will be all right once I leave?"

The thought of his departure still scared me—particularly because mutters of my name joined with curses were beginning to spread through the gathering behind us, my too-distinctive face once again dooming me this way—but I nodded. My Grace most likely did not remember me, but I felt calmer in her presence. No matter what she had suffered, the woman whom that little girl had become would not be cruel to me even while she ordered my death.

He clasped my shoulder, bowed to my Grace, and left.

Tahira and Kanzeo, who had turned to follow, halted. The little boy jolted in shock, while Tahira coolly raised an eyebrow (an even greater expression of surprise).

I agreed with them—the upward curve really did feel shocking on my mouth.

Both siblings glanced at me a moment longer, then dipped more reverences to my Grace before passing by me. They had no greeting for me, but I did not expect any.

Taking a deep breath, my pulse once again roaring in my ears, I bowed and then raised my eyes to my Grace's.

She was smiling.

Gazing at me and smiling.

Much like that little girl had done all those years before.

Oh, it was not the same smile—that princess had not yet known sorrow, while my Grace had since suffered more than I could imagine. But, as it had then, the sight of her smile, her benediction, was enough to inspire within me a feeling that I could be more than what I was...

"May the Almighty bless you, Crown Prince Eligeo tej-Shehennadem," said a woman in armor standing by my Grace's side. Her skin was pale and glittered a faint green, so she seemed to be not of the Nasimih, and perhaps not of Nademan either. "So says our Grace."

Why did she not speak those words—that astonishing, beneficent use of my title just like my Lord—herself? Unless... I briefly closed my eyes. *So that is one of the ways she suffered. He took her voice. Just as he took my confidence in myself.* Agony pulsed through my spirit as I met her gaze again. How I wished she had been spared.

Perhaps understanding something of how I felt, my Grace inclined her head, as though in acceptance, a sort of shared pain and deep sympathy tinting her smile.

There was no recognition gleaming in her eyes, but that eased some of the weight of my shame. It was already too much to stand before her laden by such sin; if she had remembered me, remembered the contrast between an eager young prince and my broken self, I would not have been able to withstand it.

Then the armored woman spoke again, "May the Almighty bless you, Crown Prince Eligeo tej-Shehennadem. In the love of my Honor Elian the Exemplar of Esteem, supporting his judgment, I welcome you to the encampment of the Quest's army. Know that you are safe here. By my will, no harm will come to you. So says our Grace."

My Honor had stated something similar, and of course my Grace would affirm his words, but... I did not understand. Why would she risk anything at all for me? The mothers who had gladly stood by her were already cursing my presence! Why—

The armored woman raised both her brows and widened her eyes. Another woman standing to the other side with a baby's carrying basket on her back directed a hard, pointed glare in my direction.

Oh! I scrambled to bow, my cheeks moist with embarrassed gloss.

Paper crumpled with the movement.

I froze, once again reminded of the purpose I had forgotten. Then, shamefully, I muttered, glancing up at her, "My Grace, I have papers..." I quailed, unable to recall how to speak with the proper etiquette.

Seeming unconcerned by the disrespect, my Grace nodded and lifted a hand, fingers bent as though prepared to receive a stack.

I scrambled again in retrieving the documents from within my ragged tunic. Then my cheeks glossed again at the warmth the papers held after so long pressed against the skin of my chest. I could not possibly proffer them—

My Grace waved her hand, drawing my attention to the midnight blue gloves covering her elegant fingers.

I wordlessly proffered them to her and then, face even more moist with gloss, removed the rest from my trousers. Using my clothes had seemed prudent at the time, but— I had not realized it was still possible for me to feel so humiliated, after everything the Gouge had done to me.

The glowers and glares from all of my branch-sisters intensi-fied, scorching hot with hatred. Even the armored woman seemed angered.

But my Grace seemed unperturbed. Her crowned head lowered, she calmly flipped through the stacks of paper I had brought, handing portions as she finished to the armored woman and reading faster than I would have thought possible for one who had been tortured as I had.

As she scanned them, I suddenly remembered the packets missing from my sleeve and panicked—until I saw a familiar bundle in a satchel near the armored woman's boots. Elacir had already proffered those, it seemed, perhaps directly to an aide.

Amid my Grace's perusal, the armored woman stirred and recited, "If it is not too much a source of hurt to you, would you answer a painful question, Crown Prince Eligeo? So says our Grace."

I stared blankly at her, before remembering protocol and quickly dipping my head. My mind was too much awhirl to notice my own dread, for she— *She cares about* my *consent? But- but* no *one cares about my consent! It is my punishment, is it not, for everyone to take what they want of me without ever letting me choose?*

The armored woman asked, "From where did you retrieve these papers? So says our Grace."

The gloss spread over my whole face. Swallowing, I tried not to mutter as I answered, "From the G-Gouge's b-bedchamber. He t-took me there... and when he was d-done... I-I used the op-opportunity to take his p-papers." My Grace seemed to be actually listening, so I described what the monster had said and the jewel he had inspected.

As I spoke, the armored woman's expression softened, filling with concern and sorrow. But my branch-sisters did not soften in the least.

I did not expect anything else. Not once had the folk of the capital ever shown the slightest hint of pity for my sufferings. Why would these branch-sisters from other towns be any different?

I concluded with the mumbled words, "I-I am s-sorry I do- do not know w-what they say. I-I cannot read well—the Gouge... he..." A prince should be a devoted student of literature, so the Gouge had used conjury to all but break my ability to read and write.

My Grace nodded, the gentleness in her eyes showing that she understood with the profoundness that came only with shared experience. Beside her, the armored woman said, "My gratitude for these papers and your account, Crown Prince Eligeo. The documents are written in cipher, so I will consider how to uncover their contents once my Lord's victory is fully achieved. But be assured that both they and your knowledge of the enemy's thoughts are valuable regardless. So says our Grace."

She thinks my intelligence was valuable... and did not my Lord act on my warning? I swayed slightly on my feet, almost dizzy with relief at the thought that the Quest had accepted my service. If my Grace ordered my execution now, I would die knowing my life was not wholly a waste.

My Grace smiled softly, then met my gaze with the full force of her own. As cold as the bluest ice, as hot as the bluest flame— her gaze incinerated my pain and misery, like a red-hot iron burning infection from a wound.

Once again, I felt filled with breath but could not breathe.

If my Lord's gaze revealed who I truly was, then my Grace's set me free of all the miseries that caged my spirit. If he saw me, then she helped me see myself as well.

I could not understand what such kindness from them meant. Giving me sanctuary was one matter, but to care to *see* me this way... Was I not nothing more than the sins of my father?

I felt so *unclean* before her...

A mutter reached my ears. A voice that I had not heard in months yet as familiar as my own.

I turned just as my siblings came into view.

They were stumbling along behind a man whose physical appearance mirrored my Lord's. His aura of power and command was considerably lesser, as was the warmth of his lavender eyes, but, still, his demeanor was princely and full of honor, and the resemblance was almost haunting. My Lord's brother, for certain, though whether he was elder or younger I did not know.

I hoped my siblings understood what blessing they had received to be brought to our Grace's presence by our Lord's brother.

My Grace bestowed a brief, resonant laugh, as bright as a tolling bell.

His eyes steady upon her, the man bowed and smiled a little in return, the slight gentle curve lightening the sternness of his expression. "My Grace," he intoned in a voice nearly as musical as his brother's, "before his departure, our Lord expressed his wish that I present before you the rest of Nademan's former heirs."

I did not react at the designation he used—it was only too accurate—but my siblings scowled. Before flinching at the glares of the mothers on guard around us.

My Grace smiled at them, and the armored woman recited, "By the Almighty's blessing, I welcome you to the Quest's encampment, Nademile. So says our Grace."

My sisters and my brother mumbled replies and only bowed when one of the mothers nudged them.

I winced.

"My gratitude, Prince Darian," the armored woman continued as my Grace turned back to the princely man. "How did you fare during the battle? So says our Grace." She conveyed these last sentences in a flat tone, but my Grace's expression showed a hint of anxiety for the first time since I had arrived.

Prince Darian—so he was a prince! A *true* prince—dipped his head. "The Almighty has blessed our Lord with triumph thus far, my Grace," he replied quietly, "and that is the greatest health for which I could ask."

My Grace smiled again, appearing pleased, and beckoned him to her side. Bending their heads together, their gazes meeting, they seemed to be conversing, but without physical speech. Perhaps with a type of magic I no longer recognized.

The sight of their closeness, of how dearly they seemed to regard one another, how much comfort their sibling bond brought them, reminded me of my own sisters and brother.

It had been so long since we had really acted as siblings, and I still could not remember their names, but, perhaps, amid the freedom of my Grace's presence, the Gouge's evil shadow was finally dispelled...

I turned toward them.

And shrunk at the way they sneered at me.

We had not seen each other in weeks—and the last time we had, the Gouge was publicly tearing away my clothes—but they only showed me hatred.

Like our branch-sisters.

Everyone was against me.

No one was on my side.

My head spun, my consciousness receding at the blinding pain, and I unthinkingly cried out, *My Honor Elian!*

He was the only person who cared what became of me. If only I could have stayed with him!

My Honor Elian!

The feel of a powerful gaze jolted me from the terrible loneliness.

Miserably, I turned back to my Grace.

She raised an eyebrow, and the armored woman said, "Crown Prince Eligeo, it is my will that you and your siblings remain here with General Palanéze." The woman gestured toward herself. "She will convey an order in the name of the Quest. So says our Grace."

Then she and Prince Darian walked through the gathering, the mothers and children making way for them before following, and within moments they were all gone.

Leaving me alone with the armored woman—who was apparently General Palanéze—and my siblings—whose names I could not recall.

I could remember my Grace's name from a few weeks spent together nearly twenty years ago but not the names of the family whom I had known since their births.

My Honor Elian, I whispered within my own mind, desperate for comfort. I did not dare to reach for my Lord's name or the Almighty's.

The general spoke, "My Grace has ordered me to convey her judgment, Nademile."

My attention snapped to her face. Though it was marked by wrinkles around her nose and lips and near her eyes like a kindly aunt, her expression was fierce, warlike. Terrifying.

Of whichever nation she had been a general, it was no idle recognition. Nor was how deeply she was trusted in serving as my Grace's voice.

I bowed and composed myself enough to answer, "I will do whatever our Grace wills." How I wished I knew the proper etiquette...

My siblings only stared in sullen silence.

The general stated, "For the sins of your father, the monarch of Nademan, who abandoned his duty when its fulfillment was most required, my Grace revokes what remains of your ranks and pronounces upon your once-royal heads a sentence of death."

I gasped. *Death? But I thought...*

"What say you, Eligeo, Ilona, Kiora, Lisson?" General Palanéze demanded, drawing a sword from the sheath at her waist. "Will you surrender with dignity or die like the shameless oath-breakers your parents were?"

Ilona screamed in outrage and hurled a slew of crass insults. Kiora crossed her arms over her chest and jutted out her lower lip in a childish pout. Lisson yelled, "Don't you dare insult our parents! And the *Quest* is the oath-breaker! You welcomed us!"

I closed my eyes, embarrassed even amid my pain. All three were past the age of adolescence, older than Elacir, yet they acted like unmannered children. What a disappointment to learn their names seconds before they spoke so about our saviors.

For the Quest truly are our saviors, I thought. *They freed us from the Gouge—who would have never given us the choice of a dignified death. For that alone is gratitude insufficient. And beyond that, to accept my service and with that acceptance redeem a shred of my soul...* I smiled, peace sweeping out from my heart at the specter of a death actually worth something. *How blessed I am to have seen a little of their glory before my end.*

My heart set and my mind decided, I bowed and answered calmly, quietly, "As our Rulers bestow sanctuary, so may they revoke it. I accept our Grace's judgment. For it would be an honor to give my life to balance something of my father's sins."

Ilona, Kiora, and Lisson stared at me, silenced. Then all three began screaming.

General Palanéze laughed loudly, drawing my gaze to her face, which was suddenly almost familial, like an aunt's, and no longer fearsome. "What an answer!" She sheathed her sword, cutting off my siblings' yelling, and grinned. "Our Grace will be pleased, your Highness Crown Prince Eligeo-nadem. If you would allow, I will escort you to your platform for the night, in my own tree. Expect to rise early tomorrow—I will begin with teaching you how to read and write again in the morning, using the methods with which our Lord aided our Grace in overcoming the Blood's theft of her literacy."

I blinked, too overwhelmed for my usual diffidence. "So our Grace will not have me executed?"

The general laughed again. "Certainly not!" Then she glanced at my siblings with a cold frown. "The three of you, Nademile, would do well to follow us, though I advise you to remain hidden. My Grace will not be pleased to learn of your disobedience." The 'my' before the reverential address was spoken with decided emphasis.

"So, what, we should follow her even to our deaths?" Ilona shot back, too foolish to stay quiet.

The general narrowed her eyes. "Without question. In allegiance to the Quest there is salvation and freedom. We were dying before; they have returned us to life. And they do not err."

At her words, six overwhelming thoughts joined together in my mind:

The Quest did not think my sufferings at the enemy's hands, or those of my siblings, even the way we had been abused, to be shameful. That had not been mentioned even once as a reason for censure, regardless of our reactions to the general's words. Character was what concerned our Rulers.

My Grace had stated that I would not be harmed because this revocation was a test. And I had passed. When my siblings had not.

Executing me would have been easier. For my Honor to give me sanctuary and for my Grace to affirm it... these were courageous acts beyond incé comprehension.

Because I had passed and because my Lord had accepted my service, the Quest would treat me as though I were more than the sins of my father, as though I were worthy of my rank.

They might even consider restoring my rank—only mine, not my siblings'—if this mention of lessons was any indication. Though, as they had already shown, they would respect my choice and consent in this matter, as no one else had.

And, finally, however my people reacted, I was safe.

For the first time in fifteen years, safe. From the Gouge, from the people of Nademan.

Safe.

Not only alive but safe.

All because my Honor had favored me with his compassion.

How I longed to see him again.

Amid all of this overwhelming change, he was the center of my world.

And I could only pray that he would survive the Quest's coming battle with the monster whose cruelty had destroyed my soul.

CHAPTER 24
FINDING BALANCE

Perspective: Count Ciro Tolmarie, mayor of Jurisso and noble of Nademan
Date: Eyyéfaz, the twenty-seventh day of the seventh moon, Narsaffe, of the year 500, C.Q.
Placement: between Chapter 50 and Chapter 51 of The Bell Tolling

I threw myself down the massive tree trunk, my desperate speed so great that my descent was more of a controlled fall than a climb. "Duke Foltariet," I called, careful to use his actual title, "please listen!"

The nobleman reached the bottom of the ladder unfurled only for him and strode off toward the northwest. Toward the Quest's camp.

I dropped to the base of another one of Ehaya's outermost trees and chased after him. "Duke Foltariet, our Grace has not yet granted leave for visitors to enter! Please do not do this!"

He dismissed me with a flick of his fingers.

A thump echoed from behind me as the squad of soldiers who my Grace had designated to be the first to return reached the ground.

They were watching, as were probably half the city-folk from the treetops, but I was too frantic to be embarrassed.

My Grace had only just ordered that no one was to be allowed inside the camp without express permission. Yet already someone was about to defy her command.

The marquis was going to ruin everything.

"Duke Foltariet!" I cried. "Please wait for her orders!"

The man finally turned his head and threw me a sneer. "And how will I receive these orders? Through *you*, Tolmarie? Can a man who cast out his own parents be trusted to speak truthfully?"

My fists clenched, my utter distaste for this man welling in my heart, but I tried to remain calm. As much I despised the admission, Duke Foltariet possessed much political influence throughout Nademan. His wife's name and his former service as the guard of the northern marches (the reason he was still habitually called 'marquis' by most of Nademan, although he had become the duke after his wife's death) had not been forgotten even under the Gouge's rule. Angering him would bring only trouble for the Quest.

"Well, what say you, Tolmarie?" Marquis Foltariet taunted. "Did you even visit your mother during your morning in my city? The loving, doting mother who would have given everything for you and whom you exiled so that you could marry a—" he used an insulting term for a woman in reference to my wife.

The Quest, the Quest, I chanted to myself. He was trying to ruin my name by provoking a reaction, and I needed to remember that. Indeed, he was probably trying to supplant me in the Quest's favor—the man had hated me ever since I mustered the daring and courage to defy the Gouge in my province. For all that he showed some level of loyalty to the Quest, he would never hesitate to sabotage any who did not bow to his whims.

He had no conception of how perceptive our Rulers the Potentates of the Quest truly were. How powerful their grasp on the hearts of Nademan was. How loyal their servants. How devoted their army. How profound their own compassion.

Still, the marquis was not someone to lightly offend. Particularly not for a junior noble like myself.

So, biting my tongue, remembering my Honor Arista, I instead replied, as calmly as I could, "Duke Foltariet, let me at least seek our Grace's will on this matter."

The marquis scoffed and increased his pace.

I resisted an urge to punch him—uncharacteristic of me, but something I often felt around this odious man—and instead took a deep breath and tightened my grip on my emotions. A good noble, unlike that stain on the name of nobility, knew how to use his emotions well. Making decisions and making reports while angry was *not* a good use of emotion.

With the practice of training, only a few steps later the wild edge to my anger was mastered, and I spoke into the commanders' mindlink, *My Grace, the marquis is on his way to the camp. He will not listen to my attempts to persuade him to do otherwise.* My tone revealed how anxious and upset I was, but not to such a degree that it would seem my judgment was affected.

As much as the Nademani celebrated candor and openness, we did not appreciate skewed judgment. One could not trade if one's judgment was impaired.

My Grace issued an order to a captain of another company and informed two others of an ambush in their path. Then she responded to a fourth's request for assistance. Then turned to aid a fifth.

How I wished I had been able to handle the marquis myself. With our Lord's, our Honor Elian's, and our Honor Kyros' departure and our Honor Arista's absence, she led the entire assault herself, and I had not been able to prevent this massive complication for her.

My Grace advised another captain and then finally answered me, *Count Tolmarie, do not worry. Let him enter, and I will address his complaints.*

The reassurance made me feel only more guilty.

She paused a moment and then said, the command of her

tone increasing in intensity until the thread of my vassal's bond to the Quest vibrated with the fury of a gale, *In the name of our Lord, the Quest has chosen to give sanctuary to Crown Prince Eligeo tej-Shehennadem and to Nadeya Tahira Enarias, whom you called the Gouge's strategist. They and their siblings are under our protection.*

I froze mid-step.

The world seemed to fade out of focus, the shades of smog and tree and yellowed grass blurring into a smear of sickly color.

Those words...

Through the many discussions of the Quest's inner circle we had been blessed enough to attend, Belona and I had learned of the true history of the Gouge's strategist. The rumors spoke false-hood—she was as much the monster's victim as any of us—indeed, even more so, for she was forced to personally confront his cruelty every single day, without respite or support. If she was ruthless, she was so only for the sake of her little brother, a sweet boy whom Belona and I had quickly begun to regard as a son (though there was but a decade between us). For as long as the Quest entrusted him to our care, we were determined to lavish our affection upon him and delight in every moment of his joy.

So, though the possibility of sanctuary for the strategist—the prime instrument of the monster's rule and the pillar of his throne—had initially rankled, I now at least tepidly welcomed the news of her wellbeing.

I had been prepared for that declaration and presumed it was why my Grace did not want anyone returning to the camp without leave.

But... what I was not prepared for... what I could not compre-hend... The former crown prince was- was- *he* was being *welcomed* in the Quest's camp? The curse of Nademan, the heir of the shamed king, the source of our miseries—*that* crown prince? *He* was being given sanctuary? Not death for his father's sins?

My head spun and my stomach roiled at the notion, and I very nearly lost my last meal.

But if my Grace has chosen something, is it really your place to disagree, Ciro? I asked myself. *They are our saviors—when they command obedience, loyalty is to obey without question. Surely there is some mystery in this matter that they know and we do not.*

Those thoughts soothed the turmoil in my spirit enough that I unfroze and ran after the marquis.

My soldiers, who had silently halted for me, followed on my heels. They were among the most loyal of my Lord's loyal divisions and had been trained by him personally, so my Grace's command for them to return in such a delicate moment made sense.

My cheeks glossed, despite the many burdens on my soul, at the realization that she had perhaps ordered me to return for the same reason.

Our Grace was of a similar age to Belona and me, a year younger, but we revered her. The wisdom quietly blooming in her gaze was beyond time.

As our Honor Arista's bravery was beyond measure.

Remembering my lieges' sacred faces, I forced myself to walk beside the marquis. I would do whatever I could, even if it were only a little, to make the coming confrontation just a bit easier for her.

The marquis curled his upper lip and sneered but said nothing and only marched faster.

I matched my stride to his, and the soldiers fell into step behind me.

As we were crossing the glade to the west of Ehaya, a man approached. Though he was dressed in black and scarlet tunic and trousers, with a putrid yellow sash crossing his torso, the colors of the enemy, he seemed beaten in a way none of the monster's soldiers were. A staff member then, one forced to attend the Gouge because serving the castle was his family's craft. A position without escape.

My heart melted with sympathy at how frightened he looked. He was nearly old enough to be my father and was not of my town, but my noble's instincts surged with a desire to protect him.

The man, beginning his fourth decade from the lines framing his hazel eyes, bowed as he neared the marquis. "Duke Foltariet," he murmured, seeming relieved by the noble's presence.

I frowned, not appreciating another reminder of how influential the governor was. Then glanced upwards, partially distracted by the plum-colored form of Inase bi-Dekecer sweeping up over the glade and toward the castle.

The marquis offered the frightened man a smile that was not quite gentle. "Nadeyi Kotariet, my dear friend, how has the staff fared during the battle?"

Nadeyi Kotariet shook slightly and wrung his hands. "Duke Foltariet," he whispered, "I have news that will displease you. Something I saw from the windows."

My full awareness snapped back to the two men as the cold trickle of a breeze swept up my spine. *No, it cannot be...*

The marquis demanded, "What news?"

Nadeyi Kotariet twisted his fingers together. "I saw the Gouge's strategist go to the Quest's camp. And I saw one of the Sholanar carry the cursed prince there as well."

The words were like the crash of a severed bough amid the silence of the forest.

The marquis' face turned so glossy that the brown skin gained a white sheen in the dim daylight.

My Grace! I cried into the commanders' link. *He knows—*

The governor emitted a long, low snarl, resembling a hunting wolf more than a man. Then he stalked north toward the camp, fists clenched at his side.

I spun around to face my soldiers. Ignoring their shaken expressions, I ordered, "Sergeants, detain Nadeyi Kotariet. The rest of you must come with me."

Ahead of us, the marquis shifted smoothly into a run, flashing like wind with his kind magic.

The soldiers snapped to attention and saluted, putting aside their questions for the sake of obedience.

I turned and sprinted, invoking my kind magic as well. But I could not catch the marquis—he had been the marquis of the northern marches in part because his kind magic was greater than others of the Nasimih. Even slowed by age, he was twice as fast as I was.

He had already disappeared past the gates, which were opened for him, before I could reach them.

"Count Tolmarie," Sergeant Frorarias said crisply, saluting me, upon my arrival, "our Grace has ordered me to convey to you that she is enthroned at the pavilion."

I nodded, murmured my thanks, and dashed into the camp.

Though the ground was clear, the army's possessions neatly packed away onto their platforms, little undergrowth at all present despite the summer month, weaving through the thick tree trunks still took too many precious minutes.

I reached the Quest's tree just as the marquis stormed toward the pavilion.

Toward where my Grace sat calmly on our Lord's throne, Prince Darian standing at her right shoulder, their expressions as serene as the cool shade of a green tree.

The sight of them, regal, resplendent, as majestic as our Lord himself, immediately soothed me, easing away much of my worries and disquiet.

But guilt still flamed in my belly.

The marquis drew himself up like a bear readying for a rampage.

My Grace raised an eyebrow, and Prince Darian stated, his musical voice sounding remarkably like hers did in mindlinks, "Blessings, Duke Foltariet. Have you still understood nothing of the curse of blood that afflicts the souls of those who murder the manipulated and kill without cause? So says my Grace."

The marquis stopped, rigid with shock, his chest half-inflated and his mouth hanging open.

I was no less stunned. Though I had not voiced a single objection, discontent had still lingered deep within my heart. But at the reminder of my Lord's wisdom from before the battle... I was no rootless man. I had a daughter, a daughter to whom I most assuredly did not wish to bequeath a blood curse. The very thought threatened to crumble my sanity. No demand for recompense was worth this.

As much as I despised him, the marquis held the same motivation: the welfare of his daughter, the sole heir of the beloved wife who had long ago passed into the Almighty's reward. Her welfare was the original reason he had tried to appease the wretched Gouge and fallen into evil.

It was the reason he now bowed and stepped aside. His eyes were hard with displeasure, but he said nothing. Threading his fingers together, he seemed prepared to wait for my Grace's convenience.

As I also was.

My Grace inclined her head. *My captains,* she then said in the commanders' link, *complete your remaining assigned tasks in the next two hours. Upon your fulfillment of my orders, report to me. It is my will that the army gathers within the camp by midday for my declaration of victory. Thereafter, we will rotate between luncheon and burial. By sunset, my Lord's triumph should be woven through the trees of Ehaya.*

All the captains, including me, murmured their obedience.

Then my Grace glanced at me and smiled softly. Lifting a hand, she flicked it in an elegant gesture of dismissal.

Understanding the unspoken meaning, I could not help the grin that split my face in answer. I eagerly bowed and only controlled my impulse long enough give instructions to my squad (who had arrived while my Grace was speaking). Then I dashed the twenty yards toward my company's tree.

The soft murmurs of mothers and high screeches of small children reached my ears, but I did not pause to look for them.

Reaching the stairs, I scrambled up to the second-highest platform, where couples with small children slept, and darted to the jugs of water and rags set aside for bathing. Not stopping to draw a curtain for privacy, I wet a rag and began scrubbing my chest-plate.

A flicker of motion caught my attention. Just as my heart suddenly warmed.

Another smile spread on my lips as I turned and beheld Belona standing behind me.

One of her blonde eyebrows was raised, teasing me about how she had surprised me, but the faint smile on her strawberry lips spoke of welcome, relief, the utter bliss of being together again…

All of my fears from the battle surged forward—the anxiety that I might fail to return and leave her to carry my duties alone, the terror that an attack on the camp might steal her from me because she would never hesitate to defend our child and our Ruler… And yet, looking into those beautiful blue eyes, seeing our sleeping baby in the carrying basket on her back, observing that the only difference between this morning and now was the wrinkles in the plain linen gown beneath her leather vest—it was impossible to remain fearful. Yes, many of those whom I loved were still in danger, and the lives I had ended and had seen end under my command today weighed heavily upon my mind, but, as long as Belona, our daughters, and our Grace were safe, all of it could be borne.

I exhaled softly, the stench of blood cleared from my nose by her rich floral scent, and took a step toward her, arms reaching for an embrace.

She took a step toward me as well, the same longing in her own eyes…

The squish of the rag in my hand reminded me of my current state.

Smiling wryly, I glanced down at my soiled and bloody armor and then back up at her. "My apologies, Belona, my love. I do not want to smear filth all over your clothes."

Belona laughed and stepped back. "Hurry, Ciro, before

Dorona realizes her father is back and has not offered homage yet," she teased.

As though in response, Dorona smacked her lips, a sign that she was slowly waking.

I grinned and quickly washed the gore, dirt, and tiny twigs and flecks of bark from my leather armor, cap, and hair. Then I refreshed the bandages on my limbs and rinsed my mouth of the faint taste of blood, a remnant from the punch an enemy soldier had landed on my jaw. Thankfully, the thick rolled strands of my long beard had shielded me from the worst of the damage and from any visible bruises.

Only once I was fully clean did I wrap my arms around my wife's waist and pull her into my chest. Removing her bonnet, I buried my face in her silky hair and savored her scent and closeness and the warmth radiating from Dorona's body in her cozy basket.

"Ciro," Belona sighed, relaxing against me.

My name in her voice lit a spark within me. I drew back slightly, gently tilted her chin up, and pressed my lips to hers. Oh, the soft feel of her mouth...

She responded just as enthusiastically, enjoying the intimacy, but just as careful to keep our touches chaste. Because, any moment—

"Buh-buh-buh!" Dorona spluttered, now fully awake and very cross.

Belona and I laughed and withdrew.

Seating myself on a cushion, I gave back her bonnet and raised my hands for the carrying basket.

Grinning, Belona deftly removed it and held it out to me, and I immediately lifted our baby into my arms. "Dorona," I cooed, gazing into those wide blue eyes mere inches from my own, "what does my soul desire? A hug from her papa? A kiss? His heart? His ring?" I removed my mayor's ring and folded the wonderful little fingers grasping for my beard over it. "Does my soul not know that she does not need to ask?"

Dorona's rosy mouth finally stretched into an eight-toothed grin. Artless, demanding, perfect.

Putting the basket aside, Belona replaced her bonnet and elegantly settled by my side. "Papa," she said in a lovely lilting tone, "was not little Dorona a good girl? We did not cry while you were away, and we waited to eat with you. Are you not proud, Papa?"

I grinned, knowing what she was really saying—Dorona had slept through the battle and so lessened the stress on her mother's shoulders. Our precocious little countess. "Of course Papa is. My soul is so brave, and that makes Papa brave." I kissed Dorona's drool-streaked cheek and savored her sweet, milky scent. "Now let us eat before the bears in our bellies roar!" I poked her belly, and my heart swelled at her shriek of laughter, which now perhaps would never be dimmed. "Roar!"

That time was the best gift my Grace could have given me. Amid the horrors of the battle, the two hours I spent with my wife and my baby poured new energy into my limbs and new courage into my heart. If not for the absence of our other daughters and our branch-mates and the dangers faced by the Quest, the world would have been truly bright, as it had rarely ever been for me.

CHAPTER 25
FINDING ATTUNEMENT

Perspective: Count Ciro Tolmarie, mayor of Jurisso and noble of Nademan
Date: Eyyéfaz, the twenty-seventh day of the seventh moon, Narsaffe, of the year 500, C.Q.
Placement: between Chapter 50 and Chapter 51 of The Bell Tolling

But *then, one glance at our Grace's face,* I reflected as the army, both soldiers and our Grace's guards, assembled in front of her throne, *will be enough to ignite hope that these overcast days will someday be behind us. A hope no one could ignite save her.*

For there was a power present in my Grace's regal features that, despite the appearance of fragility clinging to her frame, could not be rivaled...

It was a power that the marquis did not seem to understand. Though he had remained silent when she had quelled his protests before, now I spotted him walking from sergeant to sergeant and noble to noble, murmuring things into their ears that did not bode well for the Quest's reconquest. The royals and the Enarios siblings were not present, a politically prudent move, particularly considering how similar the former crown prince was in appearance to his shamed father, but still news of them was spreading like wildfire in a dry wood.

My hold tightened on Dorona's wiggling form (facing forward in my arms so she could witness these momentous events) before I forced myself to relax. This was not the correct time—if I caused a disruption, I would only exacerbate the issue. And it was my Grace's right to speak first. I would not steal that right out of inflated righteousness and pride, as the marquis was doing.

Likely understanding something of my thoughts, Belona leaned into me and whispered in my ear, "You cannot reinforce her message if you do not listen to it wholly."

I nodded and gritted my teeth but calmed even as murmuring spread through the gathering army.

When the soldiers and the guards had all found their places, the families and neighbors united together with a cautious sense of triumph amid their grief, Prince Darian sej-Shehasfiyi stepped to the front of the dais and raised a hand.

Everyone immediately quieted.

"Praised be the Almighty! Beloved is the Shining Guide! Triumphant is the Quest!" he called.

"Triumphant is the Quest!" the army responded, a thunder booming enough to rival a summer storm, Belona and I adding our voices as loudly as we could. Even Dorona gave a shriek in contribution.

"Glorious is our Lord! Glorious is his Second!" the prince called next.

"Glorious is our Lord! Glorious is his Second!" the army replied with even more enthusiasm, the grief of those lost somehow threading into their fervor.

"Long live the Ideal of Freedom! Long live the Exemplar of Wisdom!" the prince declared.

The army roared, chanting the words with all the fervor of the battle cry in the morning.

As their cries echoed through the great trees, our Grace

appeared. Lightly descending the ladder with all the ease of a child of Nademan, she walked with the lethal elegance of a warrior, though no sword hung at the belt of her formal green athar robes. Her every motion was so beautifully commanding that within moments the entire gathering was enraptured.

Stepping onto the dais, she faced the army, gracefully swept her robes forward, and took her place on our Lord's throne.

Prince Darian bowed and, at her nod, took his place a step behind her right shoulder.

The two of them together were almost too much to behold. Glorious, brilliant, the very reminder that the sun still shone far beyond our limited sights. Their faces were as youthful as many of ours, but their authority was of the Divine. My Grace represented our Lord as surely as though she *were* him.

It was why my Grace did not need anyone else to stand with her. Why our Lord's father and guardians and Inase bi-Dekecer remained in Ehaya to perform burial rites. For her authority was sufficient to rule, and Prince Darian's presence augmented it without lessening that impression. There was no difference between them.

That impression was given all the greater strength as Prince Darian then declared, "Praised be the Almighty, beloved is the Shining Guide, and glorious is our Lord Lucian the Ideal of Freedom." The words resonated so beautifully that it seemed impossible to believe that my Grace herself was not speaking. "By the Almighty's blessing and with our Lord's favor, I, his Second, say unto you, Army of the Quest, mothers and warriors alike, that Ehaya is won! We are victorious!"

The army whooped and cheered, many actually bouncing up and down in their joy. Yes, all of us *had* known this, but there was something about her declaration that made the joy real in a way we had never imagined it could be. Though the whispers of sorrow for those who had not returned already swept through the trees, our celebration was so much purer, so much louder—their sacrifice had prevented the destruction of us all.

A brilliant smile adorned our Grace's blessed lips, and all around me people began to openly weep with happiness. Tears drenched my own cheeks and fell onto the soft linen of Dorona's little cap, Dorona herself cooed joyfully, and Belona wrapped her arms around us and muffled a sob of a laugh in my shoulder.

"By the Almighty's name," my wife whispered, "the Quest came exactly when we needed them."

More tears, cool as the first breezes of spring yet slightly bittersweet, spilled down my face in response. Indeed, the Quest had revealed themselves exactly when we needed them—exactly when we were most likely to accept them. Only a few years—no, only a few *months*—earlier and we would have scorned the source of this joy.

But the Almighty had not let that happen, so there was no sense in mourning it.

Breathing deeply, I smiled up at the exalted figure of my Grace.

She allowed the army to celebrate for a long while. Only when their exultation began naturally to fade did she nod to Prince Darian, who recited, "Our Grace favors us further with these words: The Almighty has blessed us greatly in empowering our defeat of the enemy's forces so soon, not seven months after my Lord's arrival in Nademan. And soon we shall be far freer: even as we speak, my Lord and my Honors pursue him. They will not fail in their endeavors, for the Almighty is with them—the Gouge will not escape. Know this with the whole of your hearts: the Gouge will *not* escape."

The prince patiently waited several more minutes as the army cheered again and then said, "Even as we pray for the news of the enemy's full defeat, there is much left for us to do in order to secure the future survival of Nademan and to fulfill my Lord's wishes. We have spilled much blood in our efforts thus far, and borne much suffering, and we must remember and honor those who sacrificed for us. It is a time of grief. And yet a time of joy and perseverance, for in fulfilling my Lord's wishes exists our freedom, and that glorious dawn is so close, so close that we can almost taste the sweetness of unsullied water and sunshine.

"Therefore, I ask each of you to purify your hearts and follow the whispers of conscience and shame in all matters so that we might learn the errors in our actions and thus become worthy of earning greater and greater triumphs in our Lord's name. The coming days are bright with the promise of liberty, and yet they will try our devotion in ways deeper than those past. But, if our Lord prays for us, we will surely emerge victorious."

Another deafening cheer.

The prince continued, "As we yearn for those future victories, let us remember amid the burials and the feast to come the heroes of this day: my Lord, certainly, though he would laugh to be called so. My Honor Elian the Exemplar of Esteem, and my Honor Kyros the Exemplar of Strength, who would both smile."

Belona and several others shouted, "And you, our Grace!"

My Grace bowed her head, the delicate flush of her cheeks somehow adding to her majesty, and Prince Darian smiled slightly before speaking further, "Count Ciro Tolmarie, who won the battle within the city in my Lord's name—"

My face became as glossy as glass, even as I understood what she was doing.

"—and the captains and sergeants of all fifteen companies. Indeed, every one of you here and every one of those who did not return. For all of you do I proffer gratitude. Then I remember the duke of Ehaya, Marquis Foltariet—"

A smile, grim but still charmed, lightened the marquis' stern face.

"—who spoke to the city at the correct moment. And, finally, I remember those whose service was unexpected yet invaluable: Nadeya Tahira Enarias, who alerted the Quest to the conjurors' plans and whose myriad efforts are the very reason for the speed of our reconquest, and Crown Prince Eligeo tej-Shehennadem, who warned us of the Gouge's escape."

The army stared, eyes wide and mouths agape, their joy frozen into shock.

"For these reasons, I gladly bestow upon Tahira Enarias the title of 'Inase', trusted confidante of the Quest and upon Crown Prince Eligeo-nadem the restoration of royal address, though not true rank. And with still greater happiness do I affirm the haven that my Honor Kyros the Exemplar of Strength promised Tahira Enarias and the sanctuary that my Honor Elian the Exemplar of Esteem vowed for Crown Prince Eligeo-nadem. The choices to gift such favor were my Honors', and it is my humble delight to support their choices in their absence and in their place.

"In this matter, Nademile, I am well pleased, for Nademan's future must indeed be bright if a prince of the old house holds the capability to demonstrate such virtue. And it is my prayer that this virtue is evident in all of our actions. It is my prayer that my Lord will see his wishes fulfilled. Perhaps then the Almighty will bless us with his happiness, for in his favor is our freedom. May we find within ourselves the capacity to attain that blessed state.

"May the Almighty bless our Lord and, through him, Nademan and Icilia. Thus has our Grace spoken."

The army cheered once more at the evident conclusion of our Grace's speech, but this time in a daze, unable to comprehend what had just been proclaimed. Indeed, even Belona, the other captains, and I, who had heard these declarations before, were too stunned to understand.

My Honor Kyros' promise to the strategist Enarias was not all that surprising, even for the rest of the army—rumors of Kanzeo's identity and history had spread rapidly during our journey to Ehaya, at the Quest's own encouragement—but for my Honor Elian to vow sanctuary to the cursed crown prince... Why would he *do* that? Why would he give *sanctuary* instead of merely ignoring his existence if execution seemed too extreme? Why would he *champion* him when those who were already his vassals would be so hurt? Why would he act so while they still grieved those who died in his name? Why would my Honor take any risk at all for such a worthless man?

All my earlier resolve to not question my Rulers' judgment seemed brittle beneath the weight of these questions.

Those questions whirled in my mind as I embraced my family and departed immediately after the speech for the first burial rotation (the reason I had received those two hours of rest beforehand), throughout even the burials themselves, and on my exhausted return once all the hundreds of burials were complete. I had stayed all afternoon and evening, even while other companies came to and left the field, yet even exhaustion could not release those questions' stranglehold on my mind.

As the soldiers finally gathered for the victory feast, I realized I was not the only one still troubled. Whispers ran rampant in the camp as men and women crouched around campfires and on the edges of platforms and anxiously tried to piece together what our Grace's speech had meant. And when those answers did not readily come, they clenched their fists in frustration and slammed aside bowls in anger.

Standing in the center of the camp, I realized that the Quest's reconquest was beginning to fall apart.

Apparently reaching the same conclusion, Belona shifted our supper tray in her arms and stepped close enough to whisper in my ear, "Ciro, my love, you must act."

"How, Belona?" I whispered back. "I left so quickly, without addressing the marquis' poison or helping our Grace quell him, because I did not know what to say. And the hours since have not revealed the correct answer to me."

She shook her head. "You must trust that the Almighty will guide your tongue. We *cannot* let this discord spread. It is our duty to support our Rulers' choices as their vassals, and it is our duty to ensure our fellow citizens do not lose our Rulers' favor as their nobles. We *must* act. It is what our Honor Arista the Exemplar of Bravery would expect, and it is also what our Grace wills, what she ordered me after your departure to ask you to do."

Those words about duty were precisely what needed to be said, and the seal upon them that proved their worth was my Grace's command. A command that was my liege's right to give.

I sighed. "As always, my love, you are wiser than I am." I took a deep breath and adjusted Dorona's position on my left arm so she would be more comfortable. Then I strode to the nearest fire.

The soldiers, from my Honor Kyros' division, jumped to their feet. "Count Tolmarie!" a sergeant exclaimed. "We are honored! Please, sit with us!"

"My gratitude for your welcome," I said and selected a cushion for Belona. Once she was settled, I took a seat on another and waved for the soldiers to do the same. "If you would allow me, I desire to ask your opinions on a matter."

The soldiers nodded eagerly.

I recited my Lord's favored prayer for meals and raised a spoonful of chicken broth to Dorona's mouth as I collected my thoughts. Then I asked, "What are your reactions to our Grace's speech?"

They knew exactly what I meant, and their expressions twisted into scowls. "We do not know what to think," the sergeant replied. "We trust the Quest, but... why would our Honor the Exemplar of Esteem do this to us! Why would he not respect how we feel? Why would he do this to us while we still grieve the dead?"

The complaint was too eerily close to my own thoughts. As I considered how to answer, I murmured soft encouragements to Dorona until she finally stopped turning her head away and swallowed the contents of the spoon.

Then I replied, praying that my tongue would be blessed with the right words, "I have pondered his decision for most of the day as well. Before our Grace's speech, I asked my countess," I dipped my head toward Belona, "what she witnessed when the crown prince was brought before our Grace. And I can only think that our Honor saw something—something worthy of... of, well, redemption in him." A bitter smile curled my lips as the truth of those words dawned in my own heart. "Did the Quest did not redeem us as well? Did they not take risks for us and champion us when we no longer had faith in them? Did they not disregard their own griefs and sorrows, the losses of their families of which we well know, when they chose to act for our sake?"

The soldiers mumbled an agreement, gazes downcast.

I softly asked, "Would you truly ask our Rulers to abandon someone they believed worthy of redemption?"

Regret and shame creased their faces now, and I judged my task here to be complete.

Rising with a word of farewell, Belona, Dorona, and I moved to the next fire and again sat, ate a few mouthfuls, and answered these most distressing of questions for them. Then rising, we moved to the next and repeated the task. Then again. And again. And again.

There was a distinction among the companies and their families.

My Honor Elian's own troops, those who had fought by his side in the province of Adeban, seemed reluctant at all to complain, but a sort of grieved betrayal gleamed in their eyes. Yet all Belona and I needed to dispel it was a reminder that my Honor's kindness was ever-abundant, that he had never failed to give that kindness even when his own soul was burdened, and that he had tempered his words for their sake in his vow of sanctuary.

My Lord's troops, too, were reluctant to ask questions, but discontent was evident in my comrades' expressions. Until I mentioned another aspect of what Belona had heard Inase bi-Dekecer briefly report to my Grace: our Lord had met the crown prince and had given him a nod. And words of gratitude—essentially a ratification of my Honor's decision. Those troops were almost jubilant after learning that.

My Grace's troops, the companies of newer recruits who had followed her from Arkaiso, were both more openly upset and more easily calmed. They only required a reminder of the deep love and trust among the Quest, which had surely led to my Grace's affirmation of her fellow Potentate's judgment.

My Honor Kyros' troops, however, were the most difficult to satisfy. The first group to whom I had spoken were born of Zaiqan, some more were from my own town of Jurisso, but many of the rest were from Gairan herself and so respected the marquis and hated the crown prince more than the rest.

In one conversation, after Belona had split from me to address the soldiers and the guards seated on the platforms, and after Dorona had fallen asleep in the carrying basket tied to my back, a mother dared to say, "Did he not give sanctuary for no greater reason than the crown prince's presenting a pitiful figure? It is not difficult to imagine—I saw him, and he was covered in blood. Could he not have made a play for my Honor's sympathies and so successfully, well, *manipulated* him?"

I raised an eyebrow, struggling to hold my composure at what may not have been intended as but surely *was* an insult. "Do you truly think my Honor cannot discern what is true and what is merely falsehood with one glance? From the stories I have heard of his campaign in Adeban, he was generous with his kindness in allowing all folk a fair chance to prove their loyalty, but he still always knew when someone intended to hurt his vassals. And from what my countess told me today, my Honor healed the crown prince—would he not be all too aware of whether the pain was real or feigned?"

"He does not have magical maturity," the mother grumbled. "His grasp of magic is not so great."

"Through no flaw of his own," I responded. "Moreover, he is trained by the same masters as your liege, our Honor the Exemplar of Strength—whom you revered enough to follow weeks before he achieved maturity. Neither Potentate needs magic to judge with acuity and discern what is true."

She subsided, but another soldier demanded, "Do our thoughts not matter about this? Do our pain and grief not matter? It is our nation! If our Rulers accept him into their midst, who is to say they will not make him our king as well!"

Before this grievance could gain weight, I said firmly, "It does not matter what we ourselves think or feel; only our Rulers' thoughts and feelings matter. Did we not promise that when all of us—of our own free choice, not because of a compulsion like the enemy would contrive—when all of us pledged? Did we not choose their wishes and judgment over our own when we pledged?"

The group had nothing more to say and instead cowered in shame as they watched Prince Darian pass a few feet away. Though he did not look in their direction, his appearance, particularly in profile, was so like my Lord's that the treason within these doubts felt all the clearer in his presence.

With only a word of farewell, I left for the next group.

And, as I did so, a thought flared in my mind with all the force of a strike of lightning:

My Honor Elian's choice was the bravest choice of all of the Potentates'. For he had risked the Quest as none of them had. And, in doing so, he revealed the beauty of the dignity of incé, the dues of compassion and empathy to one's fellows solely because they, too, were among the children of Icilia. Indeed, kindness at its best.

And a choice in accordance with his name.

That ignited another, greater revelation:

Amid the darkness of the enemy's blood-soaked night, the other Potentates were too blinding to be seen, too complex and too beyond, and my Lord even more so. But, unlike them, my Honor's glory was soft, gentle, sweet, and so soothing that, basking in its glow, even tormented, darkened minds gained such power that they could begin to see the Light.

Was not empathy the basis of the dignity of incé and thus the most easily understood of the virtues? Had not the crown prince been freed from years of torment all because of the empathy of the

Exemplar of Esteem? Was not empathy thus the first step toward freedom?

Only by beholding my Honor Elian's glory could a soul dare to dream of freedom.

So every glimpse thereafter of the other Potentates and of my Lord himself was because of my Honor, and all the blessing of those glimpses, therefore, was his.

The truth resonated within the Quest's name: my Honor Elian the Exemplar of Freedom was the first star of the Lord of Freedom.

CHAPTER 26
CHASING ESTEEM

Perspective: Khuduya Rosalla Eminietta, citizen of Khuduren
Date: Eyyédal, the second day of the eighth moon, Belsaffe, of the
year 500, C.Q.
Placement: between Chapter 50 and Chapter 51 of <u>The Bell Tolling</u>

Like the fools they were, the soldiers opened the thick wooden double-doors to the arena and pushed Mikkel inside, ready to accept his challenge for their own amusement—they did not even pause to wonder why a young man would demand to enter such a prison. Only one remained behind to look after the gates, and his attention was more on what was happening inside the brick walls rather than outside.

I raised a finger.

At the signal, Merel teleported from where he was crouching beside me to the doors. A single well-aimed blow, and the man closing them fell to the ground, dead before he could shout a warning.

Merel cast a frantic glance in the direction of our hiding place.

Grinning fiercely, I leapt to my feet and dashed toward the doors.

A second slower, the other sixteen members of my little band followed, brandishing their weapons yet moving as quietly as a poisonous fume.

Within minutes, we were inside, and the soldiers surrounding our comrade lay slain at our feet.

I laughed wildly. "Phase one complete! Begin phase two!"

Half of our number smirked and stalked down the hallway, toward the kitchen for the off-shift staff. Both bloodlust and vengeance lifted their steps, for those staff had committed the same atrocities as our own oppressors—everything from rape to torture, all for the sake of pleasure and entertainment.

The remaining eight, though a little disappointed by our less gruesome task, fell in behind me.

Though I had never been here before—Mikkel and Camilla were the ones who had been transferred from this place—the patterns of the halls and rooms were nearly identical to my own prison's. With little effort, I found the jailer's desk by the gladiators' entrance to the arena.

The woman screeched in surprise. Jumping to her feet, she grabbed a spiked mace and charged toward me.

I stepped lightly aside and swung back with my dagger.

The tip pierced the thin strip of unprotected neck above the back of her gorget.

I turned and wrenched the blade through, cutting half the head from the neck in a spray of warm crimson blood. An equally warm, satisfying feeling filled my belly as I relished in the coppery scent.

"Nice!" Imalla whistled from behind me.

I threw a grin full of bloodlust over my shoulder. Then, uncaring of how the blood was staining my filched weapon and stolen armor, I strode forward and grabbed the six rings of keys lying in an open drawer on the other side of the desk. I tossed five of them to the slightly less mad members of my little group and kept one for myself.

"When we are done with the other prisoners..." Jonrel started.

"... you can go after whichever soldiers are near," I completed.

Our comrades were dealing with the staff, but there were surely at least another fifty soldiers who had come during their weeks of leisure for entertainment. Rapacious and lustful pleasure was, after all, how the Slicer kept his troops under his control in the absence of war.

My band-mates cheered, eyes lighting up with excitement, and rushed into the underground bowels of the arena, leaving me to follow at a slower pace. Though Mikkel had lectured all of us on the importance of stealth, my group almost seemed to be increasing the noise they made, the better to attract more soldiers.

I flipped my dagger and caught it in an attempt to remind myself that I, at least, should be quieter so I could watch their backs.

And also so I did not have to share my kills.

I doubted that most of what my comrades and I felt was what we should, what those seeking the Quest's approval and coming should feel, but it was so difficult to suppress the love of brutality that had been steeped into our very souls...

I suppose I should at least try though... With a slight grimace, I shoved down some of my giddy delight at the sight of the soldiers' corpses that my band was already leaving in their wake.

Those soldiers are monsters, and they need *to be killed so they do not hurt anyone else, but that does* not *mean we should enjoy killing them!*

As I repeated those words like a prayer, I reached the first hall of cells. It was already empty, the doors hanging ajar, so I continued onwards. I did not even blink at the filthy squalor of those tiny cages—I hardly remembered the wonder of my parents' painstakingly clean and lovingly furnished home. Though with my mind I knew that the enemy treated my fellow gladiators and me worse than animals, my heart was too desensitized to remember that it could, or should, be different.

It was not as though I was worth better treatment than such squalor.

The second hall also lay empty, as did the third and fourth, while the thumps of running feet and the clangs of swords clashing against swords came from up ahead. Blood was oozing through the channels in the stone as my comrades fought wildly against the pack of soldiers attempting to corner them. Twenty-six new faces beat at those soldiers' backs with their bare fists.

Recognizing the crazed desire for vengeance in their eyes, I strangled the war cry rising in my throat and edged around the fight to the next hall of cells. Where I would hopefully find my own prey.

The fifth hall was full of prisoners, but I did not have its keys, so I headed to the last, the sixth.

The prisoners inside, all wide-eyed and holding onto the iron bars at the front of their cells, muttered excitedly at my appearance. They had evidently heard enough of the skirmish in the hall to comprehend that the soldiers were no longer in control.

Grinning at their eagerness, I worked quickly to unlock the cells, starting with the first and moving toward the back.

When the final door swung open, the prisoners all gave me looks that were a mixture of gratitude, relief, and fierce blood-thirst. Then, heedless of their lack of weapons, they ran to join the fray.

All except one: the occupant of the final cell. A young man with a proud bearing, intense blue eyes, and an unbroken nose.

Unlike every other gladiator I had ever met, both those whom I freed and those who died at my hand, he did not seem like a broken man. Indeed, save for the gauntness of his frame, the knotted scars crossing over the patches of exposed skin beneath his rags, the greasiness of his dark hair and beard, and the gray pallor of his peach-white skin, he was the image of the nobles of the old monarch's court.

With that much regality, he probably *was* a noble.

The Slicer liked to target the nobility with even more malice than the commoners. He crushed their spirits until they were little more than rabid beasts and then, only then, allowed them the mercy of death.

So for this noble to be appear rather whole... that was stunningly impressive. It meant he was worth something, unlike the rest of us.

The noble opened his mouth to speak.

But, before he could, there was the shuffle of a leather boot.

I whirled around and jumped forward, drawing my other dagger and slashing down with both. Red stained my vision with the anticipation of spilling blood.

The soldier dashed toward me, broadsword raised as her lips twisted in a cruel sneer.

How foolish to attack alone, without armor, a gladiator who had survived the arenas.

Ducking below the thrust, I briefly leaned into her guard and slashed the top of one shoulder.

Blood spurted from the wound at each expansion and contraction of her muscles.

She shrieked, pale eyes ablaze with more anger than pain, spun, and charged me again.

I darted around the blow, following the arc of the swing, and swung my own blade so that it barely, just barely, caught her armpit.

The nick caused such pain that she dropped her sword.

The hilt slipped from her fingers.

She cursed and bent to retrieve it.

I stepped in for another slash. My red-hued gaze was on a part of the lower back that was especially sensitive to the cuts I most enjoyed inflicting—

Before my dagger could reach my target, another hand grabbed the soldier's sword and sliced it up through her throat.

The headless body slumped to its knees and then fell sideways, while the head rolled to a stop near the wall.

Chest heaving, I turned and glared at the noble. "What was that for! That was *my* kill! The only one I've gotten so far!"

He ignored the exclamation. Instead, piercing my dull hazel

eyes with his blazing blue ones, he demanded, "Why are you doing this?"

I blinked, the question like a deluge of cold water amid my battle-crazed state. "What?"

"Why are you doing this?" he repeated.

His gaze was so powerful, so captivating because of the intense life-filled quality of it, that I could not look away. "Ummm..." I began. "Ummm... because..." I exhaled a sigh, trying to gather my thoughts. "Because I want to have a name worthy of the Quest's salvation."

The intensity of his eyes only sharpened. "And do you believe what you are doing is worthy of such honor?"

I floundered, unsure how to answer—none of my comrades were ever interested in asking about anything other than the possibility of bloodshed.

"Earning the Quest's favor," the noble said quietly, "will require much more than slaughtering the enemy. Earning such divine esteem will require becoming a leader worth following, in their image, in accordance with their example, holding esteem for oneself, for others, and for the Almighty. It is what the first Quest exhorted the first monarchs to do."

As my bloodlust died, a pang of anguish, as great as what I had felt moments before the unlocked manacle fell from my wrist, racked my heart—if becoming a leader was what salvation required, I would never be redeemed. I remembered only flashes from my life before the arena, and I was not capable of more. The Slicer had stolen all of those things from me, just as he had stolen my innocence.

At the thought, the anguish grew... until, like all my pain, it was devoured by anger.

"How dare you speak of such things to me?" I snapped. "I rescued you, Count! You have no place to question my motive or reasoning. Go out and kill as you are supposed to!"

Again he ignored my exclamation. "I know the stories of the first Quest, Khuduya," he said, voice still even and quiet, "and I can help you. If you accept, I can aid you in becoming a leader worth following."

Despite how I disliked it, his calmness quenched my anger. But still I asked, narrowing my eyes, unwilling to accept what he was saying, "How do you know such stories? No one has dared tell them in over a decade."

He inhaled deeply, closing those keen blue eyes for just a moment, the first emotion he had shown other than deep focus since I had opened his cell. "I once knew," he whispered, "a man who could recite the legends without need of a reference. He would tell them to his little sister, and I censured him for it... Kyros was his name, and I did not understand what a friend I could have had until I lost every chance to gain his friendship..." He met my gaze again. "Let me support you in achieving the height of your ambition, Khuduya."

I stared, my cheeks hot as my emotions raged. I despised asking for help... and he was speaking of impossible things... yet... he was a noble. A *count*, even. Someone born with the heart to lead and trained to possess a complementary mind. If anyone among these gladiators was capable of leadership, it was he. So for him to speak of *supporting* me... I could not understand it.

If he wanted to usurp whatever clout I had in the gladiators' eyes, he certainly could. We were wild and uncivilized, but most of us treasured whatever customs we could remember, and one of those was a respect for the nobility. I might have opened their cells, but that gave responsibility more than reverence.

As I gawked at him, another pair of footsteps, these familiar, entered the hallway behind me.

"Rosalla," Mikkel panted, "there were not as many soldiers as we expected, but they are starting to rally, and, if we do not leave soon, there soon will not be any cha—" Halfway through the word, he stopped speaking.

I turned to see him standing as though frozen, his eyes upon the noble's face.

The noble smiled softly, an expression that lacked the barely restrained insanity of every other gladiator's. "Blessings, Mikkel," he greeted. "It is good to learn that you still live."

"H-how…?" Mikkel gasped like one strangled. "You were… you were supposed to be *safe*, Ensel!"

The noble stepped forward and laid a gentle hand on my lieutenant's cheek. "I promise I will tell you why. As well as tell you of your father. I was taken but a few months after you, but I can share what I do know. But, first…" Ensel let his sentence fade and looked to me.

I swallowed. Then firmly decided to deal with everything else later. "What about these soldiers, Mikkel?"

My voice seemed to snap him to attention. "We need to leave *now* if we want to stay ahead of their pursuit. All the gladiators have been freed, and we have stolen more weapons, so there is no reason to delay."

I nodded and marched outside. With a few barked orders, I gathered up my comrades, old and new, including Ensel—the possibility of tormenting our oppressors through a chase was an excellent motivator—and managed to organize them enough that, quieting all arguments, within half an hour, we were fleeing east across the plains.

And all the while Ensel's words haunted me.

I might have been liberated from my cell, but I was a slave in heart, mind, and soul.

So how could a slave like me ever dare to dream of esteem?

CHAPTER 27
PROVING BROTHERHOOD

Perspective: Prince Darian sej-Shehasfiyi, brother of the Quest Leader and auxiliary heir to the throne of Asfiya
Date: Eyyélab, the twentieth day of the eighth moon, Belsaffe, of the year 500, C.Q.
Placement: partially concurrent with Chapter 52 of The Bell Tolling

An odd sense of nausea trickled up my throat, seeming to scald my heart with its passage.

I frowned and discreetly rubbed the cloth over my heart, trying to ease the discomfort, before returning my gaze to Count Ciro Tolmarie.

Yet, though the report that he presented on Nademan's food resources was of paramount importance, all I could truly comprehend was the anguish glimmering in Malika's eyes.

Nearly thirty minutes prior, before this meeting in the commander's pavilion, she had almost fallen from our platform, screaming from a bout of unexplained pain—pain that could not be explained by anything beside her curse. Or evil befalling the other Potentates...

As much I prayed that her curse was not the cause, so much

more did I pray that the second had not happened. For if it had...
I did not dare even to consider it.

Not two hours ago, Elian had informed us that Lucian, Kyros, and he would soon be in position to strike at the Gouge. I refused to think that the battle would go poorly, that Lucian's efforts would result in anything but outright victory.

I refused to think it, but I could not help but fear it.

When Malika and I had reunited with Lucian before the march to Ehaya, I had been shocked to behold how ill he appeared. The silver of his cream skin seemed closer to the last pale light that lingered after the sun had already set, like a reminder of bygone glories, than his usual radiance—a dimness reflected in his every feature, from the limp, lusterless look of his hair and beard to the languid movements of his limbs. But worst was his presence: it had felt thin, tired, as though he was fading away before my eyes.

And in that state, he had dueled conjurors and was likely now battling the Gouge, all without his companions, his family, and his guardians able to do much more than defend his back. None could reduce the strain upon him, so he bore it all alone.

Truly, watching him confront conjury and only being able to cast shields of athar magic to defend him had become one of the worst memories of my life.

I had hardly dared to dwell upon his fading health in the weeks before the battle, nor during the horrors of the battle itself, for even smoke rising from Mount Atharras would not be so terrifying.

Nearly as frightening as his ill health was the thought of asking Lucian what ailed him. If he did not wish to speak of it—and I did not think he did, for his companions' worry mirrored my own, ever increasing as he chased the Gouge—then raising the issue might have given him cause to be rid of me.

Other than a few warm smiles and embraces, he no longer seemed to wish for my presence. Despite all the many years I had spent at his side, he had refused every one of my attempts to serve him since he had reunited with Malika and me on the march to Ehaya. I had hardly seen him outside of meals, meetings, or public gatherings. As reluctant as I was to think it during the march itself, it was as though our closeness was evaporating much as he himself was...

How I prayed that neither was true. But if our brotherhood, which I treasured above my own life, was the necessary cost for his health, even that I would give. Even Asfiya herself I would give, as our family had all those years ago. Even Icilia herself was a sacrifice I would make for him...

Summoning an image of his laughing violet eyes to the forefront of my mind, I prayed for his long life and health, desperately begging the Almighty to safeguard my brother as he endeavored to protect all of us from the enemy's cruelty.

Beside me, though her gaze did not waver from Count Tolmarie's face, Malika seemed to do the same.

"...so, in summary, my Grace," Count Tolmarie closed, "both in Ehaya and across the provinces, the captains have uncovered only half of the confiscated supplies we expected to find. The enemy burned or despoiled the rest. Thus, the supplies with which you hoped to compensate for the allegiant towns devoting their youth to your army—they have not been recovered." Nothing in his neutral tone indicated the least disrespect; the events of the last three weeks, atop the circumstances of his pledge and the months of campaign, had proved his loyalty unshakable.

Malika nodded thoughtfully. *So the towns will certainly need aid, Count Tolmarie?* she asked in my father's link.

"Yes, my Grace," Count Tolmarie answered.

She pressed her lips together. *Would you ask the captains whether they believe the farming towns on the plains could be persuaded to send that aid?*

Count Tolmarie bowed his head. "As you will, my Grace."

Malika raised an eyebrow. *You do not believe that they would be willing though, do you, Count Tolmarie?* Her piercing gaze perceived even more of the noble's hidden thoughts than I could.

He shifted slightly on his cushion, then seemed to allow himself a wry smile. "Their reluctance to respond to your attempts at communication is telling. If those attempts do succeed... from what I recall of the markets of my childhood, they will offer some dozen bushels out of grudging tribute, but no more. They were miserly even in the years of plenty before the enemy's tyranny; I can only imagine how much more so they must have now become."

And, even without the lack of hands, Malika mused, *the Dasenákder is struggling, as are the plains to the south. Hunters cannot find prey, chickens and other fowl do not have enough grain, and the crops will yield less than ever. So, following the pattern of every year prior to this one, winter will be harsher and spring paler. And as desperate as the towns are, so much more so are the cities as the more immediate targets of the enemy's tyranny.* She blew out a breath and clasped her hands in her lap. *It is quite an impossible situation.*

I could not bear the thought of despair plaguing her as the worst of her memories did. "Your coming has and will continue to change our circumstance, my Grace."

She turned to offer me a weary smile. *Not quickly enough for this winter. Because of Inase Enarias, we have won Nademan before the end of summer, months earlier than predicted, but still there are too few weeks remaining until the start of the harvest and the first winds of autumn. We do not yet have a way to purify the sky and bring back the rain the earth so desperately needs. And...*

"...even if we did, it is too late for this year," I finished her sentence. Then sighed and scrubbed a hand over my face. "Truly, an impossible conundrum."

"If I may, my Grace, your Highness..." Count Tolmarie began, then continued at our nods, "it is a wonderful problem to have. Our Honor Arista the Exemplar of Bravery confirmed yesterday that only the wretched Gouge and his closest servants are left to slay; by the pace of your reconquest thus far, you will have won both the land and the hearts of Nademan by autumn's end. We are now in a position to actually fret about starvation rather than fear that we will be brutally murdered in our beds long before we exhaust our stores."

Malika smiled wryly. *Gratitude to the Almighty, yes, but that is hardly an encouraging statement.*

He chuckled, light brown eyes sparkling for the first time in weeks. "That is why you should ask Belona to speak instead, my Grace!"

Despite the tension burdening our movements, Malika clapped a hand to her mouth, muffling a giggle, and I pursed my lips to hold back a laugh.

Despite his initial protests to Arista and Kyros, Malika and I had quickly learned that, when the count desired to be, he was among the most eloquent of the Quest's new vassals. Claiming that his wife was a superior orator was his way of championing her fortitude and ability—as well as his honesty, for, though he spoke wonderfully, she was magnificent, a rival to precocious Elacir himself.

Count Tolmarie beamed, seeming absolutely delighted, his gaze following the twitches of mirth in Malika's expression as though savoring the change. His expression showed a keen attention I had begun to see on even the city-folk's faces, no longer only the soldiers' or those of the Quest's inner circle.

For, indeed, Malika had, in the three weeks since the Battle of Ehaya, won the devotion of western Nademan. From the long days and nights she dedicated to the reconstruction of the Nademan's government to her unending patience and flawless judgment as she provided for the people's safety and recovery, she was proving herself to be precisely the ideal of rulership that the Quest of Light had promised and that Icilia so desperately needed. The Almighty's choice and Lucian's affirmation of that choice had bestowed upon us this blessing. The prudence of Lucian's decision to entrust her with supreme command over his reconquest had been well proven.

Amid the ever growing admiration that was filling my heart, I could no longer maintain any sort of distance between us, not even the use of her reverential address in my thoughts. I had sworn loyalty to Lucian's sister in the very moment I first beheld her majesty, but, instead of loving her purely, I had let my attempts at aloofness taint our bond and impair my service. I had let my jealousy deafen me to Lucian's words, privately given on the journey to Zaiqan's market, that my greatest joy would be in her surpassing me. I had let my fears deprive her of my support.

I could do so no longer. In the Quest's absence, the health that had come from their presence was receding, and she suffered countless nightmares, flashes, and bursts of sickness, as she had in Arkaiso. Her health was becoming increasingly more fragile, while her responsibilities grew more numerous by the day. She bore everything with unwavering resilience, but I was all too aware of how strained her nerves often were. The lessons I taught in Arkaiso, the chores I coordinated on the march to Ehaya, and the research I conducted regarding her curses were not enough: she needed me to stand beside her as her aide and herald, to relay her words and serve her as I would have served Lucian himself.

Such resolution was late in coming. Abominably late. Malika deserved better than me, as Lucian did. But every moment of love for her was the worthiest of endeavors, and I would not waste the moments of my life any longer, even if she did not care to return my brotherhood with sisterhood... even if she cast me aside the moment I unraveled her curses and she no longer needed me...

Blushing a deep crimson at the adoring attention, Malika smiled and lowered her gaze.

Then she froze.

And a scream of utter agony burst from her lips.

"Malika!" I shouted her name as I scrambled across the pavilion to her side and, tossing aside decorum, scooped her convulsing form into my arms. "Malika!"

She shrieked, wordless and speechless, her throat spasming wildly beneath her collar.

"Malika!" I called. "Malika! I am with you, my Sister, my

heart! Malika!" A portion of my mind knew that I was over-reaching my place—those words and this embrace were too much like Lucian's—but they were the truth wrung from my heart.

The shrillness of her cry deepened to an anguished wail. Still wordless but accompanied by a single name in the link: *Lucian!*

My lungs seemed unable to draw breath.

Lucian! she sobbed more clearly. *Lucian! Lucian, what happened to you!*

Breaking all of my bones would have been less painful than listening to those words.

"Malika," I forced past numb lips, "what do you sense?"

Malika shuddered and finally appeared to perceive my presence. But, instead of drawing away, she wrapped her arms around my shoulders and clung to me. *Darian,* she whispered, dropping my title, *I cannot sense enough to be sure, but...*

"But what, Malika?" I asked desperately.

Her brows drew together. *Darian,* she said slowly, *this is not like that first pain, the echo of what Arista suffered. That was... that was evil. This is... different.* A terrible misery dimmed her blue eyes as they met mine. *I do not know what has happened.*

I swallowed, a question forming on my tongue that I feared to ask. The truth that whatever was happening to Lucian was not born of evil brought little comfort.

An answering pain burned in her expression. *I do not know what has happened, Brother.*

That endearment in her musical voice brought tears to my eyes. "I-I could not sur-survive it if—"

Somehow, though she was still shaking, though agony permeated her presence, somehow she still had the strength to offer me a kind smile. *Do not presume that the worst has occurred, Brother. We must have faith in our Lord.*

I sighed and gathered her closer to me, savoring her scent of sweet incense and clinging to her for comfort even as I smoothed the red-gold curls that had fallen loose from her bun and from beneath her crown amid her convulsions.

Malika sighed as well and rested her head on my shoulder. *Elian and Kyros will contact us soon, when they are safe, and will explain what happened. Lucian and Arista will be well, by the Almighty's name, for the Almighty safeguards them…*

"… and defends them, the only ones worthy of divine love," I finished the sentence, paraphrased from prose written as praise of the Quest of Light, which Hasima had recited yesterday as a prayer while we broke our fast.

Indeed, she said. *Retain your faith, Brother.* Then, switching links, she began to explain the situation to the rest of her inner circle.

Remaining silent, I held her more tightly, refusing to glance up from the wonder of her beautiful face. I certainly had noticed the hesitant approaches of my father, the guardians, Elacir, Inase Enarias, Kanzeo, and Crown Prince Eligeo—likely all called by Count Tolmarie, who was also present alongside his wife and his infant daughter—but I did not let my focus stray from Malika. Her wellbeing was my priority, and, if I acknowledged the devastation building in the others' expressions as Malika spoke, I would have nothing left with which to comfort her.

Though, in truth, *she* was the one comforting *me*.

Malika snuggled deeper into my embrace—causing my breath to hitch, for I had not before dared to believe that my affection would be so welcome—then paused.

I braced myself for another attack.

Instead she disentangled herself from my arms, rose to her feet, and pulled me to mine. *Come*, she ordered and led the way off the pavilion and up the ladder to the highest platform on the Quest's tree, the whole of her circle following obediently behind.

Despite the confidence now in her walk, I remained ready to catch her should she stumble.

Gratitude to the Almighty, Malika reached the platform without mishap. She chose a spot in the center of the wooden floor, facing the east, and folded her hands over her waist. With a tilt of her chin, she gestured for the rest of us to gather around her.

Silently we waited.

Waited.

Waited.

Waited.

Then…

Watch, Malika whispered, pointing to the eastern sky over the treetops.

The smog in the east, burnished by the new yellow rays of the morning sun, rippled like muddy water hit with a stone.

In the wake of those ripples were thin lines of blue. Cracks in a wall of smoke.

Those blue lines spread, slicing across the sky, and broadened, first streaks and strokes, then circles, painting the firmament with the sleek swishes of a pen until the whole of it was awash with blue, the smog dwindling to patches, then ultimately specks that disappeared under the golden glory of the risen sun.

The rich incense of Lucian's divine-gifted magic glided on the wind, filling my senses with the ethereality of pure holiness.

The light was too much for eyes so long accustomed to a dimmed world of blackened sky and twilit earth, but I could not bear to look away or even narrow my gaze, so thirsty was I for the beauty of the sky.

"I never knew how dark the world had become," Taza whispered behind me.

"'Only the Light can reveal the true depravity of the dark,'" Hasima replied, quoting our Graced Queen Manara the Exemplar of Truth.

"As only our Lord Lucian the Ideal of Freedom could have banished the darkness," I murmured, the words spilling from my lips.

For this beauty was the Almighty's salvation and the prophecy of Lucian's birth given the form of light for all to behold. He was our sun…

... as his Second was the sky.

Though looking at her required a lowering of my eyes, I felt as though I was raising them yet higher as my gaze came to Malika.

Malika, who stood framed by a firmament as blue as her eyes, as expansive as her wisdom and compassion, as dynamic as her capacity to fulfill every role required for the greatest ruler Icilia would ever know.

In the unshrouded glory of the sun, her majesty became all the clearer, as though the clearing of the sky was also removing the shrouds dimming her grandeur.

She is my liege, I whispered to myself. *She is everything.*

On the heels of that thought came another: light, Lucian's light, as I had witnessed my brother's magic to be during the Battle of Ehaya and as Elacir had described, eradicated conjury—his purification of the sky proved this fact beyond question. So perhaps a drop of that magic was precisely what Malika's cure required...

This miraculous magic for the conjury, because only conjury can destroy the natural connection between the mind and the vocal cords and truly break someone's will to speak... and healing for the muscle damage caused by alchemy... but then what prevents recovery? What is cementing this spell, and was cementing the presence of the smog in the sky? In all recorded and observed examples, conjury's spells dissipate the moment catalysis ends... My brow furrowed as I tried to reach an answer that seemed only inches beyond my grasp—

Prince Darian, Malika stated.

My attention snapped to her.

Prince Darian, she said again, azure eyes on the azure horizon, *it is my will to leave by the noon hour for the province of Makiran, for my Lord's side.* Though my name was the only one she spoke, her words were in the collective link and quieted the excited murmurs surrounding us. *Organize the captains and prepare five companies for swift travel. Have my horse saddled and my possessions packed.*

"As you will, my Grace," I responded without hesitation.

Prince Beres, Safirile, Inasile, Crown Prince Eligeo, you will come with me, she said. *Transfer your duties to the captains who will remain here and carry your materials with you. Count Tolmarie, Countess Tolmariat, I will brief you on my orders for the command of the capital, which I will entrust to you before my departure.*

They murmured obedience. No one dared to ask why such upheaval was necessary.

Malika exhaled a long breath as she stared at the eastern sky. Then whispered, *Lucian is not well.*

And those words suffocated every breath of joy for the purified sky.

My father uttered a low, keening moan, voice cracking under the immensity of his terror and grief and collapsed onto the platform, lying prone on the wooden floor. The guardians, Elacir, Inase Enarias, Kanzeo, the crown prince, and the nobles fell to their knees, weeping and wailing.

All I could do was stand. Too numb to move, to think, to *breathe*. Lucian's health had been steadily worsening for the last six months, but he could not actually be *not* well...

Malika turned, pale cheeks sparkling with tears and lips spread with agony, walked forward a few steps, and folded her arms around my shoulders.

I gasped a sob and fell apart in her embrace.

She drew me closer, whispering soothing words even as her own heart was shattering. Stroking my back, smoothing my beard, wiping my cheeks, caring for me as only Lucian ever had.

In those moments it was impossible to not believe that she loved me.

Because her love for me and my love for her was all that ensured that we both remained standing.

I proffered gratitude to the Almighty even as I screamed, *Dalaanem! Lucian!*

"*Lucian!*"

CHAPTER 28
VOWING ALARM

Perspective: Etheqora Revera qia-Tovacera, citizen of Etheqa
Date: Eyyésal, the twenty-ninth day of the eighth moon, Belsaffe, of
the year 500, C.Q.
Placement: between Chapter 52 and Segment 5 of The Bell Tolling

Flaring my wings behind me, I let the wind filling the membranes pull me up from my flight and then squinted at the western horizon.

The ominous gray clouds building there obscured much of the light... and the smog perennially inhibited visibility... but the soot-colored splotch that had caught my gaze... no, it certainly was not a piece of cloud. It was moving much too fast to be anything but a flight of Sholanar.

"There!" I called out above the whistling wind and, very briefly lifting one hand from its grip on Astor's torso, pointed at the spot. "Do you see that movement, Afra?"

Glancing over my shoulder, I waited as Afra activated her farsight and cast it in that direction.

A few moments passed as the rest of us—even Netara and Cethor—quietly waited. The last four months had taught us all greater patience, and most particularly in this. Pausing to gather as much intelligence as we could about our enemy was not a step any of us now chose to forego.

Then Afra replied, "I see it, Revera! Sholanar soldiers!"

"Are we following them?" Netara asked over the rising wind. Her burgundy wings fluttered, the sharp winds nearly dislodging her curly red hair from its tight knot of braids at the top of her neck.

I needed but a single wingbeat to decide: "We are! If they are daring to risk travel amid a rising storm, their mission must be important! We must disrupt it!"

Everyone loudly agreed, even Cethor.

I bent my right wing and used the movement to execute a slight turn, changing our course toward the soldiers. Following behind me, using the streams of air generated by the path of my wings, my flight matched their course to mine. Within twenty minutes, our path would intersect with the soldiers'.

A smile twitched my lips at how well we had executed the delicate movement. Much better than we had when we left Potsmia.

As much as we had practiced during the winter, the months since our departure were what had truly begun to hone our skill. The skirmishes we had fought, though few in number, were so intense, so challenging, so full of peril to our lives and limbs, that we were forced to rapidly improve and learn how to better prepare and strategize. So many of our days were occupied with practice, the browning mountainsides above which we flew and fought reminding us of the weight of our purpose.

That weight made all the difference in our practice.

Here on the increasingly barren slopes, traveling away from Potsmia and crossing the border of our province, my wing-mates and I could no longer pretend that this mission was about our own vengeance. It was not about proving myself or escaping the place of our suffering or even seeing the world—it was about the reality that Etheqa was dying. Not only our own province of Zimaka but the whole land. From the people to the trees to the mountains, our country was crumbling under the influence of the Blood's governor, the wretched Broil.

The actions of a few Etheqore could not save our nation. But we owed it to her and to the shining man to try.

"Rev," Astor breathed, catching my attention, "you will need to go higher soon. Let me tie on your mask."

I nodded, trusting his judgment. He did not fly, but he knew the sky as well as I did. Indeed, the masks, thick strips of cloth capable of filtering smoke, were his innovation: after much painful reflection on the soldiers' hunt last summer, he had realized two months ago that the smoke layering the sky wreaked its greatest destruction through direct inhalation, similar to normal campfire smoke. As long as our noses and mouths were covered, with cloth finely knit enough to prevent the soot from entering our airways, we would be relatively safe. Not that we should linger amid the tendrils of smog, for the masks would not filter out smoke for very long, and the particles were injurious to our skin as well, but a little bit was bearable.

A little bit was all we needed.

Astor removed cloth from a pouch on his belt and twisted beneath the thick rope tying him to me so that he could wrap it over the lower half of my face. He centered it, pulled the strings on either end taut, and knotted them over the back of my head. Then, his thin lips curving into a soft smile, he pressed a kiss to my chin, the straight, noble lines of his beloved face bright with trust. The plates directly below his lower lip vibrated pleasantly against my skin, and his warm, clean scent filled my nose.

"You can do this, Rev," he whispered.

I returned the smile but not the affectionate gesture. I could accept the friendly kisses he had begun to offer me, but I could not yet give my own. The memories of our tragedy were even now too fresh, and time was not as quick a healer for me as I had hoped. But, still, both of us believed we could overcome our scars.

Astor settled back against me and tied on his own mask,

before leaning around me and calling out, "Cover your faces!" His light baritone voice lifted easily over the winds and my airstream.

The command was well-timed.

For, but moments later, we were close enough to the soldiers' flight that I could discern the smoky colors of their uniforms and the glare of the red skulls stamped onto their chests.

Without speaking, I tilted my wings back and flapped them hard, quickly propelling myself higher. My friends followed my cue, and we rose to just below the base of the smog-tainted storm clouds, amid the masses blowing downwards. The air sizzled above us in the huge thunderheads, a warning that we had to move quickly before any lightning began.

The soldiers passed below us, flying just a few degrees south of west. They did not look up, not expecting anyone to risk the smog, or the lightning, and we angled ourselves so that we could follow them.

Flapping the full extent of my wingspan, I waited until they were far enough away that they would not be able to hear the beats of our wings over the boom of the growing thunder. Then I led my flight to a lower altitude, one less affected by the storm's rising winds.

"What will we do when the rain starts?" Glora called.

"We will need to retreat to what shelter we can find," I replied. "But I think we will reach their destination before then. Regardless of the importance of their task, they will not risk the rain itself. Not for very long, at least."

No one contested the assertion. Indeed, we were probably all remembering the one day of the hunt on which we had thought we would escape, the day on which the soldiers had moved more cautiously due to rain. We believed our willingness to risk the illness, desperate as we were, would be enough. But that hope had been more foolish than an uncontrolled plummet. They had been too well organized and aware of the storm's movements, and, before the rain could fall, they had caught us and had—

I shook my head and refocused on our maneuver.

The soldiers flew for some minutes, occasionally shifting course a few degrees to the south or the west, seeming completely ignorant of the storm brewing behind us. Thankfully, the major wind upon which the storm sat was blowing nearly twenty degrees north of west, so the black clouds were not quite overhead. But once the massive formations in the east traveled far enough, we, too, would be under its shade.

"The storm will be here in six minutes, Vera!" Afra yelled.

"We cannot continue to take this risk!" Dalor shouted. "The lightning alone is too dangerous!"

Agreeing with them, I opened my mouth and began to bend my right wing, ready to signal a landing.

Just as I found a clump of trees large enough for our needs, the soldiers dove forward over the crest of a nearby foothill.

"We follow!" I responded and slanted my wings down in a gentler glide which aimed for the same spot.

My flight obeyed, and we descended, navigating the now-howling winds with newly developed skill, as the soldiers disappeared into a gap amid the trees.

I directed us to another gap about halfway down the hillside, thirty feet from the soldiers.

We were close enough to count them now: there were ten, a full squad. A difficult challenge, but one which our mixed flight, more experienced than before, could surely handle.

Breaking away from the wind's currents, we ducked beneath the cover of the leaf-laden branches. Though those leaves were half-disintegrated and brown, their thick clusters would still provide adequate cover.

Keeping our wing movements slow and small, we drifted beneath the trees to the ground. Cethor and I untied the ropes holding Afra and Astor to us, placed them on their feet, and landed beside them. Those of the Sholanar amongst us tucked our wings tightly against our backs, and together we all drew our weapons and tiptoed through the trees. Though Afra's steps were the quietest on the leaf litter, the rest of us were admirably silent as well. The benefit of arduous training.

Ten feet from the soldiers, we stopped and knelt behind several thick patches of nettles.

For a few moments, I blinked, unable to make sense of what I was seeing.

Then the usual warmth of my auburn scales disappeared.

Beside me, Astor's plates stilled so much that they seemed like cracked earth upon his face. Afra's skin lost every bit of gloss. And Netara's, Cethor's, Glora's, and Dalor's scales dulled to the lifeless ashy gray of a spent fire. Their faces bore the same horror as my own.

For, through the trees, the remains of a village, a caravan of the Areteen and a long-severed acquaintance of our own aerie, was visible.

The familiarly-patterned tents and wagons lay in charred and jumbled piles of wood, bodies interspersed among them. A squad of soldiers cackled as they sifted through the remnants.

But far more horrifying was what the soldiers who we had followed were doing.

Eight of them were holding four young men of the Areteen in place.

All of whom, from his gasp, Astor seemed to recognize. Despite the years that had passed.

The men were struggling wildly, but they could not dislodge the tight grips on their arms.

While the other two soldiers...

One raised a sword and held its point over the chest of the leftmost prisoner.

The other lifted a bone. A one-and-half-foot long bone. A thigh bone—a femur.

An incé one.

The soldier was holding the bone in front of her chest, her face creased in concentration. A black mist, blacker than night, pooled in her palms and slithered up the yellowed bone. The whites of her eyes turned black, and black veins spread out from her eyes over her scaled cheeks.

The bone began to shake.

A scream filled the air.

The black mist coated the tip of the bone, sheathing it entirely.

An orb of black energy coalesced at the tip.

Then a bolt of darkness flashed from the bone to the man's heart just as the other soldier thrust his sword forward into it.

Blood spurted in the air.

And screams poured from the man's collapsing body.

An apple-red light gathered above his pierced and bleeding heart. The edges wavered, but the shadow... the black bolt grasped *ahold* of it. More and more black mixed with the red... until the red disappeared amid the black.

All the while the man's body screamed as it fell.

Before it hit the ground, it dissolved—disintegrating into black ash.

The black bolt zapped back to the bone.

The soldier exhaled a delighted laugh as the black veins tainted her blue scales a harsh smoky charcoal, like blood spreading through water.

Then she pivoted to the next prisoner. He had barely a moment to exclaim in horror before he, too, was struck.

His body shrieked and faded into ash.

The soldier turned to the third. And then the fourth.

Within moments, all four were simply... gone. No bodies to bury, no graves to dig.

Mere moments had passed, and they were just *gone*.

It was the most brutal death I had ever seen. More brutal than all the broken corpses of my family and neighbors...

The soldiers gathered together and laughed as they exclaimed in jubilation. Then they and the other squad, who had watched curiously, departed.

Only then did my friends and I stir, our limbs finally unfreezing from the shock and horror of what we had witnessed.

We stared at each other.

"What *was* that?" Netara whispered.

"What *happened*?" Glora asked. Her eyes desperate, she turned to her husband, who only shook his head, his pale red scales dimmed to a dirty foggy gray.

Afra fell into Cethor's arms and began to sob into his collar. He clutched her to him, his eyes closing as tears seeped out from under his own lids.

I just stared, my scales so cold that they seemed moments from flaking away. For a horror creeped up my spine that... "We did not *act*. We did *nothing*." I had led my friends from our home to *act*... and we had been useless... we had done nothing to help those men, who had once, long ago, been our friends.

Afra wailed, and Glora collapsed onto Dalor's chest. He embraced her, though his eyes seemed unseeing, a terror flickering in them.

"Revera..." Astor whimpered, taking my limp hand. "Was that not conjury?" He wrapped both his arms around my waist and pulled me to him. He buried his face into my middle and sobbed, his body shaking against mine.

I leaned down into his form, desperate for his comfort. "Astor..." my voice broke over his name. "Almighty forbidding... How can we *do* anything about such evil?" The words fell from numb lips.

No answers came.

For a long while, an endless moment stripped bare of relief, none of us moved. So overwhelmed by grief and sorrow and horror as we were, we did not have the *strength* to move.

Even when the rain started, poisonous drops tearing leaves from branches and spattering over our skin, we were still.

Then, as the day dimmed yet further with the sun's setting and the rain grew fiercer, I managed to rouse myself enough to urge us to find shelter.

We crawled into the remains of the tents and wagons. We dried ourselves only at each other's urging.

The moment the storm ended, we buried the corpses. I gathered the mud formed from those black ashes, the only remains of the four men, and added it to the grave as well.

We waited, not one of us sleeping, until dawn.

Then we left, flying further west, in the direction Afra had seen some of the soldiers go with her farsight.

Though this was horror that we could not combat, there was no turning back. No matter how deeply they had fallen into the enemy's grasp, the other villages needed to be told. No one was safe from the Broil's regular cruelty, so no one could possibly be safe from this.

As we flew, I prayed most fervently that, somehow, somewhere, we would find the shining man.

If anyone could stop such malice, he could.

I had to find a way to warn him.

CHAPTER 29
CONTRIVING ROLES

Perspective: Inase Tahira Enarias, confidante of the Quest
Date: Eyyéqan, the nineteenth day of the ninth moon, Alkharre, of
the year 500, C.Q.
Placement: same as Segment 5 of The Bell Tolling

Unbothered by the jostling pace of my horse, I opened another ciphered letter and held it alongside the first. *Some of these combinations of runes are certainly the same...* I moved the papers to one hand and retrieved my quill, inkwell, and journal from the saddlebag.

A hand rose from its grip on my waist and stretched, palm up. "I can help, Sister," Kanzeo said timidly, as he had since we were reunited.

I passed the letters into his fingers and patted the other hand clutching the fabric of my gown and the trousers I wore beneath.

He sighed contentedly, despite the inadequate show of affection, and pressed his thin face into my back. "I love you, Tahira," he said, his voice muffled.

"I love you as well, Kanzeo," I forced through my emotionless mask.

The delight radiating from his thin body was palpable—it was only the third time I had managed to say those words since the day we were freed.

How much our world had changed.

When the Battle of Ehaya began, I had believed it to be my last day and resolved to do what little I could, despite my failure in protecting my missing brother. Ignoring the general's summons, I convinced the staff to hide according to my instructions, shouldered the sack containing all the most relevant papers within my possession, and left to search for one of the Potentates.

I never expected them to actually believe my warning. No, indeed, punishment was what I expected when I approached my Honor Kyros the Exemplar of Strength.

He had given me safe passage, respect, and my brother instead. His own sigil hung from my throat as I sought his sister, the Quest's Second and Icilia's supreme commander. And she herself had not only accepted my paltry attempts at service, my weak attempts at sabotage, but had bestowed upon me a place by her side—a place allowing me to explore my talents to their fullest while also retaining the presence of my brother. She even granted me a title.

Though Kanzeo's absence had terrified me when I learned of it, his choice to search for the Potentates was well made. Not only had he freed us but all of Ehaya and thus Nademan herself. His plea to our Honor Kyros had persuaded the Quest to accelerate their plans; he was almost as much the cause of our salvation as our Rulers themselves.

In return, all he wanted was the affection I no longer knew how to give.

But I was determined to learn, and the Quest and their inner circle were replete with wonderful examples.

Disregarding my discomfort, I raised one of his hands to my lips and kissed it—prompting another contented sigh—before returning to my work.

Although my Grace had originally asked me to help organize her forces, once the marquis of Ehaya exposed my identity, the

Quest's troops became decidedly more resistant to following my orders. They obeyed because my Grace had spoken for me, and they did not threaten me... but it was not optimal for operational excellence. Consequently, my Grace commanded me to complete an equally urgent task: decoding the enemy's papers, both the sheafs Prince Eligeo had brought with such risk and the boxes the Quest had recovered during their reconquest.

I had only once enjoyed myself more...

"Inase Enarias," Prince Darian said, slowing his horse to ride alongside me, "how goes your process?"

I considered my notes on the similarities. "I have nearly finished forming an analysis of the patterns. I now look for either an uncoded portion or a match in writing style from among my own papers."

He nodded and offered me a wry smile, an odd expression on a face only slightly less impassive than my own. "I believe you will have invented a new discipline by the time you achieve success."

Knowing the value of any praise from him, I bowed my head. "Gratitude to the Almighty."

"Gratitude indeed," he replied.

The muffled thuds of more hoof-steps on soft earth melded with our horses' as my Grace joined us. *For what are we now grateful?* she asked lightly in Prince Beres' link.

Though an answer was what etiquette demanded, the prince and I remained silent as we examined her face.

She appeared even more miserable than she had yesterday: her cheeks were almost bloodless, pale with apprehension, and the bruises around her bloodshot eyes, formed by a month of near endless tears, seemed more swollen than ever...

My Grace pushed her lips up into something resembling a smile. *Reuniting with Elian, Arista, and Kyros will help. They promised to share even more of my tasks.*

Prince Darian and I exchanged a skeptical glance. My Grace bore the demands of ruling an entire nation with greater ease than most had in wielding simple knives. She was born and blessed for these duties; their weight was not what ruined her health.

My Grace exhaled quietly but said nothing further as, after a thousand miles of journey, our destination finally came within view: the Makirani tree-town of Natrisso, located mere miles from the place where the Gouge had perished and chosen as the new seat of Nademan's crown during my Lord's convalescence. The sight brought little relief to any of us, and least of all to her.

Prince Darian straightened. "My Grace, your orders?"

She gave a list of specifications for the permanent campsite.

The prince bowed from his saddle. Upon the relayed instructions, the third, fourth, and fifth companies left our columns to set up a permanent camp, while the first and second formed a defensive perimeter—my Grace and Prince Darian trusted my information on the possibility of hidden enemy squads still roaming the forest.

The core of the entourage, my Lord's family and specifically chosen vassals, continued directly to Natrisso.

At the base of the first tree (rather short at seventy-five feet), I tucked away my materials, handed my reins to one of the town's loyal folk, and dismounted before helping Kanzeo do the same.

As I steadied him on the ground, my brother yawned and cupped his mouth. His eyes widened at something over my shoulder. Then he ran from my side to a figure in midnight blue hugging my Grace in welcome.

My Honor Kyros the Exemplar of Strength.

Though more careworn than when he had given me his sigil, as marked with misery as our Grace, he was smiling, beige face shining and gray eyes aglow, ash-blond curls tucked beneath his cap and beard neatly combed. Dazzlingly handsome.

At the sound of my brother's footsteps, he turned and, chuckling, held out his arms.

Kanzeo flung himself at him, and my Honor caught him, spun him around, and whispered in his ear.

As beautiful as his face and figure were, far more so were his character, his kindness and compassion, his strength in helping lead a nation in our Lord's absence. He had saved both of us, Kanzeo and me, without a single expectation of gratitude.

Setting my brother on his feet, my Honor Kyros called, "Blessings, Inase Enarias! I am glad to see you! How are you?"

At those words coupled with his actions, my heart, guarded and shriveled though it was, threw itself at his mercy, warming for him as a bolt of pure dedication threaded through my soul.

And, reeling, I stuttered for the first time in my life, "B-blessings, my- my H-Honor. H-how are y-you?" My cheeks glossed, and I ducked my head, having forgotten to answer his question.

His smile remained just as welcoming as it had been when I had first seen him. "I am better now that my Grace has favored our Honors and me with her presence."

I nodded dumbly... and remembered my most urgent task: "I have your pendant, my Honor!" None besides the Potentates could undo the clasp, and our Grace had asked me to keep it for my own protection until their reunion.

Still smiling, he came a few steps closer and raised his hands for the clasp. When I offered it to him, he opened it—without allowing his fingers to touch even a thread of my gown or a single hair.

How can I not be loyal? I wondered dazedly. No one except that violet-eyed boy from long ago had ever treated me with so much dignity.

A corner of Kanzeo's lips slanted upwards, his expression eerily perceptive as he watched me.

"My gratitude, Inase Enarias," my Honor said as he pocketed his pendant. "I have prayed that it served you well." Then, turning, he dipped a second reverence to our Grace. "Please, my Grace, if it is your will."

A mixture of sorrow, excitement, and anxiety glittered in her blue eyes as she smiled and led the way up the ladder into the town, her entourage walking with her.

My brother and I linked hands as we followed, warding each other against our discomfort.

Despite how my Grace, Prince Darian, the two Asfiyan warriors, and Inase bi- Dekecer (who carried the same title as me but whom my Grace called 'Little Brother') included us, we did not belong amid the ranks of the Quest Leader's family. We had no place coming to see my Lord on his sick-bed.

A pace ahead of us, Crown Prince Eligeo, shoulders hunched and scrawny arms tight around himself, seemed to feel much the same way.

And Natrisso's townsfolk appeared intent on ensuring we did not forget it, casting us glares full of loathing with every step.

Yet I felt safe during the long walk across the bridges and platforms and up the ladders. Despite the enmity surrounding me, I had utter faith in my Grace's promises. Such stark difference from the thousands of times I had walked the castle's corridors.

I wonder how their anger can be addressed…

As I pondered that question, my Grace's entourage climbed onto the final platform, the highest one, usually the mayor's home but here the Quest's quarters.

Bowing my head, I waited as my Grace greeted our Honors Elian and Arista and three more of the Quest Leader's guardians. Inase bi-Dekecer enveloped my Honor Elian in a tight, clinging hug.

My Honor Arista, as Kanzeo and I noted in shared glances, seemed much better than we had feared after hearing of the Gouge's defeat: though the channels between her plates were still an unwholesome gray, but her eyes sparkled a brilliant amber, and overall her appearance, despite the marks of grief, was one of health.

Indeed, healthier than Prince Eligeo, Kanzeo, and I still appeared.

My Grace nodded to their bows and, breathing deeply, walked into the hut. The Asfiyan princes and guardians followed on her heels. Leaving my Honors and Inase bi-Dekecer with Prince Eligeo, Kanzeo, and me outside.

Refreshing his smile, my Honor Kyros introduced us, a distinction that made me lightheaded and unsteady on my feet as I curtsied. Particularly because it came from him.

Grinning, my Honor Arista exclaimed, "Finally we meet, Nademile Enarios! I have heard much about both of you from my Grace and my Honor Kyros of Light."

Kanzeo's and my cheeks glossed.

She turned to Prince Eligeo, who resembled a rabbit ready to bolt. Tilting her head, she inspected his face, his heart, perhaps his very soul. "Hmmm... I admit that I was not as inclined as my Grace and Prince Darian-asfiyi to reinstate you. I was not as understanding because of your history, though that will indeed sound hypocritical when you learn of mine. However, I can see what my Lord likely will. You have my utmost confidence as well, Crown Prince Eligeo-nadem."

The prince fumbled a bow and awkwardly mumbled words of gratitude. Then he raised his gaze to my Honor Elian, a heart-breaking desperation in his eyes.

My Honor Elian smiled kindly and embraced the broken man (prompting such relief that it was painful to behold). "How glad I am to see you, Crown Prince Eligeo-nadem. The confirmation you gave my Lord of his suspicions about the Gouge's where-abouts was invaluable." He nodded to Kanzeo and me. "I am pleased to meet you as well, Nademile Enarios. We have prayed long in gratitude for all of you. Though it was not clear at the time, you are the reason for achieving our first triumph within one year of our meeting. May you soon be blessed with your chance to pledge to my Lord."

Though he spoke cheerfully, his smile had faded by the end of the last sentence, as had his family's.

"How I wish he was awake to celebrate this day," my Honor Kyros whispered.

"Our Grace had dearly looked forward to it," Inase bi-Dekecer said sadly, "while you were chasing the enemy."

Kanzeo and I bowed our heads, for they spoke of the anniversary of my Grace's ascension, which was today. And, instead of celebrating their triumph, all she received was the sight of his unconscious face. It was why no one dared to congratulate her.

How I wished I could ease her pain, all of their pain.

How I wished I could ease the burden on my Honor Kyros' shoulders.

Several minutes later, the Asfiyan guardians exited, and Prince Darian called, "Elacir, come! Bring the Nademani with you."

With a bow to my Honors, Inase bi-Dekecer beckoned us inside the hut.

In the main room, Prince Beres lay sprawled with such grief on his face that I could not bear to witness it. His elder son, however, wore a cold composure that rivaled my own, and masked his pain much like mine.

Crossing that room, we entered the larger of the two bedrooms, the noble couple's sleeping quarters.

There upon a bed, my Grace kneeling by his side, lay the Quest Leader.

Despite the bandages stiffening his torso and coating his hand, he seemed peaceful, calm and confident even in repose, a faint smile curving his lips.

His face is familiar...

Kneeling on the Quest Leader's other side, Prince Darian said, "My Lord, I introduce to you Crown Prince Eligeo tej-Shehenna-dem, Inase Tahira Enarias, and Nadeyi Kanzeo Enaries. You wanted to meet all of them..." His cool voice broke, and he pressed a hand to his lips.

My Grace blinked back tears as she adjusted the pendant centered above our Lord's heart.

A pendant, an emerald one, that... yes, it was a twin to my Honor Kyros', but did it not also resemble...

I grasped the emerald that hung beneath my dress at my navel.

As I stroked the round, polished surface, the realization was all too clear.

My Lord possessed that silver-cream skin and sunlight hair and beard I remembered so very well... when he opened his eyes, they would be gold-flecked violet.

Those violet eyes.

The kind eyes that had sustained me for five long years.

The respectful eyes I loved as much as my brother's.

The powerful eyes of the Quest Leader, brighter than the clearing blue sky.

Those closed eyes, the day they would reopen unknown even to my Honor Kyros' foresight.

Stifling a sob, I fell to my knees.

Even as I served my Grace and cared for my brother, my dearest wish had been to find that boy whose brotherly affection had saved me so many times.

I had found him. As he lay on his sick-bed.

How I prayed his eyes would open again.

CHAPTER 30
CONTRIVING UNION

Perspective: Inase Tahira Enarias, confidante of the Quest
Date: Eyyélab, the ninth day of the tenth moon, Thekharre, of the
year 500, C.Q.
Placement: concurrent with Chapter 55 of <u>The Bell Tolling</u>

My Grace tapped the tip of her finger against the edge of her writing desk for emphasis, the sound clear despite the crack of thunder outside. "Every report, particularly of the harvest, thus far indicates that the situation is worse than that for which we had planned."

My Honor Arista frowned. "So, if I understand correctly, between the enemy's burning of supplies and the ominous signs of the worst winter Nademan has faced in fifty years, the whole nation is on the brink of starvation."

Everyone seated in the little circle of chairs and stools, from my Grace to Safira Da'ana Birretís, even my Honor Arista herself, winced at the grim statement.

"And that brink may in turn push our people over the edge," my Honor Kyros replied. "Faneresso will not be the only ones to attach conditions to their loyalty, nor will such towns stay quiet."

Safira Birretís nodded. "From my decade of observation and

aid, I think your interpretation is correct, my Honor. Even your first vassals in Zaiqan may not stay quiet. Famine is far more destructive in Nademan, where half of the towns' food is gathered through trade, not established agriculture and hunting patterns, a consequence of their tendency to switch tree clusters every generation. Though they have not been able to move these last fifteen years, most settled fields have been ruined by drought."

The three Potentates, as well as the guardian herself, glanced at me in what was most likely a request for confirmation, so I interrupted my thoughts and said, "That seems an accurate assessment of our plight. The people truly are loyal—who they needed was a ruler who would act in accordance with her duty, and you have been her, my Rulers. But hunger has a way of blinding the mind to what is otherwise so very clear."

My Grace's lips curved in a sad grimace, her blue eyes glinting with a remembrance of her own history. "Indeed, Tahira."

My Honor Kyros shook his head. "We cannot let the situation deteriorate any further." The compassion in his voice almost brought a smile to my impassive face.

"With what resources?" my Honor Arista asked pointedly. "The sky is cleared and the rainstorms returned, but autumn is here and winter will soon be upon us. Any crops we try to have sown will not mature fast enough to save most of the people. The plains towns are proving resistant to the thought of sharing, as Count Tolmarie predicted, and we can hardly force them to do so. And even if we could, the grain would take weeks to reach most of the towns. We do not have so long, and Arkaiso has only so much food to spare. What other options exist?"

My Honor Kyros pressed his lips together. "What of the northern march? There is enough unforested land south of Icilia's border with the Burning Mountains for a little agriculture."

"As you said, Kyros," my Grace replied, "a little. We can try, but the marquis of Ehaya knows that land best, and he has been mercurial in his willingness to help since I disagreed with him about Inase Enarias and Prince Eligeo-nadem. He did not pledge."

Too accustomed to the reminder of my status as a pariah (not that providing such a reminder was my Grace's intention), I did not flinch. Instead, I mused that the marquis had been unlikely to help anyway. He had acquiesced to the Gouge too many times to have retained any steel in his spine. .

"Yet another plan that cannot work..." My Honor Kyros rubbed his face, pain more than frustration in the gesture. How I wanted to soothe it away...

Judging that my proposal was ready enough, I spoke, "What of hunting in the deep forest?"

The three Potentates and the guardian turned to look at me. "The deep forest, Inase Enarias?" my Honor Kyros asked, his soft gray eyes flicking to my face.

I suppressed a gloss, both at his attention and at the title I treasured as a sign of my Rulers' trust. "By the calculations I remember making as a child, Nademan is comprised of over two million square miles, most of which is forest. Prior to the Blood's conquest, there were one hundred twelve towns alongside the three cities; today, from your reports, there are seventy-eight. Each town and city hunts, at maximum, in a forty-mile radius from its cluster. When totaled, the number is roughly four hundred thousand square miles which are regularly used for hunting."

My Grace tilted her head. "Those numbers indicate that roughly twenty percent of Nademan's total territory is used for hunting." Her eyes gleamed with interest. "Continue, please, Inase Enarias." With a nod, she briefly thanked Safira Hasima Sareneze, who was offering us bowls of stew and plates of bread.

Muttering my own thanks, I dipped my head to my Grace, impressed by how she had divided the numbers without paper or a long pause for thought. "Much of the forest, therefore, is untouched, save for the occasional traveler. That is where I suggest we send your soldiers to hunt, beyond the range of the cities and towns. I do not think that these deeper parts of the forest are in much better condition, but the prey they produce might, even without the aid of established patterns, at least help the people survive this winter, until the land's revitalization results in a greater bounty."

By the conclusion of my proposal, all three Potentates were exchanging excited looks—or, rather, an emotion that vaguely resembled excitement, overshadowed as it was by the misery that clung to them. A misery that each of us shared.

Safira Birretís, however, raised an eyebrow. "Inase Enarias, you yourself proposed after the Battle of Ehaya that the majority of the soldiers be given orders for patrolling the forest. You informed our Grace, with which I agree, that you believe that there are likely still enemy soldiers lurking for the right moment to sabotage the Quest's reconquest." There was nothing in her tone save a respectful politeness.

The Potentates glanced curiously at me.

I appreciated how they always seemed willing to listen to my opinion, without speaking for me. "Indeed," I answered. "But, from our discussion and these reports, the famine is still a greater priority. There is little point to protecting our safety when starvation is so imminent, and these soldiers would be cautious in their attack, considering that they are isolated in what is now enemy territory for *them*. There is a major risk, yes, but it is my thought that we must take it. Your reconquest of Icilia as a whole depends on the people of Nademan being ready for war and being able to provide for your vassals in the other nations by next spring."

"That is very true," my Honor Arista murmured. Then asked, "So you do not believe the soldiers can both patrol and hunt?"

I shook my head. "My Grace's strategy for patrols requires that those soldiers scout every abandoned cluster and scale up and down every one out of five trees. As our Lord's refuge proves, it *is* possible to hide in the Dasenákder without being detected. To prevent this, your soldiers would need to scour the forest. To scour and to hunt as well... with the largest and most nutritious prey being creatures of the forest floor... I do not think your army has both the skill and the time. I fear that many squads would have to choose between bringing back food and ensuring the total safety of the forest. These missions would build skill, yes, which will be key next year, but not quickly enough for such double action."

The three Potentates gave each other faint attempts at smiles, both wry and sad, in remarkable unison. "As he said," my Honor Kyros said quietly, "'our land is trapped in a struggle for her very soul.'"

Those words were astonishingly apt in describing the sense of visceral horror in my heart at the decision confronting us. But I did not understand from where the words had come—none of the books from my childhood and adolescence contained those words—nor did I understand the anguish in their expressions.

Apparently comprehending more than I had, Safira Birretís bowed her head. "Our Lord's wisdom rings forth in every circumstance."

My breath caught. *Those are my Lord's words! Ahhh, that is why they capture the whole of the situation so well.*

"His wisdom," my Honor Arista spoke with tears in her brilliant amber eyes, "is the only guide which can aid us in such a decision.

I bowed my head as well. Though I might propose and Safira Birretís advise, the decisions, with all their weight and sorrow, were the Potentates' and the Potentates' alone.

"Very well," my Grace sighed. "We seem agreed on Inase Enarias' plan—" she waited for all of us to murmur assent— "so let us discuss the distribution of orders..."

I momentarily switched my attention to my brother, who was attentively listening to Prince Darian's lecture. Hands folded beneath his chin, sprawled out on his cushion, he stared up at the prince, his eyes brimming with adoration—and he seemed far more at ease than either Prince Eligeo (who was curled in a ball, a defensive posture, despite the matching adoration in his expression) or me. It gave me hope that, with time, the wounds of his suffering would heal and that he would have a full life in the Quest's service. Such healing did not seem possible for Prince Eligeo and me, each broken in our own ways, but how I dearly prayed it would be so for Kanzeo. He deserved better than I had given him.

"... Inase Enarias?" my Grace spoke my name, concluding a question.

I considered what she had been saying and answered, "I do think your orders should also be relayed to both the messengers and the mayors with your communication spell. It would reassure the towns that you are acting, and it would silence dissent, at least for some time."

My Grace blew out a breath. "Then we will need to split these communications among ourselves. Between the messengers and the mayors, the number of contacts required rises to over one hundred."

My Honor Arista offered her a reassuring look. "Kyros and I will handle most of them, Malika, as soon as your plan is final. Will we not, Kyros?"

My Honor Kyros dipped his head. "As you will, Malika, and as you command, Arista."

How I loved the utter respect in his steady gaze.

"And our gratitude, Inase Enarias," he said, turning to me, "for your well-considered ideas, as always." The warmth on his noble features was dearer to my heart than any treasure could ever be.

So captivated was I by that kindness, which he so generously gave to *me*, that I only returned to myself at the sound of crying.

My Honor Elian's crying.

My Grace, my Honor Arista, and my Honor Kyros tensed, exchanging upset looks, Prince Darian clenched a hand into a fist, and Prince Eligeo seemed on the verge of weeping himself, but no one said anything. No one did anything, knowing how deeply he desired his privacy, save for casting a few sympathetic glances in the direction of the ajar door.

The door that led into the Quest Leader's sickroom.

The sickroom that might be his tomb.

It was a fear that all of us felt and that none of us could escape.

Though my face was blank, my emotionless façade firmly in place, I felt the same tears prickling my eyes that were spilling down my Honor Elian's cheeks.

For I feared I had found the violet-eyed boy who had been my savior long before I knew his name only to lose him entirely.

I could only imagine how much more profoundly the Potentates and his family hurt. But no one but our Lord himself knew the answer as to when he would wake... *if* he would ever wake...

My Honor Elian's sobs grew in intensity, a lament of grief that somehow sounded musical despite the heart-wrenching pain within it.

Anguish ladened every expression, but still we did nothing, desperately trying to continue with our duties.

Is this what the future holds? I wondered, a worse agony scalding through my heart and soul than anything the Gouge had ever inflicted. *Is this what will happen to us? Our struggling to continue the reconquest for his sake despite his absence? Oh Almighty, is this all the time we were allowed to have with him?* A single tear escaped my control and rolled down my cheek. *I did not even have the chance to apologize for what I have done to his trust.*

My Honor Elian uttered a wail like he was falling to pieces, and the agony of that sound seemed to tear through the rest of us as well.

Then...

In Prince Beres' links...

Lucian is waking!

At my Honor Elian's scream, books, papers, and plates crashed to the floor as everyone leapt to their feet, and the Potentates, the Asfiyan princes, Elacir, and the guardians all scrambled into our Lord's room, terrified excitement ruling their expressions.

Only Kanzeo, Prince Eligeo, and I remained behind.

As much as I wanted to follow them, I quietly closed the door. It was a private family moment, and it was not our place to intrude.

But, oh, how I wanted to see him...

"Do you think we might get to see him?" Kanzeo chirped, breaking the charged silence. "They *did* let us come see him when we arrived, so maybe they might include us again." He grinned sweetly up at me, eyes a warm blue, and tossed his arms around my waist. "I love you, Tahira!"

I stiffly returned the embrace and patted his back. "I love you, Kanzeo," I managed, the words just as difficult as before.

He squeezed me, seeming delighted, and then tilted his head back. "So, do you think they will let us, Sister?"

I did not know how to answer. I could not see why they would. Maybe Kanzeo, for my Grace had said our Lord was fond of him, and Prince Eligeo, considering the Potentates seemed agreed that they would present him as a candidate for Nademan's future monarch, but not me. My sins were too great.

Perhaps I would be blessed with a glimpse of him from afar.

If he did not send me away in disgust.

"Tahira?" Kanzeo asked, worried now.

I forced a smile, determined to worry him as little as possible. "They will surely allow you a chance."

A solemn expression creased his features, one that seemed strange on the face of a boy of fourteen years who still demanded hugs and kisses like a very small child. "Our Rulers really do care about you, Sister," he whispered, then turned and called over his shoulder, "and they really do care about you, too, your Highness!"

From the corner of the room into which he had retreated, Prince Eligeo jolted, flashing a startled look at my little brother.

Then, noticing my gaze, he seemed to withdraw deeper into himself. He did not even respond to Kanzeo.

I crinkled my brow slightly. My reverence for the Potentates' decisions, and particularly for my Honor Elian's bold choice, had transformed my distaste for the crown prince into a slowly burgeoning respect... but I still could not understand how he would be able to bear the weight of Nademan's crown, as the Potentates seemed to want. Though newly freed herself, Nademan was soon to enter a nearly endless war in the Quest's service. That seemed too much for Prince Eligeo's shattered spirit.

Yet, as Count Tolmarie had so well explained (I had listened to his countess' report alongside our Grace), he was the only choice for my nation's monarch. The only choice, so we would have to trust our Lord.

Our Lord, who was awake and recovering, if the sounds of exultant joy from his room were any indication.

Suddenly overcome with longing, I tightened my arms around Kanzeo and bent to press my face into the side of his head.

He sighed happily and melted into me.

I exhaled quietly, letting myself savor his sweet, still child-like scent. As the apathy the Gouge had forced on me thawed, it was so wonderful to no longer need to strangle my yearning for affection...

The door swung open just as I stepped back.

Through the crack between the door and the frame, there was revealed the form of a man wreathed in light, seated upright, his silver-cream face crowned by sunlight curls so neatly arranged beneath a cap that it did not seem as though he had just woken. His eyes were the gold-flecked violet of my long-distant memories.

He was elegantly raising a flask to his lips as those eyes touched my face.

Then Safira Sareneze stepped out and closed the door, then walked toward the tiny kitchen.

My pulse pounded in my ears like the beats of a drum... for it was *him*. I had known it, yes, but to see those eyes...

Though I knew Safira Sareneze was gathering a meal for our Lord, I could not move. I only distantly noticed my brother's concerned questions and Prince Eligeo's standing to help the guardian.

Oh Almighty, may he have enough mercy for me that no disgust dims his gaze...

Just as I proffered this prayer, gripping the emerald pendant hanging beneath my dress, the door opened again...

And General Palanéze, standing in the doorway, spoke, "Inase Enarias, Nadeyi Enaries, our Lord asks for your attendance."

Kanzeo squealed, quietly, with excitement, but all I could do was nod.

Then follow her into his room...

It did not seem a good omen that everyone, from my Grace and my Honor Kyros to Prince Darian, was fidgeting.

Still numb, I curtsied, deeply, and stood quietly, head bowed, beside my brother as our Grace began to recite the introduction.

There was such an uproar in my mind that I could not even focus on the honor of my Grace *herself* introducing us to our Lord... it was a clear statement of value and trust—even royalty would rarely receive such honor in the Quest of Light's court— but I could hardly process the moment! For his gaze was on me, piercing through to my soul, seeing the stain of my sins and the corruption of my treason...

In the upper edge of my vision, as my Grace completed the introduction, a slow smile began to curl my Lord's lips... a pleased smile that held all the newly restored light of the sun, breathtaking with grandeur, full of a satisfaction that seemed oddly like what I felt when a plan came to fruition...

Leaning back into his cushion, my Lord spoke, "Blessings, Sister. The Almighty has finally reunited us."

Sister?

Sister?

Sister!

Those words, echoing in my ears... were not what I expected.

To not only acknowledge our history but to repeat that endearment...

Almost heedless of the rest of his family's exclamations and my brother's awe, I fell to my knees. "So... I truly did meet you?"

My Lord chuckled as his guardian set a bowl in his lap. "Indeed, yes." Then, casting an amused look at his companions, he began to narrate the story of how we had met.

He remembered it just as clearly as I did.

He had not forgotten me.

He had not forgotten me.

He had not forgotten me.

From my initial reaction to our conversation to the unspoken promise of his return and the emerald, he remembered our meeting as I did, and it seemed to have meant much to him, which was comforting for it had meant the world to me...

And, somehow, what he had learned of me since had not tainted those memories...

As he completed the story, his beautiful smile dimmed. "How I wish you had not suffered such tragedy between that meeting and this one, my Sister."

The utter, heartfelt sincerity of those words pierced my heart as keenly as his gaze. He expressed sorrow for my pain, but... "I wish I had not betrayed your confidence, and all the ethics we discussed," I whispered, unable, for once, to suppress my grief. How deeply I did not deserve his kind regard...

Kanzeo shuffled closer to me and hugged my shoulders, but, for once, his touch did nothing to content me. In that moment, all the burden of the last five years weighed so greatly upon my soul that I feared I would be crushed to pieces beneath it. There could never be redemption for me.

But my Lord shook his head. "Tahira, you did not betray me. Indeed, as Malika said, you have my gratitude for what you have done for us." Amusement sparked on his shining face. "I promised you that someday I would come for you. But, rather, it is you who came for me. And, as I did then, I welcome you to my family."

For a moment, I could only stare. *He alone knows just how grotesque my sins are... yet he, the Lord of Icilia, does not despise me. Indeed, he... loves me. He* loves *me. And... by saying that I came for him, is he not saying that I* saved *him? That my service was valuable and that he accepts it wholly? And, and, he wants* me *to be part of his family? His blessed and sacred family? He actually* wants *me as a sister?* The relief and untarnished joy brimming in my heart at this realization was equal only to what I had known when my Grace reunited me with my brother.

So, my heart melting like ice drenched by the rays of the sun, I let the smile building within me free, allowing it to curl my lips in the widest expression of joy I had given since he and I had met all those years ago, permitting the pure happiness of it to relax the stiffness of my posture and soothe away years of pain, anguish, and apathy.

His violet eyes sparkled as he observed this change.

Around us, my brother exhaled a sigh of unspoiled bliss, and my Lord's companions exchanged truly excited glances, these unsullied by sorrow.

"So, Malika, Elian, Kyros, we have a new sis—" my Honor Arista began.

As her lips formed the word, a bolt of unmitigated terror shocked me like a burst of lightning. *I do* not *want my Honor Kyros to see me as his sister!*

Before I could react, my Lord cut sharply across her words: "No. Not your sister, my companions. Only mine."

"What?" the Potentates gasped.

"What do you mean?" my Honor Kyros added, confused (how I wished he was not, but it was only to be expected).

"Inase Enarias has our names, as does her younger brother," my Lord stated, "but only I will call her Sister, should it please her."

Once more, I could hardly comprehend the words. Permission to use his name—that was an honor that not even Count Tolmarie had—so to receive it for both Kanzeo and me... but, even more than that, his insistence on the exclusivity of the address of Sister meant... it meant...

It meant he *approved* of my blossoming affections for his companion. He knew how I felt about my Honor Kyros and *approved*. And that meant that, if *Kyros* was willing, I could try to court him. Actually court him!

My heart full of gratitude, my relief and joy restored, I bowed my head and answered, "There is no greater blessing." Then I nudged my star-stricken little brother, prompting him to repeat the words.

"Excellent," my Lord said, placing aside the bowl he had somehow emptied amid his narration. "Now, come, tell me of these strategies you have designed."

Once again touching the emerald that had so long anchored his memory in my mind, I dazedly rose, walked a few paces to where Prince Darian beckoned me, and knelt beside him, opposite my Honor Elian and my Honor Kyros. Kanzeo joined them, immediately snuggling up to his hero.

My Lord—no, my Brother, *Lucian*—smiled at me, an invitation to begin.

I composed my thoughts and started to speak of how I had manipulated the Gouge's strategies and planned for my Lord's reconquest.

As I did, I looked up into his shining face.

Those violet eyes assured me that I had finally found him and that his brotherly affection had not faded. Nor would it ever. Indeed, though the secret was as yet only between his eyes and mine, he was willing to entrust his own divine-bonded brother's heart to me. Just as he was willing to embrace my blood-born brother as his own.

How the Almighty had blessed me with the honor of receiving his gaze.

CHAPTER 31
CHOOSE THE DESPISED

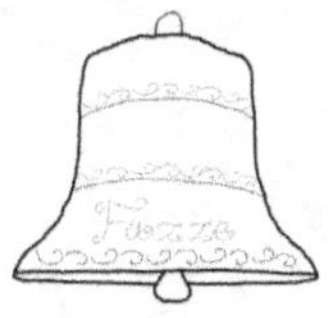  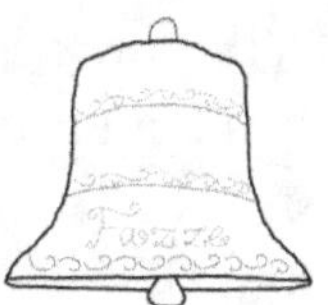

Perspective: Honored Elian the Exemplar of Esteem
Date: Eyyélab, the ninth day of the tenth moon, Thekharre, of the year 500, C.Q.
Placement: between Chapter 55 and Chapter 56 of <u>The Bell Tolling</u>

Though the discussion affected me as well, for the decisions were made in my name alongside the rest of the Quest's, I kept most of my concentration on the swirl of my magic. Eight hours had passed since Lucian's waking, but I was only now sure that his body would be able to accept my healing. His recovery was truly miraculous, particularly in its speed, but only now had it proceeded so far.

My ungloved hands pressing gently against the cool skin of the side of his chest, under his midnight blue robes and the blanket covering his form to his shoulders, I trickled more power into one rib and winced as a wave of pain rolled over Lucian. So deeply connected to him as I was through my healing, I felt everything he did, his body made almost my own by the magic.

Nothing of that pain showed on his face, however. Smiling with evident approval, he was listening to Malika's, Darian's,

Tahira's, and the guardians' report on the movements of his forces as though nothing physically troubled him.

Such absolute discipline was not something I could manage as the agony searing through his body worsened the pain pulsing through my own wings.

I carefully set one rib fragment to healing, slowly threading it through the torn flesh.

Just as I finished with it, the rim of a cup of water appeared at my lips.

"Drink, Elian," Kyros prodded.

I sipped at the cool liquid, thankful for the refreshment. I had only started an hour ago, but already the strain was fraying at my nerves. At least I had had the sense to rest my elbows on the edge of the bed and place my knees on a pillow so that I could maintain my position for as long as I would need.

"Elian," Kyros whispered, crouching beside where I knelt at Lucian's bedside, "if it is in accordance with your judgment, would you answer a question?"

I nodded, startled, despite the pain, by the reverence in my brother's voice. I might have been the one between us who wore our Honored King Naret the Exemplar of Love's crown and ring, but he possessed magical maturity and I did not. He had no need to revere *me*.

Kyros rested a hand on my shoulder. "In the weeks since we reunited on the march to Ehaya, I have watched you heal even broken bones and organ tears with no more than an hour's effort each time. But, from what I sense of your catalysis and your use of power, you are preparing for a much longer endeavor. What is... what is the reason for that?" There was a note of fear in his rumbling voice with which I was only too familiar.

I sighed. "His bones, Kyros," I spoke in a low voice, "were more than fractured—in places the ribs are fragmented into multiple pieces, and, between the battle and our movement of him to Natrisso, some of those fragments have moved. It is truly the Almighty's miracle that none of the pieces have pierced his lungs. Particularly because I could not return them to their places while he was unconscious. And additionally I am worried that his unconsciousness may still have lingering effects on how well his body can accept my magic. It is better, and less painful, to be careful." Less painful for Lucian, I meant—I usually performed healings quickly precisely because the extended period of connection exacerbated my own suffering.

Kyros exhaled a heavy breath. "That is quite frightening," he murmured. Then he pressed a fatherly kiss to the side of my face. "We are blessed to have you, Elian, my Brother." He gave a gentle squeeze of my shoulder, before he stood and stepped back to Malika's side, a few paces to my left, at Lucian's right hand.

I ducked my head to hide a shy smile as my scales flared. A year had passed, but I had not forgotten how incredible it was to have anyone at all care for me. *I* was the one blessed.

Beneath the cool but severely bruised skin that my fingers touched, another fragment shifted into the proper alignment, and more of the internal sores closed. Kyros' benediction, for certain, aiding my magic.

Biting my lower lip, I focused on the next fragment. If I moved it just so, one rib would be almost complete...

"Elian?"

I jolted but kept my hands and my magic steady with the aid of both instinct and practice. "Yes, Malika?" I replied.

"I beg your pardon for disturbing you," Malika said and waited until I nodded my understanding to continue, "Lucian, Arista, Kyros, and I are in agreement that we should shift the soldiers' focus from patrols to hunting in the deep forest. All that remains is your choice. If it pleases you, would you give your own opinion of this plan?"

I decreased the flow of my healing magic and considered the matter. Pressing my lips together, I answered, "Could we, perhaps, ask them to do a bit more than just hunting? Maybe dig burrows for rabbits as well on their way? I tried it during one summer and found much more to hunt and eat closer to my hut in the autumn. Rabbits breed very quickly."

Some whispering occurred around me, and a word, "sustainable," lingered on the air.

Then Malika returned, "We will include it. Would you have any other recommendations?"

My scales flared at the note of admiration in her beautiful voice—a voice *I* had been blessed enough to help her regain. "N-no," I squeaked.

"Then do you give your approval, Elian?" she asked.

"Yes, Malika," I managed to utter.

"Excellent," she said. "Then, if it would be in accordance with your wishes, my Lord, Arista, Kyros, and I will inform the mayors, the captains, and the messengers."

"With my favor, Malika," Lucian said warmly. "It is a well-designed plan, and I am pleased. We will need to arrange for more resources soon, as the land is still recovering and will provide less and less bounty as winter begins, but I pray it will last the people until then and form the foundations of prosperity in the coming years."

Glancing up, I smiled at how Malika, Arista, Kyros, Darian, the guardians, and even Tahira were beaming, overcome with delight at his approval.

It was so wonderful to see all of my family so happy. Especially Malika. She had been sorrowful for too long, and too long had we been deprived of Lucian's beneficence. It was so wonderful to listen to his voice alongside hers.

Letting the adoring smile pulling at my lips spread across them, I concentrated again on my task and finished assembling one rib. A bit more magic held the bone in place and nudged it to continue healing. Then I switched to the nerves, blood vessels, and various tissues. The stings and pricks of connecting them were too much like my feathers being yanked out.

I winced, shuddering at how much it hurt, but, though it was *his* pain and though I knew from my magic that he felt it, Lucian did not react at all as he listened to more reports.

Once the flesh seemed as healthful as magic could render it, I moved to the next rib.

Three more left... then his collarbone and his hand...

Even amid the strenuous work and the endless pain, I could not help but note how Lucian's skin did not warm. My hands were hot, the thin scales filming the sides of my palms like chips of flame against sunbathed rock, but the cold of his skin was reminiscent of freshly fallen snow and far less meltable.

It must be a quality of the Muthaarim, Lucian's kind, I thought, *which he shares only with the Shining Guide's original people and the first Quest. Prince Beres' skin heated after a while when he let me heal those injuries in the moon of Kadsaffe.* I bit my lower lip again. *It is so difficult to tell if there is infection or inflammation here... Oh Almighty, I beg of You succor...*

Sometime later, after I had painstakingly rebuilt two more ribs and solidified the flesh around them, a soothing, blessed hand briefly touched my shoulder.

I slowed the flow of my magic to a trickle and looked up again.

Lucian smiled at me and flicked his gaze toward Malika.

I turned my attention to her.

"If you would allow, our family," Malika was saying, "Elian, Arista, Kyros, and I will seek our Lord's wishes on this matter and return to you with his choice."

I blinked, my tiring mind not able to grasp the meaning of the formal words.

Perhaps noticing my confusion, Arista bent slightly and whispered in my ear, "Malika is respectfully asking everyone to leave so we can discuss who Nademan's next monarch should be."

Oh. I nodded in understanding. Our family surely understood that this was a decision for the Quest alone, but, because they had essentially helped rule Nademan during Lucian's convalescence, it was only proper to use such deeply deferential words.

Without raising a single question, Darian, the guardians, and Tahira quickly dipped reverences and slipped out the door, closing it behind them.

It was the first time the five of us had been alone since our lesson on the Quest's lore in Arkaiso, the day before my birthday.

More than four months since we had been alone together, all five of us physically present.

As much as I loved the rest of our family and our vassals, how I had missed those moments encircled by the presence of the ones who held my heart...

The same contented smile that curved my lips dawned on Lucian's, Malika's, Arista's, and Kyros' beloved, sacred faces as a warmth swirled among us, one laden with the impression of secrets whispered and quiet smiles shared... Soft chuckles, shrieking sobs lightened by kindness, the sweet taste of a free breath, the perfume of incense and roses, the bright flashes of shining eyes giving me all of their attention... The feel of the greatest security I had ever known. The greatest blessing in the world, which the Almighty had deigned to bestow upon my lowly self.

"How has only one year passed?" Arista breathed, speaking aloud my own thoughts. "It is as though you have always been a part of me." Her dark amber eyes brimmed with an affection made desperate by grief as she wrapped her arms around my neck. "I never want to be without you."

Overwhelmed by the comfort of her strong grip, I pressed my bearded chin down over her forearm and leaned my cheek into her touch, softly kissing her sleeve. "I missed you when we were apart," I mumbled, daring to speak what was truly in my heart. The slight brush of her form against my already-irate wings poured streams of fiery agony down my back, but I did not care. I could suffer at other times, but every second with my sister was a treasure and any comfort I could offer amid her grief was an honor.

Arista tightened her hold on me, and Kyros lightly clasped my upper arm. "I missed you, too, Elian," he said affectionately, his rumbling voice caressing my name.

"The days were long without you," Lucian added quietly, cupping my other cheek above my beard with the tips of his elegant fingers and, in one touch, dispelling all of my pain, anxiety, exhaustion, and physical stress. "I prayed every night for your health and happiness."

My heart soared as my body could not at their words, overwhelmed by a sense of utter wellbeing. And then the best came:

"I thought of you always, Elian," Malika confided, leaning toward me with a warm smile, her words all the sweeter because they were now spoken *aloud*. "How I prayed that the Almighty would soon reunite us, my friend."

It was one of the best moments of my life. Embittered only by the secrets I still kept and the trust I still withheld. If only I could be sure that my parentage and my curse would not steal a future full of such moments from me!

His thumb gently stroking the cluster of warm, glowing gold scales on the ridge of my cheekbone, Lucian pierced my gaze with his.

The physical connection forged between us by my healing magic became suddenly one of our souls.

And for just one moment, it was the eternity of my pledge once more, my very being resonating in tune with his—

The pressure abruptly faded as Lucian removed his gaze from mine and glanced at Malika. "Speak your question, my Sister," he said.

She grinned, blue eyes sparkling with enthusiasm. "If it would be in accordance with your wishes, I beg that you reveal to us your choice for Nademan's future monarch." Formal words, yet full of sweetness and affection as only my family could make them.

He smiled back at her, violet eyes twinkling. "It is my wish to know your opinions." His gaze swept over Arista, Kyros, and me. "All of yours, my Sisters and Brothers."

I squeezed my lips together to suppress a squeak of excitement. How honored I was that the Quest Leader himself wanted to know who I thought should be crowned! That little orphan from Bhalasa could never have dreamed that such exaltation would be possible for him.

"Malika," Arista said with a smirk, leaning most of her slight weight onto my back in the space between my untied wings, "you should speak first."

Malika chuckled and dipped her head. Then, pausing a little to organize her thoughts, she spoke in her divine-blessed voice, "I have always supported choosing Crown Prince Eligeo tej-Shehennadem for Nademan's throne. My reasons are five in number: first, he understands the depth of his people's desperation and torment better than anyone else because he himself has suffered directly beneath the enemy's fist. Whose empathy would be greater than his?

"Second, he has the disposition and essential training for rule. He was eleven years old when Nademan fell—his mind was already firmly set in the ways a monarch must think, and, based upon his actions during the Battle of Ehaya, his instincts are for service, as a crown heir's should be. His heart is ever focused on his duty, much as mine was, despite all I suffered.

"Third, as Arista and Prince Darian both can attest, the prince is intelligent and willing to learn. Though the Gouge broke his ability to read and write, as the Blood did mine, Prince Eligeo has labored day and night and is finally able to pen his own thoughts, instead of merely copying from prepared texts. Yes, we will not be able to ask him to master disciplines at Elian's, Kyros', and my speed, but we can expect him to grasp the basics and to continue his studies in acknowledgment of his limitations even after he is crowned.

"Fourth, restoring his position would ensure that the same royal house remains in power in Nademan, thereby granting stability. By this I do not mean political stability—he is much hated, so his rule will require much effort to strengthen. What I mean is magical stability: by retaining the same bloodline that our

Rulers the Quest of Light established, the connection between the people and Nademan's magic will pass seamlessly to the next generation. And, of course, it would be better to restore our Rulers' works wherever possible instead of creating them anew.

"Finally, Prince Eligeo will be loyal to you and to that which you represent. On the day of the battle, after he delivered the Gouge's papers to me and after the arrival of his siblings, I ordered Taza to test the former royals. At my direction, once I had left the platform, she told them that I had decided to execute them for the sins of their father." Malika exhaled a laugh and shook her head. "Prince Eligeo did not hesitate to accept my decision. He did not even question why I would decide so when Elian and I had already promised him sanctuary.

"Thus, in my lowly opinion, my Lord, Prince Eligeo would truly be the worthiest choice if it would please you to bestow your favor. May all be as you wish."

Upon the conclusion of Malika's argument, there was silence as each of us considered her words.

Then Lucian glanced at Arista. "What is your opinion, Arista, my Sister?"

Arista shrugged (the movement not spilling more pain down my back only because of Lucian's touch) and rested her head on top of mine. "I questioned Malika's support whenever this issue was discussed in the spring and the summer because I suspected that the depth of the shamed king's corruption penetrated deeper than we knew." Despite the casualness of her tone, her words were as weighty as boulders and tinged with the all-too-familiar echo of heartache. "I worried that the prince himself had absorbed some of the mistaken notions of his father, as he was a child old enough to have been trained in his father's ways at the time of Nademan's fall, and I worried that the prince's own torment had corrupted his thoughts, that the pain and fear had broken him into the Gouge's true servant. I have seen both before in Zahacim. But, when I met Prince Eligeo upon Malika's arrival in Natrisso, I used my Quest-gifted magic to assess his heart. He is capable of true freedom, Lucian, as far as it is within my right to know, and I add my voice to Malika's petition."

Malika beamed. Arista was the only one of us who had previously opposed her argument.

Lucian nodded and raised an eyebrow in my direction. "Elian, my Brother?"

My scales flared at the attention. But thankfully my voice was steady as I answered with all the heartfelt sincerity the words required, "I believe in him, Lucian. He should not be blamed for the sins of his father, and he deserves his own chance at fulfilling his promise. It was why I chose as I did, and it is why I now add my voice to Malika's petition." My lips curved down as I dropped my gaze, unable to hold his, a shame burning my heart that even the presence of my family could not fully ease. "I cannot bring myself to truly be ashamed of my choice, and for that I am sorry. I risked your entire reconquest for one man, and I did not even ask you first."

Lucian stroked my cheek again but did not respond, instead glancing up at Kyros. "Kyros, my Brother?"

Not seeming as decided as the rest of us, Kyros sighed and wrung his hands. "I have seen his heart as Arista has, and I agree that he is capable of true freedom. I know you acknowledged his service on the day of the battle, Lucian, and I know he has given every effort to the lessons Malika has arranged for him since the Battle of Ehaya. He is certainly loyal, especially to Elian—" My scales flared at the mention of the prince's obvious and overwhelming adoration for me. "—and he is certainly capable. But... I worry for him. We have been treating him as though he will become king these last months, because of your acknowledgment that day and because we thought to use this time to prepare him, but he still seems... shattered." A fatherly sort of sympathy filled his voice. "He lacks strength, Lucian. He will need more help than only education if you choose to crown him. That poor man needs so much support."

I frowned, troubled by what he was saying. "Kyros is correct, but... is there any other choice?"

"There is Count Ciro Tolmarie," Arista replied, mentioning a man for whom I prayed much in gratitude as she snuggled further against me, enveloping me in the blissful warmth and sweet perfume of her presence, "who is much respected by our army, the province of Zaiqan, and, as the months pass, by the rest of Nademan as well. But I do not think the thought of the throne has even occurred to him. My liege's bond tells me that all he wants is to eventually return home to Jurisso and live peacefully with his wife, his daughters, and his neighbors. He does not have the expansively generous heart required to rule a whole nation."

A small knowing smile curved Lucian's pale lips.

"Countess Belona Tolmariat is another choice," Malika said, "but she has the same desire as her husband. She would not be happy as queen in Ehaya, and her unhappiness would taint her rule." Her lips twisted wryly. "No other mayor or captain has enough skill in ruling for this war-stricken age, so the only other choice is Marquis Foltariet, and he is still upset over our decisions to protect Tahira and Prince Eligeo. Though he has not openly disobeyed me, we have not spoken since he quarreled with Prince Darian and me after the victory speech. Because of both that incident and his impertinence on the morning of the battle, I do not believe he is a worthy choice."

"Also," Arista added, "half of Nademan, particularly those who adore Count Tolmarie, hates him." She chuckled with just as much wryness. "And all of Nademan hates Prince Eligeo. His face is too much like his father's to be easily looked past."

"This is true," I said, speaking to clarify the matter in my own mind yet addressing my words to Lucian, as was our custom, "but your choice is not about who is liked most. It is about who is most worthy, most loyal, and most devoted to this nation. Who will have the determination necessary to uphold the endeavors of providing support for your war and rebuilding the people's lives and hearts." I tilted my cheek slightly into Lucian's hand, carefully avoiding the bandage covering his palm as I savored how the comfort of his touch was liberating me from my usual agony. Without it, I could not have fully enjoyed the peace of Arista's embrace or offered whatever solace I could to her. I had been willing to suffer for it, but the pain would have lingered in my mind and corrupted the purity of my joy. So I prayed in gratitude that Lucian's kindness had saved me from even the possibility of taint without drawing attention to what I still did not dare to reveal.

"Indeed," Malika agreed.

"And only Prince Eligeo fulfills those requirements," Kyros said with another sigh. He folded his hands over his waist. "He needs someone to stand at his side, Lucian, if you choose him. Even his own siblings do not care for him, so he is all alone, save for us."

"I could continue to speak with him through a communication spell after our departure," I offered. "It is something I was already considering asking leave to do."

"Because he adores you, Hally!" Arista teased, the Zahacit word for brother sweet in her beloved voice, then laughed and kissed my cheek.

My scales heated again, both at the affection and because she was right. Elacir cared deeply for me, treating me much the way Kalyca did Kyros, but Prince Eligeo looked at me with stars in his eyes. Not at Lucian, not at Malika, but at *me*. It was overwhelming and embarrassing, but I did not correct him or refuse him the affection and acknowledgment he seemed to crave, for I was unwilling to break his already shattered heart. He needed me, and I was happy to support him.

Kyros shook his head. "It is a worthy idea, Elian, but he needs more. Someone to stand with him every day, who he believes needs him in return."

I had no answer for that. I cared for the prince, already beginning to regard him as another brother, as I did Elacir and Darian (every fear of jealousy between us was now healed by love), but there was little equality between us as Potentate and vassal. And I could not remain in Nademan.

"Indeed, Kyros," Malika said, touching his elbow, "but that is a matter to reserve for a later discussion." Once Kyros nodded, she bowed her head to Lucian. "My Lord, if it is your wish, we would beg the favor of your choice."

The small knowing smile Lucian had worn amid our discussion deepened to a sweeter but narrower curve, the corners of his lips just slightly turned up, the lines framing his mouth and mustache deep creases, the silver of his cheeks a sunlit radiance, and he lowered his gaze to the glint of the ruby ring that adorned the silver-cream hand still resting on my cheek.

Malika, Arista, Kyros, and I waited, entranced by the peaceful joy and the glow of silver on that blessed face, which had been too long silent and dim in repose.

Then Lucian raised his gaze to mine, smiled fully, dazzlingly, and said, "Elian, your choice was the one I prayed you would make."

I startled, the top of my head bumping Arista's chin and my hands shifting slightly on his side before I controlled myself. "Truly?" I breathed

He chuckled softly. "Yes, Brother. Prince Eligeo is a man for whom it is worth risking our reconquest, and he is the one to whom I intend to entrust Nademan after our departure. The Almighty's blessing is upon him."

Like Malika, Arista, and Kyros, I could only stare at him in shock. Yes, we had thought this would be his decision, and all of us besides Kyros had just argued for it, but to know for certain... and for him to say it so simply, so lightly, as though it were only to be expected...

The kind laughter I had so missed during his convalescence rang from his lips. "Malika, Elian, Arista, Kyros, as you yourselves mentioned, I declared my choice when I spoke of gratitude to him during the battle. He understands the importance of our war as no other does, having suffered the very heart of this evil, and his eyes discern most clearly the stark difference between the faithful and the faithless. He is the best choice for the throne, as you yourselves have said. And, Elian, I told you my view of your choice on that first night after we left Ehaya in our pursuit of the Gouge."

There was silence as we stared at him.

Then Malika smiled with wonder bright in her beautiful eyes. "It is one matter to guess at your choice and quite another to listen to you declare that we are in accord."

Lucian arched both brows. "Of course we are in accord, Malika. Your judgment is mine. There is no difference between us. So the Almighty has ordained."

She beamed, blushing a lovely pink.

I smiled at her happiness—those words were the reassurance she had wanted, that she had ruled exactly as he would have—and then expressed my own wonder, "You spoke of it, but I did not understand it then. Your view on my choice, I mean."

Lucian's gaze slid to me, and he chuckled again, seeming pleased as his thumb again stroked my cheek. "Yes, but you did understand what you were choosing when you saved him," he said, his tone light but the timbre of his voice deep, resonant, and rich, "and that has rendered it a choice worthy of your rank and power. A bold choice, a brave choice—the bravest and boldest any of us has made so far, I think."

I gasped, unable to believe what was reaching my ears. "How can that possibly be true? Arista held the Gouge—" even after what he had told her, which I did not mention for her sake— "and you slew him! And Kyros fought most of the soldiers, and Malika ruled Nademan!"

Despite the anguish in her eyes, Arista laughed and, briefly removing my cap, kissed my head. "My choice was not as brave and bold as yours. Nor were Lucian's, Malika's, or Kyros', in truth."

"Indeed," Kyros said, offering me one of his rare, truly bright smiles.

"Certainly," Malika said, smiling as well. "Without a guarantee of how any of us would react, much less our inner circle and our people, you risked your name and your honor for this man because of compassion, justice, and the esteem of incé. That is truly worthy of the Quest, Elian. It is why I championed your choice and why I indicated to Belona that Ciro should do so as well."

"As Malika says," Lucian added. "For the sake of virtue, you risked everything to protect him, and that is a choice that pleases the Almighty, as it does me. The rest of us have only made expected choices, the sort we knew would be praised and would please others, but you have made one that was unexpected, received blame, and displeased an entire people. All for the sake of the Light. And, so, I am proud of you. You are the first of the Quest to show Icilia the meaning of freedom."

All I could do was gaze up into their shining faces in wonder, lips parted, eyes wide, scales brilliant gold, unable to think of any words to say. I had never expected such praise! I had never expected to ever feel such a sense of belonging. I had never expected to ever dare to think that the Almighty's own Chosen might care for me.

My friends laughed and all whispered, "I love you, Elian."

Then, while I still stared, Lucian nodded to Kyros and ordered, "Call the crown prince. Tell him that the Quest wishes to speak with him."

Kyros bowed his head and left the room.

Arista squeezed me once more and kissed my cheek, then stepped back to Malika's side.

Shaking myself, I returned my attention to my magic, intending to tie off the healing for now, like thread in sewing a seam, and return to it once Lucian would allow more.

Only to find that, somehow, amid the Quest's discussion, the last rib had been fully assembled and the flesh around it stabilized. Even the pieces of his collarbone were knitted together and healed. Even the deep, nerve-damaging cut on his palm. Not a single blood vessel or nerve or tissue connection was out of place. The bones, muscles, and ligaments were even strong, as though already fast on their way to regaining their previous vitality.

After forty-nine days, Lucian was fully healed. And, like his waking, it was truly miraculous.

Lucian stroked my cheek once more and, bending as he could not before, whispered in my ear, "Do you not know, my beloved Brother, that your touch itself is my cure?" He pressed his lips to my forehead, atop the centermost cluster of gold scales just beneath the edge of my midnight blue cap. "I pray to the Almighty in gratitude for your love, for all the health I have is your gift to me."

My scales flaring so brightly that the glow edged my vision, too stunned to muster words to speak, I dipped my head, removed my hands, and smoothed down his clothes and blanket. When Arista finished retying my wings, I rose to my feet and walked with her to our places at his left hand.

That was where I was standing when Prince Eligeo entered.

His hands shook where they were clenched over his waist as he tried desperately not to cower, and the first face to which he looked was mine. Only once I smiled at him did he seem to remember himself enough to bow to Lucian.

Lucian inclined his head and smiled in his lordly way. "Crown Prince Eligeo tej-Shehennadem," he said, his tone warm, "in the Almighty's name, the Quest has chosen you to sit upon the Throne of Conscience as Nademan's next monarch. Will you accept this duty with the whole of your heart and soul and in love of the Almighty and loyalty to the Quest?"

Before my very eyes, the prince somehow composed himself, inhaling deeply and straightening, his posture becoming as regal as we could hope. Elegantly he bowed and answered, "As you wish, my Lord. It would be my honor to serve Nademan in this way."

Malika, Arista, and I exchanged triumphant glances, and Kyros wore an expression of pride.

We had truly chosen well. As I had chosen well that day.

Remembering again how Lucian had supported my choice, I beamed as I watched Prince Eligeo kiss Lucian's hand and listen intently as Malika explained what was now required of him, his eyes full of the quiet fire only duty and devotion could bring.

The crown prince truly was worthy of Nademan's throne, and I was glad to have protected him.

This bold and brave choice I had made, this demonstration of virtue that brought the first light of freedom to Icilia's darkness, was entirely because of Lucian's grace.

CHAPTER 32
INTENDING HONOR

Perspective: Crown Prince Eligeo tej-Shehennadem, Heir-apparent to Nademan
Date: Eyyélab, the sixteenth day of the tenth moon, Thekharre, of the year 500, C.Q.
Placement: concurrent with Chapter 56 and, partially, Chapter 57 of The Bell Tolling

Tossing aside my cap, I twisted my fingers in the newly trimmed strands of my hair and slammed both elbows on the writing desk's low top. The words scrawled on the page blurred as I blinked back tears.

Too stupid, piteous little prince, too stupid...

The Gouge's voice, haunting me from beyond the grave, dripped poison in my ears that seemed more real than any assurance my saviors had provided...

Isn't that why you lost your right to rule? Because you were too stupid to protect your people? You'll always be too stupid, Eligeo.

Cowering in my chair, I hid my face in my hands and tried to ignore the voice. But, after so many years of torment at his hands, death did not prevent him from being a part of me, a disease I would never be rid of...

Don't think there is any way out of this trap—and even if there was, you'll never find it! Always too stupid...

Tears spilled down my cheeks, as they seemed to keep doing at even the slightest upset, though I was now safe, nourished, and loved.

Yes, loved, as hard as that was to believe. Even a broken heart like mine could not mistake the expressions of affection the Potentates often bestowed upon me: my Honor Arista's lessons on ruling and writing, my Honor Kyros' attempts to find clothing that fit my frame, my Grace's involvement of my opinion in the new governance of my nation, my Honor Elian's quiet questions about my health... my Lord's decision to place Nademan's crown on my head... these were not casual actions, the careless gestures of fickle hearts. No, the Potentates truly cared for me. They had not merely deigned to not cast me aside but had instead championed me.

Even at the expense of their promise.

My mind was not so far gone that I had not come to understand the weight of what my Honor Elian had done when he offered me sanctuary.

My name, as I well knew, was one that the people of Nademan cursed every morning and every night—the speaking of ill wishes toward my father and me was almost as much of a daily ritual as praying for the Quest's coming, and the years that had passed since my father's treason had only heightened that hatred. With every day, my people were newly reminded of what might have been different, what cruelties might have been avoided and what joys retained, if only he had not neglected the whole of his duty. And I, as the heir of both his throne and his blood, as well as his face, carried all the weight of their blame.

That blame was what had made my Honor Elian's choice so full of risk. Though his own soldiers, the men and women who had fought for months beneath his command, bowed at his decision, the rest of the Quest's soldiers had grumbled. Exchanging looks and mutters of complaint, they simmered with discontent, displeased with our Honor's decision but unwilling to speak openly of their anger for respect of the Potentates whom they served. But, though the soldiers were relatively quiet about their disagreement and quickly abandoned it, the city-folk had raised a furor, demanding at the very least a public disavowal and preferably my execution. And the people of Nademan were certain to be just as upset.

From what my Honor Elian had said to me since that day, he had been well aware of the people's anger in those moments. Yet he had not allowed it to rule his decision, instead choosing so smoothly that it did not feel like a choice.

"I chose to protect you, Prince Eligeo," he had declared only yesterday, in response to my doubt-filled questions, "because I understood something of your pain. My heart knew compassion for your circumstance, and my soul knew that shielding you was just and abandoning you was not. Just as I knew compassion for our people and could not ignore the reasons for their rancor. I chose in accordance with what would best form balance. And as my Lord stated both that night and since his waking, my choice was the one that fulfilled the esteem of incé and respected the rights and dignity that belong to all of us. I would not have regretted it even if the people of Nademan had abandoned my Lord because of it, nor would have he himself. The Quest truly is with you, Prince Eligeo; please do not doubt us!"

How could I doubt anything when I looked up into the divine face that had been my salvation?

But, away from the comfort of his presence, I could not escape those doubts.

Those doubts were not trifling.

The people of Nademan—my people, the people my Lord wished me to rule—hated me. They blamed me in the place of my father for the sins he had committed, and the dishonor of his name and face blackened my own. Even though they loved the Quest, how could my people ever feel anything other than hatred for me?

They were not wrong to hate me.

I had lived fifteen years past the murder of my father, as his heir the regent of Nademan even uncrowned, and I had done *nothing* for them. I had done nothing to fulfill the duty that was the sole purpose for which I was born... Until my Lord's coming. And what I had done then, bringing papers and news of the Gouge's movements, was nothing compared to the weight of my unfulfilled duty.

How would I ever be able to fulfill it?

I was... without question... a broken man. My mind quavered beneath the burden of my torment, my heart overflowed with misery, my soul was heavy with sin, and my body was racked by the lingering effects of fifteen years of hunger and the terrible, *intrusive* injuries the Gouge had wreaked upon me. Even with safety, nourishment, and love, I might never fully recover. The damage went too deep. So how could I ever rule? How could I give enough of myself to my people to care for them as duty required when there was not enough to give?

Why would my Lord wish to entrust his reconquest to such a man?

My lips spread wide with pain, and I shook my head, a fear greater than anything conjury had ever inflicted rising in my heart: that he would regret that wish. He would regret ever thinking I was worthy of rule.

And my Honor Elian would regret ever having shielded me.

That thought hurt worse than anything I had ever suffered.

At least my people will see their desire granted when that comes to pass, I thought wretchedly. *I will not survive my Honor's affection turning to dislike. It would have been less painful to die at the monster's hands than to perish in the Quest's disapproval. But that is the only future I can have.* The edge of the precious pages I had wasted caught my gaze. *Well, that is presuming I can even write this pledge. Otherwise I will not have even this much chance to try to serve them. I will fail at the first task my Lord set me by rendering myself truly ineligible to be considered for the office of crown heir.*

The pledge for crown heirs was not like other pledges: from the Potentates to citizens without rank, all proffered loyalty through scripts designed by the Quest of Light and bound by the receiving liege's magic, without change or variation save what each office required. Such was the law—except in the matter of crown heirs. Each crown heir, as the Quests' custom dictated, because of the immensity of what ruling meant, especially for those without the divine favor of the Quests, was required to write his or her own pledge—a pledge that was supposed to be original, unique, eloquent, and written without help (save by one's spouse, if one was married). It was not idle custom—all prior accomplishments and existent qualities were weighed equally with the pledge, and it was possible for even heirs-apparent to be rejected if their pledges were inadequate. And, according to the lore, it was not even the monarch who wholly decided this but the nation herself.

Whatever I wrote for my pledge would be judged by Mother Nademan herself. By the Quest Leader himself. Indeed, by the Almighty!

It was guaranteed that I would fail.

I sighed and rubbed a hand over the coarse skin of my face. *But my Lord still wishes it, so I must try. I cannot, I simply cannot appear before him in an hour without anything at all. I would embarrass him during the triumphal speech!*

But if I could not write anything in the six days he has given me, how can I write anything in one hour?

Ruined as I was by this question, I almost did not notice the quiet sound of the room's door being opened.

When I realized what I had heard, I leapt to my feet and spun around, arms already crossed over my torso to protect as much of myself as I could.

"My apologies, Prince Eligeo," said a man whom I had rarely heard speak, the Quest Leader's father, Prince Beres sej-Shehasfiyi, "I did not intend to alarm you."

Though his voice was soft, gentle like his every regard of me had been since my Grace had introduced us after the Battle of Ehaya, I still quailed beneath his gaze. He was going to hate me as well after I embarrassed his beloved son.

Prince Beres glanced around the tiny bedchamber, the one assigned to me by my Lord's guardians out of the three this hut boasted. The quarters had actually been intended by the towns-folk for them, but the guardians had, at my Grace's orders, allowed me a room as they had Inase Enarias and her brother. The room was hardly larger than my hole in Ehaya's castle, but I had treated it with respect and kept it clean. That, at least, could not be disappointing to the prince.

Unlike the rest of my unworthy self—

"May I be of assistance in helping you write your pledge?" Prince Beres suddenly spoke.

I startled, jumping a foot in the air, and nearly tipped over my inkwell. "I-I b-beg your p-p-pardon," I stuttered, "but- but- h-how can you h-help m-me?"

The prince nodded as though I had given some sort of wise opinion in a discussion of equals. "It is true that no one can overtly help you. But I remembered that the crown heirs I knew would spend days in the library prior to their pledge. You do not have a library, so, should it please you, I thought I might serve as your reference." His lavender eyes, usually distant and cloudy with grief, glittered with an odd hesitance.

Almost as though my acceptance mattered to him.

Which was absurd. My opinion, good or bad or neutral, mattered to no one. I did not at all merit the address of 'Prince,' particularly from the Potentates and their inner circle.

But, still, I dipped my head and asked him to take a seat on the only other cushion in the room, while I resumed my dreaded place in front of the little writing table.

I deeply admired the prince, the Quest Leader's own father and a powerful magician, and I would not lose the opportunity to spend time in his presence. I wished too much that he would deign to treat me as a son, a distinction too high for me to covet.

Prince Beres elegantly seated himself, each movement so very much like his sons', and met my gaze. "What troubles your ability to form the words you require?" he asked softly.

I took a deep breath and spoke slowly, as my Honor Kyros had taught me, to reduce the stutter that emerged when I was upset, "I do not know what would truly be persuasive enough considering... considering who I am." The shame of my identity felt like it would crush me, a massive tree trunk falling ominously toward my head. "I-I... I cannot see what I can actually do that would matter. I have little to offer my people."

Prince Beres bestowed another thoughtful nod. "It seems," he said in that baritone voice that was so like my Lord's, "that you are thinking as many crown heirs initially do: in terms of plans for your rule."

I blinked. "Yes, your Highness."

"Prince Beres-asfiyi," he lightly corrected, "and, after today, Prince Beres will suffice with the change in your rank." Without waiting for a response—not that I had one—he continued, "From the many pledges I have read and from the few I was privileged enough to observe, I have come to realize that the better pledges are not about what a crown heir plans to do but rather about what the throne means to you. There is a place for announcing plans and declaring visions for your rule, but it is not here. The pledge is much more important than such things, for plans and visions can change with circumstance and so are not a worthy basis for your plea for the nation's trust. What instead truly *is* a worthy basis of consideration is your heart.

"Hearts, Prince Eligeo, do not change—at least, not the core of them. People motivated by greed are always greedy, and those motivated by love of brutality are always cruel, no matter what else may transpire in their lives. The same is true of those driven by wholesome and beautiful things, like love of virtue, the Quest, and the Almighty. Knowing *that* about one's ruler—knowing the core of their hearts—well, Prince Eligeo, the acceptance of your pledge is a commitment to your heart. It is trust that the core of you is worthy of belief, that it will shape your rule well. Thus, I would advise that you know your core and let that be the substance of your pledge."

I exhaled and nodded, frantically trying to process what he was saying. "So," I spoke carefully, "I should look for my core? And write of it?"

He offered me the faint trace of a smile. "Yes, Prince Eligeo."

I fidgeted with my fingers as I racked my mind. *Was* there anything at my core? For so long I had been little more than a hollow, animate shell.

As that thought occurred to me, so did another... *The reason I bowed when my Lord told me the night after his waking that he would make me crown prince, the reason I dipped my head when my Grace and my Honors hinted at it, was because it is a chance to fulfill the duty for which I was born. Is not my lack of fulfillment of that duty, my inability to ever fulfill it, the first and greatest reason I hate myself? My royal duty—that is the only thing that has ever mattered to me, and the Gouge knew it, too.*

Trying to silence the sound of my tormentor's voice, awakened at the mere mention of him, I glanced up at Prince Beres. "Duty," I whispered. "That is my core. I do not deserve it, nor do many believe I should have it, but I am born for it, and I love Nademan with every particle of who I am."

That faded smile bloomed, for a brief, fleeting fragment of a second, into a full smile. "Excellent, Prince Eligeo," he praised, sounding like his exalted son. "Now, if you would allow, one more consideration."

I nodded, dazed by his approval.

"As you well know," he said, "our Rulers the Quest of Light named each of Icilia's nations with what they perceived would forever be the source of salvation for those people, the cure to the excess or deficiency of their most dominant quality. Asfiya's salvation is ever in purity as Nademan's is in..."

"Shame," I murmured, finishing his sentence as he seemed to want. "Conscience."

"Exactly." Another faint smile. "The best pledges I have read or heard showed remembrance of this part of the lore. And I would say that such remembrance is even more important in this age, for it is an age in which the Quests walk amongst us. An age of salvation. Thus, an acknowledgment of Nademan's salvation is only fitting. Particularly because you are the first monarch that our Rulers the Quest of Freedom will crown."

My breathing hitched at the momentousness of his words—I did not deserve such honor, nor was I ready for it—but I nodded again, understanding his point.

An idea began to form in my mind.

Words that were suitably eloquent... that conveyed what I must... that truly reflected what dwelled in the core of my heart and the foundation of my soul.

Turning, I seized my quill and scribbled rapidly across a fresh sheet of paper, paying little attention to grammar or misspellings in my frenzy to simply *write* what my heart and soul knew—

Frantic minutes later, I shook my sleeves down over my ink-spattered hands and offered the page to Prince Beres.

The prince read the words, so very slowly, while I squirmed on my cushion.

Then he lifted his eyes and again—again!—offered me that sweet smile that was so like his son's. "Let me fix your grammatical mistakes. Then memorize it, for it has my approval."

I nearly cheered! My Lord had ordered that his father's approval was all I needed to seek for the ceremony, so this meant I was almost done! At least with the writing.

Exhaling what could possibly have been a laugh, Prince Beres brought out his own quill from a pocket, dipped the nib in the inkwell, and made several careful notes on the paper in his neat hand. Then he placed it back in my fingers and had me read it aloud several times, until I had memorized it.

The words rang with the truth of my soul.

So I was dazzled beyond measure when my Lord approved and when the people of Nademan celebrated my rise to the office of crown prince. For finally hope had kindled in my heart that I would be able to honor my Lord's and my Honor Elian's choice.

It was a dream beyond my boldest imaginings made true, a prayer I had never dared to whisper answered, a hope too exalted to possess given form.

And the Almighty had blessed me with it because of my Honor Elian the Exemplar of Esteem, who had rendered the freest, wisest, bravest, strongest, most compassionate choice of all the Potentates for my sake.

Through his shining face was our Lord's promise of freedom bestowed.

CHAPTER 33
THE RESONANT PROMISE

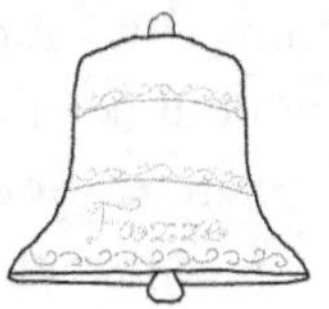  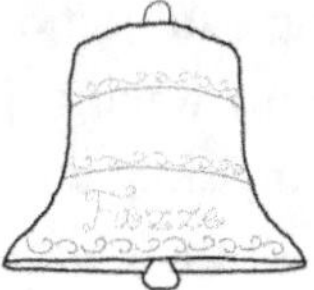

Perspective: Lord Lucian the Ideal of Freedom
Date: Eyyélab, the sixteenth day of the tenth moon, Thekharre, of
the year 500, C.Q.
Placement: after Chapter 57 and Segment 6 of <u>*The Bell Tolling*</u>

Gratitude to the Almighty welled in my heart for the miracle unfolding before me: despite all the sorrow that burdened their souls, my family and my people were laughing, expressions as joyous and serene as I had ever seen them wear.

After the triumphal speech and the wonder of Nademan celebrating my Quest, my companions had ushered me from the tree-tops of Natrisso to a grand pavilion, a series of tents constructed within the boundary of the town to shelter all six hundred and thirty-three members of my inner circle, my army, and the towns-folk as we partook of the feast they had prepared.

The triumphal feast, as my soldiers called it.

As my captains served the bread, the broth, and the bowls of fruit, everyone had sat in silence, quietly watching my counte-nance with a solemn dignity and a tempered exuberance.

It was not the ambience I had wanted. I had wanted all to

remember that the Quest Leader's presence was one of easy comfort and welcome familiarity.

So, once I had recited the prayer and sipped my first spoonful of broth, I stated, "I have a complaint to raise."

My family startled.

"It is quite a grave matter," I continued, voice calm as though pondering a subject of scholarship, "something that has disturbed me since my waking. Indeed, every night without fail, this matter troubles my sleep and hinders my rest, in a manner it did not for all the months of the previous year. Yet I fear that there is no answer to this difficulty, though I would wish to listen to your opinion regarding the matter."

As I had spoken, the faces of my companions and the rest of my family lost considerable color, glow, vibration, gloss, and silver, and my soldiers and my people seemed as agitated as troops watching an enemy force approach.

"What troubles you so, my Lord?" Malika asked, already pale cheeks almost colorless with an anxious fright.

For a moment, I savored the utter beauty of her voice, the one I had so deeply yearned to perceive with my senses for so many years, the sound that represented holiness itself to me. Then I replied, in an entirely even tone, "It is difficult to sleep at night when one's face glows like a lantern."

Everyone blinked.

Then Arista choked on a reluctant laugh. "Lucian! That was not amusing!"

I raised an eyebrow. "Was it not? From your silence, I had thought such gravity appropriate."

The calmly delivered words were the catalyst for a strangled burst of relieved laughter, and with it finally my family and my people relaxed, shoulders slumping as they whispered to each other about my rather alarming attempt at a jest. And that in turn sparked easy, comfortable, and relaxed conversation, between friends, family members, and even those not yet acquainted.

On the far end of my table, soldiers and townsfolk openly

laughed and ate and approached my companions, while my family themselves laughed as though they had not spent weeks upon weeks fretting about my health or hovering at my bedside.

On my left, Arista teased Elian and Elacir, swiping their caps and ruffling their hair while also encouraging them in their attempts to design new recipes for the army's campfires. Our brothers laughed and offered her adoring smiles, relishing her affection and wishing to add however they could to the happiness of her expression and comfort her amid her grief.

To their left, Tahira selected choice bits of bread and fruit for her brother, which he returned with a continuous stream of affectionate words and hugs—they had joined us on the path between the speech and the feast, and my companions' welcome was shielding them quite well from the soldiers' and the townsfolk's discontent.

Opposite them, my guardians laughed together, casting frequent devoted glances in my direction as they celebrated my success with stories of my childhood.

On my right, Malika, Kyros, and Darian spoke in quiet voices, smiling brightly among each other and occasionally chuckling, as tender and loving in their mellow way as Elian, Arista, and Elacir were in their boisterous one.

Every few minutes, all of my companions, my guardians, and my confidants sought to engage my father and Eligeo, both of whom sat silently, one between the two groups on my right and one between those on my left. Neither prince had much to say, both lost in their pain, but my companions, Taza, Da'ana, Elacir, Kanzeo, and even Darian, Hasima, and Tahira tried to include them, laughing and jesting, telling stories and offering comments on the food, sometimes even succeeding in evoking a smile.

That was what I had wanted. Camaraderie, affection, fellowship. All within my sight, at ease in my presence, remembering that I was their brother and friend as well as their liege and ruler. They belonged with me, as I did with them. With whom would they be familiar if not with me?

To whom would they come for comfort and salvation if not to me?

From whom would they receive freedom if not from my divinely blessed hands?

Even as joy crinkled my eyes and curved my lips in a quiet smile, my heart yearned for those distant from my sight yet not from my prayers, the people of Icilia who wandered lost and alone, their paths bleak and dark, uncertain or unknowing of my coming.

With the inhale of a breath, I raised my awareness from my physical form and spread it across the land, over tree and plain and river and hill and mountain, until the whole of Icilia unfolded within my vision.

It was a vista of diametric contrast between Nademan, where the brightest of celestial lights shone amid drops of starlight, and the rest of the seven nations, where the starlight flickered, almost extinguished, smothered by darkness.

Without hesitation I plunged into that darkness.

Though the sun shone bright in the heaven, beneath the clouds of smog there was little distinction beneath day and night. And regardless the enemy cared nothing for shame, for even the slightest particle of decency, perpetrating the cruelest evils as easily under the pale light of day as beneath the black of night.

What I saw as my awareness encircled Icilia could not have been recounted, such was the depth of horror I perceived. Such was the violence inflicted upon children, upon women, upon men, violence and murder and torture beyond reckoning. Beyond the perception of sorrow and the belief of grief.

That was every day and every night in Icilia.

It was a reality that burned my heart with every moment that I lived. A weight of suffering that seemed only to increase despite every person I freed and every mile I reconquered.

It was my burden, and I was grateful for it.

Who would care for their miseries if not I?

Weakened as I had been by my illness these last months, I had spent too long unaware. Now that the wellspring of my life was filling once more, even now being replenished by my companions' united joy, I gave as much time as I could to sharing so fully in my people's torments. Though I could not possibly physically save them at this moment, so great was the physical distance and so long was my task, I hoped that perhaps, someday, a few of them would be comforted to learn that the Quest Leader had been present with them amid their agony. As Belona had been. As my companions had been once their initial horror had passed.

Oh Almighty, Liege of my soul, I beg You to grant them that knowledge and that peace in the hereafter if not in this life. And may my own soul be at peace regarding those I could not save. They have sinned, yes, but You have entrusted them to me, and wholly do I love them, as You do.

A single ray of sunlight touched my soul, musical laughter in my ears and incense in my nose, a loving reminder that the Almighty had crowned me the mother of Icilia and that a mother's prayers for her children never went unheeded.

I smiled softly, with both my lips and my heart.

Then I concentrated my attention upon a powerful little light, the blazing spirit of my beloved Kyros' darling sister, sweet and vivacious Kalyca. Though she dearly missed her brother, and actually the whole Quest, even me, she was feeling supremely satisfied as she watched the countess and a number of family heads once again apologize for how members of Tresilt's recalcitrant faction had sneered at her that morning. To Kalyca, this seemed a proper vindication of how poorly they had once treated her brother and of how deeply they needed to display loyalty toward him now. The countess and her faction reported regularly to me and fulfilled the orders I gave, but in Kalyca's mind this was not enough.

Chuckling to myself, I ascertained that she was as spiritually, emotionally, and physically well as she could be and that she remembered my counsel. I savored the feel of her spirit and prayed for the little girl I loved as I did Darian...

Once I was satisfied with her wellbeing, I moved my focus west and north to where a ragged group of women and men of the Ezulal and the Nasimih slept uneasily beneath thorny bushes, decrepit weapons clutched in blood-encrusted fists. What armor they had seemed inadequate to protect them, as evidenced by the numerous injuries that riddled their limbs, several of which were an angry red or sickly blue or even black with infection.

As much as their physical condition smote my heart, I was much relieved that Rosalla Eminietta and her comrades still at all lived. Their attempt at liberating the gladiators imprisoned in another arena had been at least partially well-meant but rather ill-planned and ill-prosecuted. How I prayed that my guardians, Amalna and Faqehen, as well as one among their own number, would someday succeed in convincing them of the value of their lives. Each of them had a place in Icilia that was not to be disregarded, and Rosalla herself had much capacity for true freedom…

With another prayer in my heart, I let the core of my awareness fly south and slightly east, across the icy breadth of the Anharat (the chill of which I well remembered), to another group, women and men of the Sholanar, Areteen, and Nasimih, who attacked a flight of unsuspecting enemy troops, swords and spears raised and war cries on their lips. An auburn-scaled woman, Revera qia-Tovacera, issued commands in a booming voice as her sister, Netara, shifted the angle of her wings to facilitate their comrades' strikes. Within moments, the enemy squadron perished, and Revera dove to cut the ropes binding a group of Nasimih women to a burning tree.

The sight evoked another chuckle. How blessed I was by the inspiration Revera had derived from my actions and presence, and how pleased at the way in which she prospered. The days I had given to rescuing her aerie, though a delay in my journey to find Malika, had been well spent indeed. Her loyalty and the intelligence she gathered would someday be a great boon to the Quest. How I prayed that the Almighty would safeguard her and unite her with my Quest…

Contented, I swept my awareness north toward Asfiya, where I inspected the barrier around the athar orchards for any cracks or weaknesses, before returning home to my companions.

After years of seemingly endless darkness, at least one part of Icilia now shone with the light and happiness of the Almighty's promise.

With an exhale, I lowered my awareness into my physical form and opened my eyes.

A slight furrow disturbed the serenity of my brow.

In the awareness of Icilia that buzzed ever beneath the planes of my mind, shadows lurked. Shadows that hid evils, plans and movements of the enemy, horrors that I did not yet know...

The whole of Icilia was given unto me to rule and protect, yes, but the Almighty alone truly knew all. The Almighty chose to reveal and to conceal, to bestow awareness and to revoke it, to display and to veil, and in these matters, as in all things, I submitted myself to the Almighty's will. I did not raise question or complaint, letting nothing mar my trust in divine guidance.

For in revealing and concealing was the Almighty's beneficence. By displaying certain matters to my awareness and veiling others, the Almighty tested my faith, and, through these trials, my holy qualities were further refined and purified, so that I rose higher in divine-blessed power and comprehension and became better and better able to care for my people.

Furthermore, by expanding and limiting my awareness, the Almighty lightened the burden upon my soul. There were many evils that I needed to see to understand my people's plight, but there were uncounted others the sight of which would provide no benefit. Chief among them was the enemy's movements. The Blood and his governors had many cruel plans, and I would address each when I arrived at the correct time when and reached the correct place from which victory was most likely. Learning of these plans too early would trouble me unnecessarily, while I was unable to act, and though I certainly possessed the capacity to bear unimaginable burdens and yet still beam with gratitude and joy, it was the Almighty's kindness to preserve me from such excess tribulation.

Moreover, by giving and restricting certain things from my perception, the Almighty empowered my own free choice. A choice could only be considered fully free if it was made without duress, gave due deliberation to virtue, cause, means, and consequences, and, most of all, was in accord with the soul of its maker. A choice that was not true to oneself was not truly free. And therein lay the question posed to me: in the absence of full information, would I still retain my faith in my judgment and my trust in my capacity for perseverance, both gifts of the Almighty? Would I believe that the divine love within my heart would guide me truly? Or would anxiety over needing to choose well lead me toward doubt, uncertainty, and a wavering of my confidence? Thus, in limiting my gift of near omniscience, the Almighty urged me to remain true to myself. And, with each such choice, my glory grew all the brighter and became all the stronger a guide for my people. It was a chance I would not have had if I knew every aspect of every choice, for then there would be no need of faith or trust, no trial or refinement of my heart, as the information itself would be the judge of which path to take. Therefore, in respect for my free will, the Almighty bestowed upon me opportunity to choose in accordance with my soul and so revealed the esteem I held for myself.

My soul resplendent with these beliefs, I did not consider further the Almighty's revelation and concealment of the enemy's plans and instead returned the entirety of my attention to my family and my people.

How delighted I was to witness their happiness.

Once Tahira, Eligeo, Kanzeo, Belona, and Ciro had been among those lost in the darkness, as had my own companions. But the Almighty had saved them through my hands, and to behold their laughter, both here in Natrisso and far away in Ehaya, was a wonder.

At least the Quest of Freedom has restored the Light in one of

I swallowed the last mouthfuls of my meal, savoring the dried blueberries, and then relaxed on my cushion, leaning onto the thick pillow placed between my back and a wooden board (which my companions had arranged for both distinction and comfort). Resting my crowned head against the soft linen, I continued to watch.

Although I was silent, I was in no way ignored. Even while my senses had observed in great detail locations far distant from this one, I had responded to smiles, questions, comments, and jests and had eaten the portions Elian had selected for me. To my family and my people, I seemed an active participant in the celebration, as present as they were, engaging in their conversation and sharing in their mirth.

Sharing in their joys and their sorrows as I always would…

A rough palm slid beneath the fingers of my right hand, and I glanced in that direction to behold a sight of such beauty that my heart immediately soared as though on Sholanar wings: Malika tipping her head back in laughter, cream cheeks suffused with a rosy glow, full lips red with undimmed smiles, and azure eyes sparkling like stars, her crown shining as though lit from within by moonlight. My sister, my heart, my Second joyful despite all the burdens she had lifted in my absence, her hand gripping mine with the assurance that she would always champion me.

Around her, my family had paused to cherish her happiness, Elian staring as though overcome and Darian beaming with the same steady brotherly love that he had always given me.

Indeed, in my brother's lavender eyes I saw that he was at last beginning to fulfill my wish, pass the trial I had set before him, and attain the lofty rank which I had long prayed he would.

The same was true of my companions—in accepting my love and their duties, fulfilling my wishes, passing my trials, and so rising in holiness and power, they were becoming who they were meant to be. Malika's prudent governance, Kyros' steady command, Arista's brave heroism, Elian's bold choice for the sake of esteem... Only through them, only through Malika, could my Light be seen.

Though war raged around us, this moment was one of untainted happiness, both for my family and my people and for me. And truly that was my greatest triumph.

Gratitude to the Almighty.

PRONUNCIATION SUPPORT

This guide is for selected names.

The Quests

Aalia—Aaah-lee-ah

Manara—Muh-naa-ruh

Naret—Naa-ret

Lucian—Loo-see-uhn

Malika—Maa-lih-kah

Elian—Eh-lee-uhn

Arista—Uh-ris-tuh ('ris' rhymes with miss)

Kyros—Kai-ros ('Kai' has the same sound as the 'i' in fine; 'ros' has the same sound as 'most' without the 't')

Izzetís—Izz-eh-tees ('Iz' rhymes with fizz, 'tees' is said with extra emphasis) [Elian's former surname]

Fazálli—Fahz-aal-lee ('aal' is said with particular emphasis) [the name of Lord Lucian's sword]

Family, Guardians, and Vassals (those with repeated mentions, in order of appearance)

Darian sej-Shehasfiyi—Deh-ree-uhn sehj-Sheh-haas-fee-yee

Beres—Beh-rez

Taza Palanéze—Taa-zuh Pah-luh-neh-zehs ('neh' is said with extra emphasis)

Ilqan—Il-qaan ('Il' rhymes with 'fill')

Revera bia-Tovacera—Reh-veh-rah bee-uh-Toe-vaa-ceh-rah [in Revera's second and third chapters, 'bia' is replaced with 'qia' (qee-uh), an indication that she is married, like the use of 'Missus' rather than 'Miss']

Kalyca Dinasietta—Kah-lih-kah Dih-naas-ee-et-tah ('Ka' has the same sound as 'cast'; 'et' has the same sound as 'set')

Elacir bi-Dekecer—Eh-laa-seer bee-Dek-eh-cehr ('seer' has the same sound as 'seer')

Tahira Enarias—Tuh-hee-rah Eh-naa-ree-uhs

Kanzeo Enaries—Kan-zee-oh Eh-naa-ree-uhs ('Kan' rhymes with 'can') [the difference in surname is because of gender]

Eligeo tej-Shehenkorom—Eh-lee-hee-oh tehj-Sheh-hen-nah-dem

Rosalla Eminietta—Roh-saa-luh Em-in-ee-et-tah ('et' has the same sound as 'set')

Ciro Tolmarie—Cee-roh Toll-maa-ree

Belona Tolmariat—Beh-loh-nah Toll-maa-ree-uht [the difference in surname is because of gender and marriage]

Dorona—Doh-roh-nah

Astor—As-tohr ('As' has the same sound as 'pass'; 'tor' has the same sound as 'tore')

Netara—Neh-tah-ruh

Afra—Af-rah ('Af' has the same sound as 'laugh')

Cethor—Ceh-thor

Glora—Gloh-rah

Dalor—Dah-lohr ('tor' has the same sound as 'tore')

The World (in rough order of appearance)

Athar—ut-hur ('ut' has the same sound as 'but', 'hur' sounds similar to 'her')

Icilia—Ih-sill-lee-ah ('sill' has the same sound as sill)

Zahacim—Zah-haa-sim

Khuduren—Khoo-doo-rehn

Bhalasa—Bhuh-lah-sah

Etheqa—Eh-theh-kah

Nademan—Naa-deh-muhn (the accent is on 'deh')

Asfiya—As-fee-yah ('As' rhymes with 'mass')

Koroma—Koh-roh-mah

Incé—een-seh (because of the noted accent, 'seh' is pronounced with particular emphasis)

Dalaanem—Duh-laan-ehm

Khuduya—Khoo-doo-yah

Etheqora—Eh-theh-koh-rah

Potsmia—Pots-mee-ah ('Pots' is almost pronounced 'Potes')

Nademan's provinces and cities, west to east

Adeban—Ah-deh-baan

Zaiqan—Zai-kaan ('Zai' has the same sound as the 'i' in fine)

Arkaiso—Ar-kai-soh ('Ar' has the same sound as 'are', 'kai' has the same sound as the 'i' in fine)

Pethama—Peh-thah-muh (the accent is on 'thah')

Gairan—Gai-raan ('Gai' has the same sound as the 'i' in fine)

Ehaya—Eh-haa-yuh

Makiran—Maa-kih-raan

Tadama—Tuh-dah-muh (the accent is on 'dah')

Buzuran—Boo-zoo-raan

Nadeya—Naa-deh-yah [the address for Nademani women; equivalent to Miss or Misses]

Nadeyi—Naa-deh-yee [the address for Nademani men; equivalent to Mister]

THE GLOSSARY OF THE SACRED TONGUE

Common Words:

Incé

A word used in Icilia that combines the meanings of "mortal" and "human"

Dalaanem

The formal address in the Sacred Tongue for the Quest Leader; translates to "my Lord" (literally, "my guide")

Chapter 1—Darian 1:

Lord Lucian the Ideal of Freedom:

A'Qahre rad beleqas Isilia on he eyeh ru a'laètaqqe é a'Raèdalaan thaner. Onó zaler rasehem a'Qahre rad adiniqas a'ajeh é a'Dalaane-é-Fazze, a'Ewaràwalaane ó a'dinile é a'Zahràdalle ai a'Arafàwalaane é Isilia, a'Kairie é kairiese ai a'Sheheh é Shehile. Elàkan la raëh fazer an a'lalaëh eïla a'Raah-é-Fazze.

The Almighty has blessed Icilia on this day through the ascension of the second Quest Leader. Unto my lowly head the Almighty has bestowed the crown of the Lord of

Freedom, the Heir to the gifts of the Shining Guide and
the supreme ruler of Icilia, the Liege of lieges and the
Monarch of monarchs. There is no path free from the
darkness save for the Quest of Freedom.

Prince Beres sej-Shehasfiyi, Prince Darian sej-Shehasfiyi, and the
guardians of the Quest Leader:

> Aalimas a'Qahre! Aalimas a'Raah-é-Alaah! Aalimas
> Dalaan Lusian ma-Fazélaah!

> Praised be the Almighty! Praised be the Quest of Light!
> Praised be Lord Lucian the Ideal of Freedom!

Lord Lucian the Ideal of Freedom:

> Fazálli

> The name of Lord Lucian's sword, which means 'freedom
> that is born of goodness'
> (literally: Free Goodness)

Chapter 18—Darian 5:

Prince Darian sej-Shehasfiyi and General Taza Palanéze:

> A'Qahre ediniqasimas u'haseh onó am, Ajaanem.

> May the Almighty bestow wisdom upon you, my Honor.

Lord Lucian the Ideal of Freedom:

> A'Qahre beleqasemas Ajaanam Kairos a-Majéalaah e
> a'archel purer é enalheham. A'naaleh é a'Qahre ai
> a'husneh é a'Zahràdalle ai a'loreh é a'Raahile enpure-

qasemas u'am zilu am banàkanerad onel am aneqasu
kanne. A'Qahre ideqasemas am u'beleh onó a'Silàretet é
Isilia, be am kaneqas ó Dalaanam ai Fidaanam ai ó
Raaham.

May the Almighty bless your Honor Kyros the Exemplar
of Strength with the full grandeur of your potential. May
the Almighty's praise and the Shining Guide's love and
the Quests' favor infuse you so that you become who you
are destined to become. May the Almighty render you a
blessing unto the Land of Icilia, as you are to your Lord
and your Grace and to your Quest.

Graced Malika the Exemplar of Wisdom:

*Ne a'onàmirile é a'Qahre, a'Zahràdalle, ai a'Dalaana-é-
Isilia, efikrerim likelam ai qabeham! Melchelam
kaneqasemas é alheh ó a'Qahre.*

*By the names of the Almighty, the Shining Guide, and the
Lady of Icilia, seek your fulfillment and your future! May
your promise be of worth to the Almighty.*

Honored Kyros the Exemplar of Strength:

En manarrel ó a'Qahre, em azeqas a'taëh é albelem ai
rohehem ai a'jameh é nohehem ai zatelem an a'labiëh é
Isilia. Em rad wuldemiz é he husner retet, em rad eleqas
a'raëh é a'Raahile, ai em efikreqas a'beleh é a'Zahràdalle.
Tharel kuseqas hayànohilëm, qanel aleqas qalàzazatelem,
ai fazel kureqas neràrohilëm zilu em banàkanemas ke
a'Qahre aneqas. Saleh unpureqasemas puràtaëh idel em
kaneqas.

In devotion to the Almighty, I offer the whole of my heart

and soul and the sum of my mind and body for the service of Icilia. I am born of this beloved earth, I have chosen the path of the Quests, and I seek the blessings of the Shining Guide. Purity sharpens my thoughts, hope lightens my tongue, and freedom hones my actions so that I may become what the Almighty intends. May peace suffuse all that I am.

ACKNOWLEDGMENTS

At the fulfillment of this complement to the first volume of a'Silómizze é a'Raah-é-Fazze, the Archivist proffers gratitude to the Almighty, to the Lady of Icilia, and to the Guardian of Names for the blessing of this chance to behold the glory of the Quest of Freedom. May the Lord of Freedom be pleased with this praise of his name.

***

My first and greatest thanks are to the Almighty, Who has bestowed upon me the blessing of writing this story. Patience in difficult hours, gratitude for every victorious step, and fervent prayer are what have created *The Resonant Bell*, from the first sparks of inspiration to the final efforts of compilation, and are what have ensured that this story fulfills the intention in accordance with which it was designed. Thus, I proffer all my gratitude to the Almighty and, under divine auspice, the Lord who transforms dust into gold and bestows blessing unto those desperately seeking his favor.

My second offering of gratitude is to the Prince of my community, who has supported my endeavors at every footstep. His acceptance of a copy of *The Bell Tolling* gave me strength when I despaired of success. I have no less appreciation for my mother — who gladly devotes all her energy to helping me shape details about the lives of the Quest's people — for my father — who happily lavishes all his knowledge on helping me forge the theoretical and theological foundations of the Quests' Civilization.

Third is my praise for Lee Contreras, who designed *The Resonant Bell*'s beautiful cover, from the clouds to the bell and the watch-tree, dedicating hours of loving effort and listening to bringing my wishes to fruition. No less do I honor Mary Reid, who edited *The Resonant Bell* with great patience and kindness and, through hours of discussion and dozens of keen suggestions, brought my vision to completion.

I also offer acclaim to Mustafa Pishori, who drew the intricate frame that adorns the edges along with his friend, Murtaza Shakir.

Fourth is my tribute to my friends—Malia, Mrs. Battles, Dr. Post, Patrick, Mary B., C'Sherica, and Hussaina—who helped me develop various elements of my story and writing through their thoughtful answers and eager interest. No less is the salute given to my beta readers—Mrs. Battles, Andrew B., Edith P., and Lydia —who were patient with the winds of my creativity and offered critiques of my story and writing that, in various ways, strengthened both the narratives and my conviction to publish this volume. I also equally extol Mari Galloway and Maxine Smith, who patiently waited to see their commendations for *The Bell Tolling* on the back of this book.

Fifth is the depth of my regard to the University of Dallas and her professors and students, who, throughout my five years there and in every interaction thereafter, deepen my understanding of the Divine, ethics, politics, and human nature as a whole. Similar is my regard for the Women's Society of Cyberjutsu, who have supported me in numerous areas, from my writing to my career to my confidence as a woman.

Sixth is my recognition for all those who have purchased copies of *The Bell Tolling* and *The Resonant Bell*, particularly those who pre-ordered Book One, and for my active followers on social media, who have done much to bolster my confidence in the public success of my writing endeavors.

If I have forgotten a name in these lists, I ask that you forgive me. My thanks remain true, regardless of mention.

Seventh, I thank you, dear reader, for deigning to peruse this book. I pray that this story meant something to you, that you gained both adventure and inspiration from the writing, and that you felt hope sparking in your heart as you witnessed the resonance of the rise of the Quest. May that hope help shield you amid these difficult times.

In particular, I thank those who have understood that they are the recipients of the dedication of this book.

Eighth, I pray for the people of Ukraine, who suffer atrocities, horrors, and the seizure of their freedom all because of the whims of a heartless tyrant. For many months have the profits of *The Resonant Bell* been devoted to the people of Ukraine's aid.

Lastly, I voice my gratitude for the Quest of Freedom and for their vassals — for Darian, Tahira, Eligeo, Ciro, Elacir, Kalyca, Kanzeo, Revera, and Rosalla, who have given their voices to the narration of this book. Through their eyes we have been blessed to behold the exalted glory of the Quest of Freedom and to witness the path by which a recognition in oneself of a need for Divine Blessing entirely transforms the heart and the soul. And, as the source of such grace, in many ways it is for Lucian, Malika, Elian, Arista, and Kyros that this book was written. May the second Quest be pleased with the praise of their name.

And above all, may the Almighty bless all of us.

AUTHOR'S BIOGRAPHY

Amena Jamali lives a life animated by the coolness of shrewd logic, the vibrancy of ambitious passion, and the exaltedness of deep morals and philosophy. Her lenses of choice for viewing the world are faith, gratitude, empathy, love, and clear-sighted rationale and strategy. She is many things: devout Muslim, dutiful daughter, patriotic American, thoughtful political activist in the making, blossoming cybersecurity professional, and—not least of all—a writer of epic fantasy.

That last, her epic fantasy writings, holds the essence of all of her hopes, ponderings, and dreams, the substance of her musings about philosophy, and the explorations of her ideas about politics. As her writing evidences, she cares deeply about the power of truth, respectful and reverent discourse, and the formation of a truly inclusive and empowering society that values free choice and the pursuit of virtue for all.

Because of what this story means to her, it is her wish that her books are found to be a source of hope and enlightenment. She prays that every reader falls in love with her characters, as she has, and that their story sets her readers free.

To learn more about Amena's books and to connect with her, please visit www.amenajamali.com. There one may find links to the social media platforms that Amena uses, a form for subscribing to her newsletter, and bonus chapters!

In addition, please support Amena's publication of the books of *The Lord of Freedom* by leaving a review of *The Resonant Bell* on Amazon and on social media!

AUTHOR'S WORKS

Previously Published Books in *The Lord of Freedom* series:

Book One — The Bell Tolling (2021)